THE POSSESSING

Avily Jerome

THE POSSESSING
Published by Dragontail Press
P. O. Box 54550
Phoenix, AZ 85078

ISBN 978-1-7321879-9-3
Copyright © 2020 by Avily Jerome
Cover design by Kirk DouPonce, Dog Eared Design

Available in print from your local bookstore, online, or from the author. For more information on this book and the author visit: www.avilyjerome.com

This is a work of fiction. Names, characters, and incidents are all products of the author's imagination or are used for fictional purposes. Any mentioned brand names, places, and trademarks remain the property of their respective owners, bear no association with the author or the publisher, and are used for fictional purposes only.

Brought to you by Avily Jerome

Library of Congress Cataloging-in-Publication Data
Jerome, Avily
The Possessing/Avily Jerome 1st ed.

Printed in the United States of America.

For my family, the reason I do all I do.

ONE

"They're coming for your son." Pastor Floyd gazed at me from across the wooden desk in his office.

I tamped down the panic that rose in my chest. "Who's coming for Beck? And why?"

Pastor Floyd smiled, but dark circles highlighted his puffy eyes and crow's feet, and the lines around his terse lips made his face look gaunt. How long had it been since I'd seen him? He'd performed Beck's dedication when Beck was eight weeks old. I'd been to church a few times since then, but I hadn't been in… a couple months, at least. But he seemed to have aged years.

The lines etched in his features made him appear sad. "You already know the answers to both of those questions."

Bookshelves lined the wall behind him, blinds covered a window to my left, and his various degrees and certifications and a couple of ornamental crosses adorned the opposite wall.

Pastor Floyd's eyes looked tired—more so than I remembered.

Why, though? The city had been quiet for almost a year. Ever since I'd defeated Dionysius and thwarted his plan to use his army of half-demon monster spawn to take over Phoenix.

The memory of a cold chill crept up my back, and debilitating nausea threatened to overturn my stomach. I pushed both sensations away. They weren't real. Not anymore. I couldn't feel demons now.

I took a deep breath and refocused my attention.

I did know the answers. Sort of.

The *why* was easy. Beck was descended from a very particular and strictly controlled bloodline that had been bred to produce the future antichrist. But I wasn't. Only my late fiancé, Trent, had been part of that line.

I picked up a decorative letter opener from Pastor Floyd's desk and tapped it against my leg. "Isn't Beck... I don't know... tainted or something, since he's mine?"

"We'd hoped that would be the case. But the demons' options are thinning. They're running out of candidates to fulfill their plan. Other than Beck, we know Mr. Harding was a potential fulfillment of their prophecy, but now that he's aware, he's not willing to participate in their plans. I've uncovered three other potentials over the last year and have discussed the ramifications with them. There are others—I'm certain of it. The demons wouldn't leave something like this to chance. But finding them all has proved more challenging than I expected."

That explained why he looked so haggard.

"The plan only works if the potential is willing or ignorant," he continued. "Beck is young enough to be groomed for the role. If they can get to him..."

He trailed off and gazed at me, his expression both calculating and pitying.

I knew what he *wasn't* saying. My stomach tightened. "They're going to try to kidnap him, like they did with Trent when he was young."

Pastor Floyd nodded.

"How do you know?" I asked.

"I have pieced together the bits and pieces through painstaking research and interviews."

That was possibly the most useless thing he'd ever said while still directly answering my question.

Apparently, he recognized that fact too.

He brushed his hands over the leather cover of the Bible on the edge of his desk, almost like a self-soothing gesture. "I don't know when they'll come for him or who they'll send. But I fear your respite is at an end. You must be on your guard at all times."

I breathed deeply. "What do I do? I can't quit work and be with him all day every day. I still need to pay rent and eat and—"

"I'm not suggesting you quit your life," Pastor Floyd said. "Just be wary. Can you still sense them?"

"I... don't know. There are times when I get that nauseous feeling, like I used to when they were around, but then it's gone, and I'm not sure if I just imagined it or if it's just residual trauma or whatever."

"Trust your instincts, Jack."

"You think they're still following me? Monitoring me?"

I glanced around at the unassuming office with its minimalistic, functional furniture and sparse decorations, as though a demon might pop out from one of the beige walls.

"I absolutely do. Be on your guard. Be wary of anyone new who comes into your life. And if something doesn't feel right, it probably isn't."

"How…"

I stopped, trying to sort out my thoughts, feeling the room for any hint of demonic activity, but there was none. I knew there wouldn't be—there never was, here. This place always had an atmosphere of peace, as though a demon-proof bubble surrounded it.

But still, I hadn't felt anything in almost a year. "I can't feel them. I can't go into the other dimension. How can I fight them when I don't know who or what they are? How can I protect my son if I don't know when or where the threat is coming from?"

Pastor Floyd inhaled, long and slow, before repeating, "Trust your instincts, Jack."

He stood and motioned toward the door.

I followed his implication and pushed up from the worn chair and turned to leave his office.

"You know where to find me if you need me," he said, opening the door to usher me into the hall. "I'll learn what I can, but you know more than you realize. You have the information and the resources—use them. And Jack… one last thing."

I waited while he tried to sort out his thoughts.

"There's something else going on. I believe there are other demons, like Dionysius, who are going to come for Beck and try what Dionysius tried, to lift him up as the antichrist. But there's something else… something new. I don't know what it is yet, but it feels very wrong, very dark, and it's coming our way. Be careful."

He closed the door to his office.

I stepped out onto the bush-lined sidewalk that led to the main sanctuary and the parking lot. Why did he have to be so cryptic? What did he mean, I knew more than I realized? Why couldn't he just tell me what I needed to know?

"Jack. What are you doing here?"

I snapped my head up and looked into a pair of sea-foam green eyes.

My heart stuttered. He was just as gorgeous as I remembered. "Hi, Chase," I said. My voice squeaked a little more than I was proud of. "Pastor Floyd asked me to come by."

Chase took a step back, giving more space than I wanted from him. "Oh? What for?"

"I… do you want to grab coffee or something? We should catch up."

"I'd like that." Chase smiled.

"I have to pick up Beck from the nanny. Meet you at our—I mean the coffee shop down the street—in twenty minutes?"

A flicker of something flashed in Chase's eyes at the mention of Beck. He'd never come right out and said it, but I knew my pregnancy was why we'd drifted apart.

I couldn't blame him. Dating a pregnant woman—not to mention the possibility of raising someone else's kid—well, it probably wasn't exactly how he'd seen his future. After all, he was a pastor. Nothing he said or did made think he judged me, but still, it had to have crossed his mind. How would it look?

Besides, we hadn't even been actually dating in the first place, so there was nothing to break off. It was fine.

Chase fell into step beside me as I walked toward my truck. "How is he? Beck, I mean?" he asked.

"He's good," I said. "Starting to crawl. Well, scoot. There's some forward momentum, at any rate."

"I can't wait to see him. I'll wrap up here and meet you there in a little bit."

I nodded and hurried out to my truck—my new truck. I missed my old truck, a compact green Ranger, but I'd had to get something with a back seat when Beck was born, so I'd upgraded to a gorgeous, fully loaded, dark green Ram.

I climbed up into the cab and pulled out of the church parking lot, suddenly realizing how much I missed it here. I'd never been a church goer, but a year ago… a year ago, this had been the only place I'd felt safe.

Maybe it was time to start going back.

I closed off that line of thought and headed to pick up Beck.

Beck's nanny, Gen, opened the door to her apartment and put her finger to her lips. "He just went down," she said. "I know it's late, but he refused to nap earlier."

"It's fine," I said.

Gen was a grad student, majoring in early childhood development. She and my sister-in-law, Cameron, dated for a little while. It didn't work out, but they were still friends.

Sister-in-law wasn't technically accurate. Cameron was Trent's sister. But she was closer than a sister to me, and I trusted her judgment when she'd recommended Gen. I hadn't regretted it for a minute. Gen was priceless. She had a few other kids that she cared for part-time while she took online classes, and somehow managed to juggle a social life, too.

"How was he today?"

"Perfect, as always." She grinned, leading me through the living room of her apartment. The smell of freshly baked cookies wafted up from a candle on the half wall that separated the living room from the kitchen and dining area. "He's trying to push up on all fours instead of just doing the army-crawl thing. Next thing you know, he'll be pulling up on furniture. He'll be walking in no time."

"Don't say stuff like that. I'm not ready for a toddler."

Gen smiled and tucked Beck's toys into his diaper bag. "I'm sure you have plenty of time."

Two other people about Gen's age sat at her kitchen table. "Jack, this is Oscar and Cadence. We have several classes together. We're working on a group project about societal reform." She turned to them. "This is Jack—Beck's mom."

Gen trotted into the back room to get Beck.

The girl, presumably Cadence, raised a sculpted eyebrow and tossed sleek blonde hair behind her ear. "The cop."

"Guilty," I said.

"Agreed," Cadence sneered.

Oscar's eyes widened. "What the hell, Cadence? That's so disrespectful."

I gave him a quick once-over. He was tall, well-built. Olive skin and dark, curly hair.

Cadence shrugged. "I respect those who have earned my respect, and so far the police aren't on that list."

Snobby little twit, with her petite, slender frame and full lips that lost some of their appeal when she sneered like that.

My jaw tightened. "Let me guess, you're on the side of no police whatsoever."

She lifted her chin. "The police force in America is inherently flawed. Police brutality is out of control. We don't need the police anymore. If you have gangrene, you cut the limb off, not try to heal it."

"Big words coming from someone who's never had gangrene," I said.

Cadence crossed her arms and leaned back far enough that I almost hoped she'd tip the chair over entirely. "So, you're saying there's no corruption in the system?"

"Not at all. There's corruption in all systems. But there's also two sides to every story."

"Bullshit," Cadence said. "We've all seen the videos. You can't say some of those things are justified."

I leaned against the half-wall, forcing my demeanor to remain calm and professional. "A few years ago, I was part of a squad that was tasked with keeping the peace at a protest. A new tech company was trying to set up a factory here, but they cut a lot of corners, and there were injuries. Technically, everything was legal and up-to-code, so they won the lawsuits against them."

"What does this have to do with anything?" Cadence demanded.

"I'm getting there. Protestors surrounded the building, demanding a union, demanding more oversight, and demanding the factory be closed down. The protests lasted for over a week, pretty much nonstop. Anyway, on the third night, a man in the crowd threw a smoke bomb."

"Oooh, scary," Cadence sneered.

"Shut up and let her finish," Oscar said.

I gave him a small smile before continuing, "Turned out to be harmless, but we didn't know that at the time. We tried to break up the protestors to get to the guy who threw the bomb, and some of the cops on duty were pretty aggressive in their attempts to get to him. But the cell phone videos that turned up later on the news only showed the aftermath—the cops shoving their way through what appeared to be a peaceful protest. No one saw the guy with the smoke bomb, only the unnecessary aggression of the cops. Instead of a 'thank you,' we got beer bottles and insults thrown at us."

"That's disgusting," Oscar said.

Cadence leaned forward in the chair. Damn. She didn't fall on her ass.

She rested her forearm on the table between the textbooks and laptops that covered the surface. "But if the police hadn't been there in the first place, he wouldn't have felt the need to throw the smoke bomb."

"You don't know that. And neither did we. And we didn't know if it was a toxin or if he would throw something else."

"Okay, but if you hadn't been there, and he had thrown something toxic, then the other protestors would've done something. They could've solved it peacefully without the cops butting in."

"That doesn't usually end the way you think it's going to." I pushed up from the wall, towering over her. "That's how we get lynchings. Mob rule deciding what's best."

"That's sort of the topic of our project." Oscar tapped the laptop in front of him. "What kind of reform do we need at a systemic level in order to achieve the most good for the most people? Personally, I think we need *more* police, not less. Police are overworked, and too much expectation is put on them to always have their bodycams and never screw up, even when people are shooting at them or attacking them or threatening them, and they don't know what will happen. If we had more police, then there would be more people to share the workload."

"And less accountability." Cadence twisted in her chair to glare at him. "You can't just throw a bunch of new cops out on the streets without proper training."

"I didn't say I didn't think they should get proper training!"

I'd heard all these arguments before—from both sides—and there was no perfect solution.

"But they're not getting training now." Cadence frowned. "Adding more would make the problem worse, not better. We need to scrap the system we have and start from scratch. Preferably without the power-hungry bullies who currently infest the law enforcement profession."

Oscar turned to me. "Are you a power-hungry bully?"

I smiled. "Not that I know of. But I've known a few." Unfortunately, this profession does attract that type."

"So, you agree that police are out of control," Cadence said.

"Some are. I've had to testify against people I've worked with, and one is even doing time now. It sucks. We're supposed to be able to count on each other. It feels like a betrayal, even though accountability is necessary. And there's a lot of gray area around what is and isn't an appropriate use of force. Sometimes you need someone who isn't afraid to either hurt or get hurt to go into places like gang territory and crime rings."

"There is never an excuse to use excessive force," Cadence said.

I thought about killing Dionysius. To the casual observer, it would appear I picked a fight with him—stabbed him and shot him while he was only defending himself. But that wasn't what had happened. To the casual observer, he looked human. Any video would've shown a man, not a demon. And anyone who knew what he'd done, what he was still doing… "Sometimes you don't know the whole story," I said quietly.

Gen came out of the bedroom carrying Beck. "If all cops were as good as Jack, we wouldn't have to have this discussion," she said. "But I think the problem goes deeper than that. Law enforcement is set up under a flawed system. Even if every law enforcement officer were perfect, they're still operating under unjust laws. In order for police reform to be effective, we have to start further back. Reform the structure of our entire society."

"How would you enforce it?" Oscar asked, at the same time that Cadence said, "Exactly! No more cops, no more government."

I took Beck from Gen. He was still groggy and nuzzled against me. I held him close and inhaled his scent. I never knew I could love anyone like I loved this little bundle in my arms. No way was I letting any demons get their hands on him.

"People are basically good," Cadence went on.

"You just called all cops power-hungry bullies." My arms tightened around Beck and I had to consciously relax them. "Are they basically good after all?"

Cadence narrowed her eyes, but went on. "We want to do what's right, for the most part. If we were free to govern ourselves—not this fake democracy, but really govern ourselves—then the world would be a better place."

"But if there's no government, what do you do about the people who aren't basically good?" Oscar demanded again.

Cadence slammed her palm against the table, making Beck jump. "Shut up and let me finish. The power structures set up in the formation of this government are what cause the abuse of the very things that are supposed to set us free. It's only when we get rid of the biased power structure that we can even hope for equality."

"That's a totally asinine assumption," Oscar said. "There won't be equality in that kind of society because there will always be people who abuse whatever system is in place to put themselves on top."

Cadence leaned her chair back again. So close to tipping all the way over… But no such luck. "Without a government-orchestrated system, there *is* no top. It's all flat, and therefore we are all equal. If it's all flat, then we can focus on making sure there's nobody in need. Nobody oppressed."

Gen shook her head and pulled Beck's half-finished bottle out of the fridge. "You can't have a completely government-free society. Someone has to take care of things like roads and infrastructure. And if you want equality, or to make sure no one is in need, someone has to ensure that food and stuff is distributed equally. What we need is a leader who is strong enough to make sure that no one climbs over others to get to the top, wise enough to know where they're needed, and kind enough to let us each live and let live."

"That's a dictatorship," I said. I hadn't planned on saying something—I enjoyed listening to the discussion—but that was exactly

11

what Dionysius had pretended to be. A benevolent dictator, who would save us from ourselves and anyone else who tried to hurt us. All we had to do was let him have unlimited power.

"Is that bad, though?" Gen sat down across from Cadence. "Plenty of countries have dictatorships. They aren't all bad. Some of them are really pretty good. There's no way to avoid bad people abusing power, but with one person in ultimate control, if it's the right person, it could really solve a lot of problems with inequality for the overall population."

"The problem with a dictatorship is that power corrupts," I went on. "Even if you found a single person who was truly invested in the lives of their people, who genuinely wanted the best for them, and who had the power to enforce equality—which is impossible because people are still human—they would eventually die. And others would strive for that power. And anyone who seeks power is not someone you want having all of it."

"So, we vote on who would be the best person for the job," Oscar said. "Oh, hey, we already have that!"

"But nobody agrees on what's best." Cadence stood and grabbed a wine cooler from Gen's fridge. Maybe if she drank enough I'd get to see her fall over in the chair.

She sat back down, all four chair legs firmly on the floor. Damn. "So," she went on, "it becomes a war for who sucks less. Having nobody at all is better than electing the lesser of two evils."

"Or we just find a benevolent dictator who will never die," Gen grinned.

I smiled, but again, that was a little too close to Dionysius for my liking.

"I'd love to stay and hear what you come up with for your project, but I need to get going," I said.

"Thank you for your invaluable perspective and for your service to our city," Oscar said.

"Try not to racially profile or abuse your power," Cadence sneered.

I strapped a still-dozing Beck into his car seat and turned to glare at her. "I swore an oath to serve and protect, and that is what I do, every single day. Even people who insult me, hate me, and would get rid of me if they could."

I seethed as I hefted Beck's car seat carrier up over one arm and his diaper bag over the other. "Thanks, Gen. I'll see you tomorrow."

I swear, having a kid put me in better shape than Academy training ever did. I stewed over Cadence's attitude all the way to the coffee shop. Give her a few years outside of her happy little bubble of academia and see if she changed her tune at all. Or put her in a position when she wasn't one of the privileged she claimed to be so against. Not that Oscar was much better, with his sycophantic idealism. More police wouldn't solve the problems in the system, either, especially not with the current lack of budget for proper training.

Even Gen, with her lack of understanding of how the world worked and her hope for a benevolent dictator to make things better, was getting on my nerves.

Sometimes it was easier to deal with demons. At least then I knew where I stood.

I forced myself to calm down as I drove toward the coffee shop. I hadn't had a conversation with Chase in way too long, and I didn't want it tainted by all the things I wished I'd said to wipe the smirk off Cadence's face.

I pulled in to the coffee shop parking lot and released Beck's car seat. He looked so peaceful. So much like his father.

Warmth rushed over me. I had bigger things to think about than a couple of grad students arguing over the state of the government.

Inside the coffee shop was the one person who might be able to help me make sense of the cryptic warnings and vague portents of doom that threatened my son.

TWO

A blast of cool air-conditioning hit me when I walked into the coffee shop, a reminder that even though it was technically fall, the stubborn desert summer still lingered. Chase was already sitting at a table by the window, well distanced from anyone else in the shop. Another pang of nostalgia shot through me. He was the one who first called this place "ours."

He smiled at me when I walked toward him, lugging the baby carrier. I set the carrier on the floor and slid into the chair across from him. He pushed a coffee toward me.

"He's getting big," Chase said.

"Yeah, they do that."

"Are you okay? Holding up okay? Back to work… everything?"

"I'm good. Thanks." I took a sip of my coffee and pulled away quickly. It was still too hot to enjoy.

"Good. You know I'm here if you need anything."

"Thanks," I said. It was nice of him to say, but we both knew I'd never ask.

"Why did Floyd want you to come in?" He took a sip of his own coffee, then removed the lid and stirred in another creamer.

"He said they're coming back and they're after Beck."

"Demons." It wasn't a question.

A weight lifted from inside me, and I remembered how much I loved talking to him. From the moment I'd met him, he'd always believed everything I said at face value. Never thought I was making it up or embellishing things. Never thought I was crazy.

He faced every puzzle with that same detached scrutiny, investing all his energy in finding answers, reasons, and solutions. He was the reason I was able to do what I did a year ago—travel though an extra dimension and kill a bunch of demons and rescue a bunch of girls from a demonic trafficking ring that was using them to incubate their demon spawn.

He was the one who'd made it possible for me to continue living after Trent died.

I don't think I even realized how much I'd counted on his quiet strength until that moment, which came as a stark reminder of my the last several months without it.

I shoved back the tears that tried to form in my eyes and focused on the conversation.

"Exactly," I said. "Pastor Floyd told me he'd been in contact with three other potentials and they knew what was going on. The demons' plan is unraveling, so they're scheming to kidnap Beck and raise him to be their chosen one."

Chase poured yet another creamer in to his coffee cup. A wave of surfer-blond hair fell over his forehead, and he pushed it back. "What are you going to do?"

"I have no idea. I can't feel the demons anymore. I can't get into the other dimension. The only reason I could before was because part of my soul was attached to the demon that killed Trent. Now he's dead, and I… I'm lost. I don't have any clues, anything to go on. I don't know who they are or what they have planned for my son, only that he's in danger."

"I see. And Floyd didn't have any suggestions?"

"He said to trust my instincts."

"That's it?" His gorgeous green eyes looked into mine, seeing into me, through me.

I nodded. "The problem is, I don't know what my instincts are saying. I don't know how to sense the demons anymore, let alone how to fight them. I know they're everywhere, but I can't shoot them, and the sword won't work on this side."

"You still have the Hamet sword?" Chase asked.

"Of course. The demon I got it from made it seem like it was important. It's not something I'm going to just get rid of, even if I can't use it."

"That's wise. You never know when you may need it. I think there's more to that sword than we yet realize."

"There's one more thing I don't quite get," I said.

"What's that?"

I glanced down at my son, still dozing in his carrier. "Why now? Nine months of pregnancy, and the last two I could barely move. Plus, the first few months when he was a newborn, I was still recovering.

15

There were tons of opportunities to take him if they wanted to, and I would've been powerless. Or at least an easier target. So, what happened now to make them suddenly ready to try it? Now that I'm back at work, getting back into shape… why now? What are they planning?"

"Floyd didn't know any of this?"

"If he did, he wasn't sharing. He just wanted to warn me they're coming. And there's something else, something new, or old, he doesn't know." I sipped at my coffee again. Not having copious amounts of creamer to cool it down, it was still a little hot, but cool enough to drink.

"We have a lot of work to do, then. I'll see what I can find out from Floyd. And from any other sources I come across. Let me know if you uncover anything in any of your cases."

"I don't even know where to start looking."

"You didn't know last time, either."

A smile twitched my lips. "True, but at least I had Trent's old case files."

"That's a start. Maybe there's something in one of those cases that didn't get wrapped up. Some lead you can follow."

"Yeah, okay. That's a good idea. Thanks."

"That's what I'm here for," Chase smiled.

And just like that, we seemed to be back to normal. Back to how we were when we were following leads and uncovering evidence last year.

Maybe that camaraderie, working together, was all Chase wanted. More than a year now since Trent's death. I could start really dating again, but I could also be content to be friends. Partners on this mission, whatever this mission turned out to be.

I sipped my coffee, enjoying the moment of companionable silence. Until it was broken by Beck wailing.

"Good morning, handsome," I cooed, reaching down to free him from his seat, and picked him up. He immediately started rooting, looking for food.

I didn't have any qualms about feeding him in public, but at the coffee shop, across the table from the hot pastor I was interested in… yeah, no. That wasn't going to happen.

"Well, I should probably get him home," I said.

Chase reached across the table to tousle Beck's head. "He looks a lot like you."

"Really? I've always thought he was the spitting image of Trent."

16

Chase shrugged. "I didn't know Trent, so maybe. But I still see so much of you in him."

"Thank you. And thanks for meeting me. It was good to see you."

Chase stood and lifted Beck's carrier up onto the table to make it easier for me to put him back in. "You look good, Jack. Motherhood suits you."

I finished strapping Beck in and came around the table.

Chase pulled me into a hug. Man, it felt good to be in his arms again. I hadn't realized how much I'd missed that.

"Call me if you find anything," I said.

"I will," he promised. "You too."

⌗ ⌗ ⌗

Beck was super annoyed by the time I finally got him upstairs to our apartment. He grabbed my shirt and nuzzled at me, his wail reverberating off the thin walls.

"Hold your horses, it's coming." I flopped onto the couch to feed him. While he nursed, I pulled out the notes I had on the case from a year ago.

Dionysius used to be the lead demon in this area. The demons were very territorial. Technically they were supposed to be on the same side, but it was really an every-man-for-himself kind of arrangement. They all sought to be the most powerful. Dionysius had planned to take over the city and enslave everyone in it by using his demon minions to spawn a breed of half-demon monsters for his army.

I'd killed him and at least most of his spawn, but not before he killed my best friend, Bridget. Sharp pain stabbed through me at the memory. It was her wedding day. She was so happy. Happy to be getting married to who she thought was the man of her dreams, happy to be carrying his child. And I'd done nothing. I didn't know how to tell her that her fiancé was a demon and her child inhuman spawn. So, I'd gone along with it, agreed to be her maid of honor. By the time he'd killed her, there was nothing I could do. I should've acted sooner. Should've done something else to protect her.

Wiping away a tear, I vowed for the millionth time not to make that mistake again.

I turned my attention back to my notes.

Dionysius's plot was only one piece of a much bigger plan. The demon prophecies foretold that their great leader would come from a specific line of people and would rule the world. Their chosen one was, in pop culture terms, the coming antichrist. They were carefully manipulating that bloodline, trying to ensure that the antichrist would be pure and fulfill their prophecies.

My fiancé, Trent, was a direct descendant of that bloodline.

And now Beck.

Satiated, Beck pulled away and smiled up at me, milky drool leaking from his lips, his big brown eyes bright.

I grinned at him and lifted him up to my shoulder to burp him.

Case notes littered the coffee table and couch around me, making less sense the more I looked at them. I read through them all again, even though I'd been over them dozens of times in the last year. I had to be missing something.

There were no dates attached to any of the prophecies. The antichrist could've been Trent or his father or Beck or any of a dozen generations. The prophecies might not be fulfilled for another thousand years, so what made this day, this child, so special?

And what was the new thing Pastor Floyd was concerned about? How did it tie in to what happened last year?

I set Beck on his blanket on the floor with some toys while I opened up the files on the flash drive Trent had left for me.

But this was all old news. The trafficking was all Dion's doing. As far as I knew, missing persons reports had gone back to normal after I killed him. There would always be crime, but the rates weren't unusually high like they had been a year ago.

I pulled up news reports. Both for Phoenix and across the country, specifically looking for upsets in local governments, and scrolled through article after article. I was about ready to give up for the night, when a familiar name popped out at me.

Brandon Harding. One of the potentials, who I'd rescued from Dionysius.

A year ago he was a state representative or something from Chicago. Now he was running for senator in Illinois.

It could be coincidence—run of the mill political ambition—but it could also be orchestrated by the demons, positioning him in a seat of power that could very easily be upgraded. Pastor Floyd had mentioned him—said that he knew what was going on—but I'd assumed Pastor Floyd meant it was because we'd told Harding everything after I'd rescued him from an underground demon lair where he'd been imprisoned by Dion last year. Was there more? Did he know what was happening now?

I glanced at my watch. It was getting late Chicago time. But I needed to talk to him. Looking through my notes, I found his personal number. He'd given it to me after I'd saved him.

I called and a woman answered the phone.

"May I speak to Brandon please?" I asked.

"He's busy," the woman said, her tone curt and suspicious.

"Can you tell him it's Jack Davidson calling? I have a feeling he'll make time."

The woman sighed audibly, and the phone went silent for a few moments.

Beck scooted toward the shoes I'd kicked off. In a minute it would be in his mouth. Retrieving the shoe, I tossed it down the hall toward my room and went to the kitchen to get a cracker for him to gnaw on.

"Jack?" Harding's voice came over the line. "How are you? It's been a long time."

"About a year," I said. "I'm okay. I was just doing some work, and I saw you're running for senator. Congratulations."

"Thanks," he said. "It was not an easy decision to come to, but after… everything that happened last year, I realized I'm in a unique position to do some real good in this country."

"That's great," I said. "Actually, that's kind of why I called."

I was pretty sure he didn't entirely understand the scope of what had happened to him. I'd explained that he was one of the potential men bred to be the antichrist, but… well, I couldn't blame him for not fully grasping that. Still, I had to find out if he knew anything.

"I've gotten reports that there has been an increase in demonic activity lately. Have you noticed anything where you are? Has anyone approached you—anything seem fishy about anyone connected to your campaign? Anything like that?"

"No, nothing. I mean… I didn't know who—or what—they were before, so there's always a chance they've infiltrated my team without my knowledge, but no one has approached me about rethinking my position on becoming the antichrist. At least not this week."

I chuckled. At least he could have a sense of humor about all this. "Okay. Well, you have my contact info, right?"

"I do."

The cracker box was almost empty. I'd have to put those on my list when I hung up.

"Give me a call if you notice anything. I have a bad feeling that things are going to get worse before too long."

"I will. Good to hear from you, Jack."

"Thanks. You too."

I hung up the phone and stared at the wall.

I hadn't known him well, so it was hard to tell whether he sounded normal or not. So much about him reminded me of Trent—his voice, his looks, even some of his speech patterns. Something felt off about the conversation, but I couldn't quite put my finger on it.

Or maybe everything was fine, and I was looking for things to be suspicious about.

I slammed my hand against the wall, scraping my palm on the rough stone of the backsplash hard enough to break the skin.

Damn it. I did not have time for this.

Beck started to fuss. He was really a pretty easy baby, but he needed me to stop working and pay attention to him. I scooped him up off the floor and carried him on my hip while I rinsed the blood from my hand and nuked myself some leftovers for dinner. After he was down for the night, I pulled the Hamet sword from my closet and sat on my bed, running my fingers over the blade.

Except in this dimension it wasn't a blade. The metal it was made of bent and crumpled like rubber, bouncing back into place as soon as I let go.

The rubber-metal smacked against my hand where I'd scraped it, making it bleed again.

I wiped my hand on the leg of my jeans and continued to study the sword. In this dimension, it was little better than a toy. Something about the way it had been made was designed for the other dimension, and here it was… incomplete. Like there was a missing ingredient.

In the other dimension, a formidable weapon I'd used to slash demons into oblivion without my arm getting tired. Like it was made just for me.

But I could no longer get to the other dimension. I was powerless. Powerless to stop the onslaught of demons. Powerless to fight back.

Powerless to protect my son.

I closed my eyes and squeezed the hilt, feeling it mold to the shape of my hand.

Pastor Floyd said to trust my instincts. What did that mean? How did I do that?

The sword seemed to grow warm in my hand, but my room got cold. My eyes popped open. The air around me seemed to shimmer. A familiar sense of nausea made my stomach roil as goosebumps rose on my arms, and the hair on the back of my neck stood on end.

The Eyes were back.

THREE

I gasped and dropped the sword on my bed.

The sensation of my skin crawling and goosebumps raising on my arms diminished but didn't go away. I could still feel the presence of a demonic entity in my room, but it wasn't as strong without the sword in my hand. So subtle I could almost believe I'd imagined it, if I hadn't known the feeling so well.

I picked up the sword again, and again the sensation of the demon's presence filled the atmosphere.

"I know you're there," I said. "What do you want?"

Silence.

Was it because I couldn't hear it, or because it didn't answer?

The energy shifted slightly, like lightning in the air concentrated on a certain spot, then drifting away, like the thing was moving. Before, it had felt like it was in front of me, and now it felt like it was moving away. Toward the door. The hall.

Toward Beck.

Terror clutched my stomach and yanked. Gripping the sword, I ran after the demon.

It stopped inside Beck's room. The cloud of energy drifted a little more. It almost felt like it was standing over the crib, looking down at him the way I'd done so many times.

They all look the same. The demon's voice reverberated in my head.

I gasped. So, I could hear it. Only as long as I held the sword? I couldn't be sure—I didn't know if it had said anything before.

"What do you mean?" I asked.

A jolt of surprise shot out from the demon.

I'd almost forgotten what it felt like to sense their emotions. To almost be able to read their minds.

It seemed surprised I could hear it.

"What do you mean they all look the same?" I demanded again.

The boys. The ones we're after. They have a mark.

A mark? I glanced at Beck over the side of his crib. I couldn't see anything except a shadow crossing his face.

Wait...

That wasn't a shadow. It wasn't visible before, but now—because of the sword?—I distinctly what looked like a very faint birthmark on his forehead. A symbol.

"You won't take my son," I said.

You won't be able to stop us.

Trust my instincts.

I prayed this would work.

I thrust the sword into the area where it felt like the demon stood.

Shock and pain rippled through it, and then... it disintegrated. I don't know how I knew, but I did. The air felt dead, like I'd switched off a heat lamp. It had turned to ash, the way the demons in the other dimensions had when I'd killed them over there.

I stared at the sword. It worked *through* dimensions. Helped me sense the other side.

I couldn't believe it.

Had it done this before?

No, of course not. I would've noticed. So, what changed? What was different now?

I could figure that out as I went along. In the meantime, I was just grateful to have something on my side.

I might stand a chance after all.

I gripped the sword and closed my eyes, focusing on the other dimension that seemed just out of reach. There—another demon, just out of my range. In my second bathroom, just on the other side of Beck's bedroom wall.

The demon that had haunted me last year, the one that had stolen a piece of my soul and trapped it in the other dimension, had told me there were rules. That they had to respect certain boundaries if I set them. Who made the rules? Enforced them? I had no idea. But they were there.

"You're not welcome here," I said. "None of you. You will not enter my apartment or come near my son."

The thing seemed to whoosh backward, until it was in my neighbor's apartment.

You can't keep us from your son.

"You will not come in my apartment. And you're not welcome at Gen's, either."

You have no authority over Gen's home.

Shit. The thing had a point. Maybe I could get Gen to disinvite them or something. That had zero potential for backfiring.

But in the meantime, I'd make damn sure they stayed out of my place. "Get out and stay out. If you set foot in here, I'll kill you."

I dropped the sword, surprised to feel energy running through my system. Before, when I'd accessed the other dimension, it left me exhausted, sometimes catatonic. But now, power ran through me.

I picked up the sword again. A shock, almost like static electricity, energized me.

Trust my instincts.

Still didn't know what that meant, but I was getting there. And my instincts said the sword was much more powerful than I'd previously believed. Somehow, Chase had intuitively known that, as well.

I'd probably get more than a few weird looks down at the station, but I was going to be carrying this sword with me everywhere from now on.

Take that, demon scum.

###

The next morning, when I dropped Beck off at Gen's, I lingered for a few minutes, trying to determine the best way to ask my very weird request.

"Hey, Gen... you remember last year, all the reports about the Prince and the demons and stuff, and the giant monsters that were terrorizing the city?"

Because that didn't sound insane.

"Yeah, of course. Did you know there are whole forums dedicated to proving it was all a hoax? Like that it was some giant conspiracy? But I knew people who died. I—why?"

I gave her a little half smile. "Okay, so you know it was a real thing that happened. I can't really talk about it much, because... because I can't. But I have reason to believe that there may be another attack. And I know this is going to sound weird. But would you say something for me, out loud?"

She raised an eyebrow, but nodded.

"No demons are welcome here," I said.

"No demons are welcome here." She stuck her hands in her back pockets, an obvious attempt to not cross them or otherwise indicate that she thought this was ridiculous.

"Leave my apartment and do not return."

She stared at me for a long moment before repeating my words. "Thank you," I said.

She nodded. "Did that... do anything?"

I pulled the sword out from where I'd sheathed it to my back using my shoulder holster and clutched the hilt.

The apartment felt clean. I could sense demonic presences, but they felt far away. "I think it worked," I said.

She stared at me, her mouth gaping at the sword. And especially when it bent like a toy as I put it back.

"I..." she paused. "I trust you, Jack. And I'll take care of your son. But any time you feel like explaining what's going on, feel free."

"Thanks," I said. "I'll tell you what I can when I can. Just keep Beck safe."

I kissed Beck and hurried to work.

I stepped into the precinct and was blasted with a shock of air-conditioned atmosphere. It wasn't supernaturally hot like it had been last year, but Phoenix was experiencing the traditional mid-October heat wave. And the captain liked it cold, so the AC would stay on long past when everyone else shut theirs off entirely or switched to heat.

"Morning, Jack."

I smiled at my coworker, Ken, but it was half-hearted. He still hadn't given up his crush on me. He wasn't quite as obvious about it as he'd been before, but he'd brought me meals several times after Beck was born and was constantly offering to help out.

"What's new?" I asked him.

"The usual. Sex. Drugs. Rock and roll. Mostly drugs. Got an uptick in violent incidents over the last week. Something new on the streets—we haven't been able to pinpoint it in blood tests yet, but it's making people super violent."

Warning bells rang in my head. Violent how? Was it related to demonic activity? Or was I just being paranoid again? There was plenty of non-demon crime in a city this size, and I had enough to deal with at the moment without going off on potentially unrelated rabbit trails. "Sounds fun. Good luck with that." I hurried past his desk.

"Hey, Jack?" he called me back.

"Yeah?"

"Why are you wearing a sword?"

"Working on a theory."

"What kind of theory?"

"Can't say. It would bias the results," I said.

Not bad for coming up with an excuse out of my ass. I hurried away toward the captain's office and knocked on the door.

"Come in," the captain called.

"Hey, Captain," I said. "If you don't have anything urgent for me, I'd like to go through some of the case files from last year."

"Sure," he said. "Anything in particular you're looking for?"

"I'm not sure yet," I said. "Maybe it's just that we're coming up on the anniversary of the day the Prince tried to take over, but I have a nagging feeling we missed something that may come back to haunt us."

"I understand."

His smile suggested he was indulging me because of the trauma I'd faced last year, but I'd take it. I could handle his pity if it meant I could try to get information that would help me with whatever Pastor Floyd was warning me about.

I'd been working for about an hour when the captain burst out of his office and charged toward my desk. "We've got an armed robbery in progress," he shouted. "One civilian injured, at least one more being held. All hands on deck. Let's go!"

FOUR

I followed the captain out of the precinct and raced with the others toward the scene of the robbery, a pawn shop tucked into the side of a mountain—or what passed for a mountain here.

We surrounded the front of the building—there was no back entrance—and the captain demanded that the perpetrator come out with his hands up.

A man stumbled out a few moments later, hands raised. He had something—some type of bulky, metal object—tucked into his pants. He walked slowly toward us.

The sword at my back seemed to vibrate.

I ought to stay in position, gun ready, but the sword hummed at me, calling me. I reached behind my back with one hand and grabbed the hilt.

Almost immediately, the nausea and chills that assaulted me when I accessed the other dimension and when I felt demons near, as I had in my apartment, swept over me.

I stared at the man, focusing my attention through the sword. I didn't exactly understand it, but somehow the sword was acting like a conduit, letting me feel things more strongly.

I looked at the man who still walked slowly toward us.

He was definitely human. But... also demon.

How did that work? He couldn't be both.

The man stumbled to the side, heading toward the mountain. What was he doing?

"Stop!" the captain yelled.

He didn't stop.

The captain raised his voice, his weapon ready. "I said stop! Don't take another step!"

He still didn't stop.

He stumbled another step, then another, almost into the mountain, and then… disappeared.

The captain fired off several rounds into the side of the mountain. Dust flew up into the air and a rabbit bolted into a different clump of brush. But the man—the man was nowhere.

I tucked my gun into its holster and grabbed the sword hilt with both hands, focusing on where the man had disappeared.

There.

I could barely make it out, but I knew it was there. The line of scorched earth that indicated a portal to the other dimension had been opened.

The thief had taken whatever he'd stolen and escaped through a portal to the demon dimension.

But that wasn't possible.

Humans couldn't travel in the other dimension. I was the only one who had, as far as I knew, and that was only because I was partially connected to a demon who had grabbed on to me.

Demons could take humans with them, though. Humans would pass out and eventually die in there, but if a demon carried them, they could be transported. That was how Dionysius had kidnapped so many girls without a trace. His minions had taken the girls through portals and carried them to their safe houses and underground labs for experiments.

That meant this thief had to be either working with or for a demon on the other side. The demon had to transport him through the other dimension to wherever he was going. That, or something had happened to him, similar to what had happened to me, and he was somehow attached to a demon and therefore could travel through their dimension like I had.

"Canvass the area," the captain shouted. "He can't have gotten far. I don't know how he did that, but we're going to get him!"

Officers swarmed over the hill and spread out behind the pawn shop. Paramedics rushed in and retrieved a forty-something woman who had blood streaming down her arm.

The captain waved at me. "Jack, you get in there and talk to the pawnbroker. Find out what she knows."

I nodded, sheathed my sword, pulled my gun, and jogged toward the door.

Ken followed me.

I acknowledged him, and we stepped inside. It was a smallish room. The clerk, a scrawny young woman with big boobs and wine-red

29

hair stood behind the counter, her hands up. She looked like I could break her slender frame in half—but at the same time there was a hardness to her, like she'd be scrappy in a fight. Someone I wouldn't want to underestimate based on her size.

The usual array of instruments and knickknacks lined the walls, and cases of jewelry and weapons sat arranged with small aisles between them all along the floor.

One case, near the back wall, was shattered.

I went one way, Ken went the other, and we quickly cleared the building, then I approached the clerk, holstering my weapon.

"Are you hurt?" I asked.

She shook her head.

"You sure? Do you want the paramedics to check you out?"

"I'm fine," the girl said. "Just a little freaked out."

"Are you up for answering a few questions?"

She rubbed her hands up and down her arms. "Sure. Of course. Whatever you need to know."

I pulled out my notepad and pen. "Okay, Miss—" I glanced at her nametag. "Joy. I'm Detective Davidson, and this is Lieutenant Richmond. Can you tell us what happened?"

"I opened the store. Went through my daily routine, like I always do. Bell on the door jingles, and that woman walks in, looking for a trumpet for her kid who's in band. So, I show her the instruments, and she sees the prices and gets all twitchy, like she expected instruments to be cheaper."

Joy rolled her eyes, then waved back toward the door. "Anyway, then this guy walks in. I knew there was something off about him, like he was on drugs, maybe? Anyway, I ask if I can help him and he ignores me. Walks straight to that case over there, pulls a handgun from under his shirt, and smashes the case with the butt. The alarm automatically goes off, and he freaks out and starts firing. Hits the woman in the arm."

I nodded to encourage her to keep talking.

"Right, so I duck behind the counter and press the panic button. He fires off a round or two, then goes back for something out of the case. Then he starts having this weird schizo conversation with himself. Saying he can't touch it, he tried and it burns. Something like that. He starts screaming like he's being tortured and flails on the ground for a couple minutes, and I'm watching through the glass on the counter, but I don't want to move because God only knows what he'd do next, and then he stands up, grabs a towel or something from that pile of linens in the corner and picks up whatever it was, stuffs it

30

in his pants, and goes for the door. That's when he hears sirens, and he stops and waves the gun around again. You guys surround the place, he went out, and you came in. That's it."

"What did he take?" I asked.

"Hell if I know. I just work here."

"Don't you have an inventory list of what's in the cases? Can we take a look?"

Joy nodded. "Yeah, sure, hang on a sec."

She unlocked the door behind her labeled Office and disappeared inside, returning with a huge photo album. She set the album on the counter and flipped through it. "Case number seventeen," she muttered, scrolling with her finger along the pages. "Here we go. Here's all the things that were in that case, with pictures and pawn tickets."

"Thanks," I said.

I took the book over toward the smashed case and nodded for Ken to join me. We couldn't touch anything until photographers and forensics got here to document everything, but we could look.

Together we matched up the inventory with what was still left until only one picture remained unaccounted for.

It was a statue of a woman. Looked like an ancient goddess thing. Gold, according to the pawn ticket, about eighteen inches tall. Not solid—it was hollow inside—and inset with lapis lazuli for her eyes and a belt around her waist. No details on its origin, whether it was an antique or imported or anything.

Just a statue.

Probably worth a fair penny, being gold and having real lapis lazuli, but nothing to set it apart from anything else in the store.

So, what was important about it? What made it desirable enough that a demon helped a human steal it? Or hired a human to steal it? Was there something happening in the demon dimension to make things like this statue, whatever it was, and my sword act strangely?

No, it had to be the other way around. The human had to have gotten help from the demon. A demon wouldn't need to use a human at all. A solid one, anyway. There were different kinds, I'd discovered. The real, physical, live ones, and, in a sense, their ghosts. The real ones, like Dionysius and Chet and the others, could come into this dimension, appearing human but having supernatural strength and abilities. On the other side, they looked like monstrous gargoyles, but here it was impossible to distinguish them from regular people unless you had special sensitivity or had your soul trapped partially in the other dimension. Those were the ones who could breed with humans to create the half-demon monstrosities. One of those could've traveled through dimensions and opened up a portal inside the pawn shop, taken what they wanted, and left again through the portal without ever setting up off an alarm.

But one of the ghosts…

When I killed one of the demons like Dionysius or their mutant hybrid spawn, that creature's spirit was trapped in the other dimension. They could no longer access this dimension, although they could still influence it. Their dimension was outside ours, or on top of it—at any rate, they couldn't come into this dimension, but since their dimension was sort of layered over this one, they were still part of it.

One of those would need a human to get the statue. Would that work? Could they ride a human body into this dimension in much the same way that we could ride them into the other?

I'd have to ask Pastor Floyd about that.

But what on earth could a demon want with a statue? How would it help them? They had no need of or desire for material possessions, so even though it was gold, it wouldn't do them any good. And why *that* statue? It was clear they were after that thing specifically, and that it was somehow powerful enough to make their human minion balk at grabbing it.

So, what was it?

I turned back to Joy, who stood with her back pressed against the wall behind the counter, hands still rubbing her arms.

"Don't touch anything until after forensics gets in here," I told her. "I may have more questions. And we'll need copies of any video surveillance you got."

"Sure," she said, nodding.

I held up the photo of the statue and the pawn card. "Can I take these? Or make a copy of them?"

"I can copy them," she said.

She took the album and disappeared into the office, returning a moment later with copies of both the picture and the pawn card.

"Thanks," I said.

Ken followed me out.

"You were pretty quiet in there," I said. "What are your thoughts?"

"I'm not sure yet, but all of this with the guy disappearing into thin air reeks of the supernatural entities we encountered last year."

I nodded. "I was thinking the same thing."

"My question is, what is that thing?" Ken asked. "Why did they go to so much trouble to steal it? Is it some sort of magical artifact? What does it do?"

32

"My questions exactly." I tapped the copy of the pawn ticket. "That's what we're going to find out."

Back at the precinct, I gave Ken the task of checking out the person who had sold the statue to the pawn shop, Ellie Malone.

I watched the footage of the robbery, which happened pretty much exactly as Joy said.

After about the third time through, I studied mug shots, looking for anyone who matched the description of the perp.

"Got anything?" Ken asked, sitting down on the edge of my desk.

"Nothing. You?"

He shrugged. "I talked to the owner of the pawn shop. The statue came in about a week ago. The woman who brought it was stout, fidgety, and wanted to sell not pawn. She didn't have provenance on the thing. Said her grandfather gave it to her when he passed a month ago, and she needed the money because she'd gone into debt with funeral expenses."

"I don't suppose we have any information on the grandfather?"

Ken picked up my stapler and absently turned it over in his hands. "Nothing much. Background check on both of them was pretty standard. She's divorced, one kid, shares custody with the ex. Clean as far as criminal record. Grandfather was a vet—Gulf War, I think— Alzheimer's."

"Okay, thanks. I'll do an image search and see if I can figure out what the statue is. Let me know if you find anything else out."

"Will do," Ken said.

He shuffled back to his desk.

I stared at the computer screen for the next couple of hours but found nothing. Still no closer to understanding the stupid statue's importance. I rubbed my eyes and arched my back to try to relieve some of the stiffness.

"Jack!" the captain called me from his office.

I stood, stretched, then walked in. "What's up?"

"Any luck on that statue?"

"I've got nothing. It seems to be one-of-a-kind. Which may be why it was valuable enough to steal, but I've got nothing conclusive. The shop paid the previous owner a few hundred for it and was charging triple that. So, it's pricey, but not really more valuable than half the other stuff in the shop, so no reason that I can figure out why it would be the one thing he grabbed."

"I've had people interviewing the clerk as well as the owner, and none of them seem to have any idea, either."

33

"Maybe we could call one of those TV shows where they have experts in those sorts of things," I suggested.

"Yeah, do that," the captain said. "Can't hurt to ask around. Somebody's gotta know something."

"Okay," I said. "I'll fire off a couple emails, and then I need to get going."

The captain nodded. "Good work today. But listen—if we don't find something in a day or two, shelve it. I don't want to waste too many hours on an ugly-ass statue that no one cares about except the guy who stole it."

I nodded and made my way back to my desk. On one hand, he had a point. Under normal circumstances, I'd assume it was an heirloom or something that someone wanted to get back but couldn't afford to pay for.

But the guy who stole it clearly had demonic help and he disappeared into a demon dimension.

That meant it was connected to something bigger, something worth killing for, and I had to find out what.

FIVE

"Jack!" the captain shouted from his office.

I jumped up from my desk and hurried that direction. I stopped just inside the door, leaning against the frame. "What's up?"

"We've got a murder. Body dumped in a ravine down by the airport."

"I'm on it."

The scene was already cordoned off when I arrived and made my way down the steep hill to the bottom of the ditch. A jogging trail ran along the top edge. A woman in spandex shorts and a neon green sports bra stood next to the cops on the scene.

One of them saw me and waved me over. "Detective, this is Cassie Holt. She found the body."

"I totally thought it was, like, just some homeless person at first." She twisted her fingers together so hard I worried they might fall off. "But then, I don't know, it was just, like, way too still. Too stiff and unnatural. So, I went down there and he was, like, totally dead."

"Totally dead. So, not just a little dead."

She narrowed her eyes at me, and I quickly put my professional face on. "Thanks, ma'am. You can finish giving your statement, and then you're free to go."

I made my way down to the body and crouched down. Male. Lying face up, eyes closed. Older—fifties or sixties I guessed, based on the weathered condition of his skin, although that could be off. He wore a white gown, like a hospital gown, but with full coverage. Blood stained the front, making a pattern that looked like it had been drawn or maybe written. Pulling on my gloves, I shuffled closer and lifted the gown at his neck.

36

A symbol had been carved in his chest. It looked like an ankh, but without the arms of the cross—just the post with the loop on the top.

I didn't see any more obvious wounds, so it looked like that was the most likely cause of death, but there wasn't nearly enough blood for him to have bled out. He might also have a stab wound in the back, but there wasn't any blood on the ground, and there was no staining that I could see from this side, so that seemed like a less likely explanation.

Forensics arrived a moment later, setting to work photographing and collecting any possible evidence.

"He wasn't killed here," I said, stepping out of their way. "Pretty sure he was dumped."

I turned to address the other cops. "There's no vehicle access anywhere around, so he must have been killed close by. Check for a blood trail or any other evidence of how he might have been brought here."

Of course, that was completely disregarding the possibility that he'd been dragged through another dimension…

I mentally kicked myself. I dealt with murder all the time, and I hadn't had a demon-related death in a year. What were the chances I'd have a portal-jumping thief and a dead guy dropped from another dimension in the same day?

"Here!" someone shouted.

Relief flooded over me as I stepped carefully over the sparse weeds between the body and the trail toward where the tech stood. Kneeling, I examined the blood spatter on the ground just to the side of the path.

More blood smeared the ground nearby, heading in the direction of the airport. A few of the others and I followed the trail as it looped around the lot between the airport and the industrial area a few blocks west. The blood spatter stopped right next to the fence that surrounded the part of the airport where UPS and FedEx and other shipping planes were housed.

What in the world? Or the underworld?

Where had he been killed? In the airport somewhere? How had they gotten the body out without being seen?

"There's blood in there," someone said.

I looked to where he pointed, at a splatter on the ground inside the airport perimeter.

"We've got to get in there," I said.

My phone buzzed, and I glanced at the caller ID.

Shit. Gen. I was late to pick up Beck.

I answered the phone. "Hey, I'm on a case. I'm so sorry, I'll be there as soon as I can."

"Don't worry about it. I just wanted to check. He's fine here for as long as you need him to stay."

"Thanks, Gen. I'll call you when I'm on my way."

It took forever to get the clearances to get inside the airport, but at last we found the scene of the crime—a hangar. A plane from the UAE had arrived a few hours earlier and was parked just over the pool of blood that had presumably come from our victim. Airport personnel swore it hadn't been there when the plane landed, and no one saw anything—or anyone—suspicious.

A headache started to form behind my eyes as I questioned about the fifth person who hadn't seen a thing.

"I've been here all afternoon," a man identifying himself as Joe Dunkle said. "I monitor from over there"—he pointed to an office behind a window—"make sure the safety and security protocols are followed, that kind of thing."

"A guy got murdered in here, and you saw nothing?" I asked.

He shrugged. "I don't know what to tell you. I was gone for maybe half an hour on my break—it's documented—but there was no one in here at the time. Pilots and crew were gone, and they hadn't come to unload it yet."

"But it's been unloaded now?"

"Yes, ma'am."

"Any idea what was on the plane?"

"Not a clue. We get shipments a couple times a day from all over the world. Could be anything."

Great. This guy was a wealth of information.

"Thanks."

We finished gathering evidence, then headed back to the precinct.

All the work from the robbery that morning still sat half-finished on my desk. It would only take me a minute to wrap that up.

I reached out to the celebrity antique experts as well as a couple auction house appraisers, sending them the picture of the statue, then shifted gears and input everything I had on the murder near the airport into the system. Finally, I wrapped up my paperwork for the day and stood to stretch.

"Hey, Jack, you headed home?" Ken asked, appearing by my desk.

"Yeah. I've got to pick up Beck."

"Do you want to hang out later? Get a drink or something?"

"I can't. I have plans."

Plans to work. But whatever. Definitely not plans to hang out with him.

I kept a copy of the picture of the stolen statue, hoping maybe Pastor Floyd would have an idea. Whenever I heard from him.

# # #

As I was leaving Gen's apartment with Beck, my phone rang.

I glanced at the name in surprise. Isaac Reyes. I hadn't heard from him in a couple weeks.

"Hey, Doc," I said.

"You can call me Isaac," he said.

I grinned. "I know. But I always think of you as Doc."

He gave an exaggerated sigh. "Well, as your doctor, I prescribe dinner out. Tonight, if you're free."

"Who am I to ignore a doctor's direct orders?" I shifted Beck's car carrier so I could unlock my truck. "Beck too?"

"Of course," he said. "I just found out about a little hidden treasure of an Italian place near the Biltmore that I've been wanting to try. I'll text you the address."

"Okay. See you in a few."

Isaac had worked with me on the case last year. He was the one who first figured out that the demon spawned from the kidnapped girls weren't normal. He was one of the best labor and delivery doctors in the Valley, but I'd decided I didn't want a guy I sometimes went out with to deliver my baby. That just seemed too weird.

Beck and I arrived at the restaurant where Isaac waited outside for us.

He grinned, flashing his brilliant white smile and deep, gorgeous dimples. He slipped one arm around my waist and kissed my cheek, then took Beck's carrier with his other hand. "You look gorgeous, as usual."

"I just got off work and I look like I got run over by a truck," I said.

"A really, really pretty truck," he said.

I laughed.

Isaac was one of the few people who could really make me laugh, deep down to my core. His deadpan humor was exactly what I'd needed after Bridget's death and during my recovery after I'd nearly died in the demon dimension battling Dionysius. We went out every few weeks, and shortly after Beck was born, he'd hinted at wanting to be more, but at the time I wasn't ready, leaving us in an extended phase of maybe-more-than-friends-but-not-actually-dating.

He'd made a reservation at the restaurant, and we were led right to our table. The interior was dimly lit, with elegant chandeliers above every table and smoky glass atop wood walls separating the tables from one another.

This place was not going to be cheap.

That was another thing I liked about him. He had plenty of money, and he was ridiculously generous, but he never showed off or acted condescending about anyone else's status or situation.

And he didn't really care what anyone else thought. This restaurant wasn't typically the kind you'd bring an infant to, but he never thought twice about me bringing Beck on our dates.

We sat and he lifted Beck from his carrier. "Hey, buddy! You're getting so big!"

Beck gave him a slobbery smile, which he returned, cooing and talking baby talk, before he handed Beck to me.

"Wine?" he asked.

"I probably shouldn't. I'm still breastfeeding."

"Good for you. Do you mind if I do?"

"Of course not."

He leaned over to kiss my cheek again. Friendly, affectionate—exactly personifying where our friendship had settled.

The waiter came and took our drink order, and Isaac turned to me. "What's new?" he asked.

"I may have had a demon encounter today," I said.

His eyes widened. "I thought you couldn't feel them anymore."

"So did I. But… remember the sword?"

"Of course."

"When I'm touching it, I can again. Not in the same way, but it's like it gives me access to at least a glimpse of the other dimension. Like, I can sense if there's one around, and yesterday… well, let me start at the beginning."

Between drinks and appetizers, I told him about my conversation with Pastor Floyd, the demon I'd killed in my apartment last night, followed by the robbery at the pawn shop this morning, and what I'd found—or rather not found—in my research this afternoon.

I left out the murder at the airport—it was fishy, but as yet unconnected.

"Did you see your pastor friend?" Isaac asked.

The waiter arrived just then with our meal, and I waited until he walked away to answer.

I didn't have any reason to be ashamed. Isaac and I weren't exclusive by any stretch. And yet I couldn't help feeling a twinge of guilt admitting that I'd seen Chase. The way Isaac looked at me, like he was looking through me—he always seemed to know what I was thinking, and right now I had a feeling he knew how weird it was for me to tell him about the other man in my life, even though there wasn't really anything to tell.

Maybe because seeing Chase twisted me up inside so much that I couldn't really articulate my feelings to myself, let alone justify them to someone else.

"Yeah," I said once we were alone again.

Beck reached for my plate, and I grabbed his tiny hands to keep him from burning himself.

"I ran into him on my way out of Pastor Floyd's office. We grabbed coffee and spent a couple minutes catching up. Nothing huge."

"Okay."

There was something in his tone—not jealousy, exactly, but certainly a wariness—as if he didn't want to say too much about Chase with me.

I reached over and took his hand. I didn't even know how I felt, I couldn't exactly explain it to him. But I wanted to reassure him that nothing had changed between us.

"You know if you need anything, all you have to do is ask," he said.

"I know. I don't even know what I'm dealing with yet, but if there's anything, I'll call."

"Good." Isaac finished off his glass of wine. He gestured toward my plate. "You going to finish that?"

I pushed it toward him. "Help yourself."

Between bites, he told me about a recent delivery where he'd had to perform an emergency C-section because there was a twin that had somehow not shown up on ultrasounds. "It shouldn't even be possible with technology the way it is, but the mom hadn't gotten the routine care she should've, and hadn't even seen a doctor since near the beginning of her pregnancy."

He went on, telling me about the details, allowing me to just relax and enjoy his company with no demands on my time or energy. My heart warmed. He always knew how to make me feel comfortable.

Beck was starting to fuss by the time we finished our dinner. "I need to get him home," I said. "Want to come over this weekend? Movie marathon or something?"

"I'd like that," he said. "I'll be on call all day Saturday, but maybe Sunday?"

41

"Sunday it is," I said.

He paid for our meal—no matter how many times I protested, he always insisted—and generously tipped our waiter, then walked me to my truck.

I secured Beck, then went around to my side and turned to Isaac.

He pulled me into a tight hug and held me for several long seconds, then pulled away slightly and dipped his head toward mine.

I lifted my face to accept the kiss and lingered there for a long moment, opening my mouth to the gentle teasing of his tongue before pulling away. "See you Sunday," I said softly.

He grinned. "Till then."

I headed home, suddenly ready to sleep, even though it was still early evening. I fed Beck and tucked him in, then went to my room and sat on my bed, holding the sword. I closed my eyes and felt the sword's energy pulsing through me, connecting me to the other dimension, making my body ripple with nausea and prickle with unnatural heat. I could sense demonic presences, but not close. Maybe somewhere else in the apartment complex? I wasn't sure, but at any rate, they weren't close enough to worry me.

I just wished I could go back there, even for a little while, to do some recon. I had to find out what the deal was with that statue.

I fell asleep still holding the sword, and woke a few hours later to my phone ringing. I sat up, blinking, trying to orient myself to what was happening.

The phone rang again and I grabbed it.

The precinct.

"Hello?"

"Jack, why weren't you picking up? This is an emergency." The captain.

"Sorry, it's the middle of the night, I'm trying to wake up. What's going on?"

"We found his body. The perp from the pawn shop. He's dead and… it's ugly."

"I'll be right there. I have to get a hold of my nanny and drop Beck off first."

He gave me the address and then I called Gen.

"Hey, Gen, I'm sorry to wake you in the middle of the night. There's an emergency at work. Can you take Beck?"

"Jack, I'm so sorry," Gen's voice rasped and her breath was ragged. "I think I got food poisoning. I've been throwing up all night. I can't take him right now. I'm really, really sorry, I wish I could, I just… I can barely move."

42

"No, don't apologize. I'm sorry you're sick. Get to a hospital if you don't get better soon, okay?"

I hung up. Who else could I call at this hour?

I called Cameron.

"Hey, Sis. I'm sorry to wake you—"

"Are you okay? What happened? Is Beck okay?" Cameron's voice was immediately alert and engaged.

"I'm fine, I just have to go in to work and Gen's sick. Can you watch Beck for a few hours?"

"Yeah, of course. Bring him over."

"Thanks. I owe you."

"You never owe me anything." Cameron yawned. "That's my favorite nephew there."

"I'll see you in a few," I said.

I dropped Beck off, and then drove to the crime scene. Cop cars surrounded an open field, lights flashing.

I walked toward the cluster of activity, ducking beneath crime scene tape and showing my badge to anyone who didn't know me.

"Jack, I'm glad you're here," the captain said.

He nodded toward a lump on the ground.

Not a lump. A body. Sort of. But it looked like it had been turned inside out.

I stifled a gag. The mass of flesh and viscera that lay piled on top of a skeleton stank like it had been there for a week.

"How do you know it's the guy from the pawn shop?" I asked.

The captain pointed to the shredded clothes beneath the body. "Same outfit from the video surveillance," he said. Then he pointed to a hand that stuck out from the rest of the body, bent at an unnatural angle, but still intact. "Fingerprints match the prints we found on the case at the pawn shop," he said. "We matched the prints from the pawn shop earlier to a petty thug named Jefferson Sezate. Facial recognition from the video suggested a probable match. And there's this."

He bent over and pointed to the perp's rolled up pant legs, where shards of glass like the ones from the broken case were nestled.

"Dental records will tell us for sure," the captain said, "but pretty sure he's our guy."

"So, he breaks into a pawn shop, steals one specific, obscure item, and then winds up dead," I said. "We have to figure out what that statue is."

"Agreed," the captain said. "Any luck on that?"

"Not yet. I've contacted—"

"This is now a federal case," a woman's voice interrupted me. "We'll take it from here."

Oh, goody. That voice was familiar in the worst possible way. Could this night get any worse?

SIX

I turned, plastering on my fakest smile. "Agent Escobar. What a joyous surprise."

FBI Agent Desiree Escobar's smile was like a feral cat's. She clearly loved interloping on my territory once again. She should've been grateful. I solved her biggest case for her. Which was also my case. But she still looked like she'd try to strangle me if I so much as irritated her.

"Hello, Jack. It's been awhile."

I decided to forego small talk. "Why is this federal? You guys don't have enough cases of your own? Or you just miss me doing your job for you?"

Her eyes narrowed ever so slightly.

Good. I was getting to her.

Her tone was all business, though. "He's wanted across state lines."

That was new. The captain didn't say anything about that. Maybe he didn't know yet. Wouldn't be the first time the feds had withheld information.

"Well, you found him. Congratulations."

She turned to the captain. "Who found the body?"

"Local man and his dog," the captain said. "Dog freaked out and started whining, trying to bolt away from here—which is weird, usually dogs want a closer look—and then the guy smelled it."

"Obviously the guy was dumped here," Desiree said. "Any idea how he got here or who left him?"

"Not yet," the captain said. "We're still gathering evidence. No sign of tire tracks or blood trail to give an indication of how they got him here. As far as we can tell, he just appeared."

Appeared.

Ten bucks said he was transported through the demon dimension, and a portal was opened to toss him out.

Stepping away from the crowd, I pulled the sword from my back and held the hilt, closing my eyes and focusing on the other dimension.

I could feel the other dimension stronger now. Keeping my mind centered on the dark, tainted sensation of the other side, I opened my eyes. The scorched line from the opening of the portal was visible, even though it was dark, which meant the hole ripped between dimensions was either very fresh or had been frequently used.

"You're still playing with your toy sword?" Desiree's voice reeked of condescension.

"Yeah, it's like a security blanket. Makes me feel comfy." I went back to ignoring her and focusing on the demon dimension.

There were no demons nearby, that I could tell. Apparently, even in the other dimension they cleared out after they dumped a body.

"There's no way this guy has only been dead for a few hours," Desiree said to my captain. "Are you sure you've identified him correctly?"

"Of course not," he said. "We just got here. But based on fingerprints and the evidence we have from the crime scene this morning, we're pretty sure."

"How does someone decay that quickly?" she asked. "He looks— and smells—like he's been dead for days."

I knew how. He'd died in the other dimension. Things were... accelerated there, in a way. The whole dimension was like a gothic mirror image of our world. Some things were stronger—more complete—like my sword. But other things, like bodies... well, it didn't usually take long for them to be rendered totally unidentifiable.

Which begged the question... why was he dropped here?

It wasn't like demons cared if their dimension was littered with carcasses. There were no *Adopt-a-Dimension* campaigns to clean up their area.

Which meant someone—or something—wanted him found. They wanted us to know he was dead. Wanted us to know what they could do.

Why?

And how did that relate to the statue?

I needed to talk to Pastor Floyd again. Maybe he'd seen something like it.

In the meantime, I should get back to being a cop. There was nothing else here that I could find with the sword.

I replaced it in the holster at my back and turned back to Desiree and the captain. "What was he wanted for across state lines for?"

Desiree narrowed her eyes, as though weighing how much she should tell me. But apparently good sense won out. "Murder."

"Who did he kill?"

"A man in New York named Sean Burke, one in St. Louis, Ben Polin, and one in Dallas, Paul Winchcomb."

"What did they have in common?" I asked.

"Nothing, that we can find, except they all look like they could be brothers. Dark hair, brown eyes. About six-four, well-built."

My stomach seemed to fall out of me.

Three men who looked like they could be brothers. And who matched the description of Trent.

"We're looking into whether they may have been adopted or had the same sperm donor or something. Or whether our perp was a serial killer going after this particular type for a reason."

"Do you…" I choked down the lump that rose in my throat and swallowed to get some moisture back in my mouth. "Do you have pictures?"

Desiree nodded. She pulled up a series of pictures on her phone.

My hunch was right.

They could be Trent's twins. Quadruplets. Whatever.

Something nagged at the back of my mind. I rubbed my temples, trying to remember.

"Do you know something?" Desiree asked.

"Maybe." I kicked the ground, sending up a puff of dust. "Hang on, it'll come to me."

Three men. Three men who could be potentials. Like Trent.

Pastor Floyd had talked to three men and warned them of their possible connection to the line that would produce the antichrist. And now three men were dead. The same three? No way to know for sure until I talked to Pastor Floyd.

And there was no way I could tell Desiree the connection.

"I've got nothing," I said. "But if I come up with something, I'll sure let you know."

Desiree eyed me. "You sure you don't want to share anything?"

"I may have a hunch, but not something actionable yet."

"Great. Looks like we're working together. Again." She sounded about as thrilled as I felt.

"Can't wait."

"Ditto," she said dryly. "I don't think there's anything else we can do here tonight. I'll come by your precinct in the morning to share notes."

"Okay," I said. I didn't have much choice. The captain would be all too willing to lend me out to the feds.

"Make sure I get detailed reports of forensics and everything else your people find," Desiree said to the captain. "I want to know how they did this to him—it's not normal."

No shit.

I picked my way over the deserted lot to my truck.

Desiree followed me. "Hey, Jack."

I turned, but didn't answer.

"You talk to Chase lately?"

Was she asking because she wanted to know or because she wanted me to confirm it? Either way, it would never get old messing with her.

"Yeah, I just saw him the other day. We had coffee at our special spot. Caught up. Why?"

"Just wondering if he mentioned me."

"Nope. Why would he?"

"We've been seeing each other pretty steadily for a few months now."

"That's nice for you," I said.

I picked up my pace and climbed up into my truck. The door slammed a little harder than I'd intended, but the last thing I wanted was to hear how happy she and Chase were together.

I couldn't blame him. She was beautiful, intelligent, successful, shared his faith—and didn't have a kid.

Still, I wished he'd said something. It would've been nice to not get my hopes up that we could reconnect.

I got to Cameron's apartment just before dawn.

She rubbed sleep from her eyes and gave me a hug. "Everything okay?"

"Yeah. Or no. I mean—I'm okay. But there was a murder. And... it may be related to the demon activity that we were dealing with last year."

"Related how?" she asked.

I wondered how much to tell her. She knew the details of everything that had happened last year. She'd even gone undercover for me and let herself be kidnapped by one of the demons who was spawning demon half-breeds. I didn't want to worry her unnecessarily, but the more she knew, the safer she'd be.

49

"I've been warned that they may be coming after Beck."

She slapped a hand over her mouth, her eyes wide. She nodded slowly and breathed deeply. "How can I help?"

"I don't know yet. I'll keep you informed of anything I come across. I'm going to go home and get some sleep, but if Gen is still sick, any chance you can watch him later? I'm going to need to go in to work in a few hours."

"Of course," she said.

I went through the same sequence with her that I had done with Gen, banishing demons from her apartment, then headed home.

⸭⸭⸭

Desiree was waiting in the conference room when I arrived at the precinct a little before noon. She looked perfect, as usual. Did she not actually need to sleep ever?

I smiled and sat across from her with my notes.

"What do you have on our vic from last night? Sezate?" She folded her manicured hands on the table.

"You remember Brandon Harding?" I asked.

"Senator or something?"

I nodded. "Illinois. Not senator yet, but he's starting his campaign."

"Wasn't he here last year?"

"Yes. He'd been kidnapped by the same trafficking ring that took all those girls."

Desiree tapped perfectly manicured nails on the scuffed conference table. "Why?"

"Not conclusive, but I think they wanted to use his position of political power to further their organization. I rescued him."

"Of course you did. Just an all-around hero," Desiree smiled, her voice syrupy.

Ignoring the barb, I slid his picture toward her.

"Oh..." She sat up straighter, suddenly interested in what I had to say.

Brandon Harding looked so much like Trent that I'd mistaken him for a minute when I first saw him—and that meant he looked eerily similar to the three murdered men.

Her gaze traveled from the picture of Brandon Harding and bored into me, genuine concern reflected in her eyes. "Do you think he's in danger?"

"Probably," I said. "Given his connection to the ring last year, and now these other murders—I'd say it's worth putting a guard on him, at least until we know whether or not he's connected. My guess is Sezate

50

was just a pawn, so even though he's dead, Harding may still be in danger."

"I'll take care of it. What else do you have?"

"Preliminary report from the ME. I haven't looked at it yet." I opened the folder and slid it to the middle of the table between us.

"Skin looks like it was torn with a jagged knife, but no fragments were found to indicate what type." Desiree scanned the page, summing up the findings. "Cause of death is inconclusive due to the amount of damage to the body. Organs punctured, skin pulled almost entirely from the skeleton and stuffed inside the chest cavity, but it's not clear yet how much of this was post-mortem."

She looked at me. "Who does something like this? And why?"

I shook my head. "I wish I had an answer. But I think it's a message. He killed three people and stole a statue and then was brutally murdered. We need to know what the deal is with that statue. Why it's so important, and to whom."

"Maybe the statue was a coincidence," Desiree said. "Maybe this was a revenge killing. Or maybe it was to keep him quiet about the other murders, and the statue theft is just a side gig."

"Possible," I said, "but it wasn't on his body. Plus, he disappeared right in front of our eyes right after he stole it. That means he had help. Someone got him out of there, and until we find out who and how, we have to assume that everything is important."

"Fair." She flipped through the file again. "I'll keep trying to figure out if there's a connection—genetic or otherwise—between the murdered men or between any of them and Sezate. You see what you can find on that statue."

I nodded. "You got it."

It was harder to hate her when we were actually working together. The fact was, she was actually pretty good at her job. A little too happy about being in charge, but she was hardly the worst person I'd ever had to report to.

I still hated her off the clock, though.

I took my notes and returned to my desk. More image searching. Looking in history textbooks and scouring descriptions.

Still nothing. Nothing useful, anyway.

I took a break and tried to find a match for the symbol that had been carved into the other guy's chest. Another great big pile of nothing except wasted hours, so I went back to the statue.

Tons and tons of statues. Gold was usually reserved for statues of goddesses, but I couldn't find any image that exactly matched the stolen one. And I didn't know enough about history or ancient cultures to even begin to narrow down where it might be from.

I needed help.

Who would I even ask about something like this? Pastor Floyd was the first person I thought of when I needed obscure religious knowledge, but this seemed more historical than religious. I knew a history professor at ASU, Ron Wilkins. Maybe he could help.

I called him. "Hey, Ron, it's Jack Davidson. Do you have time to meet me? I need some help with something."

He agreed to meet me for dinner. I stopped to pick up Beck and then met him at a little Mexican restaurant not far from the campus.

He was waiting on a quaint little bench out front when I got there.

"Jack, good to see you!" Ron hugged me, his beard scratching my neck. He looked older. How long since I'd seen him? He had to be pushing sixty by now.

He looked down at the carrier where Beck dozed. "Well, well! When did this happen?"

"A little more than six months ago. This is Beck."

"Congratulations. Trent's? Stupid question. Of course it is. You named him Trent's last name."

I nodded. "I don't know if you heard…"

He patted my arm. "I know. I saw it on the news. I'm very sorry for your loss."

I choked back the emotion that rose in my throat. "Thanks. How's teaching?"

"Oh, you know. Kids get stupider and more entitled every semester. But I'm tenured, so I'll hang in there for a few more years and then retire."

"Sounds idyllic," I said.

He chuckled and led me inside. "That's the goal. But you didn't come here to talk about my classes. What can I do for you?"

We seated ourselves at a table in the corner. The rich scents of chilies, spices, and roasting meat permeated the air. I pulled out the file with the picture of the statue. "This is connected to a case I'm working on. It was stolen from a pawn shop. This specifically—it was the only thing taken. The guy escaped and was later found murdered. He didn't have the statue on him when his body was found. We think it's related to why he was killed, but we don't know what it is or why it's important."

He pulled glasses out of his pocket and peered more closely. "This the only picture you have?"

Our waitress brought chips and salsa and water.

"Yeah. Sorry," I said when she was gone. "It's from the pawn broker's inventory records. Here's the weird thing. I can't find it anywhere. I've done about a bazillion searches, and I can't even figure out what it's supposed to be or where it's from. Best guess is an idol of a goddess, but which one?"

He studied the picture a little more. "Gold and lapis lazuli?" he asked at last.

"Yeah. Hollow."

"Not hollow, probably. At least not originally. Look at the detail work on the face and body. That was carved, not cast. My guess is it was carved in wood and overlaid with gold, but it's old enough now that the wood rotted away and left it hollow."

Finally getting somewhere. "Good, that's good. That helps. How old are we talking? Any idea what civilization she might be from?"

"Features look… Mesopotamian, maybe? I can't tell much from this photo—it's a horrible picture, Jack—but that's going to be my best bet. Can I have this?" He waved the copy I'd brought.

"Sure."

We ordered our dinner. Beck woke up, and I pulled a bottle from his diaper bag.

"He looks like you," Ron said.

"People keep saying that, but I just see Trent."

"That's good. It's nice to have that part of him with you." He tapped the picture. "I'll look into this a little more and get back to you if I find anything out."

"Of course. I appreciate it."

We chatted about mundane things for awhile—school and Beck and other things—while we ate.

Finally, we said goodnight and Ron walked me to my truck.

"It was good to see you, Jack."

"Thanks. You, too. And thanks for your help."

I climbed into my truck and started the engine. And my phone rang. Chase.

SEVEN

Why was Chase calling me?

"Chase, what's up? Are you okay?"

"Of course. Why wouldn't I be?"

"I don't know." My mind flashed back to Desiree and her determination to let me know he was hers. "Except for the other day, we haven't really talked in months and you never call. I just assumed something must be dire."

"No. Not dire. But something did happen."

"What is it?"

"Floyd went out of town. He left an envelope on my desk for you."

"Oh. Okay. Are you at the church now?"

"No, I just stopped in to grab my laptop and saw it. I'm home now. Do you want to stop by?"

"Yeah, sure. Can you text me the address?"

"Oh. Right. I forgot you've never been here. Sure."

"Okay, thanks. I'm in Tempe,. so I'll be there in like forty-five minutes or so."

I hung up, pulled out of the restaurant lot, and headed in the direction my GPS told me to go.

Floyd went out of town? Where did he go? Did he find another potential?

Why would he leave me an envelope and not call me or meet with me? This was weird, even for him.

This time of night, the traffic wasn't bad, so I made good time getting to Chase's. He lived in a condo in a gated community. Nice, but not overly ritzy. I didn't know exactly what I expected of a pastor's home, but it was a little surreal to see it.

54

His décor was sparse—bachelor pad, but not gross bachelor pad. Just… plain. Simple wood furniture that looked a little bit country, a few pictures on the walls, presumably of family members, and a crocheted purple-and-teal afghan draped over the back of a beige couch.

"Come on in," he said. "Have a seat."

"Thanks." I glanced around, trying to decide what the best place to sit was. Recliner was probably his vegging spot. But couch seemed intimate.

I settled on the very edge of the couch, setting Beck's carrier down next to me.

He went to the kitchen and got me a glass of water, then sat next to me on the couch.

He handed me an envelope with my name scrawled across the front.

I tore it open.

Inside was a folded piece of paper with just a few lines in the middle.

Jack,

I may have found some new information. I have to check into a couple more things first. This is important—don't trust anyone. No matter how closely you work with them or have worked with them in the past, no matter what you think you know about them, don't tell them anything until I have a chance to talk to you.

Floyd

I glanced at Chase. Did that include him? Isaac? Desiree?

"What does it say?" Chase asked.

"He may have a lead, and he'll talk to me about it when he gets back." I took a sip of the water he'd brought me.

"That's it?"

I shrugged. "He's not really known for being overly communicative, is he?"

"True. But… he could've sent that in a text."

"Does he even know how to text?" I asked.

Chase grinned and nodded toward the letter. "That is definitely more his technological comfort zone."

"There's a reason it's a classic," I said.

We sat in awkward silence for a few more moments before I stood up. "I should get Beck home. It was good to see you."

He stood and opened the door for me. "You too. Maybe we can do coffee next week sometime."

55

My heart stuttered. Was he asking because he actually wanted to see me, or because he was trying to get information out of me?

On the other hand, Pastor Floyd trusted Chase enough to get the letter to me. But he had to know about Chase dating Desiree, right? So, who was I not supposed to trust?

I really hated being this paranoid.

"Sure," I said. "Let me know when's good for you, and I'll try to work it in. And let me know when Floyd is coming back."

"I will as soon as he tells me."

I smiled, trying to look like everything was fine and normal as I made my way out to my truck and buckled Beck in.

Don't trust anyone.

Except my instincts. Do trust my instincts.

My instincts said to trust Chase. More than anyone else, I did trust him. So, what was I supposed to do with those two conflicting pieces of advice?

Nothing really, except keep things to myself until I knew more—or until Floyd returned my calls or came home and filled me in on whatever he was finding out.

⚏ ⚏ ⚏

The next day was Saturday, so I took Beck to the park. It was more for me than for him, but I figured the fresh air would do him good. I pushed him for almost an hour in the jogging stroller Trent's parents had gotten me for my baby shower.

I should go see them. We'd never been particularly close, even when Trent was alive, but we were on good terms and they doted on Beck. They lived out in Queen Creek—a solid hour from me—so, I didn't get over there often.

I called Trent's mom after lunch. "Hey, Deanna, it's Jack. Beck and I have some spare time today. I was thinking maybe we could come over for a bit."

"Oh, that would be so nice," Deanna gushed. "Dave, Jack and Beck are coming over," she said slightly away from the phone. "Jack, you're staying for dinner, I hope?"

"Sure," I said.

I went home and showered, then headed to Deanna and Dave's.

Deanna didn't skimp when she provided food for people. Tonight was no exception. Chicken and rice and broccoli and fruit salad and homemade brownies for dessert.

"Jack, honey, you're looking too thin. Eat a little more. You're still breastfeeding, right? You need the extra calories."

That after my third helping.

I took another brownie, just to appease her.

Also because she made damn good brownies.

"How's work?" Deanna asked.

"It's fine. Working on two cases at once right now. First one's a little strange. Guy who is wanted for at least three murders robbed a pawn shop and then wound up dead."

"Oh, that's too bad. I mean… I guess a serial killer getting what's coming to him isn't so bad… but still…"

I smiled. "I know what you mean."

"What about the second?" she asked.

"Another murder, this one seems to be ritualistic. Guy was drained of his blood and had a symbol carved in his chest."

Deanna put another brownie on my plate. "Oh, that's so icky. I can't believe people nowadays."

I decided not to tell her that ritualistic murders have been happening literally since the beginning of time. Besides, she wasn't wrong. It was pretty icky. I handed her Beck and stood to clear the table.

Dave shoved his chair against the wall, propped his feet up on Deanna's chair, pulled out his magazine—something about racecars— and settled back to half-listen while he browsed.

I put the leftovers in Tupperware and loaded the dishwasher while Deanna cooed at Beck.

She was a good grandma. I needed to make spending time with them a higher priority.

"I saw Cameron the other day," I said. "My nanny was sick, so I asked her to watch Beck for a little bit."

"Oh, honey, you know you can call us to babysit anytime."

"I know. But it was the middle of the night, and I had an emergency at work. I couldn't bring him this far in that amount of time."

"Of course not. Well, still, if you ever need us…"

"I know. Thank you," I said.

We stayed a little longer before I nestled Beck into his carrier and prepared to go home.

Deanna walked me to my truck.

"Jack… I wanted to talk to you about something. I'm not quite sure how to bring it up, but I… well, it's like this. You're a beautiful young woman, and, well, it's been a year now since Trent's death. I know… I know at some point you'll want to start seeing people again, and I just want you to know, we're okay with it. Not to rush you, of course. But some day… It would be good for Beck to have, you know,

57

a father figure. We still want to be part of your life, and we want you to feel comfortable, whenever you're ready, to introduce us to… whoever comes along."

I gave her a hug. "I've been out a few times. Nothing serious. But I promise to let you know if there ever is someone worth talking about. Thank you."

She nodded.

She was more of a mom than my own mom ever was. It seemed really weird to be talking to her about my love life, though. Still, if I ever did get serious about anyone, they were family.

I wondered who it would be, if I ever did bring someone home. Chase, the upstanding pastor, or Isaac, the hot doctor? Or neither?

#̶ #̶ #̶

I woke up early the next morning to my phone ringing.

Isaac.

"Hey, Jack, I'm really sorry to call this early. I have to cancel our movie date—I have a mom in labor, and it looks like it's going to be long and complicated. I'm not sure when I'll get off."

Was it Sunday already? I had forgotten that we'd made plans. "That's okay," I said, grateful that he hadn't just shown up when I'd totally spaced on him coming over. "We'll do it another time."

"I'll call you later this week, okay?"

"Sounds good. Thanks," I said.

I hung up and lay in bed for awhile, but couldn't go back to sleep, so I decided to go to church. Chase's church. There wasn't really another one I was familiar with, and at least I knew a few people there.

Beck and I sat in the back so I could take him out if he got fussy.

Desiree sat in the front row. Next to Chase.

I should've expected that.

Maybe I should just go.

But then Chase stood up to preach. I hadn't heard him speak before. Usually when I came, Pastor Floyd was in charge of the preaching, but with him out of town…

I found myself mesmerized with Chase's teaching. He spoke on guarding ourselves from spiritual attacks using spiritual weapons.

I suddenly felt awkward without my sword. I'd left it in my truck. Even I would feel weird carrying a sword into church, and besides, Chase's church was safe. But his talk reminded me how much more secure I felt when I had it on me.

The service ended, and Chase stepped down from the pulpit. Desiree clung to him the second he got back to his spot, so I didn't stay to say hi. I would have to see Desiree at work—I didn't need to stay to watch her drooling all over Chase, too.

I strapped Beck into his car seat and started to climb into the truck, but I stopped, looking at the sword on the passenger side.

Spiritual foes needed spiritual weapons—but the demons I'd fought could also be fought with actual weapons, like that one.

Unless that was a spiritual weapon.

Or maybe it was both.

It worked on spiritual creatures, but only in their dimension.

I sat in my truck and took hold of the sword's hilt.

Immediately, I could feel the demon dimension overlaying my own with its hot, dark, oily taint. There were no demons nearby. They couldn't come into this protected area.

That was why I felt safe here.

A knock on my truck's window startled me.

I jumped and looked out the window to see Chase.

And Desiree.

I slipped the sword down to the floor on the passenger side and rolled down my window. "Hey, Chase. What's up?"

"You left pretty suddenly. I just wanted to make sure you're okay."

"Yeah, of course. I just… need to get Beck home for his lunch and a nap."

"Right. Okay. Well, I'm glad you came today."

Desiree slipped her arm through Chase's. "So am I."

I ignored her and kept my focus on Chase. "Yeah, it's been too long. I really enjoyed hearing you speak. It was good."

"Thanks. Are we still on for coffee this week?"

From the corner of my eye, I saw Desiree's jaw tighten. Clearly they couldn't be too serious—or else the two of us getting coffee was strictly a business meeting in Chase's mind.

I smiled as sweetly as I could. "Of course. Just say when."

I left before I could get into any more conversation with either of them.

EIGHT

Gen was feeling better Monday morning, so I dropped Beck off a little early. Only one other child was there so far—a black-haired kid about four years old. I hadn't seen him before. Leaving Beck in Gen's capable hands, I headed out, but I didn't go straight to work. I needed to figure something out.

First stop, the pawn shop. I parked at the far end of the nearly empty lot and walked slowly toward the building, sword in hand. A rabbit bounded from one bush to the next, scurrying away as I got closer to the side of the hill where Jefferson Sezate had disappeared.

The scorch mark, revealing the tear in the wall between dimensions, was fading. Barely visible now.

I reached out with my fingers and felt the place in the air where the rip in dimensions was still healing. A buzz, like static electricity, met my hand. I stood there, letting the air crackle over my fingers, trying to sense the other side. The hair rose on the back of my neck, and the all-too-familiar nausea churned in my stomach.

What do you think you're doing?

The grating voice echoed in my head, and then its presence coalesced. It stood just behind me, as though looking over my shoulder.

I pretended not to hear.

Come, Jack. I know you can hear me. What are you doing?

I looked toward where its voice came from, and stumbled back.

I hadn't seen one since last year, when I'd emerged from the other dimension after killing Dionysius. But there it stood, like a giant, six-fingered gargoyle. The image was hazy—translucent almost. Like a ghost. But visible. And solid. He was still alive—which meant he could come through to this dimension and take on human form, if he wanted.

"How… how did you know I could hear you?"

I was in your apartment. I heard you then. There was no reason to believe you'd suddenly lost your ability. His voice grated in my head, like nails on a chalkboard.

"I killed the one that was in my apartment, and you're not the one who got away."

I left before you noticed me. You have not answered my question.

I debated how much I should reveal. "I'm investigating."

That much is obvious. What do you hope to accomplish with your investigation?

"I'm trying to figure out how Jefferson Sezate got into your dimension in the first place."

Much the same way you did.

"That's not possible. What happened to me was a one-time deal. I was able to get there because a demon attached itself to part of my soul and brought me with it."

Yes.

"So, there's no way Sezate got in the same way I did."

And yet he was here. You saw him come into this dimension yourself. But that still doesn't answer my question. What do you hope to accomplish?

"I'm investigating his murder. Obviously I can't prove he was ripped apart by demons, but if I can figure out how he got here, then maybe I can at least figure out why he was killed."

And what will you do with that information?

This was weird. Demons weren't really known for small talk. "Why are you so interested? You guys don't usually interfere with our petty human squabbles. How does my investigation profit you?"

Mere curiosity, Worm. Carry on. I wish you the best of luck.

It faded away, presumably traveling outside the bounds of where I could sense it.

A gust of wind blew dust into my face, and I squinted, still trying to sense where the demon had gone.

That interaction made no sense. It was watching me. Grilling me. And then it pretended it was just curious and walked away. These things were not curious. It knew I could sense it, and it wanted information from me.

That meant I was a threat.

But how?

I had nothing. No leads, no clues. I still couldn't access their dimension, at least not in more than a hazy, incorporeal way. So, why did they care what I was doing or how my investigation was going?

But that only confirmed what I already knew. I was on to something big.

I left the pawn shop and headed in to work. I had just arrived when Ron Wilkins, the professor, called me.

"Jack, I may have something."

My heart jumped. I really needed some good news. "Go on."

"I reached out to an old colleague of mine, Dr. Brantley. She's an archaeologist who works primarily in the Middle East. She's going to be in town doing some guest lectures for various classes over the next couple of months, and she would love to talk to you about this statue."

"That would be great. Please feel free to pass on my contact info. I'd love whatever help she can give me."

My phone rang again.

Yippee. It was Desiree.

"Davidson," I answered in my most professional tone.

"Jack, it's Agent Escobar."

Damn it, I hated when she one-upped me.

"How can I help you?" I asked.

"You have anything on that statue yet?"

I slipped into my desk chair and turned on my computer while I talked. "Sort of. I reached out to a history professor contact of mine, and he said it looked like it might have ancient Mesopotamian origins. Obviously he couldn't come up with anything conclusive without seeing it in person, but he's going to put me in touch with an archaeologist who has worked in that area. I'm going to set up a meeting next week. Hopefully get something more."

"Good. That's good. We'll need it. There's been another robbery and murder."

She couldn't have led with that?

"Where?" I asked. "Here?"

"No. California. But same MO. Guy robbed an antique store, took just one item, and disappeared right outside—before the cops got there—but the antique store owner said the perp walked toward the alley, then seemed to wink out of existence. His body turned up a day later—mutilated and turned inside-out, just like Sezate's."

"What was stolen? Another statue of a woman?"

"No. Yes. Statue, but not of a woman. This one was a bull."

"A bull? Like... a cow?"

"Yep. Also gold, about ten inches long, six inches or so high. Jasper for the eyes."

Gold woman with lapis lazuli accents, gold bull with jasper.

"Do you have pictures?"

"Yeah, I'll email them to you."

"Thanks. I'll show them to the archaeologist when we meet. Any idea yet if our two dead thieves were connected?"

"It's too soon to know for sure. We're running background checks."

"Okay, keep me posted," I said.

"You too," Desiree said before hanging up.

I cleared some space on my desk, so I could pull out the file for reference and opened my email. I had no training in art appreciation, let alone ancient artifact recognition, but the style and shape of the bull looked like it matched the statue of the woman.

I called Ron. "Hey Ron, there was another robbery in another state that may be related to the case I was telling you about. Can I send you pictures of the stolen piece?"

"Of course," he said.

I printed out a couple copies for my file and started writing notes about the possible connections between artifacts. Ron called me back about half an hour after I forwarded the email from Desiree.

"Jack, where did you say this was from?"

"The bull was stolen from an antique store in Burbank. Why?"

"That guy had no idea what he had. Do you know if he had any provenance on it?"

I leaned back in my chair and stretched my legs out. "I can find out. What is it?"

"Unless I'm very mistaken, that is ancient Mesopotamian. I mean, it could be a good knockoff—it's hard to tell from the picture—but it looks like it was looted from a burial site. It matches other statues known to have been buried in that area around the seventh or sixth century BCE."

"That's... old," I said.

"And rare and extremely valuable. No wonder someone wanted it. I just can't figure out how it would end up in an antique shop and not selling for millions on the black market."

"Unless it's not real," I said. "Like you said, it could be a knockoff. We won't know until we recover it."

"Right. Of course."

"Thanks, Ron. I'll call you when I know more, okay?"

I hung up and spent the next hour researching statues of bulls. Turns out they're everywhere. Tons of ancient religions had bulls as prominent icons. Something to do with fertility and strength in a lot of them. I found several images that looked similar, but nothing conclusive.

My phone rang.

Desiree again.

I clicked over. "Hey Desiree, what's up?"

"Another robbery. This one in New York. Auction house. But the same thing. Only this time the guy appeared and disappeared *inside* the building. He didn't set off any of the alarms going in or out. He *did* set off the one that housed the artifact itself. It was in a glass case with lasers and a signal that goes straight to the police station, video cameras, and guards on-site. He shows up on a camera coming out of a hallway, walks straight to the case, shoots the glass, steals the artifact, and walks back down the hallway. No sign of him before or after that."

I rubbed my eyes. I needed more coffee. "No idea how he got in or out? Where does the hallway go?"

"Loading dock. But it was completely sealed. Locked up and guarded. And he doesn't show up in the videos of that area at all. Just coming out of the hallway."

Of course, I knew how he'd done it, but that wouldn't go over well on a police report. Even after everything that had happened here last year, the idea of people using a demon dimension to travel wasn't something most people actually believed was a real thing.

I stood and made my way to the break room to refill my coffee cup. "No other offices with windows or anything down that hall that could explain how he got in and out?"

"Nothing. And Jack?"

"Yeah?"

"We haven't found his body yet. He might still be alive, and he might still have the artifact."

"You keep saying artifact. What did he steal, exactly?"

"A star."

"A star?" My skepticism had to be palpable, even through the phone.

"Gold. About a foot across. An eight-pointed star, inlaid with onyx, lapis lazuli, and jasper. Auction house has provenance that claims it was handed down through an Islamic family who managed to escape Iran before ISIS destroyed that area. Family heirloom or something, but they need money to start their new life, so they're putting it up for auction."

I had to shift papers again to make room for my coffee. I really needed to clean off my desk. In my spare time.

"Pictures?" I asked.

"Already sent," Desiree said.

"Okay, hang on." I pulled up the email and printed copies.

Gold. Lapis lazuli and jasper. Iran—that was the same geographic area where ancient Mesopotamia was, right?

There had to be a connection between all three of the stolen items.

But why now? These things had been around for thousands of years—why were they just now suddenly being collected? And how many more of these artifacts would be stolen before we could stop them?

"Who was the thief?"

"We're working on that. No matches in facial recognition yet."

My phone beeped again. How many phone calls could I get in a single morning of work?

I didn't recognize the number.

"Desiree, I need to go. I've got a call on the other line. We should meet in person and go over our notes. Tomorrow?"

"Sure," Desiree said. "Over coffee? At the place by your precinct?"

I noticed she specified the one by my precinct and not the one that I went to with Chase. It might not mean anything—but it probably did.

"Perfect," I said. "Ten okay?"

"I can't, I have meetings all morning. How about after lunch? Maybe one?"

"See you then," I said.

I clicked over to the other line. "Davidson."

"Hi, is this Jack? I mean Detective Davidson?" a woman asked.

I sat up straighter in my chair, my curiosity piqued. "It is. How can I help you?"

"My name is Megan Brantley. I got your information from a colleague of mine—"

"Ron Wilkins," I interrupted.

"Yes. He told you I'd be calling?"

"Yes. I wasn't expecting to hear from you so soon, though."

"I wasn't really expecting to call so soon, but he forwarded me the picture of the artifact, the statue of the woman that you're investigating, and I couldn't wait."

Artifact. There was that word again.

"You know what it is?" I asked.

"Not conclusively, but I have some ideas. I'm flying into town tonight. Can you meet me tomorrow morning by any chance?"

"Tomorrow morning? Ron said you weren't coming until next week."

"I'm lecturing next week, but I like to get in early and get acquainted with a place if I'm going to be staying awhile."

"Great, then. Tomorrow morning is perfect," I said. "Where are you staying?"

She sent me the address of the Air BNB she would be renting while she was here, down by the ASU campus, and I found a coffee shop nearby.

"Great. I'll see you in the morning," she chirped.

It wasn't until after I hung up that I realized I hadn't asked if Ron had forwarded her the images of the bull. Probably not, or she would've mentioned it. And now I had pictures of the star too. If I was lucky, she'd recognize them and help me figure out how they were connected.

Then again, how often was luck on my side?

Not often enough, that was for sure.

I rubbed my eyes. I'd been on the phone all day. Was it time to go home yet?

I glanced at my watch and groaned. It wasn't even lunchtime.

"Jack," the captain lumbered out of his office and tossed a pile of papers on my desk. "We got an ID on the murder from the airport. Guy's name is Rusty Hodge. Worked at the airport—he was one of the guys unloading the plane. He clocked out, everyone thought he went home. Single, homebody. He had the next couple days off, so no one even noticed he was missing until he didn't show up for work."

"Okay. I'll see what else I can find out," I said.

The captain went back to his office, and I started reading over the file, but my brain felt like mush.

Screw it. I had to get out of this office. I started packing up my things.

My phone rang again.

Gen.

"Gen, hey, is everything okay?"

"Not really. Beck is sick."

NINE

"Sick? Sick how?" I demanded.

"He's running a fever. I think you should come."

"I'll be right there." I shoved all the papers I'd been working with and the pictures I'd printed out into my file and thrust everything into my briefcase.

I stopped by the captain's office. "Beck is sick. I need to go. I may have to take tomorrow off, I'll let you know."

"Keep me posted," he said, only half looking at me, his gaze absorbed by something on his computer screen.

"Jack, you leaving already?" Ken popped up from his desk to block my path.

"Yeah, I've got to run."

"I may have something on that statue that was stolen from the pawn shop. I talked to the woman who sold it, and she admitted she didn't sell it just because she needed the money, but she wouldn't tell me her real reason over the phone. I have a meeting with her on Wednesday."

"Wednesday? Why not sooner?"

"I tried. She wasn't available. You want to come with?"

"Yeah, I would. Thanks. I appreciate it." I tried to give him a genuine smile even as I shoved past him.

Once inside Gen's apartment complex, I could hear Beck's wailing from halfway down the stairs. He was never this upset. He must be really sick. I glanced at my watch. His pediatrician's office was open for another couple of hours—good. I wouldn't have to take him to the ER.

I pounded on Gen's door, and she opened it, relief flooding her face. Two toddlers, a blond boy with drool dripping down his face and a black girl clinging to a purple blanket played with toys in the sectioned-off portion of Gen's living room.

Gen held Beck against her shoulder, jiggling him gently. "Jack, I'm so sorry to have to call you out of work, he just…"

"I know. It's fine. Thank you." I took him from her. His face was red and warm, but he stopped wailing when I had him in my arms.

"Hey, big guy," I cooed. "It's okay. Mama's here."

Gen gathered up his things while I snuggled him to calm him down.

"I'm probably going to take tomorrow off work, so I'll call you tomorrow night and let you know how he is," I said.

The pediatrician's office squeezed Beck in. The nurse practitioner who took his vitals smiled and talked in a soft, soothing voice as she asked me about symptoms.

I repeated to her what Gen had told me. Symptoms started suddenly—he threw up, started to fuss, and the fever started to get worse through the afternoon.

"Vitals look good," she said. "I'll run tests for flu and a couple other things. Chances are it's just a virus. I'm going to give him something to bring the fever down."

She checked a few more things and promised to call me when she got test results back.

# # #

I fell asleep that night on the recliner—Trent's chair, that I rarely used—with Beck on my chest. His breathing was raspy but steady, and his fever was present but not overly hot.

I woke up several times during the night.

Beck was restless, and neither of us slept much.

Morning came way too soon, and even though I was technically taking the day off work, I still had the meeting with Dr. Brantley.

I bundled Beck into his car seat and began the long drive to Tempe.

I was five minutes late getting to the coffee shop. Only a few people populated the industrial-themed space.

A woman stood from where she sat in a plush chair by the window and came toward me. "Jack?"

I nodded.

"It's so nice to meet you. I'm Megan Brantley."

She was younger than I expected. Maybe only a few years older than I was. Dark hair styled in a sexy pixie cut. Light blue blouse and gray slacks. Professional, but not overly dressy. I liked her.

I took her extended hand. "Jack Davidson. And this is Beck. He's not feeling great, so I couldn't leave him with the nanny today."

She smiled at Beck. "He's cute." Then she led the way back to where she'd been sitting.

I took the chair opposite her and pulled Beck out of his car seat, letting him snuggle against me. He dozed against my chest while we talked.

"I saw the picture you gave to Professor Wilkins," Dr. Brantley said. "I'm very intrigued. It's impossible to tell if it's real or a replica, but even if it's a replica, it's still much more valuable than something you'd expect to find in a pawn shop. Wilkins was right about it being Mesopotamian, or modeled after that style. If I'm not mistaken, it's a goddess. Like I said, probably worth a fortune."

"There's more," I said. "I didn't mention it when we were on the phone yesterday, but there were two more robberies, same kind of thing. Stolen by a petty thief. One in California, one in New York. The one in California, the robber is confirmed dead. No word yet on the one in New York, but I don't have a lot of hope for him."

"What was stolen?"

I pulled out copies of the pictures Desiree had sent me. "This bull was stolen from an antique store in Burbank." I swiped over to the other picture, "And this star was stolen from an auction house in New York."

Dr. Brantley gasped. "Oh… my…" She stopped, her face almost glowing. "Do you have any idea what this means?"

I shook my head. "Pretty much why I called you. I've gathered they're connected, but I have no idea how."

"If I'm not mistaken, these are all related to the goddess Inanna."

Inanna. Tension drained from my shoulders. I had no idea who Inanna was, but just having something to go on made this whole investigation seem less hopeless.

"I've never heard of her," I said.

"She was the most prominent goddess in some ancient cultures. She was known for love, fertility, justice, power. She later came to be associated with other goddesses, like Ishtar and Artemis, but she was originally her own entity." Dr. Brantley pointed to the first picture. "The statue may very well be her, or it could be modeled after one of the lesser goddesses. But these other statues—they are some of her well-known symbols. The bull and the eight-pointed star are both common to her."

"Okay, they're all connected, but that doesn't explain the deaths. I mean, it's not uncommon for criminal masterminds to kill their lackeys when they're no longer useful, but these murders... this was not normal."

"Define *not normal*," Dr. Brantley said.

"You sure you want to know?"

"You'd be surprised the kind of things I've seen."

I shrugged. "Okay, uh... flayed. Skin mostly removed, almost like they were torn inside out and the skin was stuffed inside the chest cavity. Intestines were kind of... on top."

Her face remained remarkably neutral. "That... that sounds familiar, but I can't quite place it." She pulled out her phone and typed something on it. "Just a note to myself, so I can look it up later. Go on."

I hesitated. I obviously couldn't tell her everything, but if she was going to help me, I couldn't keep it from her, either. "There was also some weirdness about how they got in and out of the places they robbed. They seemed to appear out of nowhere, committed the robberies with no concern whatsoever about being seen or tripping alarms, then seemed to disappear again without a trace."

"Interesting."

"So, what are you thinking?" I asked. "About the artifacts and how they're connected? I feel like there's more going on here than just trying to find a matching set. If that were the case, all three pieces could've been purchased pretty easily. The thefts and the murders— there's an urgency here that makes me think this points to something bigger."

Dr. Brantley nodded slowly. "There were a lot of mystical beliefs held about gods and goddesses. In ancient times, people believed the gods lived in another realm—on another plane of existence, so to speak."

That sounded eerily reminiscent of the demon dimension.

"In this other realm, they had great power, but their power was limited on Earth. People built idols, which were sort of—I don't know, a gateway, I guess? Not only were the idols physical representations of the gods in this realm, but it was believed the idols became a means for the gods to access, influence, and be part of this world. That's why sacrifices were such a huge part of ancient worship—people thought they really were serving the gods by serving their idols."

"So, let's say for the sake of argument that the stolen idol is real and not just a replica, what would that mean?"

"It would mean that someone who believes in Inanna is trying to get a hold of her idol so that they can use it to worship her."

"But why would they kill people to get them?"

71

"I'm not sure yet. I'll look into it. Probably something to do with giving her power, bringing her to life."

Perfect. It wasn't enough that I had to deal with demons in an alternate dimension, now I had to deal with gods and goddesses too?

Unless…

Dionysius had told me that the demons were once thought of as gods. He wasn't just named after the Greek god Dionysius, he *was* that god. So, maybe Inanna was kind of the same—a demon trying to reestablish her power, take control of her territory, which was what Dionysius had been doing—but instead of spawning half-demon monsters, she was using her idol.

"You look like you're thinking hard." Dr. Brantley took a sip from the cup in front of her, and I suddenly realized I hadn't had coffee yet. No wonder I couldn't think straight.

I smiled. "You could say that. Just trying to put some pieces together."

"I'd like to help, if you want or need me to," she said. "I'll look into this more anyway, because if these artifacts are genuine, it's the find of a century. And I have extensively searched that region—I think I could be of use putting some of the pieces together."

Pastor Floyd's warning echoed in my head.

But I needed help—there was no way I could research this kind of thing. And I didn't have to trust her to accept her help.

"I would really appreciate it," I said.

I glanced at the clock on my phone. I needed to go to make my meeting with Desiree.

"I'm so sorry to cut this short, but I have another meeting across town," I said. "But I would love to talk more."

"I'm in town until Christmas," she said. "I'll keep you updated if I find anything."

"Thanks," I said. "I'll do the same."

I packed Beck into his seat and made the long drive back to my side of town. I reached the coffee shop before Desiree did and took the opportunity to feed Beck. He seemed to be feeling a little better, though the fever persisted.

I was just burping him when Desiree walked in.

"Hey, sorry I'm late, I got held up in—is that your kid?"

I nodded. "This is Beck."

She sat down across from me and held out her arms. "May I?"

I raised an eyebrow. She was the last person in the world I'd expected to show an interest in my maternal endeavors. But I passed him over anyway. "He's not feeling great—that's why he's not at his nanny's."

Desiree's whole demeanor softened as she held Beck. "I've always liked babies," she said. "Toddlers, not so much. But if they could stay this size forever…"

I grinned. "I never really thought about it until I had him. I liked kids okay, but I was busy with my career. Didn't really think having kids was something I wanted. But then I found out I was pregnant, and… well, I wouldn't give him back."

She laughed. A genuine, friendly laugh.

It was moments like these when I thought we might actually be friends… but give it another minute, and she'd say something snarky about how I'm a lesser cop or how she and Chase had such an idyllic relationship, which would put us back in the antagonistically civil zone.

"I might some day, but I want to make sure I find the right guy who will be by my side the whole way."

And there it was.

Good, we could get back to normal.

"What did you find out about our perps?" I asked.

She shifted Beck slightly and handed me a file from her briefcase. "We have an ID on the one from New York. He left fingerprints all over the scene. Robert Earl. Zero connection that we can find. All three have criminal histories, but nothing major or violent. No known associates with one another, no link other than the way the crimes were committed. And two out of three dead the same way. You get anything?"

"Yeah, actually. The artifacts themselves are definitely connected. They're ancient Mesopotamian—or really good replicas—all associated with the goddess Inanna."

"I've never heard of her."

"She later became associated with Ishtar and Artemis, among others."

"Those I've heard of."

"Right," I said. "Anyway, the bull and the eight-pointed star are both associated with her. So, the statue is possibly the goddess herself, and the other two are linked to her power or her domain or something."

"Good, they're part of a set. That will make them easier to trace," Desiree said. "I'll check collectors and dig sites and so forth for reports of anything matching these having been stolen."

"Something's weird, though," I said.

She raised her perfectly sculpted eyebrows and waited for me to continue.

"Let's say, for the sake of argument, that we find out these things were all stolen from the same place, like an archaeological dig. Whoever stole them must have known how valuable they were. But one was in an antique shop—had been there for a couple of years, just sitting around waiting for a buyer. One was handed down from someone's grandfather and just showed up in a pawn shop. Only one was being sold for its actual value, through the auction house. And yet all three are stolen at almost the exact same time."

"And?" She jiggled Beck on her knee, and I couldn't help being a little bitter at how well he was doing with her.

"So, why now? And why steal them? I mean, whoever wanted them could've just bought them. The one at the auction house had the bidding starting in the thousands of dollars. The other two—a couple hundred. You'd make a fortune reselling them as a set, especially if you could prove they really are as ancient as we think. So, why steal them, and why now?"

"That's actually a good point," she said.

"Awfully kind of you to say so." I simpered.

Man, I hated her. If she weren't holding my son I might actually kick her in the shins.

"I've already had all three artifacts put on watch lists on black market sites, but so far nothing."

"I don't think they'll turn up there. Whoever wants them, wants them for a reason. And I think it's time-sensitive. They needed to get all three—or more—together right away. The archaeologist thought they might be used in some sort of worship—trying to give the goddess power or bring her to life."

She blinked slowly a couple of times. "Do you have any other ideas?"

I didn't. Even knowing what I knew about the other dimensions and my suspicion that an actual goddess might be our thief, I had no idea why she would want these things or what she planned to do with them.

I needed to talk to Floyd. If I could get a hold of him.

"My archaeologist contact promised to keep in touch if she finds anything," I said. "Maybe she'll have an idea what these things could be used for or if there's a sale on ancient artifacts coming up somewhere. And I'm meeting with the woman who sold the statue to the pawn shop tomorrow, so maybe that will give us some insight. But until those artifacts show up again, we may be at a dead end. What about the murders? Anything to indicate how they were killed?"

Desiree shrugged. "Not a lot. Some kerf marks that indicate a weapon of some kind was used, but it's not definitive what. Cause of death appears to be... you know... being flayed and having their insides pulled out of their rib cages and their skin stuffed in. But everything's still... intact. Just switched places."

I stifled a gag. My ability to tolerate gore—even the description of it—was diminished since being pregnant.

Or maybe it was because I'd dealt with so much of it last year that I'd become overly sensitive to it. Whatever the reason, her description made me want to hurl.

"They could be anywhere," I said. "The murderers, I mean. And we still don't have the body of the third."

"Maybe he'll show up alive," Desiree said.

I canted my head. "I didn't really figure you for the optimistic type."

"I try not to let it get the better of me. You're probably right, though. There's no way they're going to let him live long enough to talk."

Desiree's phone rang. She glanced at the screen. "It's my boss. Excuse me, please." She stood and handed Beck back to me, then walked outside.

I touched his forehead, but he didn't feel feverish at the moment.

The captain's number flashed on my screen as it rang. "Hey, Captain," I answered. "What's up?"

"We found another body. Same as the last one."

TEN

"Where? I'm on my way."

He gave me the address, and I called Cameron. "Can you watch Beck? He's still feeling a little sick, so I can't infect Gen's other kids, but I have a work emergency."

"Sure. I'll be at my apartment."

I tucked Beck into his seat and made for the coffee shop door, almost crashing into Desiree on my way out.

"They found another body," we both said at the same time.

"I need to drop Beck at my sister-in-law's. I'll meet you there," I said.

She nodded and we both hurried to our cars.

Twenty minutes later, I pulled up at the same empty lot where we'd found the first victim, Jefferson Sezate. A gas station across the street advertised cheap fountain drinks, while a medical marijuana dispensary in a run-down strip mall on the other side of the lot promised the best prices in town. I parked in front of the dispensary.

This body was in almost the same spot, right in the middle of the empty lot on the corner.

I grabbed the sword from my passenger seat and jumped from my truck. Clutching the sword hilt, I felt for the other dimension. It seemed like the same portal had been used—the scorched opening was fresh, but not new.

I'd felt this before—the more a portal was used, whether that be frequency or volume, the longer the rip between realities remained open. It was like the fabric had to take time to heal itself, and the worse the wound, the longer it took.

"Do we have an ID?" I asked.

Desiree eyed the sword but didn't comment. "Robert Earl."

76

"The guy from the New York auction house."

She nodded. "Matched his fingerprints. He's still unrecognizable. Same as the others—looks like he was turned inside out."

I forced myself to look at the body, at the way the skin was peeled back over the skeleton, starting in the chest and pulling all the way around, to be stuffed inside from the back, which pushed the internal organs out the front.

How? And why?

I took a step closer, my hands still clutching the sword's hilt.

The body felt… strange, somehow. Tainted. Oily and dark.

Demonic.

Was it just because it had been through the other dimension?

When Chase first met me, and part of my soul was trapped in the other dimension, attached to the demon, he could hardly bring himself to touch me, because I felt empty, he had said. Was that what I was feeling now? Or was this something else?

I further inspected the tear between worlds. I could almost see through the portal. It was a strange sensation—not like it had been before, where I could actually walk through the portal and exist in the other dimension—almost like looking through a window. Through the corners of my vision, I could make out the red, barren landscape.

The demon dimension fit sort of on top of ours, but distinct. The people and buildings that existed clear as day here were shadowy and insubstantial there—more illusion than something corporeal. When I'd been there before, I could walk through buildings and over mountains like they weren't there. Physics worked differently too. Once, I ran across the entire city of Phoenix in a matter of minutes, and another time, from Nevada back home in one stretch. Plus, I was stronger and more focused there.

I squeezed the hilt a little tighter and peered through the portal, trying to see what was on the other side, but it was like looking through pea-soup fog at night.

Squinting, I took another step closer.

Something moved.

I gasped. A being—like the demons, but not quite the same—stared at me.

This one was a female. I'm not sure how I knew, any more than I'd known the others were all male, even before I'd seen them, it just had a distinctly feminine presence.

I hadn't seen a female demon before. She had similar, grotesque gargoyle-like features and claws, but her eyes were red instead of the yellow I was used to. And she wasn't as tall. Now that I was closer, I could tell she had breasts. Also, six arms. And… wings.

Her red eyes widened, as though she suddenly realized I could see her, and she leaned forward. Curiosity poured out from her as she peered at me.

"If you're done playing with your sword, we could use your help over here," Desiree's voice cut my concentration.

The other dimension was gone. Even though I still held the sword, I could no longer make out anything beyond the portal's black, scarred line.

I turned and smiled at Desiree, as if I hadn't just been staring into space while holding my toy sword. "What can I do for you?"

"We have a witness. Homeless man, over by the tree. Can you interview him?"

"You got it."

I pulled out my pad and pen and walked over to the man who sat under a scrubby tree by the road. "Hey, there. I'm Detective Davidson. What's your name?"

He clenched his fists and rubbed his knuckles against dirty khakis. "B-Brian."

"It's nice to meet you, Brian. I have a few questions I'd like to ask, but I'm starving. Would you like to hit the McDonald's down the street with me while we talk? I'll buy."

Brian nodded, and I led the way the half block down to the restaurant.

He ordered several meals' worth of food, but I didn't say anything. This might be all he ate all week, and I needed him to feel comfortable enough to tell me everything.

We sat in a corner booth. I nibbled at my fries while he scarfed down the first of his sandwiches, then tore into the second.

About halfway through his second burger, he finally looked up. "What do you want to know?" he asked through the half-chewed food spilling out of his mouth.

"You saw how that body got in that lot?" I asked.

He choked down his bite and nodded.

"Can you tell me about it?"

"You won't believe me."

"That's okay. I don't have to believe it. I just have to write down everything you say." I kept my posture open and relaxed, my smile friendly, in an attempt to ease him into speaking freely.

That seemed to loosen him up a little.

78

He took another bite and talked around his food. "I'm sitting there, taking a little rest, and there's this huge flash of light in the sky."

The portal opening. I'd seen that before.

I scribbled the note into my pad, so he'd know I was paying attention. "Go on."

"Now, this is where it gets weird." He ran a hand over his shaved, but also balding, head. "This guy appears out of nowhere. Pretty sure he was beamed down—that's the only explanation for the light and then him just appearing. But there was something wrong with the tech. He wasn't dead when he got off the transporter. He was normal. He stood there for a second, looking confused, and then…"

He covered his mouth, like he was going to hurl everything he'd just eaten. He took a sip of his Mountain Dew and a deep breath, then looked me in the eyes, dead sober. "Then he exploded. He screamed, but it only lasted for a second, and his body flipped inside-out, like something was tearing him apart from the inside. It all happened so fast, and then he was just on the ground. I… I didn't go closer. I didn't touch him, I swear."

I nodded and looked him in the eye. "I believe you."

"I don't believe in aliens or transporters or spaceships," he said after a moment. "I don't believe in anything. But that's the only thing I can think of that makes sense."

Was believing in spaceships more or less crazy than believing in demons and alternate dimensions?

"We're going to find out what happened," I said.

He nodded and shoved another bite of burger into his mouth.

I handed him a $20 and my card. "Thanks for your help. Call me if you think of anything else, no matter how weird it sounds, okay?"

"Sure," he mumbled.

Desiree was overseeing the retrieval of the body when I got back.

"What did he say?" she asked.

I handed her my notes.

She stepped out of the way of a tech who rushed past a little too closely and scanned the page several times. "Huh."

"Yep."

"Is he high?"

"Not that I could tell. But plenty freaked out. I don't know what actually happened, but he's convinced this is what he saw."

"That's going to make it harder."

"Yep."

"Okay. We'll be on the lookout for spaceships with broken transporters, I guess."

"It's as good a place as any to start," I said.

She cracked a half-smile. "I've got to go. Keep me posted if you find out anything else."

"I will."

Beck still had a slight fever when I picked him up. The doctor had said it could take a few days for him to battle off the virus whatever it was—all the tests had come back negative, so she said it was probably just a run-of-the mill cold—but I was still worried. He hadn't really been sick yet. Probably every mother since the beginning of the world had had a panic attack the first time her kid got sick, and the doctor didn't think there was anything to worry about, so I was trying to trust her judgment, but I couldn't shake the feeling that something was really wrong.

I sat in the recliner again and snuggled him until he fell asleep, then called Pastor Floyd.

He didn't answer.

I tried one more time before leaving a message. "Hey, it's Jack. Just wondering if you're back in town yet. I have a few things I want to ask you about regarding a case I'm working on. Thanks."

⽗ ⽗ ⽗

Gen called me early the next morning. The other kids she had scheduled for today—a set of siblings—had called to cancel, so she said she could take Beck.

Good. I hated to keep asking Cameron—she had work and school and stuff she had to rearrange every time I called her to babysit.

I really should find a backup sitter. I just didn't have anyone I trusted as much as Gen. And Cameron—Cameron was family. It was kind of one of those unspoken things in families like hers that you helped family out. But I hated to impose, even if Beck was her nephew. And in a pinch I could ask Deanna and Dave, but that was a couple hours round trip, so not something I could do on a regular basis.

But I really needed to not have to worry about him. There were murderers and demons and goddesses on the loose.

I dropped Beck off with Gen. Her study buddies, Oscar and Cadence, were there.

"Good morning, Detective," Oscar said. He was way too peppy for this early in the morning.

Cadence seemed to be less of a morning person. She didn't even say anything nasty.

Why were they here? Late night study fest, or something else?

None of my business. I was just grateful not to have to worry about Beck for today at least, and headed to work.

The morning was slow—mostly trying to track own any possible sales of the stolen artifacts. There were none. I knew there wouldn't be, but I had to be able to tell Desiree I'd exhausted all my resources looking.

Ken sauntered over and sat on the edge of my desk. "Hey, Jack, you about ready to go?"

I stared at him blankly for a few moments, my brain churning as I tried to remember what he was talking about.

Oh! Right. We were interviewing the woman who had sold the statue to the pawn shop.

I quickly threw a smile on my face to cover the fact that I'd forgotten. "Yeah, let me just wrap up here real quick."

I saved my notes and logs of the places I'd searched and emailed it all to Desiree, then grabbed my badge and gun.

And my sword.

Ken gave me a funny look when I slid it under my belt—that worked better for riding in the car, I'd discovered, even though it bent—but he didn't say anything.

So, I didn't, either. Let him wonder. I didn't need to explain myself to him, and I felt better knowing it was with me.

At least I knew I could kill through dimensions if I had to, and it gave me a glimpse to the other side, so that was helpful, no matter how many funny looks I got.

I climbed into Ken's cruiser beside him.

"This reminds me of the time we went to go see that lady who thought she was an alien nanny, remember?" he laughed.

I pulled the seatbelt across my chest and snapped it into place. It smelled like body odor. Gross. Who had he had in here? "Yeah, she was a piece of work."

She definitely was, but she wasn't wrong. She'd been coerced by demons into using her closed-down daycare facility to house their demon spawn. Of course, Ken only knew a sliver of the reality of that one.

"I like working with you," he said.

"Thanks. You're a good cop. I'm glad to know you have my back," I said.

"Always," he said. His tone had a note of wistfulness to it.

Not this again. When would he realize it was never going to happen and move on?

The drive wasn't far—the woman lived just a few minutes from the pawn shop. That made sense—she'd taken it to the first place she thought she could get rid of it.

Ken knocked on the door.

A woman answered. Short, stocky, with reddish brown hair and a perpetual sneer.

"Ms. Malone?" Ken asked. "I'm Lieutenant Richmond. We spoke on the phone about the statue you sold to North Valley Pawn."

"Oh. Right. Yeah, come in."

Immediately, I was assaulted with the stench of old food and cat urine. We walked into a house stuffed floor-to-ceiling with debris.

Classic hoarder. Not as bad as some I'd seen, but still, pretty bad.

That raised another question. Why, when she clearly thrived on hanging on to everything, had she sold that one particular statue?

Ken and I sat on the edge of a couch between stacks of magazines and cats.

The cats weren't actually in stacks—they were just flopped over everywhere, lounging. I saw at least five of them just in the living room.

To his credit, Ken didn't bat an eye at the stench or the clutter. He smiled at Ms. Malone and leaned forward, as though she was the most important person in the world.

"Can you tell me about the statue?"

Ms. Malone shrugged. "What do you want to know?"

"Where did you get it?"

"I told you on the phone. I inherited it from my grandfather."

"How long ago was this?"

"I dunno. A couple years." She brushed cat hair from her leg, replacing it with cat hair from her hand.

"Do you know where he got it?"

"Not really."

"What can you tell me about him? Was he overseas recently? Did he travel much?"

Her gaze wandered to the wall behind Ken, not really seeming to focus on anything in particular. "He was a vet in the first Gulf War, then he spent like thirty years as an accountant. Got Alzheimer's and lived his last few years in a home. All his stuff was boxed up in storage. When he died, I had to go through everything."

"And this statue was in storage with his things?"

She nodded. "All wrapped up in this old blanket, stuffed in a trunk, buried at the bottom of a mountain of other crap."

The irony that she was referring to someone else's storage as a mountain of crap was not lost on me. I kept my hands firmly in my lap, trying to minimize my contamination. I would still need to shower and change before I picked up Beck, though.

"Did you ever have it appraised?" Ken asked.

She shrugged. "No. Why would I? Nothing he had was worth anything, that I could tell. I just thought it was cool, so I put it on my shelf."

"So, you didn't know what it was until you sold it?"

"I still don't know what it was."

Ken glanced around the room, at the shelves stuffed full and the stacks of everything.

"You have some really nice pieces in here. Is that Navajo?"

Ms. Malone followed his gaze to the large urn that sat atop one of the shelves. "I used to work at the Museum of Natural History, and we'd get shipments in sometimes that were interesting but didn't have enough cultural or historical relevance to put on display, so they'd go for auction."

"That's lucky for you. May I ask you something?"

She shrugged.

"It seems like you like to collect things, and that you don't get rid of much. May I ask why you sold that statue?"

"Well, like I said on the phone, I needed the money."

"Right, of course. It just seems... you have a lot of nice collectibles in here. It seems like you could have sold any number of things for much more than you got for that statue. Why was that the one item you thought should go?"

Her eyes shifted and she looked at the floor. "Didn't like it."

"Why is that?"

Her head snapped up and her eyes narrowed at him. "I just didn't, okay? Why is it so important? Can't I just have a preference without having to explain myself?"

I touched Ken's arm to subtly ask if I could interject.

He nodded.

"I'm sorry we bothered you," I said. "It's just... well, you know the statue was stolen. A man died. So, the more we know about the statue itself, the more likely we are to find it and bring the killer to justice. Anything you can tell us—no matter how strange, or how seemingly unrelated—could help."

She looked at me and took a deep breath. "You won't believe me."

That was what Homeless Brian had said, too. If only they knew just how far down I'd already fallen into *unbelievable.*

"We've seen a lot of weird stuff," I assured her. "Just tell us."

She sighed and looked at the floor again. "I got rid of it because it was haunted."

ELEVEN

I could feel Ken tensing up beside me. He'd had the same sort of reaction when the woman we'd interviewed last year claimed that aliens had asked for her help. Anything supernatural made him twitchy.

I ignored him and kept my focus on Ms. Malone. "Haunted how?"

"It would... like... move. On its own. I had it up there," she pointed to the top of a shelf where a handful of other dolls—porcelain, kachina, antique—sat in a semblance of order. "It knocked the others off the shelf. My Madame Alexander collectible shattered, and the kachinas always seemed to end up facedown on the floor."

"Are you sure it wasn't one of the cats?" I asked.

Ms. Malone smacked the couch, sending a flurry of cat hair and dust into the air and startling the mangy creature that was settled beside her. "It wasn't the damn cats! I've never had a problem with any of my dolls. I put that thing up there, and all of a sudden, every night, things were getting knocked over. It moved too. I put it on the edge, in the back, and in the morning, it would be front and center. The cats didn't do that. And other things moved. Like the mirror that was on that wall fell off, and some of my book stacks were knocked over. Every night, something would happen. And since I got rid of it—nothing."

It might still be the cats.

But she definitely believed she was telling the truth. She was absolutely convinced that her statue was haunted. And given what I knew, I couldn't say for sure that it wasn't.

"I think that's all for now," Ken said. "Detective, did you have any other questions?"

"Not at the moment." I handed Ms. Malone my card. "Call me if you think of anything else, okay?"

She nodded and stuffed my card into her bra.

Ken stood and led the way out to the car. Once we were inside, he blew a long breath out of pursed lips. "Alien nannies, haunted statues, people disappearing into thin air... what next?"

"You have to admit it's weird," I said. "A hoarder getting rid of something because it's possessed?"

"It has to be the cats."

"If so, then why did they only disturb the dolls when the statue was there?"

He threw the car into drive and squealed away from Ms. Malone's house. "Who knows? Maybe the statue was used to smuggle catnip or something. They must have been attracted to it for whatever reason and knocked the other dolls down trying to get to it."

That explanation made perfect sense. It would write well into a report.

And yet... I knew it was wrong.

I couldn't say for sure the statue was *actually* haunted, but there was something going on with it that defied rational explanation, and a haunting made about as much sense as anything else.

When we got back to the precinct, I called Desiree and told her what Ms. Malone had said. "Ken—I mean Lieutenant Richmond—concluded that the cats must have been attracted to it for some reason and they knocked over the other dolls, but it does make me wonder if anything weird was going on with the other two artifacts."

"I'll get you contact info on the others," Desiree said. "You're welcome to ask them."

She forwarded the information, and I called the first contact immediately.

I was right.

The owner of the antique store where the bull was stolen from said he'd noticed some things in the case had been shifted or knocked over a few times, but he hadn't paid much attention. He didn't check every case every day, and sometimes customers bumped displays, or minor earthquakes and even street sweepers rattled things enough to make them shake, so he hadn't thought much about it.

He didn't have any information on the provenance of the item—he'd gotten it from an estate sale in a box of other random knickknacks with no paperwork.

I called the owner of the star that was taken from the auction house next. He was a little more helpful.

"My grandfather was a construction worker in Iran," he said in heavily accented English. "He was helping to build a mosque, and when they dug the foundation, they found what seemed to be a tomb. They reported it to the government, but no one seemed to care. My grandfather and the others on his team divided up what they found, and the mosque was built on top of the site. Later, during the war, the whole town was destroyed, including the mosque, and everything underneath it was buried in piles of rubble. My grandfather gave the star to my father, who gave it to me. My wife and I left Iran two years ago, but it has been hard to transition, and we finally decided to sell the star in order to invest in our business. We are starting a restaurant."

"Oh, I'm so sorry. We will do everything we can to recover it for you."

"The auction house is insured, so it might not be as much as we could have gotten for it, but at least we will not be left with nothing," he said.

"That's fantastic," I said. "I hope your restaurant is profitable for you. One more question, if you don't mind—did you ever notice anything strange about the star? Weird things happening around it, or to other things near it?"

"I hadn't thought about it, really—I always thought it was... what is the word... coincidence? But there were times when it fell over, though no one had touched it. And we had other things break or crack—like our dishes that were given to my wife by her parents for our wedding. Sometimes our furniture moved slightly. We live near a train station, so I assumed it was just... what is the word... vibrations. I do not think an object could have such power."

"I'm sure it is coincidence," I assured him. "I just have to investigate all possibilities."

"I understand. Let me know if I can be of further assistance."

"I will. Thanks. And please, call me if you think of anything else."

Well, that was something. All three artifacts had weird, haunted behavior attached to them. And they were all connected to the Mesopotamian goddess Inanna.

What that meant, I had no idea. But it was something.

I went home that night and, after putting Beck to sleep, sat on my bed with the sword. I didn't really think it would help me figure anything out, but what I'd said to Desiree was true—it was like a security blanket. It was the only connection to I had to the other dimension, and it was powerful—powerful enough to kill in that dimension even when I had it here. It made me feel safe.

So, I sat, gently running my hand up and down the blade, thinking. Trying to piece together what I knew. It wasn't enough.

I called Pastor Floyd again, and still no answer.

I stared at my phone for a long time, trying to decide whether or not to call Chase. Desiree had made it pretty clear that she had dibs. But he wasn't remotely interested in me anyway, so it wasn't like I was trying to start anything. I just wanted to ask if he'd heard from Pastor Floyd.

I decided the need for information outweighed the discomfort. I called.

"Hey, Jack, good to hear from you!" Chase's voice sounded like he meant it. "What's up?"

"Have you heard from Pastor Floyd since he's been gone?"

"He's emailed a couple times," Chase said. "Said he's been looking into a few things but he'll be home soon. I'm still planning to preach this Sunday, but he should be back sometime next week."

"Did he… did he say anything about me? Or Beck?"

"What's wrong?" His voice instantly filled with concern.

I ran my hand absently over the surface of the sword blade. "Nothing new. He just said he was looking into stuff, and then I haven't heard from him since. And this case… there's something wrong, but I can't quite piece it together. And I don't see how, exactly, but I can't help feeling like it has something to do with what Pastor Floyd told me."

"Do you want me to come over? Look through your notes with you?"

I thought about what Pastor Floyd had said about not trusting anyone. But this was Chase. He couldn't have meant Chase… could he?

Despite Pastor Floyd's warning, I *did* trust Chase. More than anyone else I knew. And he was one of the few people I could talk to about what was going on in the other dimension.

"Jack? You still there?"

"Yeah, sorry. I was thinking. I would like you to come over, but I know it's late, and I don't want to bother you…"

"I'm still at church. I was just wrapping things up. It's no bother. I'll be there in a few."

"Thanks."

I kind of hated that my stomach still fluttered at the thought of seeing him.

After double-checking to make sure Beck was still sleeping, I started a pot of coffee and quickly tidied my living room. I'd always been pretty minimalistic and modern with décor and furnishings, and my apartment was always neat, but since having Beck, burp rags, toys, pacifiers, and other debris reigned supreme. Some days I just didn't have the energy to care.

But I didn't want Chase to have yet another thing to disdain me for, so I shoved things into my room and ran a dust cloth over the more obvious things, like the TV and bookcase.

Chase knocked just as I got the apartment to a level of cleanliness that wasn't totally embarrassing.

I opened the door. "Come in. Coffee?"

"Sure, thanks. Usually I don't drink it this late in the evening, but I have a feeling it's going to be a long night."

"Same," I said. "I have a lot to fill you in on."

"Desiree has told me a little," he said. "But she obviously doesn't know what we know about spiritual activity."

"You… you guys hang out a lot?" I was a little afraid to know the truth, but that would be better than the assumptions my imagination would come up with.

Chase just shrugged. "We see each other at church and Bible study, and we go out sometimes. Nothing major."

A weight lifted, and suddenly I felt like I could breathe. "Cool. Yeah, we're working together again, because I have the local contacts, but the case is connected to others across state lines."

As soon as I started talking, I couldn't stop. I told him everything, from the robberies to what Dr. Brantley had told me about the connection to the goddess, to the bodies being ripped apart from the inside-out.

Chase blanched at my description of the bodies. "Can I see those pictures? Of the artifacts, not the bodies."

"Yeah, of course." I pulled them up for him on my phone.

He scooted in closer so our arms were almost touching as he examined the images. "There's something in the back of my mind—I know it's there, like this is familiar, but I can't quite place it. Can you send me copies of those? I'd like to do some more research. Where did you say the statue of the star was from?"

"I don't know the exact location. Iran somewhere."

"Hmm. That whole area has seen the rise and fall of many nations in its history. This could be a relic from any number of ancient civilizations. Mesopotamia covers a lot of ground, both geographically and culturally."

"You know anything about the goddess? Inanna?"

"I've heard the name, but I'm not really familiar with her or her followers. I'll look into it."

"I think maybe I saw her."

His head jerked toward me and his eyes narrowed. "What do you mean?"

"In the other dimension."

"I thought you couldn't access the other dimension since the other demon died?"

"Oh. Shit." I mentally kicked myself for cursing in front of him. He never said anything, but I still always felt disrespectful when I let something like that slip. "Sorry. I forgot that part. I can, sort of, when I'm holding the sword." I went to my room to retrieve the sword. "When I'm holding it, I feel a connection, like the other dimension is just out of reach. I can sense it in a way that's similar to when I could cross over before. I can't reach in—but the sword can. I killed a demon in Beck's room."

"And you saw her? Inanna?"

"I mean, I don't know that it was her, obviously, but I saw something. I was holding the sword—after the second murder—and I could sense where the portal had been opened to dump the bodies. So, I was looking through, but it was really dark and hazy, and I couldn't see much, except a figure with red eyes. And she was staring at me, like she was curious."

"But not a demon?"

"She might have been. I don't know. She was like the demons, but not. I don't know how to explain it."

"And she was curious?"

I nodded. "I'm not sure if she could tell I was looking in and that's why she was curious, or if she was just curious about our investigation or what, but it felt like she was looking right at me."

"I... don't know what to do with this information."

"Me neither. That's why I want to talk to Pastor Floyd. He knows stuff, but I can't get a hold of him."

"I'll try calling him in the morning," Chase said. "May I see the sword?"

I handed it to him, and he held it by the hilt.

"I don't feel anything," he said.

I reached for it and held it, closing my eyes and concentrating. It was there—the other dimension. Still hazy and unfocused when I opened my eyes, but slightly stronger than before. "I can. There are demons over a few apartments and down a level. They're not really doing anything—it kinda feels like they're just hanging out. They're not paying any attention to me."

He took the sword again and closed his eyes. "Still nothing," he said.

"Maybe it's one of those things that you don't feel it until you've already felt it. Like… remember those 3D images in the nineties? How you'd try for hours and not be able to see it, and then all of a sudden you'd get it, and then you couldn't not see it? Maybe it's like that, and it's there, and once you change your perception enough to see it the first time, it will always be in focus."

"You come up with some of the weirdest analogies," he said.

"Yeah, well, you knew what I was talking about, so it worked."

"Fair enough." He smiled.

I grinned back, enjoying the easy camaraderie that felt like it had a year ago.

Until Beck cried.

A shadow seemed to pass over Chase's face as the reality of my life settled over him.

I stood without a word and went to get my son. My top priority. And the one thing in this life I would protect above all others.

I came back out, jiggling Beck.

"Whoa." Chase's eyes darted from the sword in his hands to me and Beck and back.

"What?"

"I felt it… just for a minute. There was a surge, like something pulsing through me, something dark, and… oily. Tainted."

"That's what the other dimension feels like to me," I said. "Can you still feel it?"

He shook his head. "No, it's gone now. It was just there for a minute, when you… when you came out with Beck."

TWELVE

My world stopped turning for a moment.

Beck?

No. That wasn't right. Beck was a baby. Innocent. I propped Beck against my chest and held him with one arm, clutching the sword hilt with the other.

Chase was right. There was some sort of darkness attaching itself to my son. Not a demon, but still demonic. It clung to him through dimensions.

Nausea bubbled up inside me, threatening to drown me in my own vomit.

Not my son.

How had I not felt it? How had I not known?

"You can't have him!" I screamed. "Do you hear me? I won't let you have him!"

From somewhere beyond the dimensional wall, I felt a rumbling laughter. Dark and sinister, and feminine. No words, just that demented, sadistic laugh.

"Jack, what is it? What's going on?" Chase asked. He grabbed the sword from me.

I collapsed onto the couch, clutching Beck to my chest, sobs shaking my whole body.

Chase scooted closer and wrapped his arms around me, Beck between us. "It's okay, Jack. We're going to keep him safe. We won't let anything happen to him."

"I can't stop them, Chase. I don't know what they want, and I can't get into the other dimension. I can't investigate, and I don't… I don't know how to do this."

"We're going to figure it out," he said, smoothing my hair.

"What if we can't?"

"We will."

"I'm going to take some time off from the office and work from home," I said. "I just... I just don't trust Beck out of my sight right now."

"I understand," Chase said. "I'll come by after work tomorrow and bring you dinner. And I'll try to get a hold of Floyd and let you know what I find out."

"Thank you," I said.

"In the meantime, is there anyone who can stay with you? Help you out a little? Your sister?"

"Cameron? Yeah, she could probably spend the night with me. She's got work and school. But Isaac might be willing to come over too."

"Isaac? Dr. Reyes?"

I nodded.

"You still see him?" I thought I detected a hint of jealousy, and despite everything, that made me smile.

"Sometimes," I said.

"Good. I'll feel better if you aren't alone, at least until we figure out what's going on." Despite the strain in his voice, I knew he meant it, and that somehow was stronger than if he'd objected. It meant he was more concerned about my safety than my relationships.

"Thanks."

"I'll sleep on the couch tonight, and you can call Isaac in the morning."

"Okay." Ever the gentleman. One of the things I loved about him.

I got some extra sheets and blankets for him, then took Beck with me into my room. Even if his was just across the hall, I didn't want him out of my sight.

I took the sword to bed too. If anything came near my son, they'd have me to deal with.

Chase was gone when I woke up the next morning. His sheets and blanket were folded neatly on the end of the couch, and there was fresh coffee—minus one cup—in the pot.

I smiled, glad he was that comfortable in my home. I called in to the precinct and told the captain I was taking some time off but I'd be able to work from home a little, then pulled out my laptop and started going over all the files from the case.

Beck woke up, so I fed him and set him on a blanket on the floor near my desk to play while I turned back to my notes.

There had to be something I was missing.

It had to do with the goddess. And the goddess had something to do with the demons, and what they wanted my son for.

But what would a goddess need a baby for? What could he do for her that the demons or the other potentials couldn't?

The other potentials.

Pastor Floyd had told me he'd spoken to three of the potentials, and then Desiree told me three men who looked like they could be Brandon Harding's brothers had been murdered, ostensibly by the same guy who'd stolen the statue from the pawn shop. I'd just assumed they were the same three men Pastor Floyd had talked to, but what if they weren't? What if there were more of them out there?

I made a note to ask Pastor Floyd what the names of the men he'd talked to were. Beck started fussing, so I paused to feed him and put him down for a nap, then I emailed Desiree and asked if any others who fit the description had been killed recently.

Beck woke up again, so we spent some time playing together before he was willing to let me set him down again.

Finally, early in the afternoon, I called Brandon Harding.

"Detective Davidson," he answered, not even waiting for me to say hello. "Why are you calling me? Again?"

I suddenly realized I had no idea what to say.

"Just checking in to see if you're okay," I said after a moment.

"Sure. Why wouldn't I be?"

Why, indeed? "There has been a resurgence in demonic activity. It may be related to the case last year when you were kidnapped. There have been a few murders, some of whom may be other potentials."

"Potential antichrists." His voice sounded dry. Not entirely believing.

"Right," I said.

"Listen, Detective, I know you're trying to help, but… I can't fully explain what happened last year, but I know that I'm dealing with some PTSD-related false memories. I'm working through it with the help of a therapist, but I really don't think rehashing this nonsense is helpful."

Rehashing this nonsense.

I couldn't blame him. I didn't want to believe it myself. After Trent died, there were a lot of things I tried to explain away with that very same diagnosis. Even checked myself into a mental hospital and tried every drug in the book to deal with it.

But eventually I'd had to face the fact that the demons were real, and they were coming for me. Brandon Harding, though… Maybe I was worrying for nothing. He was already clued in to the plot, so they

96

couldn't use him anymore, and if they weren't still haunting him, if he was trying to get his life back on track…

"I'm sorry to have bothered you," I said. "And just… be careful. The people who kidnapped you may still be trying to leverage power through you and through your position. They're very dangerous. They've killed before, and they won't stop if they think you're in their way. Watch yourself, okay? And call me if anything weird happens."

"Sure, Detective," he said.

He sounded patronizing, but I didn't care. At least he knew he could call me if anything did happen.

That was one more closed door in my research, though. I still had no idea what the demons—or goddess—wanted with Beck or how they were planning to achieve it.

Beck started fussing again, so I picked him up to comfort him. Someone pounded on my door, making me jump.

All the possible worst-case scenarios flashed through my head.

But demons wouldn't be likely to knock, and plenty of people knew I was home today.

I peeked through the peephole.

Isaac. Relief and confusion intermingled and rushed through me.

I opened the door. "Hey, what are you doing here?"

"I brought lunch." He held up a bag from the Chinese place around the corner.

"Thanks. What's the occasion?"

"Your pastor friend called me. He said you'd probably forget to eat today and suggested that I check on you."

"Oh. Well… he's not wrong. Come in."

Isaac came in and traded me the bags of food for Beck. "Hey, little buddy," he said.

Beck actually smiled at him, and he plopped on the couch. I went to the kitchen and put the food on plates. So, Chase had called him?

I wasn't sure what to make of that. Happy that Chase was concerned enough about my well-being to ask someone who he knew would care? He knew Isaac would drop everything if I were in danger, so did that prove how much he really did care, or how much he didn't, since he was willing to let Isaac be the one to take care of me?

I returned to find Isaac making faces and Beck giggling. A spot of warmth grew in my chest. Isaac genuinely loved Beck. As much as part of me still held on to the thought of Chase, I couldn't deny that Isaac would make an excellent dad.

I handed Isaac a plate and offered to take Beck, but he declined.

"Does he eat food yet?" he asked.

I shrugged. "You can try, but mostly he just slobbers on it and spits it back out."

"I've dealt with worse." He offered Beck a nibble of rice, and true to form, the rice ended up in a drool puddle on Isaac's lap. Isaac didn't seem to mind, though.

"Your pastor friend sounded really worried about you," he said after a few minutes. "Tell me about this case."

"I kind of told you already." I drenched a pile of chicken in sweet and sour sauce.

"Only a little. Fill me in. Help me understand."

I explained about the statues and the goddess and my frustrations with trying to put the pieces together.

"I just don't get why they need Beck. I mean, they've killed three other potentials, but Brandon Harding is still alive. What could Beck have that those others didn't? And I don't even know for sure who *they* are, and even if I did, I can't access their dimension, so it's not like I can go question them."

"I think you need to focus more on the goddess," Isaac said. "Let's assume, for the sake of argument, that she's real, and she travels in the other dimension. What was she like? What did worship of her involve? If someone were trying to revive her cult, what would they need?"

Good questions. Things that had been in the back of my mind but that I couldn't articulate.

I called Dr. Brantley and put her on speaker so Isaac could hear.

"Detective, I was just thinking of calling you. I may have found something," she said.

"Oh? What?"

"I've been researching Inanna, and I think I may know what the statues are for. Can you meet me?"

My tension must've been visible, because Isaac reached over and took my hand.

"Sure, where do you want to meet? Same coffee shop?"

"Actually, if you don't mind, I'd like to come to you. There's some stuff I came across in my research that I don't really want to talk about in public."

My heart stuttered for just an instant, Pastor Floyd's warning not to trust anyone ringing in my head. I quickly shoved it aside. I had my gun and my sword, if anything happened. Plus, Isaac was here. He would protect me with his life.

The absolute certainty of that hit me like a slug to the chest. No matter what, I could trust him. And that complete and unquestioning belief in him made me confident enough to accept Dr. Brantley's suggestion.

"That would be great. When do you want to come?"

"I can be there in an hour, if that works for you."

I glanced at Isaac.

He nodded. "I can stay," he mouthed.

"That would be perfect. I have a friend here—he knows everything."

"Okay, cool. I'll see you in a bit."

I texted her my address, and true to her word, she showed up an hour later, almost to the minute. I was putting Beck down again when she knocked, and Isaac opened the door.

"Hi, I'm Dr. Brantley. You must be Detective Davidson's friend."

"Dr. Reyes," Isaac said.

"Nice to meet you."

I came out from my room and shook Dr. Brantley's hand. "Thanks for coming over."

"Thanks for having me." She nodded toward Trent's recliner. "May I?"

"Of course."

She took off her suit coat and tossed it over the back of the chair before sitting down and smoothing her pant legs. "It's been awhile since I researched something this interesting and unique, and I'm excited that I get a chance to share it."

I brought coffee for everyone, and we sat around the coffee table, where Dr. Brantley spread out a mass of papers and photocopies of artifacts.

"Okay, where to start," she said, almost talking to herself.

She set a map on the top of the stack.

"This right here is the border between Iran and Turkey," she said, drawing a line with her finger. "This is Iraq, and this is the Tigris river. And this," she pointed dramatically to a spot near where all three countries met, "this is where I believe the statue came from. The area has been torn apart by wars for centuries, but specifically, in the last fifty years, there has been a lot of unrest."

Great. History and politics. Two of my favorite things.

Dr. Brantley took a drink of her coffee and scooted the recliner in a little closer to the table. "In that time, a small town was uncovered, and archaeologists—not me, unfortunately—were able to salvage some of the artifacts before they were forced out of the country and the area was bombed."

She grinned. "Now, here's where it gets interesting. The town is believed to have been destroyed around the second century AD. But, there are certain artifacts and holy relics that predate that by about eight hundred years. They uncovered a temple, and many of the artifacts recovered from that temple are consistent with art and religious icons from Nineveh."

She pointed to a place on the map a little way south of where she believed the statue was from. "This is where Nineveh was located. Excavations of the site have been interrupted many times throughout the years, but artifacts from Nineveh are in museums all over the world. Anyway, historically, Nineveh was destroyed in about 612 BCE. Burned and razed to the ground. The people were slaughtered or taken captive, but it is believed that some refugees made it out alive and headed north."

She pointed on the map to her original location. "They tried to rebuild here, including their places of worship, using artifacts salvaged from the temple in Nineveh."

"Artifacts like the statue of the woman, the bull, and the star," I said.

"Exactly," Dr. Brantley said.

"You said you found something out about the goddess herself?"

"Right. Yes. Okay. A lot of this is conjecture, but I think it's a reasonable deduction based on the evidence. Inanna, as she was originally called, before the Mesopotamian culture was absorbed by conquerors, was known for conquering other gods' territories."

So, she *was* like Dionysius.

"But her center of power was in Nineveh," Dr. Brantley went on. "In fact, the name Nineveh may even be a translation of her name, and she was most likely the primary deity of that city. When Nineveh was destroyed, she lost much of her power. Relics survived, and I believe that her true followers are now trying to gather as many of those relics as possible in order to revive her."

"Wait," Isaac broke in. "You believe this goddess is real? And that she actually can be revived?"

Dr. Brantley looked him dead in the eye and in all seriousness said, "I believe a lot of things. At any rate, her followers believe it. Remember what I said about the idols being representations of the gods here? From what I've been able to piece together, the gods need something physical to attach themselves to in order to enter this dimension. But when they do, they can affect things, like people's perceptions and their environment and even possibly the weather."

100

Isaac gripped my hand but his eyes remained on Dr. Brantley. "You think that's possible?"

Dr. Brantley shrugged. "I'm not sure. But there's mountains of evidence to support the fact that people believed the gods could increase crop yields and send plagues and other things, depending on whether they were appeased or angered. Even some of today's common beliefs are based in these early religions and forms of worship."

"What kind of things?" Isaac asked.

"Things like that the alignment of the planets—that are named after and supposed to be attached to gods—can influence behavior."

"So, her followers are attempting to revive her by gathering her idol and her other artifacts." I ran a hand—the one that wasn't holding Isaac's—through my hair.

"Right," Dr. Brantley said. "Whether or not she is real and can be revived remains to be seen, but in any case, her followers believe it, and they have already killed three people in their attempt to gather these artifacts, yes? Whether or not she's real is inconsequential at the moment—her followers need to be stopped."

"Agreed," I said, though I, too, wondered how much Dr. Brantley really knew or believed. She was accepting all this stuff a little too easily. "So, on the assumption that her followers are trying to revive her, what would that involve? Just… like… collecting all the pieces and creating an altar or something?"

"Possibly also that," Dr. Brantley said, "but that's much too mundane. They're killing people. This is not just a matter of putting together the puzzle pieces. There's usually a ritual or sacrifice of some sort involved in this kind of worship."

"A sacrifice. Something more than the murders of the men who stole those artifacts."

Dr. Brantley nodded, her expression grim. "More than likely. Animal sacrifice has been part of ritualistic worship across cultures since the beginning of time, but based on the violence they've already proven themselves willing to commit, I fear something much worse is in store for this. Early religions often required human sacrifices to achieve their purposes."

My throat tightened. Nausea roiled my stomach, the way it did when there were demonic presences around. "Human."

Dr. Brantley looked at me. "More often than not, someone innocent. Infants, especially first-born males, held an incredible amount of power."

Firstborn male infants.

101

That's why they were after Beck.

THIRTEEN

But it was more than Beck being a firstborn male child. Hundreds of firstborn male babies were born every day. Maybe thousands. There was something specific about my son, some reason they were threatening him. Was it because of his bloodline? But why? What could that possibly have to do with some ancient Middle Eastern goddess?

I needed to talk to Pastor Floyd.

"How would that work, exactly? Not the details of the ritual, but the... I don't know, philosophy behind it, I guess?"

"What do you mean?" Dr. Brantley asked.

"Why would a sacrifice give the goddess power? I mean, for the sake of argument, let's say Inanna is real and she's been trapped in an alternate dimension for several thousand years, and now her followers are trying to get her out by doing this ritual. How does the sacrifice help? What is it that would magically make it so she can break out of her dimension into ours?"

"That..." Dr. Brantley stopped and cocked her head to one side. "That's a really good question. I don't know. I'll research it." She tapped a note to herself on her phone.

Beck hollered from the other room, and I jumped up to get him, returning with him on my hip.

"Okay, one more question." I sat back down next to Isaac. "Well, probably like a thousand more, but one more immediately. Why now? She's been trapped since the fall of Nineveh, which was what, twenty-six hundred years ago? Surely there have been remnants of her followers throughout history. Why suddenly is she trying to get out now?"

"Well, now her artifacts have been found," Isaac offered.

"But at least some of them were found thirty years ago when that town was razed," I said. "People had no idea what they had. They ended up in pawn shops and antique stores. A serious follower could've bought them from the owners any time over the last thirty years, but now, all of a sudden, they're all stolen at once, and people are dying. Why?"

"Something must have happened," Dr. Brantley said. "Something to make them believe that the time is ripe."

"Like what?" I asked.

"That's what we need to figure out, I guess," she said. "I'll look into it from a historical and archaeological standpoint. And you could look at it from a current one. Like, breaking news, political unrest, crimes—anything that seems remotely related could be a clue."

She glanced at her watch. "I should get going. I have to give a lecture this evening. But I'll be looking into this as soon as I can."

I stood and shook her hand and walked her to the door. "Thanks for coming all this way," I said. "I appreciate the work you've done on this."

She smiled. "My pleasure. I'm thrilled to have a mystery to solve."

The door clicked closed behind her, and I locked it. I decided to give her the benefit of the doubt and assume she'd be less thrilled if it were her son who was potentially the target of a goddess-worshipping cult that wanted to sacrifice him to open the wall between dimensions and let her into our world.

I sat back on the couch next to Isaac, and he put his arms around me, pulling both me and Beck into an embrace.

"So, what do you think?" he asked.

"I think Inanna sounds a lot like a demon," I said. "It's weird, because all the demons I encountered were male. All their spawn were males. I even asked about it one time and I kinda got the impression that there were no female ones."

Beck started to squirm, so I set him on his blanket on the floor with some toys, then sat back down with Isaac. "The creature I saw when I looked into the other dimension was female. And based on all the descriptions, Inanna fits with what Dionysius told me about how the demon realm operates. She's territorial—steals domains from others. She can't access this dimension without some kind of help, like an idol—that's another thing I need to ask Pastor Floyd about—and she's trying to take over the world. Or at least some part of it."

"Perhaps there is more than one type of demon," Isaac suggested. "Maybe the ones you saw were a specific kind, and Inanna is something else?"

That made sense.

"Yet another thing I need to ask Pastor Floyd."

"Go ahead. I'd like to hear what he has to say too."

I called.

Still no answer. I was beginning to worry. I thought about contacting Chase, but I didn't really want to while I was with Isaac. Technically, there was nothing to hide on either end, it just felt weird. Besides, he said he'd call me when he talked to Pastor Floyd or when he found something else out, so me calling him would only be bothersome.

"How long has he been gone?" Isaac asked.

It took me a moment to reorient myself to the conversation. "A little over a week."

"You look worried."

"I am. He went to go search for information specifically about who was threatening Beck, and he hasn't answered calls, from either me or Chase. Ever since Bridget…" I paused, the memory of my best friend choking me. I'd thought I had time. Thought I could convince her. I didn't act, and I'd gotten her killed. The guilt, coupled with the ache of missing her threatened to overwhelm me.

Taking a deep breath, I forced the words out. "Ever since Bridget died, I automatically assume the worst when stuff like this happens. What if he's lying in a ditch somewhere? Or worse, is being held captive in a demon dimension?"

"Have you checked to see if any bodies matching his description have turned up?"

Why hadn't I thought of that sooner? All my worrying and a simple search would have at least put me a little more at ease.

"I haven't. I'll do that first thing, next time I go into the office. But that may be a couple days. I don't want to let Beck out of my sight right now."

"I understand," Isaac said.

He pulled me closer and ran his fingers down my face. "I don't like it when you worry so much. I want you to feel safe."

I nestled into his embrace and leaned my head against his shoulder. "I do feel safe with you. It's just… there's so much outside of my control. So much that could happen."

"I know." He tilted my chin up and leaned in for a kiss.

I kissed him back, lingering for a long moment in the security I felt whenever I was with him.

Isaac pulled back. "Jack, I… I've been wanting to say this for a long time, but I didn't think the time was right. But maybe it will never be right, so…"

I stiffened, not sure where this conversation was about to go.

"I love you, Jack," he said. "I have for a long time. I think you already knew that, but I've never said it. I just kept waiting—waiting for Beck to be born. Waiting for you to adjust. Waiting for… I don't even know anymore. The point is, I love you, and I want to be with you."

I opened my mouth but no words came out.

"Sorry." He pulled back and raked a hand through his dark hair. "I know that's sudden. I just… I want to be the one you call first when you're dealing with something like this. I want to be the one to talk you through it, to protect you, to be by your side. I want to be the one who knows when you're worried or stressed. I want to be the one who you can count on for anything, ever."

My thoughts tumbled over one another. A part of me did love him. He was one of my best friends, and I knew I could count on him. But was that enough? Could I commit to him? Let go of any thought of anyone else? "Isaac, I don't know what to say."

"You don't have to say anything right now. I love you, and that is not going away. Okay? Whenever you're ready, I'll be here."

He leaned in to kiss me again.

So naturally, that was when Beck chose to announce he was hungry with an ear-splitting screech.

I planted a quick peck on his lips and stood up. "Sorry."

"It's okay," he said. "I should probably get going anyway. I'm on call tonight."

I picked Beck up and walked Isaac to the door. He gave both of us a hug.

"Thanks for coming over today. I appreciated having a second person here for that."

"My pleasure. I mean that, in every possible way." He brushed my face with his fingertips, gazing at me with an intensity I now realized was deep longing. "Let me know what else you find out."

"I will," I promised.

"And remember, anything you need, I'm here."

"I know."

He kissed me again, and I shut the door behind him. He was a good man. A smart, rich, handsome man who loved me. So why did I want to call Chase the second he was gone?

I resisted the urge and called Pastor Floyd again, instead.

Still no answer.

And he'd given no indication of where he was going, so I had no idea where to even start looking. As soon as I had a chance, I'd check for John Does around the country that matched his description.

For now, I spent some quality time playing with my son and got myself some dinner before settling in to snuggle and try to relax before going to bed.

Chase called me early the next morning. "Can I come over?"

"Of course," I said. "I'm staying home from work again, so I'm here."

"Good, I think I found something."

"Cool. I need to fill you in on everything I learned from Dr. Brantley too."

He arrived a few minutes later with fresh coffee. From our place. I wondered if that was as significant to him as it was to me. I doubted it and tried to shove the thought away.

"Come in," I said.

Beck was feeling better—less fever and generally better demeanor. He sat on the floor with a squishy ball that rattled.

Chase and I sat on the couch. I still had Dr. Brantley's pictures of the maps and the various artifacts. I recapped the theories about Inanna and how her followers wanted to resurrect her.

"That makes sense with what I found," he said. He pulled out some notes and his Bible. "I've been looking into demonic activity since... everything last year. And I've discovered some things. Like possession. I mean, I knew about that, obviously—it's all through the Bible, and there are plenty of documented cases, but I didn't really know how it worked, and a lot of things didn't make sense after meeting Dion and knowing he could come into this dimension directly."

"Right," I said. "That didn't quite make sense to me, either."

"I think what's happening is that the demons who are disembodied—the ghosts of the Nephilim, if you will, like the one that attached itself to you—can attach themselves to things on this side, and affect the world that way. So, they can inhabit a person or animal or sometimes even an object and use that as sort of a portal into this world."

"The woman who sold the statue to the pawn shop—she said it was haunted. That it knocked over her other statues and stuff. Could that be what happened? It was possessed by a demon?"

Chase nodded. "It's very likely."

"So, Inanna—or her followers—are trying to gather up the artifacts that are directly related to her. Dr. Brantley said the idols were supposed to be physical representations here of the gods from the other side—so Inanna could, theoretically, inhabit her idols and use them to come into this world."

"Yes."

"But if she needs an idol to access this world, then that means she's not a demon with a physical form like Dionysius was, she's a spirit. Trapped in the other dimension. So, she's dead. Or, sort of dead. At least, her true demon self that could've inhabited this world is dead, and now her spirit is trying to get her followers to create this gateway or whatever for her to come back."

"It seems like it, yes."

"Where has she been all this time? Why is she just now trying to make her comeback?"

"I don't know. I'll ask her next time I see her."

I smiled at his dry tone. "I'm serious, though. She was destroyed in what, six hundred BC?"

"Whoa. Wait a minute."

"What?"

Chase closed his eyes and held up a hand.

I gave Beck his ball, which he'd rolled toward my feet, and waited for Chase to finish thinking.

"You said Dr. Brantley thought Inanna might be where the name Nineveh came from."

I nodded.

He grabbed his Bible and flipped through the pages. "Here we go. This is from the book of Nahum, an Old Testament prophet, with regard to the destruction of Nineveh. 'And Huzzab shall be led away captive, she shall be brought up, and her maids shall lead her as with the voice of doves, beating on their breasts.'"

"What does that even mean?"

"That's the question. This word, *Huzzab*, has a lot of different interpretations. The word itself means, like, 'it is established' or 'it is decreed.' Some people believe it means that it was decreed that Nineveh would be destroyed and her people would be carried away. But the word is used as a proper noun, like a name, so others believe it was the name of the queen at the time or a primary goddess."

"Okay." I nodded to encourage him to continue.

"But what if it's both? What if it really is referring to Nineveh, the goddess as well as the city? What if when it says she's carried away it's being literal—her idols and artifacts are carried from the city? That's why her maids—or priestesses—are in mourning. Because she, Inanna, was literally taken captive?"

"And that's why she's been missing all this time." I stood to retrieve Beck's ball, which had rolled to the other side of the couch, and handed it back to him. "Because she was destroyed when Nineveh was sacked. Her artifacts were torn apart, and now that they have all been uncovered, she can put herself back together. As long as those things were buried, she was still a captive, but now..."

"Now she can put them together and be free."

FOURTEEN

"That means there must be more." Again, I sifted through the pictures of the various artifacts that still sat on my coffee table. "Something new. Something recent. Because these three artifacts—the statue, the bull, and the star—were uncovered like thirty years ago. So, there must be something else, some key piece that has been uncovered since then, which triggered her escape, and her need to gather all the rest of the artifacts."

"That's both encouraging and incredibly depressing," Chase said.

"Agreed. At least we know what to look for now. But we have no idea how many pieces there are to this puzzle or how many more people will die by her trying to get them all. I need to make a couple calls. Do you want to stay and see what I can find out? I'll make lunch."

"Thanks, but no. I should get to the church. Floyd isn't back yet, so I need to be there more often."

"Okay. I'll let you know what I find out. Thanks for coming."

When he was gone, I called Dr. Brantley and told her the connection to Nineveh we suspected. "Is there any way you can figure out how many more pieces there are to this—whatever it is? Or if any other discoveries have been made recently that would tie in to this?"

"Discoveries like this have a procedure. If something related to Inanna has been found, there's documentation. I'll see what I can find."

"Thanks," I said.

I hung up and called Desiree.

"What've you got?" she asked.

"Just a theory so far." Beck was still playing happily, so I took the opportunity to step into the kitchen and refill my coffee while I filled

112

her in. "I've been talking to my archaeologist contact and a few others, and we believe that there is a sect of people, who worship the ancient goddess Inanna and are trying to revive her cult. The artifacts that were stolen come from a larger collection. What about you? Anything new? Similar robberies or deaths? Ancient Mesopotamian artifacts randomly turning up?"

"Two more deaths—not bodies turned inside out like the thieves—just regular deaths. But they all matched the description of those three victims who look like Harding. And here's the weird thing. They all died the same way. Knife wounds to the chest in the shape of a symbol, and they've all been drained of their blood."

"Oh, shit," I said.

"What?"

"The airport."

"What?" Desiree's voice held an equal mix of curiosity and impatience.

"There was another murder at the airport. I've been so focused on the Inanna murders that I haven't looked into it much, but there was a man who worked at the airport who was killed in the same way. The symbol—did it look like an ankh without the arms?"

Desiree sucked in her breath. "Yes."

Two more potentials dead.

A ritualistic symbol carved in their chests. Their bodies drained of blood.

What in the world was that about?

"These people are serious and very dangerous." I settled on my couch and gazed at my son, all the worst-case scenarios of what the demons would do to him if they got their hands on him running through my head. "I don't know how many pieces of this artifact they need to collect, but they have no qualms against killing people, and I have a feeling they're not done yet."

"If they're collecting artifacts, they must be putting them somewhere," Desiree said, though it sounded more like she was thinking out loud than talking to me. "I'll look into recently rented warehouses and such. The problem is, they could literally be anywhere. And we have no idea where they'll steal from next."

"It will be someplace with ritual significance," I said. "Inanna's original seat of power was in Nineveh."

"There's no way I can get any sort of jurisdiction over there," Desiree said. "I can contact some friends in the government, but the likelihood that we'll get any sort of cooperation whatsoever is... pretty close to nil."

"Well, if you have any contacts internationally that you can at least get the word out to, let them know what we suspect and that there may be murderers on the loose. Maybe they'll be a little more willing to share some information."

"I'll see what I can do," Desiree said. "If we had any idea at all where they're going... Well, that's neither here nor there. Thanks. This is at least something to go on."

"Let me know what you find out," I said and hung up.

I needed to talk to someone who knew more about this stuff.

I called Pastor Floyd, but he still didn't answer. Where *was* he? What was he doing? I *really* needed to find out what he knew!

But even he only had so many contacts and resources, and as far as I was aware, they were all human. I needed to find out what was going on in the demon dimension.

I picked Beck up to feed him before his nap. He seemed to be feeling better. His fever was gone. I weighed my options. I still hated the idea of letting him out of my sight, even for a minute. But I couldn't protect him if I had no idea what I was going up against, and there were certain things I couldn't ask anyone else to do for me—not Chase or Isaac, and certainly not Desiree. They wouldn't know how, even if they wanted to help. Some things I just had to do myself. Things I couldn't do while carrying Beck around.

I finally resigned myself to the fact that the only way to really protect him was to get to the bottom of this puzzle. After wrestling with my own decision for what seemed like an eternity, I took him to Gen's.

Then I went to the last place I'd encountered a demonic stronghold.

The daycare where Dionysius was housing all his half-breed demon spawn. Here, it had just looked like an ordinary building, but on the other side of the dimensional wall, it had been a full-on fortress, complete with housing for the demons and underground labs for their experiments.

I'd burned it to the ground in both worlds.

In the real world, it was still abandoned. Fencing blocked the charred remains from trespassers.

I pulled out the sword and clutched the hilt.

Even now, a year later, I could still feel the scars in the dimensional wall where demons—and where I myself—had torn holes to travel through dimensions. They were mostly closed now, and I had no way to open them from this side. Portals were created from that world into this one, not the other way around.

I circled the perimeter while holding the sword, trying to sense the other side. Trying to see if I could sense any demonic activity here.

I felt... something. Far into the interior of the wreckage. Something was there. Walking around the fence, I found a spot between panels that was wide enough for me to squeeze through, and made my way through the rubble until I found a scar in the wall that seemed thinner, less healed than the others. I gripped my sword and leaned in toward the other dimension.

"Hello? Who's there?"

A pulse of emotion—fear and surprise, followed by anger and hate.

"I know you're there," I said. "Come here."

The demon sidled closer, but I still couldn't see it. The hate mingled with curiosity now.

"What are you doing here? This fortress was destroyed," I said.

Because you destroyed it. The thing's voice echoed in my head.

"True," I said. "Which still begs the question, why are you here? Rebuilding?"

A wave of antagonism pulsed out from it.

"Or just hiding?"

Seething hatred, as bad as anything I'd ever felt from the one attached to my soul, oozed over me.

"Interesting," I said aloud, as the explanation dawned on me.

What is?

"You can't go with the others, wherever their new base of operations is."

How do you know that?

"Where are they?"

I will not tell you.

"*Will* not or *can* not? Did they abandon you? Or did they exile you? Show you where they were but tell you not to join them?"

The thing edged closer, and now I could see its vague outline through the haze of the dimensional wall. *I know where they are.*

"Tell me."

Why should I? What's in it for me?

I shrugged. "I won't kill you when I take them down."

The demon stepped closer. Bolder, almost arrogant now. *I've heard the rumors. You can't get in here anymore.*

"Don't believe everything you hear." I lunged with the sword, nicking his shoulder.

He jumped back, hissing, electrified with rage.

"I've made treaties with demons before. You help me, I'll help you."

I heard about that. A hint of trust edged into him. *What can you do for me?*

"Tell me who is in control of this region right now and where to find them, and I'll protect you when I go after them."

He paused for a long moment before finally stepping forward and nodding. *We have an agreement. I will not fight them—the only help I will be is in information. And you will see to it that I am not killed when you battle them.*

"Deal," I said. "Who took over after I killed Dionysius, and where are they headquartered?"

No one is in charge. Not yet. When you killed Dionysius, you left a... power vacuum. Others have tried to take over, but none have garnered enough followers to keep a hold on this area. Until now. Something is coming. Maybe it's already here. They're building a new fortress, like this one used to be.

"In your dimension or in mine?"

Ours. But corresponding to something in yours.

"What?" I stepped over a charred log, a little closer to where the demon stood.

The Museum of Natural History.

"The museum? Why the hell would they be going there?"

How should I know? I don't care about human interpretations of history or art. I just know that's where they are.

A museum? Filled with dinosaurs and stuff way more ancient than anything related to Inanna? What would make that a good place for a demon fortress? In the human dimension, there were probably security guards and things, but it was a public campus. Pretty much anyone could get in and out without too much trouble.

The daycare made sense, because Dionysius needed a place to house and care for his demon spawn. So, there must be a reason they were congregating at the museum. But...

"If there's no one in charge, who decided where to build the fortress? Who is leading that project?"

I don't know.

"No hint? No suspicions?"

A demon called Dumuzi is gathering the forces. He has not said who he is taking orders from. But the others fear him. They do as he says. This fortress they're building—it will be more formidable than this one was, and will have protections from... well, from you.

"I thought you guys didn't fear me anymore because I—because you thought I couldn't come over there."

116

A wave of mixed emotions wafted out from him. Arrogance, quickly replaced by confusion, then topped with frustration and irritation.

They don't want to take any chances.

So, they did fear me. They didn't know whether or not I could make it back there.

"Why not you? Why aren't you there? What did you do to piss them off so bad that you're exiled and not allowed to play with the other demons?"

I refused to obey Dumuzi.

"Why?"

I don't trust him.

"So? None of you trust anyone, as far as I can tell. You all just follow whoever has the most power."

Dumuzi is... different. There's something ancient and sinister about him. I fear what will become of us if someone even more powerful than he takes control of this region.

I relaxed a little and rested the sword on my shoulder. "You mean someone worse than Dionysius? That guy had no qualms about killing his own followers and turning them against one another as a show of power. And you think this Dumuzi is worse than that?"

Far, far worse. Whoever is giving orders—it is a power that goes beyond any I have seen in thousands of years. It will destroy us as well as you.

"Great. Okay. Well, you enjoy your little hideout here. I'll be back when I need to know more."

Wonderful. I can't wait. But a hint of curiosity and almost anticipation laced his words, so the sarcasm lost a little of the sting.

I walked back to my truck and drove slowly toward Gen's to pick up Beck, pondering what the demon had told me—both intentionally and by letting too much slip.

I had two new leads to follow. The Natural History Museum and a demon—or other entity—with enough power to terrify demons.

Had to be Inanna. But that didn't explain why she was coming here. Was it just to fill the void left by Dionysius? If that were the case, the demon at the daycare would've followed her. What was she planning that made it worth being exiled in order to not be part of it?

Why here? That part still made no sense. Her seat of power had been Nineveh. If her minions were building a fortress, wouldn't they be building it there? Or maybe they were building it there, but this would be like an outpost or something. Literally on the other side of the world.

It just didn't add up. None of it did.

One thing that the demon had let slip fell into place in my mind.

They were still afraid of me. Because the sword could get through? Because I'd killed Dionysius? Neither of those things made me much of a threat, at least not to the plan at large. And yet they were building a fortress that they thought I couldn't penetrate. Me, specifically.

What did they know about me that I didn't? And how could I use that against them?

Gen's study group was at her house again when I arrived to pick up Beck.

"Good afternoon, Detective," Oscar said. "Can I get you anything? Coffee? Water? Soda? A snack?"

"Hey," I smiled. His obsequiousness was a little over-the-top, but I couldn't deny appreciating the gesture.

"He's a little fussy again today," Gen said, handing Beck to me.

I held him and noticed the faint flush of his cheeks.

"I wonder if he's allergic to something here?" I said aloud.

"I have a dog," Oscar volunteered. "I'm really, really sorry if it's my fault."

Gen shook her head. "It's probably not that. You weren't here the first day he got sick." She turned to me. "I don't think I've gotten any new cleaning products or anything, but I'll look around and see if there's anything that's a likely culprit."

"Thanks," I said.

But the fever still had that vaguely otherworldly feel to it. As if he was being attacked. But there had been no sign of demons at Gen's apartment—I'd checked.

A million thoughts swirled in my head, and I couldn't make sense of any of them.

But one thing was for sure. No demon or goddess was getting my son. I would take the fight to them, one way or another. And that meant figuring out how to get back into the other dimension to even the playing field.

I kept Beck in my room again that night, wanting him to be near me, and the sword on the floor by my bed, within easy reach. I wasn't taking any chances.

My phone rang, yanking me from sleep.

The clock by my bed said it was three in the morning.

I blinked trying to read the caller ID.

Pastor Floyd.

FIFTEEN

I was instantly fully awake. "Pastor Floyd! Are you okay? Where are you?"

"Jack, I need you to come quickly. I'm at the church."

"I'm on my way," I said.

I called Cameron, who was more than willing to take Beck. In the middle of the night. Again. I needed to buy that girl a present to show my appreciation. Something nice. Like a Ferrari.

I sped to the church. Chase's car was in the parking lot, but I didn't see any sign of Pastor Floyd's.

Armed with my gun and my sword, I ran toward the main building. "Pastor Floyd?" I called out.

No answer.

"Chase? Pastor Floyd? Where are you?"

I almost ran into Chase as I rounded the corner toward the building that housed Pastor Floyd's office.

"Jack, you're here. Have you seen Floyd?"

I shook my head. "He called me and told me to get over here, but I haven't seen him. Is he in his office?"

"Everything is locked, and the alarms are all set. I don't know where he is."

Together, we circled the building, following the sidewalks lined with plants that gave the property a desert-oasis feel, calling Pastor Floyd's name. The unassuming buildings—the main sanctuary across from the smaller office building—were all dark. No movement disturbed the shadows, no sounds other than our voices broke the silence.

Nothing.

"Where could he be?" I asked.

A yell split the night, coming from the alley behind the church property. Chase and I both took off at a run, heading for the sound. We reached the alley, but there was no sign of anyone. I could feel it, though. Something dark. Demonic.

I gripped my sword and closed my eyes.

I could feel the taint in the air, the rip where the wall between dimensions had been torn. Opening my eyes, I turned to look at the area. As before, with the sword in my hands, I could just make out the tear in dimensions and the bleak landscape on the other side.

She stood there, her red eyes gazing at me,

In her arms lay the limp, barely conscious figure of Pastor Floyd.

"Inanna," I breathed.

Curiosity mingled with disdain as she looked me over. "You must be Jack," she said. "I've heard a lot about you. I thought you'd be... more formidable."

"Give him back," I ordered.

"Or what?" Inanna asked.

"Or I'll come in there and take him back and kill you while I'm at it."

She laughed, a deep, scratchy sound. "You can't come in here, not anymore."

"I'll find a way. I know it's possible. Even if I have to force another demon to carry me—"

Oh, hell. I was such an idiot.

"That's how they did it," I said. "The guys who robbed the pawn shop and the antique store and the auction house. They were carried through by demons, or possessed..."

Pastor Floyd's eyes shot open. "Possessed," he moaned before his eyes fluttered closed again.

"So, it can be done."

Inanna straightened, her full seven feet or more of stature imposing over Pastor Floyd's frail form. "Only if the demon wants to or is ordered to, and I certainly won't be giving any orders."

"You think I need your orders? I have allies in your realm." Okay, slightly bluffing, but she didn't need to know that.

Her red, glowing eyes narrowed.

I took a step toward the opening and raised my sword, swinging it into position.

Her eyes fell on it for the first time, and she jumped back, a hiss escaping her mouth. "Where did you get that?"

"Like I said. I have allies. Now, give him back."

Inanna looked at the sword, then at me, then at Pastor Floyd.

121

She lifted a hand and drove her long, clawed fingers straight through his chest, then shoved him through the portal into me.

I tumbled backward, Pastor Floyd on top of me.

"Call 911," I gasped.

Chase fumbled with his phone as I rolled out from under Pastor Floyd and tried to put pressure on the wounds.

Blood spurted out of five holes, making a sort of circle in his chest.

"You're gonna be okay," I said. Tears streamed down my face. "Just hang on. The ambulance is on its way."

"Jack," Pastor Floyd sputtered, blood and saliva spurting from his lips. "Jack, listen. She's killing... them all. All the potentials."

He coughed and another jet of blood squirted out from the hole nearest his heart. "She's not just trying to escape. She's trying to take over... everything. She wants... this entire dimension. Absorb it into hers. Be goddess of... everything."

"How? How is she going to do that?"

He choked, and his eyes fluttered closed, but he opened them again. "Beck... Beck is the key."

His eyes closed and the blood slowed to a trickle.

"What do you mean? Pastor Floyd? What do you mean, Beck is the key?"

He didn't answer.

Sirens wailed up the street, and a moment later an ambulance screeched into the alley. Chase waved his hands to show them where we were, and a pair of EMTs jumped out and rushed to Floyd.

I stepped back so they could work, but deep down I knew it wouldn't matter.

I picked up my sword and stepped toward the hole between dimensions, but Inanna was long gone.

An hour later, I sat at the precinct with Chase as we gave our official statements.

"I don't know. It was dark," I said. "She came out of nowhere. Definitely a woman, but she was... tall and solidly built. I couldn't see hair color or anything. She had something on her hand, some kind of blades."

Chase and I had briefly practiced what we would say, staying as close to the truth as possible but without actually mentioning demons. Chase truthfully said he didn't see anything at all—just the blood after Pastor Floyd had been stabbed.

Finally, we were allowed to leave. Chase followed me to Cameron's to get Beck, then home.

I put Beck in his crib, then flopped onto the couch. I needed a shower. And a nap. But I had time for neither. "I... need to get to work. I need to figure out what Inanna is going to do."

"You need to sleep first," Chase said. "Go to bed. I'll stay on the couch. I don't think you should be alone right now."

I nodded and let him help me up. Then I showered and slept a few hours, until my mind wouldn't let my body rest anymore.

Chase was still in my living room. He sat on the couch with a cup of coffee and his Bible.

"Find anything?" My whole body felt numb. Bridget. Now Pastor Floyd. Who else would I lose?

"Not really." He leaned against the back of the couch and closed his eyes. "That's the thing about prophecies. They're really obscure until they're not, and by then it's usually too late. And Inanna herself, other than possibly being related to Nineveh, isn't mentioned. I did find some interesting things about ancient idol worship. Namely sacrifices."

Sacrifices again. This could not be good.

I grabbed coffee and sat on the couch next to him. "What have you got?"

"I was looking into Canaanite worship—they developed some of the earliest forms of organized religion. Their idols were huge—taller than humans. Massive structures made of bronze, formed in the shapes of their gods. They were hollow, and fires would be built inside, heating up the entire statue. The people would lay their sacrifices on the idol's arms where they would be burned by the hot metal."

"What did they sacrifice?" I was almost afraid to hear the answer.

"What *didn't* they. Harvests. Animals. Children."

The nausea churned inside me again. "Children."

He nodded.

"Is that what she's planning to do to Beck?"

"I don't know."

"Pastor Floyd said she wanted to incorporate this dimension into hers. Be goddess of everything. Can she do that? Would it work?"

"I don't know."

"If she could do it, how would she?"

"I don't know. But all sacrifices, all power—everything throughout history—indicates that blood is involved. Blood is life. Blood is power. If Inanna really plans to destroy this reality and make it hers, there will be lots of blood."

"Of course there will be." I sighed, struggling to get out from under the weight of the feeling of impotence that smothered me. "So,

123

we need to figure out what she's going to do and how she's going to do it and stop her before she gets a chance."

"Right," Chase said.

I leaned my head against the back of the couch. "I need to get into the other dimension. If I can get in, I can get information. Were you listening when I was talking to Inanna?"

"Sort of, but I could only hear your half of the conversation."

"I can get in if I can get a demon to possess me. I can use them to walk through the other dimension, like the thieves did to get to the artifacts."

Chase sat up straight, a look of horror crossing his face. "Jack, no. That's a terrible idea."

"Why? Why is it terrible? I have a contact. A demon who is ostracized from Inanna's followers. We have a truce. I could get him to possess me and use him to access the other dimension."

He clenched his fists so hard his knuckles turned white. "That's not how it works! If you let him in, he will be in control. You won't be able to control him. He'll control you. And there will be no coming back from that."

"How do you know? I still have the sword. I can use that."

"These things never go how you plan or expect. Please, please trust me. Don't do this."

"I can't just sit here and do nothing. I have to get information. I have to figure out what they're planning to do and how so I can stop them. Hell, I don't even know what Inanna is, let alone how to take her out. I'm useless here. I have to get into the other dimension. I don't have another choice."

"Jack, please. Messing with spiritual forces is nothing to play with. Last time, you didn't have a choice. Last time it was something that was done to you. If you do this…"

He closed his eyes and inhaled. "Promise me you won't do this. We'll find another way."

I stood and paced to the other side of the room. "I can't promise that. My son's life is at stake. I will do whatever it takes—and I mean whatever it takes—to keep him safe."

"How will he be safe if you're possessed by a demon? Or dead?"

"Cameron or her parents will take care of him if something happens to me. But I will not let him be sacrificed so some goddess can make this world her own."

"Let me at least try to find another way first. Will you do that?"

I took a deep breath. "Fine. But I won't sit around waiting forever. I did that last time—I didn't know what to do or what action to take, and Bridget died because of my indecision. I won't let that happen again."

"Thank you. Just give me a little bit of time to figure something else out."

"How much time?"

"A day or two."

"Okay."

Chase left a little while later. I had promised… but I still needed to make my contingency plans.

I dropped Beck off with Gen and went back to the daycare, pulling my sword as I approached the ruins. I ducked through the hole in the fence and walked toward where an exterior wall used to be.

"You there?" I called out.

The demon slunk out of the shadows of the rubble and came toward me. *I don't have anything new since the last time you were here,* he hissed.

"I didn't figure you did," I said. "I have another question."

What?

"Inanna."

Shock registered through him before he got it under control.

"So, you lied to me before. You did know who was in charge."

No. I only just heard her name a little bit ago.

"Then you lied to me just now when you said you didn't have anything new. Whatever, I don't care. Do you know about the humans who stole the artifacts for Inanna?"

The demon nodded slowly. *I've heard rumors.*

"How did they get in and out of your dimensions? I thought I was the only human who could travel through your dimension and still be conscious."

The demon glared at me, his emotions wary and suspicious, but didn't answer.

"Were they possessed?" I asked.

A jolt of surprise jumped out from the demon, quickly suppressed. *What makes you think that?*

I touched a charred beam. "They got inside locked buildings, stole things, and disappeared as though they were never there. But in my experience, when people are transported through your dimension, they pass out and are unconscious. Sometimes they wake up, but if so, for only moments at a time. Even after they're returned to this dimension, they're groggy and out of it for awhile—certainly not capable of theft. So how did these people get in and out? They had to have been similar

125

to me. Except instead of having part of themselves taken by a demon, they have a demon inside them. Am I wrong?"

He writhed, as though not wanting to answer. *You're not wrong.*

Okay. Good.

"So, hypothetically speaking, if I wanted to travel through dimensions, I could get a demon to possess me."

The demon narrowed his eyes and studied me, no emotion that I could sense pulsing out of him.

Hypothetically, he said at last.

"How would that work, exactly?"

I doubt it would be appealing to you.

"Probably not. Explain it anyway."

The demon took a step closer. *It starts with your mind. You have to open your mind and let other thoughts drift away. Relax completely and allow it to happen. I would—I assume I am the demon in question?*

I nodded.

You remember being here—how you could still see humans, like ghosts of themselves?

"I remember."

When your mind is open and empty, you sort of—I'm not sure how to explain it, but you can sort of create a bridge from your dimension into this one. Tearing down the wall, mentally speaking. When I take hold of your mind, I would essentially be grabbing onto it and merging with it. I would then travel through your mind into your body. Once we are one, I will be able to travel through your dimension, in your body, and, if the door is opened, you will be able to travel through mine.

"You'll be able to travel in mine while you're inside me, but if you went through a portal while you weren't attached to me, you'd die, or whatever it is that you guys do when you turn to dust, right?"

Correct.

"Okay, one thing doesn't add up for me." I tested the sturdiness of the partial wall and then leaned on it, trying to seem casual. "I've heard about possession and stuff. But I've never heard of anyone before me traveling through dimensions the way I did, even possessed."

It doesn't happen. It's possible, obviously, but it is not a thing we do. What happened with those men who stole those artifacts was... unprecedented, even for us.

"Then how did they know it could be done?"

There are many ancient secrets, forgotten even by us, that are now being uncovered.

I filed that away for future reference.

"Okay, but it can be done. People can traverse your dimension if they're possessed."

126

Wariness tinged with grudging respect seeped out from his carefully controlled emotions. *It still takes work. The door must be opened. And you still must go through an existing portal—just because you are possessed doesn't mean you can wander in here anytime you want.*

"What do you mean, the door must be opened? Isn't that the same thing as opening the portal?"

No. Opening the portal allows demons into your dimension. *To allow you into ours, the door must be opened from the other side. Blood is required.*

Blood. Like a sacrifice? I would ask him about that in a minute. "But you can make a portal, right?"

I cannot. I am not corporeal in your world. If you remember, Dionysius and others could open portals to go through, but Nephilim spirits and those like me could not.

Damn. He was right. But finding a portal shouldn't be too hard. There was the portal that they'd dumped the bodies through in that empty lot.

Oh, shit.

The bodies.

"What happened to them?" I asked.

To whom?

"The thieves. They were torn inside out and dumped in a field. How—how did that happen?

The demon laughed, his cold, cruel mirth sending chills down my spine and into my stomach, making me want to heave.

Come, open your mind. I will show you everything you want to know.

He stalked toward me and reached—not through the portal, but through the dimensional wall, sticking his fingers into my head. Cold, slimy, dark—his claws like tentacles wrapping themselves around my mind.

SIXTEEN

I screamed and tried to pull away, but he was already latched on, swimming into me.

Instinctively, I raised the sword and slashed.

It tore through the demon's arms as if they were nothing.

He screeched and stumbled back. The claws in my head seemed to dissolve, leaving me free.

And suddenly I could see clearly into the other dimension. He stood there, as solid as if I'd crossed through a portal. He hissed, holding his stumps of arms against his chest, as he walked backward, seething.

My breath came in quick, panicked gasps.

What had I almost done?

And yet… even though he couldn't be trusted, he might still be my only shot. I couldn't get into the other dimension without him. And I had to get there. I needed answers.

"I thought we had a truce," I said at last.

I didn't break the truce, the thing hissed. *I did what you asked.*

"You tried to take me over."

You wanted to be possessed. What did you think it would be like?

"I wanted us to help each other."

How does that help me? You wanted to use me.

He wasn't wrong. I *did* want to use him. I guess I thought that because he was a demon it wouldn't matter. Not that I was worried about his feelings, of course. He was a demon.

"You want power," I said. "I offered you that. In your dimension, especially with this sword, I am powerful. I would have protected you. But it does me no good if you're driving. I have things I need to accomplish."

You are stupider than I gave you credit for. Your sword would be useless if I were with you. I can't touch it, so you couldn't, either.

"What do you mean? I could use it before."

The demon glared at me. Disdain wafted from it, even through the blinding pain pulsing from its severed arms. It turned and disappeared into the rubble of the demon fortress, where I couldn't get to it.

He couldn't touch it? What did that mean?

I ran my hand over the smooth, metallic blade that bent like rubber. I'd first acquired the sword as a truce symbol, given to me by the demon who controlled a large part of Nevada. He'd told me it would help defeat Dionysius.

It'd been wrapped in some kind of cloth. He'd never actually touched the weapon itself. The Hamet Sword, he'd called it. What did that mean? And if the demons really couldn't handle it, then this one's intel about me not being able to wield it if I were possessed rang true.

Could I wear gloves, maybe? I made a mental note to get some, and then questioned that decision. It was only by touching the hilt that I was able to sense the other dimension at all. If I had gloves on, would I still be able to do that?

I stopped by a hardware store on my way home and bought a pair anyway. I picked up Beck and got him fed and settled on the floor with his toys, then tried my theory.

I was right.

With the gloves on, the sword was less useful than a cheap plastic toy. I sensed nothing.

But if I were possessed I wouldn't necessarily need to sense the other dimension with the sword, the demon would do it for me.

But that led me back to the original problem of handing over control, which was not something I was willing to do.

So, here I was again at square one, with no idea how to get the information I needed or stop the demons from attacking.

And Pastor Floyd was gone. The aching hole inside widened, accompanied by an extra dose of guilt at feeling frustrated that any information he might have uncovered was lost to me.

I thought about his last words. Inanna was killing all the potentials, and somehow Beck was the key.

I needed to find out more about the sacrifice and what she planned to do. How it worked and how Beck could be connected.

I called the two people I could think of who could help me and invited them to dinner.

Chase and Dr. Brantley both showed up that evening, almost at the same time.

I actually cooked. I couldn't remember the last time I'd done more than throw a couple things together, but I made lasagna—Trent's mom's recipe. One of the few things I knew how to cook well.

"This smells amazing," Dr. Brantley said, seating herself at my small table, her stack of notes beside her.

"It does." Chase smiled, but profound grief shone in his eyes.

I pulled him into a hug and spoke softly into his ear. "I haven't said it yet—I've been so wrapped up in everything else—but I know how much Pastor Floyd meant to you. I'm so, so sorry."

His jaw was tight, but it seemed to be an attempt to hold back the emotion not an angry reaction to my words. "Thanks."

I sat across from Dr. Brantley, and Chase sat on the end of the table to my left. I held Beck on my lap with my left hand so I could still eat.

Chase folded his hands on top of the table. "Do you mind if I say grace?"

Dr. Brantley and I both bowed our heads. Chase said a quick prayer, thanking God for the food and asking for wisdom for the night's discussion, then he started shoving lasagna into his mouth.

Dr. Brantley grinned at me. *He's cute,* she mouthed before taking a bite.

I know, I mouthed back, my lips quirking in a smile.

We ate in silence for a few minutes before Dr. Brantley got us down to business.

"I imagine you didn't ask us both here just to chat," she said. "Can I safely assume we're all up to speed on what we all know?"

I nodded. "More or less. We're at least all on the same page with investigating this whole thing as a series of supernatural murders intended to bring back the goddess Inanna."

"Great. Glad I don't have to beat around the bush. I've been looking into the early goddess worship and practices themselves. I told you before that blood was a huge part of those rituals, but I've been studying why."

"Oh, good," Chase said between mouthfuls. "I've been looking into it, and I've hit a wall. The Bible has a lot to say about blood sacrifices, and how blood is life and blood is used for atonement, but I wasn't sure why that translated to other religious practices or how it worked."

Dr. Brantley nodded. "One thing that isn't really clear from the Bible references is that blood itself is intrinsically powerful. Not just because it keeps us alive, but it's... how do I put it... it has its own frequency, in a way. Blood is, for lack of a better term, magical. I'm not saying I believe in magic in the traditional sense, but there are things that we can't explain with science, and blood is one of them. We know how the cells work and how they pump through our body with oxygen and nutrients and all that—but we really don't understand why that makes us alive."

"Magic," I said at the same time Chase said, "God."

Dr. Brantley smiled. "Either way. But from what I can tell, the ancients believed that blood was powerful magic. They used it to appease the gods, and it seems as though the gods themselves needed the blood, which is why they accepted those sacrifices in exchange for favor. I'm not entirely clear on what they used the blood for, but somehow it gives them power."

Chase held up a hand and closed his eyes like he was thinking.

Dr. Brantley and I both stared at him and waited.

"Jack, do they bleed?"

"What?" I asked.

"The demons, do they bleed? When you killed them?"

"Wait," Dr. Brantley said. "Back up. What?"

I'd forgotten that I hadn't really told her about the other dimension or demons. I still wasn't sure how much I trusted her, but so far she knew more about Inanna than anyone else, so I had to extend a certain amount of information to get her knowledge in return. She'd accepted the goddess theory, and we'd been on that train, but she didn't know my backstory. I gave her a brief rundown of my experience last year while she listened, expressionless, absorbing my words.

I couldn't tell if she actually believed me, but she didn't interrupt or ask questions, she just waited until I finished telling her about killing Dionysius and about the demon who'd attached itself to me dying, removing me from the other dimension permanently.

I tore off a piece of bread and held it up to Beck to gnaw on to give myself time to process Chase's original question. "When they're in human form in this reality, yes, they bleed. Not in the other reality. Neither the ones like Dionysius, who were still alive and able to come through the dimensional walls, nor the spirits. In the other dimension, there is no blood."

Chase nodded. "Blood is life. By taking the blood of humans, maybe they're... I don't know, enhancing or extending their lives?"

"They're already immortal. They don't get diseases or die of old age," I said. "I can kill them, but I've only done it with the Hamet sword—I don't know if other weapons would work. My gun didn't work in the other dimension."

"Okay," she said. "That's new. That changes things."

"How do you mean?" I asked.

"If that other dimension is the same reality where Inanna lives, the blood makes sense. I told you the ancients believed that idols were the gods' way of affecting this reality, remember? So, if it's the same dimension, then the blood magic could be used to sort of make the idol itself into a permanent portal."

"How would that work?" Chase asked.

He drained the last of his water, and I stood to refill his and Dr. Brantley's cups, one-handed, with Beck perched on my hip.

"This is all conjecture, obviously," Dr. Brantley said, "but I'm thinking that the blood sort of ties the two together. The blood opens the door between realities and allows them to enter this reality while staying in theirs."

"So even though they can't come all the way through the portal, it's like… I don't know, reaching through a window?" Chase said.

Dr. Brantley nodded. "Exactly."

I set water glasses back on the table and sat down. "Okay, but what about blood makes that happen? And if that's true, is it any blood? Or would one kind of blood work better than another?"

"I have no idea," Dr. Brantley said.

"At least we have a working theory," Chase said. "The goddess is trying to reestablish her rule, so she's collecting artifacts that were part of her original idol. Putting the pieces of her portal back together. And she needs blood to trigger it so she can step through."

"Beck's blood," I said.

Dr. Brantley paused with her fork halfway to her mouth and looked at me. "Your son? Why?"

"That's what I'm trying to figure out." More backstory. I told her about Trent and the potentials, which now included Beck, apparently.

"Oh," she breathed.

"What?" I asked.

"That makes sense."

Hope and terror warred for prominence inside me. "What does?"

"Bloodlines can be tracked to specific geographic locations. If Beck really is part of some specific genetic line, then his ancestors may have been her original worshippers. They may have been part of those who built the idol in the first place. His blood, more than any other, would be powerful enough to open up the portal into the idol. Well, his and the others in his line."

"Is that why she's killing the other potentials? The reports I got from Desiree said the bodies were drained of their blood."

"Could be," Dr. Brantley said. "I wonder, is she using them as she gets them, or saving them for a giant baptism of blood at a ritual to be performed later?" That last part sounded more like she was talking to herself than us.

She tapped out a note to herself on her phone.

A moment later, her phone rang. She blinked. "Excuse me, I have to take this," she said.

She stepped into the living room, out of earshot.

I looked at Chase. "What do you think?"

"I think I need to figure out more about the nature of gods and goddesses," he said. "I had always assumed they were basically demons, like Dionysius. He'd set himself up to be a god and was worshipped as one. But he could come freely into this dimension. What's different about Inanna? Why is she trapped there?"

"Could be she's already dead," I suggested. "I mean, dead on this side. Her spirit is there, which is why she needs the idol to influence this dimension. Also why she wants to make this dimension part of hers. She can't rule it if she's not in it."

"Maybe," Chase said. "I still need to do some research."

Would the research never end? I couldn't handle *maybe* and *not enough to go on* for much longer. I needed to *do* something. "Let me know what you find out."

Dr. Brantley came back into the room, her face flushed. "You guys up for a field trip?"

I bolted to my feet. "Absolutely. Where are we going?"

"The Natural History Museum."

SEVENTEEN

I froze. Bile bubbled up inside me, threatening to choke me. "The what?"

"The museum. In Mesa," Dr. Brantley said. "I have a connection there. He knew I was in town, and thought I'd be interested. It's... you guys are going to want to see this."

I nodded slowly. "Let me call Gen and see if she can take Beck."

Gen was free and happy to have him, so I started getting his stuff ready while Dr. Brantley gathered her things and Chase stuffed the leftover food into Tupperware and stuck it in the fridge for me.

I grabbed my sword and gun, and Chase carried Beck in his car seat. Dr. Brantley led the way out of my apartment, trotting down the stairs ahead of us.

Chase grabbed my hand. "What's wrong?"

"Let's ride together. I'll tell you on the way," I said. "I'll drive because I have the car seat."

We dropped Beck at Gen's and headed toward the museum, planning to meet Dr. Brantley there.

"Can you tell me now?" Chase asked when we got to the freeway.

"Remember the daycare? Where Dionysius had his fortress set up?"

"Yeah."

"I went there a few days ago. I met a demon."

"You mentioned you had a demon contact."

I nodded. "He is... not welcome with Inanna's followers. I had a plan."

"Jack, tell me you didn't. You promised."

I kind of equal parts loved and hated that he could read my thoughts so well.

"I made a truce with him. Told him I'd protect him from the others in exchange for information. And then... I talked to him—didn't do it. I just asked him about letting him possess me so I could travel through the other dimension."

"But you're not possessed," Chase said.

It wasn't a question. He would've felt it if I was.

"I'm not," I said.

Even though he knew, he still breathed a sigh of relief at my confirmation.

"I would have, though. Except... it doesn't work the way I thought it would. He was going to take me over entirely."

"That's what I tried to tell you." He visibly relaxed in the seat next to me.

"I know. And I should have listened. But I didn't. And now that demon has no arms and probably isn't going to be much help."

"He wasn't going to be anyway."

"You may be right. But that's not the point. The point is, before that, when we were still allies, he told me... he told me Inanna's followers are building a fortress, like the one at the daycare, but bigger and stronger."

"Bigger and stronger? Against what?"

"Against me. He gave the impression that they're making it Jack-proof."

"Interesting. How?"

"I don't know. It's weird. Even though they know I can't get in there, they're still afraid of me."

"That's good. We can use that. But it doesn't answer the question. Why did you freak out when Dr. Brantley told you where we're going?"

"Because the fortress—they're building it at the Museum of Natural History."

He blew out slowly through pursed lips. "Whoa."

"Exactly. So whatever Dr. Brantley's friend wanted her to see—it's not a coincidence."

"Apparently not. Should we call someone? Backup of some sort?"

"Like who?" I asked. "The only other person who knows about all this is Isaac, and there's not much he could do. And I can't exactly call for backup to museum that isn't being threatened in this dimension."

"True," he said. "Still, I'd feel better if we had some more people there."

"Well, do you want to call Desiree? And I can call Isaac."

"Desiree? Why would I call her?"

135

"She's a fed. And you guys are… like…" I paused, thinking how best to phrase this so I didn't sound like I was feeling things out, which I totally was. "You guys are kind of together, right?"

He stared at me. I could feel his eyes boring into me, even though my eyes were on the road.

"What makes you think that?" he said after a long while.

"We're working together on this case. She just made it sound like things were going pretty well between you two."

"Things between us are exactly the same as they were a year ago. We go out sometimes. We see each other at church and Bible study. I told you that the other day."

"I know, I just thought…"

"We're not together."

"Oh."

The weight that lifted from my heart at that statement was almost enough to make me forget where we were going and why.

"I guess I could still call her, if we end up needing backup," he said after another pause. "But you're right—there's not much either of them could do at this point. Let's just go see what we're dealing with."

We arrived at the Natural History Museum a little while later.

Dr. Brantley stood outside waiting for us.

I climbed out of the truck, glancing at the sword I'd left in the back seat. I really wanted to bring it, to see what I could see of the fortress here, but I didn't want to tip my hand to the demons too soon. I didn't want them knowing I was aware of this place yet.

I walked toward Dr. Brantley, and Chase came around from the other side, slipping his hand into mine, giving a quick squeeze before releasing it.

I glanced at him and smiled before I turned back to Dr. Brantley.

Dr. Brantley almost seemed to be bouncing on her toes, her effervescence a delightful juxtaposition with her professional clothes and demeanor. "This is… more incredible than I imagined. The museum gets artifacts from all over the world—on loan—for special events and exhibits. Some of the archaeologists here are renowned, and the museum is home to some pretty intense research. They have a solid reputation for accuracy, so they were one of the top picks to get this find. And Dr. Smith was actually on the team that originally uncovered it, so he was able to pull strings to get moved to the top of the list."

Yeah, yeah, I get that it's a big deal. Get to the point.

Out loud, I said, "Can we see it?"

"Yeah, of course. Sorry, I got carried away. Follow me."

136

She led us around to the back where a loading dock sat between two doors and armed security guards stood sentry at all points.

The one in front of the door to the left nodded. "Dr. Brantley."

Dr. Brantley gestured toward Chase and me. "This is Detective Davidson and Reverend Gardener."

The security guard nodded and opened the door for us. "Dr. Smith is expecting you."

It opened into the same storage bay that the loading dock did, a large, warehouse-type room with crates and boxes neatly lined in rows and carefully labeled.

"This way," Dr. Brantley said. She led us toward the other end of the warehouse where it had been partitioned off into a lab.

A man with a shock of white hair and a bushy, white beard beckoned us in. "Welcome, welcome! Any friend of Brantley's is a friend of mine. Come see, come see."

We followed him into the lab and stopped short.

A huge statue towered before us. It had to be ten feet tall, almost hitting the ceiling.

A statue of a woman, molded from bronze, with a gargoyle-like face, six arms, and wings.

"Inanna," I breathed.

"You've heard of her, then?" Dr. Smith said. "Most people haven't. She hasn't been really worshipped in thousands of years, although you always find pockets of cults springing up here and there. Usually it's a fad—goths and outcasts looking for a way to belong. Those are in every culture. But her true religion has been dead for centuries. But now…"

He trailed off, his voice sounding awed.

I walked a slow circuit around the statue, wishing I'd brought my sword in with me. The fortress was here. And now her idol—the real one—was here. If I'd had my sword on me, I could've slashed a hole in at least some of the bastards who lingered on the other side. I really hated not knowing how many were there or what they were thinking or feeling, or if they were watching me, or…

I had too many thoughts. This was not the time. Who knew how many of them were here, and if any of them were able to enter this dimension like Dionysius had been? There was every possibility I'd be overwhelmed the first second they knew I could sense them. I couldn't go in blindly. I needed more information first.

But the idol explained a lot of things. Those other artifacts… those were just tiny pieces of a larger whole.

As I walked around the statue, details stood out to me.

There were small compartments carved into her. Little ledges on each of her six hands, and small alcoves on each of her feet, like small boxes.

I pointed to her hands. "What are these for?"

"Ah, I'm so glad you asked. There is little literature from the time to indicate the true purpose, but based on other artifacts, I imagine this was more than an ordinary idol. It was almost like a temple in itself. Those shelves would be to house other relics and significant artifacts."

He stepped closer, not quite touching the statue as he waved his arms around it. "For example, see the way her middle arm on each side is extended more forward and slightly larger than the others? I believe a sacrifice would be laid there. A fire would be lit underneath—this was probably placed over a fire pit, although she's hollow, so it could also have been built inside—to burn the sacrifice. The fire would've warmed the whole statue, and her other hands would've held things like sacred oil or incense."

"So, the other artifacts would've been useful as well as ornamental," I said.

"Oh, yes," Dr. Smith nodded. "There was never any waste. I mean, you could argue that the entire thing was a waste, if you don't believe in the deity, but in their minds, each piece would've been significant."

"Have you shown him the pictures of the other artifacts?" I asked Dr. Brantley.

"Not yet," she said.

She pulled up the images on her phone and scrolled through them.

Dr. Smith's eyes widened more with every image. "Where did you get these?" he asked at last. "Do you have them somewhere?"

I shook my head. "They were all stolen from different places. Those are the images from the police files. They're all missing."

"May I?" Dr. Smith asked, reaching for Dr. Brantley's phone.

She handed it to him, and he scrolled though again, slowly.

"Yes, yes," he muttered. "The star would've fit into her top left hand—see the way it's raised and looks like it's clutching something? It probably has a place to hold incense. The bull would've been a here—see how there's a tiny hold in the bottom right hand? Blood would drip through to the cavity inside the statue."

"And the statue of Inanna? Why does the idol need an idol of herself?" I asked.

Dr. Smith chuckled. "Good question. Probably as sort of a totem. A physical representation of her human form. This statue with her arms and wings is her true form, but when she visited her people, she took on her human form in order to keep from frightening them. It makes sense that when they worshipped, they'd have both forms represented. It might belong in one of her hands or it might belong at her crown or her feet. I won't be able to tell unless I have all the pieces together."

I nodded. "So, we know there's a star, a bull, and a statue. How many more pieces are missing?"

"Oh, several. There is probably something for each of her six hands, plus something at each foot. Maybe other things too."

I did a quick count. Minimum eight artifacts needed to be placed on the main statue. We knew of three. That meant potentially five more would be stolen. Potentially five more deaths.

A quick glance at Chase told me he was thinking the same thing.

I focused my attention back on Dr. Smith. "Any idea what kinds of artifacts they might be? What should we be keeping an eye out for?"

"That's impossible to say. There's no record of this particular statue that I know of. I can look into it, but I couldn't tell you exactly. Best guess, probably a scepter of some kind. An urn, maybe two. A lion, perhaps. Her primary symbol, the mark that was definitively hers, was a stalk of reeds tied together with a loop at the top, so that might be something to look for."

Oh shit.

Dr. Brantley put a hand on my arm. "Are you okay?"

I jerked myself back to the present. "Yeah. Dr. Smith, can you draw that for me?"

"Sure," Dr. Smith said. He grabbed a notepad and a pen from the desk and made a quick sketch. "It would look something like that."

My stomach almost fell out as the dots connected in my head. "Like an ankh without the arms."

EIGHTEEN

Dr. Smith looked at me. "Sort of. Why, does that mean something to you?"

"Maybe. At least, it's a start," I said. "Any images you have that might be related or even similar to the kinds of things we're looking for would be greatly appreciated."

"Certainly. I have a few pictures in my archives I can dig out. And I'll keep my eyes open for anything else that might come up in my research."

"Thank you."

We stayed a little longer, discussing exactly where the statue had been uncovered, the political climate and how the museum had ended up with it, and what other elements of Inanna's worship might have entailed. Most of that information I filed away for later, in case I needed it, and eventually we left the museum.

"I need coffee," I said when we were outside.

"It's after eight," Chase said.

"Doesn't matter. Coffee helps me think."

"There's a little indie coffee shop and wine bar a few blocks down," Dr. Brantley said. "I passed it on my way here."

"Perfect," I said.

We met there and walked to the far end of the dimly lit space to a high table that sat in a corner of the room, as far away from other patrons as possible in the tiny shop.

"Okay, here's what we know," I said. "Inanna needs all of the artifacts that went with her idol in order to open up the portal or whatever she plans to do. There are at least five more artifacts that are not accounted for. There's no telling how many she has already. She

140

could've gathered them from all over the world before we even knew what to look for."

"What about the symbol?" Chase asked. "You looked like you'd seen a ghost when you asked him to draw it."

"That symbol was carved into the chests potentials whose blood was drained."

The waitress came over and took our orders

Dr. Brantley waited until she was out of earshot before speaking. "Ritual murders?"

I nodded.

"Where?"

"New York, St. Louis, and Dallas," I answered. "Why?"

"Oh. Oh, man," Dr. Brantley said. "I heard something—I didn't make the connection at the time. But there was a man killed at the dig site where the statue was found. The workers—they were having trouble getting the statue out. It was stuck, but they couldn't figure out why. One morning they got to the site and there was a man killed, his blood splattered on the dig site. That day, they were suddenly able to pull the statue out."

"How?" Chase asked.

"I think Inanna had to have his blood for her statue to be freed. Her followers killed him to open up the portal and allow her statue to be moved. Then again, as she was traveling, she had to unlock more doors, if you will. She—or her followers—couldn't get the statue all the way here without using the blood sacrifices to pave the way. I'll check, but it wouldn't surprise me to find if there's a trail of bodies at all the major stops where the statue rested in transit. UAE, New York…"

"Here," I said. "There was a murder at the airport, in a hangar where international shipments are brought in. I should have known they were connected."

The waitress brought our coffees, and we all smiled in awkward silence until she left again.

"That means Inanna has followers here," Dr. Brantley said. "And possibly everywhere."

"What's our next step, then?" Chase asked.

"That's what I'm hoping to figure out." I took a sip of my coffee, trying to process everything I knew and piece together what I didn't. "We need to stop the ritual. So far, our best bet has been to collect the artifacts and keep them from her. But if we can find out more about her cult—the humans who are performing her rituals—then maybe we can stop them."

Chase ran his hands through his hair. "How are we supposed to do that when the thieves can traverse dimensions and pull artifacts out of locked vaults? How are we supposed to identify her cult members unless we catch them in the act?"

"That one's on me. I will have to figure out a way to keep them safe whenever I get a hold of them. There's something going on with the sword. Remember I told you I was able to sense the other dimension when I'm holding it now?"

Chase nodded, and Dr. Brantley's eyes were riveted on me.

"I don't know how to explain it, but it's like… it's getting stronger. The other dimension is getting clearer and I'm able to see it, sort of, not just feel it. I don't know if the power is coming from the sword or what, but if so, maybe I can use it to protect the artifacts. If and when we find any."

Chase stared at me for a long moment, his hand gripping his coffee mug. "I think maybe you should practice with it."

"What do you mean?"

"Like exercising. If the power grows every time you use it, start now building up your strength—its strength—so when the time comes, you're ready."

I took a long sip of my coffee. Why hadn't I thought of that? "I will. In the meantime, let's see what we can do about collecting those artifacts. I'll start scouring police reports and see if anything like what Dr. Smith described has been reported stolen."

Dr. Brantley stirred the last half of her chai tea with a spoon. "I'll check other art galleries and excavation sites for anything that looks like it could be related."

"I'll keep looking into the sacrifice angle," Chase said. "See if I can figure out how it works or what the ritual looks like or how Inanna will transform this world if she succeeds."

"Thank you."

We agreed to share anything new we found out with each other, then stood to head our separate ways.

Once in my truck, Chase nodded toward the sword. "May I?"

"Of course," I said. I started the drive back toward home, my eyes darting toward Chase every few seconds.

He picked it up and held it in his hands, clutching the hilt the way I did, eyes closed. After several long moments, he sighed and opened his eyes.

"Anything?" I asked.

He shook his head. "Whatever's happening, it's specific to you."

"Why would that be?"

"I wish I had an answer for that. My best guess is that you bonded with it somehow."

"Like a pet?"

He laughed, but there wasn't much real mirth in it. "Something like that."

"It's an inanimate object," I said.

He shrugged. "Is it, though? If Inanna's idols have inherent power, why couldn't your sword? Or maybe whatever it is that powers it in the other dimension attached itself to you."

"That sounds creepy. And very borderline to the possession you're so concerned about."

"Maybe. But so far, the sword hasn't tried to kill you or steal your soul, that we know of. And it is powerful *against* demons, so I'm willing to give it the benefit of the doubt."

I adjusted the air conditioner, suddenly feeling a chill. Thing was, I agreed with him. And Pastor Floyd had told me to trust my instincts. So, I would keep using the sword, and if I was bonded to it somehow, maybe I could use that.

We got back to our side of town and picked Beck up, then headed back to my apartment complex.

"Do you want to come in?" I asked.

Chase paused for a long moment before finally shaking his head. "Not this time. It's been a long day and I need to spend some time in study and prayer. And I need to sleep—I have to preach in the morning."

"Oh. I forgot—I'm sorry. Okay. I guess... I'll call you if I find anything out."

"I'll do the same."

I got Beck ready for bed and rocked him to sleep. He was feverish and fussy again. Every time he came back from Gen's. Something was trying to get to him there. I trusted Gen completely, but her apartment or somewhere she went had a weak spot. Something was trying to get to Beck through her.

How? And why her but not Cameron?

And what else could I do to protect him while he was with her?

I pulled out my sword and held the hilt, closing my eyes and breathing slowly, feeling the power course through me, golden and warm, while at the same time feeling the other dimension all around me, dark and hot and red.

It was weird—I didn't actually have synesthesia or whatever would describe what I was sensing, but somehow, I could feel the colors. I slowly opened my eyes, and the other dimension was visible, as though

I were looking at it through a dirty window. I reached out my hand, but it didn't penetrate through the invisible dimensional barrier.

And yet, the dimension was closer. Stronger. Close enough that I wondered, if I were near a portal, would I be able to get through?

I glanced at Beck, dozing on my bed.

This was not the time to check that theory.

Instead, I lifted the sword, going through slow drills, swinging, lunging, slicing, practicing the moves I would use when fighting a demon.

My phone rang. Who would be calling me at this hour?

Desiree?

That had to mean it was important. I picked it up.

"Des—I mean, Agent Escobar, what is it?"

"There's another body. Here."

"Here meaning Phoenix?"

"Mesa. I know that's out of your jurisdiction, but… I would appreciate it if you'd come along anyway and lend your experience."

Mesa.

Where the Natural History Museum was.

"Text me the address. I'm on my way."

I called Cameron to see if she could watch Beck.

No answer.

I left a message and paced my apartment, but Cameron didn't call back. I tried one more time, but I didn't have a choice. I had to go.

I took Beck back to Gen's and raced out to where I'd been just a few hours before.

The body was three blocks from the museum. Cop cars and fed cars, with their lights on, surrounded what used to be an art supply warehouse but was now a hollow shell.

I parked down the block and made my way to the scene. I found Desiree in the crowd of officers and waved at her.

She trotted over toward me—how the hell she could trot on those pumps was beyond me, but she did—and waved me through the police line.

"I'm glad you're here. This one… this one is bad."

"Worse than the last one?"

She nodded, her jaw in a tight line, and led me inside the building.

The smell overwhelmed me as soon as I set foot inside. It was like if a rendering plant overflowed into a sewer and all the diseased rats died.

On top of that, the smell was coming from the other dimension too. I had the sword strapped to my back—not even in my hands—but I could still feel the taint, like rancid grease, seeping through.

I put my arm over my nose and mouth.

Desiree had done the same, I noticed, and she beckoned me with her shoulder. "This way. Watch your step."

That was when I noticed the globs of flesh and fat splattered all over the floor. I followed her to the center of the room, gingerly picking my way through the detritus.

The blob couldn't even be identified as a body. The bones were shattered, sticking out of the blood-soaked mass of skin and tissue at odd angles. Organs, fat, muscles, even brain matter were all tossed together like a salad.

Except for one thing.

A few feet away from the main mass lay a partial skull, with a partial face still attached. A man, with brown hair and a partial beard, his one eye opened wide and his mouth, with the bottom half of the jaw missing, looking like he was preserved forever in a scream of horror.

"What..." Desiree began, then stopped, stifling a gag. "What could do this?"

I had no idea.

I knew it had something to do with coming through the other dimension, but how or why...

I just shook my head.

"Will you indulge me for a minute?" I asked.

She nodded.

I took a deep breath through my sleeve, so the smell—and even the taste—were minimized a little, and pulled my sword out.

The weapon seemed to vibrate in my hands, and the taint from the other dimension became stronger. Was it getting worse, or was I just feeling it more?

When I'd gone there before, it had made me feel sick, with nausea and chills. This was the same, yet multiplied tenfold. At least. Or was it the gooey remains of the dead body that was making me want to retch?

No, this was different. This was the other dimension in addition to the body. And it was definitely stronger.

I focused. The tear in reality here was bigger. Deeper. Harsher, almost as though the other portals had been careful incisions, and this—this was shredded.

And I could see inside. Really see, not just sense.

It was almost like I could step through, like I'd done before.

NINETEEN

I took a step, almost instinctively, toward the hole.

"Jack, watch out."

I refocused my attention on my reality and saw I'd almost stepped on the body.

"Sorry," I said.

Desiree stared at the sword. She glanced around to see if anyone was close enough to hear and lowered her voice. "What... what does that thing do?"

How much should I actually divulge? There was no telling whether or not she'd believe me. And Pastor Floyd had said not to trust anyone. But how would I explain without giving her at least a little bit of information?

"It allows me to see through the dimensional wall into the spiritual realm."

Her lips tightened into a hard line, but I couldn't tell whether that meant she believed me or she thought I was crazy.

She turned back to the body. "It looks like he exploded. But there's no trace of a bomb or anything that might explain it. The smell is... just death. Really, really bad death, but not... you know... anything combustible. There's no sign of burning or chemicals or anything to indicate how this happened."

"Do you think natural causes or murder?" I asked.

"At this point, I have no idea. The first couple we'd assumed foul play because of the way the skin seemed to be stuffed inside the skeleton. But the ME didn't find anything that could definitively point to a weapon being used. And this..." She waved her hand over the body.

"What if it's a drug or something?" I suggested. "Something that, I don't know, reacts to stomach acid or natural gases and makes them blow up?"

"Good. That's good. I'll have the ME check for... anything that might explain that."

"If that's the case, we need to know what it is and where they got it," I said. "It might still be murder."

"True. Okay, at least we have someplace to start."

"We also need to find out what he stole. All the others stole an artifact before they... exploded."

"Do you think it could be something to do with the artifacts themselves?" Desiree asked. "I mean... toxic mold or something on the artifacts that made them explode?"

"Unlikely," I said. "Otherwise it would've affected the previous owners. Like the woman who had the statue and the antique store owner or any of the people at the auction house who touched it."

"Good point. Okay, so we'll go with the theory that whoever hired them to steal the artifact then gave them something that killed them."

"It's as logical as anything else right now."

She nodded and started to pick her way out of the building.

I followed.

The breeze outside, despite the warm weather that baked the smell of the city into the air, felt refreshing and cool after the putrid odors inside.

Desiree inhaled deeply, then exhaled slowly before turning to face me. "Thanks for coming out. Would you be willing to help me brief Mesa police on what we've found so far?"

"Of course," I said.

It was nearing morning by the time I finally got home. Beck was feverish, but not worse than he'd been before.

I crashed almost the second my head hit my pillow.

⚓⚓⚓

The phone rang. What now?

I glanced at the clock. I'd only been asleep for a couple of hours.

It was Dr. Brantley. "I got a call from Dr. Smith this morning. He received a package he thinks we should see."

"A package on a Sunday?"

"Delivered by messenger."

"Okay," I said. "I'll be there soon."

I hated the way my words slurred together, making me sound drunk.

I showered and made myself a tumbler of coffee, then called Cameron.

"Hey, Cam, any chance you can watch Beck today?"

"Oh, Jack, I'm sorry. I would love to but I'm at the lake with some friends. I didn't drive… I could see if someone could bring me back but it would be at least an hour before—"

"No, that's okay. Have fun. I'll call Gen. I just hate to ask her on a Sunday." I also wasn't entirely sure what was going on at her apartment to make Beck sick. But I had to weigh that risk against getting answers.

I hung up and dialed Gen. "Hey, Gen, you up? I have to go to work."

"Again?" she asked. "Do they ever let you leave?"

"Not when there are multiple unsolved murders floating around the city."

"That bad?"

"Yeah. How soon can I bring Beck over?"

"I'm here. Any time is fine."

"Thanks."

I really needed to buy that girl an extravagant thank-you gift.

I dropped Beck off and headed down to Mesa for what felt like the millionth time. Leaving my sword in my truck, I texted Dr. Brantley to let her know I was there and walked around to the back entrance.

The security guard buzzed me in, and I made my way to the lab where the statue of Inanna still stood.

On the table sat what appeared to be a crown made up of horns, with some sort of cone in the center. Dr. Brantley and Dr. Smith bent over it, examining it with what looked like binoculars—but, like, science binoculars.

That didn't even make sense in my own head. I really needed to sleep for about a month.

"What is that?" I asked.

"Detective, come on in," Dr. Brantley said. "We believe this is Inanna's headpiece."

Dr. Smith nodded, his jowls bouncing. "Yes, yes, look at this. This extension at the bottom will fit into the notch at the top of her head. It fits descriptions of her, as well. The horns represent her power and authority over the beasts of the earth, and the sacred mountain is her domain."

My stomach clenched. This… this was an artifact. Which meant if I could control it, I could maybe keep her from completing her ritual.

But how could I possibly get in my possession?

148

"Where did it come from?" I asked.

"We have no idea." Dr. Brantley pushed her science binoculars up to the top of her head.

Dr. Smith nodded in agreement, his binoculars still on his face, giving him a very bug-eyed appearance. "It arrived by messenger this morning, almost as soon as I got here."

"Can I touch it?" I asked.

He nodded and handed me a pair of protective gloves.

The moment my fingers brushed the metal, even through the gloves, a shiver ran over my skin, and a wave of nausea hit me, eerily similar to what it felt like to sense demons.

Except I wasn't holding my sword.

How could I possibly feel it so strongly? Maybe, like Chase, I was becoming more sensitive to these things. But even so… this was a whole new level. This was… evil. There was no other way to describe it.

My fingers traced the intricate lines that formed the grooves of the horns, the subtle way they made a complete circle, sticking out in every direction. There were ten in all, with the one at the front just a little larger than the others.

The cone in the center rose about twice the height of the horns.

"Is this… gold?" I asked.

"Just the overlay. It appears to be brass underneath. You can see spots where the gold has rubbed off.

I examined the crown as thoroughly as I could for someone with no experience or understanding of such things, then stepped back from the lab table where it sat.

"You said it was delivered by messenger. Do you have the package it came in?"

"Yes." Dr. Smith left the room. He returned a moment later with a large, nondescript, brown cardboard box and handed it to me.

His name was printed neatly on the top—that was it. No other identifying information whatsoever to help trace where it had come from.

Except…

On one side was a darker patch. The kind of stain left when you spill something and it dries.

I looked closer—and that's when I smelled it.

The same putrid stench from the body that we'd found last night.

That meant this box had been in that building. Possibly even when the body exploded.

"Can I take this?" I asked.

"I suppose so," Dr. Smith said. "What for?"

"It might be evidence."

His eyebrows raised. "You don't think... I'm somehow connected to... anything?"

I shook my head. "I can't comment on an ongoing investigation, but I have no reason to believe you are at this time."

He exhaled in obvious relief. "By all means, take that, and let me know if there's anything I can do to help."

Glad I was still wearing gloves, I carefully put the box into a plastic bag, then stepped outside to call Desiree.

She didn't answer the first time, so I waited a few minutes and called again.

"Sorry, I was in church. With Chase," she said when she picked up the phone. "I had to step outside to answer. I didn't expect to hear from you so soon."

Why did she have to sound so perky and like she hadn't been up all night? And I wasn't even going to acknowledge the part about her being with Chase.

"I didn't expect to call so soon. But I might have something. An artifact that may be related to the case was delivered to the Museum of Natural History this morning. The box it was delivered in may have traces of... that guy."

There was a long pause. "I see. Do you have it?"

"The box? Yes. The artifact is still at the museum. I couldn't take it as evidence without any sure connection, but I think if we analyze the goo on the box..."

"The goo on the box." Desiree sounded ill.

Good.

Not that I wanted her to be ill. It was just nice to know that she was affected by this, too, and not that she was completely cool and collected in any and every circumstance.

"Can you meet me somewhere, and I'll give this over to you? Your people probably have better resources for analyzing it, and you'll be able to compare it to the body faster."

"Sure. Where are you now?"

"Outside the museum."

"Great. I'm on my way."

I went back into the museum to wait. Dr. Brantley and Dr. Smith stood over the crown, saying words I didn't really understand.

"Dr. Brantley, do you have a second?" I asked.

"Sure."

She followed me out of the room and into the hallway where we wouldn't be overheard.

"I assume you're going to ask me to not let him put the crown on the statue?" she asked.

"How did you know?"

"Well, if we're right, and she needs all the pieces to do her ritual, there's no point in doing the work for her."

"Exactly," I said. "If you could lock it in a separate display case... but honestly it's probably not going to help."

Dr. Brantley nodded. "Still, I'll see what I can do."

"Thanks. Also, I have reason to believe this piece was transported through dimensions last night. The man who brought it... exploded. In an abandoned warehouse just a few blocks from here."

"Exploded?"

"Trust me, you don't want to know more," I said. "Anyway, I'm going to have the box analyzed, but if it turns out it was at the crime scene, then we may need to take the statue into evidence."

"That sounds very... sloppy," Dr. Brantley said.

"What do you mean?"

"On Inanna's part, not yours. Why would she risk that? Why would she have it delivered here so soon after she killed the person who brought it, with potential evidence on the packaging, and risk it falling in to your hands?"

"I don't know. Maybe she didn't realize it had evidence on it, or doesn't know how much we already know. Maybe she's getting cocky—or maybe she's just in a hurry."

"It has to be something time-sensitive," Dr. Brantley said. "Because otherwise why would she have waited thirty years after the artifacts started surfacing to collect them?"

"Maybe she couldn't before."

"Right. Because she was entombed."

I thought about the way things worked in the other dimension. If a demon built a structure there, even though it couldn't be seen here, it could be felt. The wall around the daycare was like that. An invisible forcefield in this reality, a rock wall there. If the statue had been enshrined in the other dimension, then whatever happened to trap it there might have affected this one, as well.

But that didn't explain how it had gotten taken down in the other dimension.

Unless the blood of the man they'd sacrificed was powerful enough to have broken down the tomb that kept her trapped.

"You okay in there?" Dr. Brantley asked.

"What?" My head snapped up. "Oh. Yeah. Sorry. I was just thinking."

"About what?"

"Inanna had to have been trapped in the other dimension. Possibly since the fall of Nineveh. Which is why she fell out of power as a goddess. Which means someone on the other side trapped her, and someone let her out."

"Right. Her cult. We may have an easier time figuring out who they are if we know the why. What is so urgent that she has to do this now?"

"I'll work on the who, if you work on the why," I said.

"Deal," Dr. Brantley said.

Desiree arrived a little bit later, and I gave her the box that the crown had been transported in.

She visibly gagged upon seeing the splotch on the side that I suspected was splatter. "I'll have this analyzed."

"If it turns out to have come from the crime scene, will that be enough for you to take the artifact into evidence?"

She nodded.

"Good."

"Jack, what is happening? How are these things connected?"

I took a deep breath before launching into my explanation. "I think the cult of the goddess Inanna that I mentioned before is trying to revive her worship, and they're going to use ritual sacrifices to do so. They're collecting all the artifacts related to her original idol. Dr. Smith thinks there may be as many as four more that we don't know about. The crown is one, so if you can take it into evidence, it may halt the ritual."

"Sacrifices?" Desiree asked.

I nodded. "Possibly human."

"Do we have any idea who these cultists are?"

"Not yet. So far, it's all been very nebulous. The thieves it seems were hired more or less at random—I don't see any reason to believe they were part of the cult. Just looking for a payday. Dr. Brantley is looking into the ritual itself to see if we can figure out when it's supposed to take place or how or… anything. I'm looking into her followers to see what I can find."

"Okay. I'll keep looking into related murders and artifacts."

She sounded lost. Tired.

I didn't blame her. But I also wondered how she would react if she knew it was all real—or if it were her son, or someone else she loved, who was in danger. And the worst part was, we had no idea what the next step was. How were we supposed to fight a goddess?

As much as I hated the idea, I needed to find out more about Inanna's cult. And that meant talking to the one contact I had who knew what was going on.

I left the museum and headed to the old daycare.

The sword pulsed with the other dimension as soon as I touched it. I made my way through the fence and focused on whatever I could feel from the other side.

But I didn't feel the presence of the demon.

Where was he?

"Hello?" I called out.

Nothing.

I wandered through the debris, searching with my mind for any sense that the demon was nearby, but felt nothing. Even the lingering sensation of evil seemed more muted than it had before.

The demon was gone.

And I was back to square one.

I headed to my truck and just sat there for a long time, thinking. Square one.

This all started with the robbery at the pawn shop. The pawn shop was square one.

I returned there and went inside.

The clerk, Joy, looked surprised to see me. "Can I help you?"

"This may seem weird, but can I just walk around for a little bit?"

She glanced at my sword, clearly uncomfortable with me wandering around carrying it.

I bent the tip. "It won't hurt you," I said.

"Yeah, okay," she said. She sat behind the counter, still visibly tense, but let me wander.

I gripped the sword hilt and walked to the case where the idol of Inanna had been. It was repaired now—of course—but I could still feel the impression of the broken one, like a memory in the air.

The spot where the statue had sat now held a necklace. Nothing remarkable about it—just an heirloom, from the looks of it. But that spot still held a taint that I could feel through the barrier between dimensions. As if the statue had left a residue.

But there was no tear in reality here—just the lingering impression. I walked outside to where the thief had disappeared into the other dimension. I could feel the scar from the hole, but that was it. It was no longer open.

Square one was a bust. So, I made my way to the empty lot, overgrown with weeds, where the two bodies were found. Police tape still waved in the light breeze, but other than that, it was hard to tell that this blank space between a strip mall and a moderately busy street had seen such violence.

I ducked under the police tape to the place where the bodies had been ejected from the other dimension. The scar here was deeper, but still pretty much sealed over, and I couldn't sense anything here beyond a very mild awareness of the other dimension.

Strike two.

There was one more thing I could check, and I really didn't want to. But it was my best option.

I drove down to Mesa to the warehouse where the body had been discovered last night.

It was under heavy guard, and crime scene investigators were still coming in and out.

I flashed my badge, but the guards on duty wouldn't let me through.

Damn it. I hated asking for favors, especially from people I didn't like, but I didn't have a choice.

I called Desiree. "Hey, there's something I want to check out at the scene from last night. Can you tell your people to give me access?" I asked.

"Sure," she said.

She hung up, and a moment later, the guard's phone rang.

"Yep…" he said. "Okay. You got it."

He hung up and looked at me. "You're clear."

"Thanks," I said.

The curious whispers started before I was even out of earshot, but I ignored them. I had bigger things to worry about.

The stench still permeated the building, but it was more subdued than it had been last night. Still strong enough that none of the officers on duty were in here—they all stuck to their posts outside.

The body had been removed, as had most of the large chunks, but there were still smears and splatters throughout. Gripping the sword, I stepped toward the center of the room where the body had been.

As I suspected, the tear here was still gaping. So wide I could see through it.

The other dimension was right there, within my reach.

I took a step… and walked through the hole.

TWENTY

Searing heat, like opening an oven, washed over me, and nausea roiled my stomach.

I was here.

I took another step, absorbing the landscape as it unfolded around me.

The dark red terrain, the sun that looked as if it were being filtered through rust, the physical realities of my dimension—like buildings and people—ethereal and ghostlike.

How? How had I gotten through? It wasn't possible. I hadn't been here in over a year.

Even though I couldn't explain it, I knew it was the sword. Somehow it was acting as a bridge. Accomplishing the same thing that being attached to a demon. Giving me access to the other dimension.

I wondered if I still had the enhanced strength and speed that I'd had when I was here before—changing the laws of physics from my dimension.

I took off at a jog, willing the ground to move under me, and within seconds, I'd gone what would've been a couple miles.

I circled back, trying to get a feel for the strongholds here.

It was weird to try to figure out landmarks, since the buildings and street signs barely existed, but I made my way toward where I was pretty sure the museum was.

I was right.

Looming before me, a few blocks away, stood what I could only describe as a citadel.

It towered, dwarfing the museum in the real world. I could make out the museum's front entrance, which extended out from where the portico of the citadel arched over it.

The thing was massive, built from the bricks natural to this world—crafted from the same dark red soil that seemed to make up everything here—not something from my world. Yet these bricks formed an invisible forcefield-like barrier in the real world.

It was carefully placed, so that the doors and windows lined up with the doors and windows of the actual museum. The humans would never know it existed if it didn't hamper their ability to move freely as they always had. Tall columns held up the entrance, but from this distance, I couldn't see inside.

I knew what I would see, though. The citadel would be a temple, at the center of which was the statue of Inanna.

What would it look like here? Would it be vague and ghostly, like the human structures, or more like the citadel itself, just as real here as it was there?

I needed to get a good look at it—the statue and the citadel—but I still didn't want to tip my hand. As of yet, the demons still didn't know I could get into this dimension. The element of surprise might be my only advantage.

Besides, my being here could be a fluke. There was no guarantee I could get back once I left.

I crept forward, my whole body alert to any sign of demons. I crouched down to avoid detection. The whole dimension reeked of demonic activity.

They were around, and they were close, but I didn't see any nearby or paying attention to me.

As I drew nearer to the citadel, though, the feeling of an oily taint covering my skin and nausea churning inside me increased. They were in there. Dozens of them swarmed around the inside of the building. Working? Guarding? Preparing for the ritual?

How close could I get without being noticed? And if I were noticed, could I get back to the portal at the murder scene before they caught up to me? And if not, could I create a portal? I'd been able to when I'd had part of my soul trapped here. The demon had explained to me that opening a portal only worked one way—out, not in. I could create a portal to get out, and once one was opened, I could use it to get in, but I couldn't open one from my side to here.

I decided to test the theory. Using the sword, I concentrated on the fabric that separated the dimensions and sliced a hole.

That was a bad life choice.

I opened a window right in the middle of an intersection.

A man driving through caught a glimpse of me and screeched on his brakes, making the car behind him slam into him.

I ducked out of sight. He shouldn't be able to see in here—but maybe I was just at the right spot between dimensions, or because I was from there, not a demon, he was able to see me.

I peeked through the portal. The accident was a fender-bender, but didn't look too serious. Good.

But that wasn't the only bad life choice. The tear in the dimensional wall had attracted the attention of a demon I could only presume to be a perimeter guard. He jogged toward me, his expression at first curious, then alarmed.

He stopped when he was a few feet away from me, his jaw dropping and shock emanating from him. "You!"

"My reputation precedes me," I said.

He sucked in his breath and started to turn. I assumed to sound an alarm.

With one quick step, I lunged toward him and thrust the sword into his back. His yell died on his lips as he started to crumple toward the ground.

"You'll never stop us," he managed in a hoarse whisper, just before his body disintegrated.

One down. How many hundreds to go?

I didn't know, but I couldn't stay to find out. I'd already been here long enough, and the demons would eventually figure out their sentry was missing. I needed to be long gone before that happened. I jogged back toward the building where I'd entered and jumped through the portal back into my own dimension.

A crime scene tech jumped at the sound of my shoes hitting the floor. He turned around, gaping at me. "Where did you come from?"

"What do you mean?" I asked. "I've been here all along."

He blinked at me, but I ignored him and made my way back outside.

I paused once I got into my truck, waiting for the adrenaline crash. Before, whenever I'd gone into the other dimension, it left me completely wiped out. One time, I'd been unconscious for days after. I fully expected to need a nap at least before I could drive home.

But it didn't come. My body didn't feel that bone-deep weariness. My mind didn't feel clouded. Instead, I felt... energized. Strong.

I held the sword. What *was* this thing, and how did it work? And why did it only work for me? I had no idea and no way to find out. But I wasn't going to look this gift horse in the mouth. I could get into the other dimension—and that meant I had a chance.

I would not make the same mistake I made before. Bridget died because I was indecisive. Pastor Floyd died because I didn't know what was going on. I would not let anything happen to Beck. I would not wait until Inanna took everything from me. I would take the fight to them.

I called a meeting with Chase and Dr. Brantley that evening. We met at my house and Chase brought pizza.

Dr. Brantley commandeered Trent's recliner again, and Chase sat next to me on the couch. I set my sword on the coffee table in front of us and placed Beck on the floor. He gnawed on a crust while I filled the others in on the citadel—and the fact that while holding the sword I could travel in the other dimension.

"Jack, that's huge." Chase ran his fingers over the sword, his brow furrowed.

"What are you thinking?" I asked.

He looked at me. "I don't love the thought of you going in to the other dimension and attacking a citadel on your own."

"Believe me, it's not my first choice, either. But I don't think we have any other options. I don't know what's going to happen when Inanna completes her ritual—how she's going to remake the world or what's going to happen when she can affect it. I need to attack before they're done with their preparations. I still have the element of surprise. If I get in there, I can cut them off before they start."

"What if something happens to you in there? You have no backup. We'll never know what happened to you."

"I can get out using the sword. If things don't go my way, I'll pop back into this dimension and at least most won't be able to follow me."

Chase closed his eyes, and I could swear, he looked like he was about to cry. "You don't know that." His voice was husky.

"I can do this," I said, trying to sound reassuring.

"That's what Floyd thought too."

His words crashed through me. I hadn't even considered that he might be worried, about how my plans might affect him.

I reached over and took his hand. "I'll be careful. But I have to do this."

Chase inhaled and squeezed my hand. I sat quietly, waiting for him to respond.

He was silent for a long moment before he finally spoke, his voice clearer now. "I'm having an idea."

I waited for him to form his thoughts.

"The sword works through dimensions, right? Can you just take the sword into the museum and, I don't know, attack from this side?"

My mouth dropped and I shut it. "Why didn't I think of that?"

Chase grinned. "You're too focused on action. But what do you think? Could it work?"

I nodded slowly. "I think so." I turned to Dr. Brantley. "Can you get me inside the museum?"

"Yes."

"I'll get Ken and Desiree to back me up, in case there are any demons like Dionysius, who can come into this dimension. I'll go in there and kill whatever I can, and destroy the citadel in the other dimension."

"You really think this will work?" Chase asked.

I nodded. "I think it's our only shot."

"When?" Chase asked. "Tomorrow morning?"

Dr. Brantley shook her head. "Too much risk of casualties," she said. "We have to go when the museum is closed. After five."

"Okay," I said. "Tomorrow after five."

I looked at Dr. Brantley. "You're surprisingly chill with all of this."

She shrugged. "If you're right, then we're stopping a massive war. If you're wrong, then the worst that happens is you get kicked out of the museum for damaging artifacts with your rubber sword. And let's just say, I've seen enough weird stuff to not be willing to take the chance."

I picked up my so-called rubber sword. I had two choices. Assume she was one of Inanna's minions, in which case she was going to betray me anyway, or assume she was genuinely trying to help. Pastor Floyd said not to trust anyone. But he also said to trust my instincts, and something about Dr. Brantley made me believe that she was on our side.

But even if she betrayed me, it didn't change what I had to do. "Okay, then. I'll meet you at the museum tomorrow night."

After Chase and Dr. Brantley left, I called Ken.

"Hi, Jack! What's up?" He sounded way to happy to hear from me.

"I need your help with something. But it's off the clock. Are you up for it?"

"You know I am. I'm here for you, no matter what."

Not quite how I wanted that conversation to happen, but I'd take it. "Can you meet me at the Museum of Natural History in Mesa tomorrow night around five?"

"Sure. What's going on?"

"It's hard to explain. But I have a lead on the murder case from the airport, and I think the perpetrator may be hiding out near there."

"Oh, that's weird. The museum? Why would a murderer hide out there?"

160

"It's just a hunch so far, which is why I can't do anything official. But I don't want to go alone."

"You got it. I'll be there."

"Thanks," I said.

I called Desiree next. "I may have a lead. I don't know for sure yet, but I'm meeting a contact at the Museum of Natural History. Can you join me?"

"What kind of lead?" she asked.

"Someone who may know what's going on with the artifacts."

I tried to remember how much I'd already told her about Dr. Brantley or any of the other things I'd learned.

"Okay. What do you need me for?"

How did I explain that one?

"Just in case. I have reason to believe that my contact may be a target, and I'd like backup on hand just in case things get violent."

"Okay. I'll see you there."

I gave her the details, and then called Trent's parents to ask if they could babysit. In case anything happened to me, I wanted Beck to be with family.

They were thrilled to have the opportunity, of course, so early the next afternoon, I drove out to drop Beck off.

"I'm not sure what time I'll be back. It may be late," I said.

"You have a key," Deanna said. "I'll make up the spare room, and if you get in late, you can just crash here."

"Thank you," I said. "I have one more favor to ask you, and this is going to be weird, but please humor me."

"Of course, honey. What is it?" Deanna asked.

I walked her through reciting what I'd said in my apartment and Gen's, banishing demons from entering. He was as safe as I could make him.

I held Beck, giving him an extra long, tight hug before saying goodbye and handing him to Deanna. "I'll see you tonight."

Ken was already waiting for me when I arrived at the museum.

"Want to tell me what's going on?" he asked.

"I'm about to stop a murderer, I hope. I expect it to get violent."

Ken lounged against his cruiser and folded his arms. "That's super encouraging, thanks."

I gave him an apologetic smile. "I wish I had more I could tell you. It's complicated."

"It always is," he said. "I'll follow your lead, then?"

I nodded. I didn't give him enough credit. I'd been so busy pushing away his romantic overtures that I hadn't appreciated that he

161

really was a good cop. A good man. One day, when we had a little more time, I'd tell him that. "This way."

Desiree showed up a few minutes later.

She and Ken eyed each other.

"Who's that?" Desiree asked.

"Ken. Lieutenant Richmond, I mean. I asked him to come."

That seemed to satisfy her.

"What's the plan?"

"My contact, Dr. Brantley, is going to let us into the museum through the back. I don't know exactly what is going to happen, but I suspect it will get violent."

"Okay." Desiree pulled her gun. "Let's do this."

I led the way around the back, holding my sword, but with my gun loose in my holster, ready to go. Dr. Brantley opened the door as soon as we got close.

A wave of stink hit me—a smell identical to the one from the building down the street—but not from the physical air. It was coming from the other dimension. And it was mixed with a sulfuric stench.

And there were presences. Demons. Lots of them.

"Stop," I said. "Something isn't right."

Desiree looked at me. "What?"

"I don't know," I said.

I glanced at Dr. Brantley. Her eyes didn't have that warm, welcoming look that I was used to. Instead, they were glazed over, almost as if she were high.

My sword quivered with energy.

Dr. Brantley moved forward unsteadily then fell onto her face. Where she'd been a moment before stood a demon. I recognized him—he'd been one of the ones who'd helped prepare the way for Dionysius by spreading false information. Here, he looked human, although larger than most normal humans, but with the sword I could also see his demon visage, like a huge gargoyle.

He stepped over Dr. Brantley. Had he killed her? I couldn't see a wound, but that didn't necessarily mean anything. His cadence was slow and deliberate, as he walked toward me.

"Freeze!" Desiree yelled, pointing her gun. "FBI!"

He ignored her and kept walking.

"I said freeze!" she shouted again.

He didn't stop.

I felt a familiar presence.

The demon from the daycare. What was he doing here?

He was behind me, but I ignored him—he couldn't affect this dimension.

The echo of Desiree's gun filled the little space behind the museum. Three shots, center mass. Red splotches appeared on the demon's chest, but he didn't stop. It took more than that to kill them.

Another shot fired, but it wasn't Desiree. It came from the other side of me… and it wasn't aimed at the demon.

Desiree crumpled into a heap, blood pooling underneath her.

TWENTY-ONE

I whipped around to the other side and stared at Ken. His weapon was still pointed Desiree's direction.

"What the hell are you doing?" I yelled.

The demon Desiree had wounded but was still stalking toward me. I pulled my gun and shot him in the head, killing his physical form.

Ken turned his weapon toward me. But not Ken—at least, not entirely him. The demon from the daycare had… merged with him, somehow.

I slashed with my sword, bumping Ken's arm, but not doing any damage in this dimension. I held the sword one-handed and punched Ken with the other, just grazing Ken's face. It didn't really hurt him, but it sent him stumbling back a few steps. Enough that I was able to grab his wrist and twist, making him drop the gun.

I kicked it away and threw another punch.

This one knocked him over, and his head hit the concrete hard enough to at least stun him.

Now it was just me and the demon.

I turned back around, holding my sword at the ready.

The demon just laughed, then faded away, like he was running the opposite direction.

His laugh was replaced by a chorus of other voices—harsh, metallic, demonic.

A swarm of demons hovered around me in the other dimension.

With a sound like fabric ripping, the walls between realities opened, and the demons surged through. I slashed wildly, the sword searing through those closest to me, killing some. But there were too many. I would be overwhelmed.

Another voice, this one female, spoke out over the din of demonic clamoring. "Stop."

Inanna.

The demons around me paused, waiting expectantly.

"Did you really think it would be that easy?"

"I hoped so," I said.

"You are more foolish than I expected. Strong, to be sure, but so arrogant. You knew I was building this place into a fortress. You knew we were watching you. Did you really think I wouldn't be prepared for you?"

"My mistake. I'll just get out of your hair, then." How did she know what I knew? How...

I took a step backward, but there was nowhere to go.

Inanna laughed. "You would have done well as one of my followers. Unfortunately, I don't have time to deal with converting you." She nodded toward her demons. "Carry on."

The horde advanced toward me once again.

Shit.

Shit, shit, shit.

I couldn't escape. My sword was useless in this dimension against their physical, human bodies. My gun would work, but not enough, and not fast enough.

I drew it anyway, holding it with one hand and my sword with the other. I was being overwhelmed. Tactical retreat was my only option. Maybe I could carve enough of a path to get to my truck.

I turned and fired into the demon closest to me. I didn't count my shots, just kept firing until it went down, then on to the next one, all the while slashing with my sword, occasionally striking through the dimensional walls and hitting a demon spirit on the other side.

I'd taken down a couple, but they were still coming.

I wasn't fast enough here.

Wait.

I wasn't fast enough *here*.

In the other dimension, though, I could manipulate physics. Bend the reality. There was a portal just a few feet away. Plus, my sword would work there.

A guttural yell erupted from my chest as I barreled toward the portal opening, firing and slashing. I jumped through the hole, the atmosphere changing from bright, Phoenix fall to stifling demon sulfur, and started running. Demons charged toward me, but here, my sword flashed through them like a warm knife through butter, turning them to dust.

I willed the ground to move under my feet, and in a few steps, I was back where I'd parked. I sliced through the dimensional wall with the sword and jumped into my truck, peeling out and racing down the street.

When I was far enough away that I didn't think they wouldn't follow me rather than protect the fortress, I pulled over. Panting, I called the Mesa police and asked for backup and an ambulance.

But backup wasn't really what I wanted. I couldn't go back there. I couldn't get close. I'd barely escaped. There was no way I'd get that lucky twice.

Instead, I drove to Chase's church.

The only place I knew I would be completely safe.

I pulled into the parking lot and immediately felt the sense of peace that washed over me whenever I was here. A total absence of any influence from the other dimension.

I stumbled from my truck, weary—but not from the other dimension, just a general exhaustion from fighting for my life—and made my way to the office building.

The front door was open, and I walked down the hallway and pounded on Chase's office door.

He opened it and gaped at me. "What happened? Are you okay?"

I stumbled forward and he caught me, pulling me into an embrace. I couldn't hold it in anymore, and I let all my emotions spill out onto his clean shirt.

When I could breathe again, I pulled back and looked at him. "It was a trap. An ambush. The demon from the daycare must have warned her. Or Dr. Brantley did—or both. And Ken... Ken shot Desiree. I don't know if she's alive. I escaped through the other dimension."

He stepped back and ran a hand through his hair.

"Start over."

I told him about getting to the museum and Dr. Brantley opening the door, then being overwhelmed by demons.

He took my hand, his touch soothing. "Okay. Who do we call to see if she's okay?"

"I don't know—I don't know her superiors or anything. I guess I could call the captain and see if Ken checked in."

He nodded. "Good. Let's start there."

I called but the captain wasn't in. No one had heard from Ken.

"Nothing," I told Chase.

"What about Mesa PD? You called them when you escaped, right?"

I nodded and called the Mesa PD dispatch. I identified myself and explained who I was and asked to talk to a captain or someone in charge.

I finally got in touch with someone who told me three people had been taken to the hospital. No fatalities that he knew of.

Chase's shoulders visibly relaxed. "That's good, then. She—they're alive. Can we go down to the hospital and see what we can find out there?"

I nodded. "Can you drive? I... I don't know if I can right now."

"Of course. Come on."

We drove in silence to the hospital in Mesa. I showed my credentials and explained that I worked with Agent Escobar. Local police were there—I'd need to make a statement. But they were willing to let the hospital staff tell me about her condition.

"Agent Escobar is in surgery," the head nurse on duty told me. "The bullet punctured her intestines, but the doctors are hopeful that they can repair the damage."

"And the others? Dr. Brantley and Lieutenant Richmond?"

"Dr. Brantley is in ICU. She's unconscious, but her vitals are stable. But we're not sure what happened—there are no visible signs of trauma—no head wound or internal bleeding—so we can't yet determine whether she is going to recover. Lieutenant Richmond was treated for a concussion, but was released."

A concussion. He'd turned on me and might have killed Desiree, and he got away with a concussion.

But it wasn't just him—it was the demon. Had he willfully betrayed me? How many of his actions were controlled by the demon? And how had that happened in the first place?

I pressed my hands to my temples, trying to push back the headache that wanted to overwhelm me.

Chase put his hand on my shoulder, his touch firm and soothing.

"Can I see Dr. Brantley?" I asked.

"She's not awake," the nurse reiterated.

"I know, I just... please?"

The nurse finally nodded. We left Chase in the waiting room, and she led me down a long hallway and around several corners before admitting me in to the ICU.

Dr. Brantley lay in a bed, an IV in her arm and monitoring equipment stuck to her at various points on her body.

Other than being unconscious, she seemed normal. Her color was good, her makeup and hair were a little bit messy, but she didn't look like she'd just been in a demon fight.

What had really happened? Had she betrayed us? If so, then why was she lying here? I'd never sensed any demonic presence around her, never had an inkling that she was doing anything besides trying to help. And if that were true, then this was my fault.

Just like Bridget.

"Hey, Dr. Brantley," I said aloud. "I don't know if you can hear me, but... I'm sorry. I'm sorry I dragged you into this, and that I didn't see this coming. I—"

Dr. Brantley's eyes opened, and she blinked. The monitors around her beeped and chimed.

The nurse pushed past me and rushed to her side. "Hey there. It's good to see you awake."

"Where am I?" Dr. Brantley asked.

"Arizona General Hospital in Mesa," the nurse answered. "Do you remember what happened?"

Dr. Brantley's brow furrowed. "I'm not sure. I was at the museum. I was expecting company, so I went to open the back door, and then... it felt like someone grabbed my head from the inside out, and I could see what was happening, but I couldn't control it, and then everything went dark."

"Okay. I'll let the doctor know you're awake." The nurse stalked toward me. "You, out."

"Wait." Dr. Brantley's voice cracked as she forced the words out. "Can I talk to her first?"

The nurse looked back and forth between us as though weighing the danger. "Five minutes," she said at last.

"Thank you," I said.

As soon as the door closed behind the nurse, Dr. Brantley asked, "What really happened?"

"It was a trap," I said. "They were waiting for me. Inanna and dozens of demons."

I told her everything. "I'm so sorry," I said when I finished. "I never should've brought you into this."

Dr. Brantley shook her head. "It's not your fault."

"It is, though. I asked for your help. Asked you to go to the museum and let us in. There's no way you could've known that you'd be attacked because of me. And now you can't go back there—they know you're working with me. They'll kill you."

"Jack, stop. I made my own choices."

I smiled, but it wasn't true. It was my fault. Just like when I'd gotten Bridget killed. I messed up, and people got hurt.

I had to do better.

168

But how, when the demons knew I was coming? When they'd be guarding Inanna's statue? When I had no idea what the ritual was or when it was supposed to take place? After I'd tipped my hand too soon?

"I should let you get some rest," I said.

"I'll call you when I'm out of here. We need to regroup and figure out our next move."

"Sure." Except there would be no regrouping. I'd almost gotten her and Desiree killed. There was no way I was going to let them anywhere near this again.

Besides, I still didn't know for sure whether Dr. Brantley was really on my side or not. Pastor Floyd had said not to trust anyone. I couldn't risk it. Not if I wanted to stop Inanna and keep Beck safe.

I had to do this on my own.

I asked Chase if he could drop me off at Deanna and Dave's house. They could help me pick up my truck in the morning, but I needed to sleep and spend some time with Beck, and I didn't want to waste that much time in transit.

They were all asleep when I got there, but the spare room was ready for me, Beck already sleeping in the crib in there. He stirred when I came in, and I picked him up, holding him close and breathing in the scent of baby shampoo and clean pajamas.

"I'm going to take care of this," I whispered. "I won't let anything happen to you."

TWENTY-TWO

Deanna was more than happy to take us home the next morning. She spent the whole drive talking about how much fun she'd had with Beck at the park and how close he was getting to crawling and how jealous her neighbors were of her delightful grandson.

I let her prattle on, engaging with the occasional appropriate exclamation, but letting my mind churn.

In the end, I realized it all came back to the sword. The sword was powerful, and growing stronger every time I used it. Nothing else even stood a chance against the demons. I needed to find out more about it.

And that meant going back to the source. The demon I'd gotten it from. Which could prove challenging. I'd already tried allying myself with a demon, and it had possessed Ken and nearly killed Desiree. And I didn't have any leverage. No bargaining power.

Still, I had nothing else to go on.

That would be my next step.

Chase was just arriving at the church when we got to my truck. Deanna walked to the back of her sedan to get Beck's things while I transferred him from the car seat in her car to the one in mine.

"Jack, I'm glad I caught you," Chase said behind me.

I turned around. "Hi, Chase. What's up?"

He glanced at Deanna. "Do you have a minute to talk?"

Deanna came around with Beck's diaper bag. "Hello, there."

"Deanna, this is Chase. He's the pastor here. Chase, this is Deanna—Trent's mom."

Chase's eyes widened a moment, but he quickly put on a smile and extended his hand. "It's nice to meet you."

"You too." Deanna gave me a significant glance as she handed me Beck's bag, but I just smiled.

"Thanks for the ride. We'll come out and visit again soon," I said.

I waited until she was in her car and out of earshot before turning back to Chase. "What's up?"

"I heard back from the hospital. Desiree came out of surgery and woke up a couple of times throughout the night. She's going to be okay."

It felt like a weight lifted from me. "Thank God."

Chase nodded. "I did."

I smiled, but it was short lived. "I don't know what to do next. I thought I was taking the fight to them, a preemptive strike, and I walked into a trap. I won't be able to get near the statue in either dimension now. I still don't know what she's planning, let alone how to stop her."

He leaned back to rest on the side of my truck and exhaled. "I wish I had an answer for you."

"The one thing I do know is that our time is running short. Inanna is on a deadline. So, whatever I do, it needs to be fast."

"Is there any way we could get the museum director to forfeit any of the artifacts?"

I shrugged. "I don't know. Desiree was going to try to get one of them as evidence, but I don't know if anything she found was conclusive enough to give her the right to take it. And now it will be some time before she can get back to work."

"I'm going to go down to see her this afternoon. I'll ask what she found out and if she knows anything more."

"Thanks. I have something I want to look into, so I'll keep you updated too."

He gave me and Beck a quick hug, and I dropped Beck off at Gen's, then headed once again to Mesa and the warehouse where I knew there was still a rip in dimensions.

The officer on duty recognized me and let me in. I gripped my sword and inhaled, feeling the other side. There were no demons close by.

Good.

I needed to get past them without being noticed.

Taking a deep breath, I stepped through the hole into the other dimension and paused, allowing my body to adjust to the vile weight that oppressed me here.

More dust than usual filled the red-tinted sky, and the sulfuric smell made it hard to breathe. I set out at a jog, willing the ground to move beneath me, heading north.

It had been a long time since I'd been to the demon fortress where I'd been held captive, but I was pretty sure I could find it.

Within a few minutes, I was outside the bounds of the city and any familiar landmarks. But it wasn't long before I saw the shadowy reflection of what was Las Vegas on the other side. Many of the structures were reinforced on this side.

Beyond that, north and slightly west, lay my destination.

The facility was much as I remembered it. A structure that was largely underground, with a tunnel that led to the surface.

A single guard stood sentry at the door.

I approached him. "I need to speak with Tsenaha," I said.

He gaped at me, as though trying to process seeing me here, in his dimension, aware. He encroached on my space, a show of aggression, but not an attack.

I raised my sword. "Look, I'd rather not have to use this, but I will."

He eyed my weapon, then suddenly seemed to recognize it, and stepped back quickly. "Wait here," he said, his voice gravelly.

He disappeared inside and returned a short while later, accompanied by a demon I recognized. Tsenaha, the prince of this region. He'd kept me prisoner on behalf of Dionysius, but he and I had come to an agreement after I'd escaped.

He glared at me and at the sword. "I thought we had a truce."

"We do," I said. "That's why I didn't kill your guard and fight my way in to find you."

Tsenaha bowed his head in acknowledgement. "Why are you here?"

"I need help."

"I already gave you that sword. I fulfilled my end of the bargain."

"I know. Which is why I came to you. I'd like to make another bargain. I need information."

"What's in it for me?"

I shrugged. "What do you want?"

Tsenaha crossed his arms. His claw-like nails tapped against his biceps as he eyed me. "What information are you looking for?"

"I need to know everything you know about Inanna, and everything you know about this sword."

He licked his fangs with a forked tongue. a gesture that seemed almost nervous. "Information on the sword is free. On Inanna... well, if I cross her, I risk everything I've built here. I risk my very life."

172

"Okay. What will help you secure it? Aside from me killing Inanna? Which, by the way, I'm going to do with or without you, so you might as well be on my side for this one."

"There is a demon to the west. His name is N'merygor. He controls a large part of what you humans call California."

My gaze darted that direction. Nothing grew in this dimension, but the rise and fall of foothills stretched out before me, and a mountain range rose in the distance.

"California?" I turned back to Tsenaha.

He nodded. "Not the cities, but some of the rural areas. If I control his province, then my stronghold more than doubles. Many of his followers are loyal to me, but I cannot get close enough to him to get rid of him."

"Why not?"

"Because he's expecting me. Kill him, and I'll tell you everything I know about Inanna and what she's planning."

I considered his proposal for several minutes. I really would have the element of surprise, then. And I'd broken both into and out of demon fortresses before. Plus, ridding the world of one more demon couldn't be a bad thing, and who knew when it would come in handy again for me to have a demon ally.

"Okay," I said at last. "How do I find him?"

Tsenaha gave me detailed directions on how to find N'merygor's mountain fortress. "He wears a necklace shaped like a coyote. In your reality it would appear to be gold, but it's made of an alloy that includes precious metals from this land. Kill N'merygor and bring the necklace to me to prove that he is dead."

"Couldn't I just steal the necklace and pretend I killed him?"

Tsenaha smiled, but it looked more like a sadistic snarl. "If you can get the necklace without killing him, you are more skilled than I imagine you to be. I do prefer him dead, but the necklace is the most important thing."

I considered asking why, but decided I didn't care. This was a means to an end. I exhaled, psyching myself up for my mission. "Okay. I'll see you later."

I set off at a jog in the direction of N'merygor's fortress. Reality bent under me, and it was only a few minutes until I reached the mountainous region. It didn't take long to find the landmarks. In the other reality, trees and rivers and lakes dotted the landscape, but here, I could jump over them, almost as though they were toys.

The smell of sulfur was less here, too, away from the denser demon population. Even the air felt less stifling. That changed as I drew closer to where Tsenaha had said the fortress would be.

A stone tower—in this reality—stood atop one of the mountains. That was the lookout. At least one demon would be stationed there.

I paused to get a sense of where I was and what I was dealing with. One demon sat atop the tower, gazing out over the mountains, looking bored.

There wasn't much in the way of cover. I doubted I could use stealth to approach. Surprise was better.

I waited until the sentry turned completely away from me, then ran as fast as I could and leapt up to the top of the tower, the strength of Wonder Woman coursing through me in this dimension.

I landed and thrust my sword.

The demon had just enough time to look over its shoulder at me, shock written on its face, before it disintegrated.

I crouched atop the tower to get a lay of the land. The entrance to the fortress sat about twenty feet below. Another sentry stood guard there, but again, it didn't seem particularly invested in its duty. The door was closed. I had no idea if it was locked or had special protections on it. I couldn't see a doorknob from here—but that would probably be too easy anyway.

At any rate, I couldn't risk killing the demon until I figured out how to get inside. I watched for a little while, but no one came in or out, and I didn't have any more time to wait.

I leapt from the tower on the side opposite the fortress door, where I wouldn't be seen, and circled around to catch him off guard.

He wasn't paying attention. Didn't even notice me until I sidled up beside him and thrust my sword under his chin. "I'm here to see N'merygor. Please take me to him."

He opened his mouth in what looked very likely to be a cry of alarm, and I pressed the sword tip against his throat. "I'd recommend against that."

The demon raised his hands. "If you'll allow me?" He motioned toward the door.

I took a step back, enabling him to turn, but keeping my sword at throat-level. He pressed his hand against what seemed to be a sensor, and the door popped ajar. But instead of opening it, he whirled around, knocking the sword away from his neck, making me stumble.

"Intruder!" he hollered.

"I said not to do that." I lunged, slicing through the arm he held up to stave me off and thrust through his heart.

He turned to dust.

The door remained open.

Of course, they knew I was here now, but they didn't know who they were dealing with.

I stepped inside and paused to get my bearings. This fortress was much like the others I'd been in—a long hallway lit with different colored lights. The elemental energy from which power was drawn—yellow for fire, blue for water, white for air, red for earth—all swirling behind what appeared to be windows in the wall.

A cluster of demons emerged from one of the doorways further down the hall.

I held the sword in front of me. "I am here to speak to N'merygor. I don't wish to harm you, but I will see him one way or another, so you might as well let me through."

A few of them glanced at one another as though weighing the likelihood.

"Really? There's a human in your dimension. Either you've heard of me, which means you know what I'm capable of, or you haven't, in which case you must be wondering how I got here and how powerful I am. I assure you, you don't want to find out the hard way. Take me to N'merygor."

One of the demons nodded at last. "This way."

The others parted in order to make room for me to follow. I narrowed my eyes at them. "Don't risk it."

"None of us will harm you. Yet," the leader said.

I followed him down the long hallway, trailed by the rest of the demons, through a labyrinth of tunnels that I would be hard-pressed to make my way out of when I left. I tried to remember each turn and to look for landmarks, but in the real world we were deep underground in the side of the mountain, and everything on this side looked the same. I'd have to fight my way out of here and hope I could make it back up to the surface.

At last, we reached what seemed to be the center of an elaborate maze, an anteroom lined with multiple doors. The leader of the demons rapped on the one opposite where we'd come in.

"Enter," a deep voice echoed from beyond.

The demon led me into what could only be described as a throne room. The lights on the walls were patterned into a mosaic of what appeared to be battle scenes. Demons stood in attendance at evenly spaced intervals. A throne sat against the far wall, and on it perched a demon. Around his neck hung a coyote-shaped medallion.

His eyes widened, and he sat up straighter, gaping at me.

"How did you get in here?"

"Your dimension or your fortress? Your fortress—I killed a bunch of your lackeys. This dimension—well, let's just say that was the easy part."

He eyed me for a long moment. "You're Jack Davidson."

"My reputation precedes me."

"Yes, we all heard about what happened to Dionysius. To be honest, I thought you'd be more formidable."

"Why does everyone keep saying that?"

"What do you want?" he asked.

"I need your necklace."

His hand went to his chest where the medallion lay. "Over my dead body."

I shrugged. "If that's the way you want it."

He growled and waved a hand.

His minions turned on me, the lust for death clear in their yellow eyes.

I swung the sword, slicing through the first one, then sweeping back and cutting through two more.

The sword seemed to grow stronger and sharper with every demon I killed. And... so did I. Energy surged through me, and no matter how many demons I cut through, I didn't tire. Eventually, I had cleaved through all the demons surrounding me, and I approached the throne.

N'merygor gaped.

"All I want is the necklace. There's an easy way and a hard way. But honestly... it's not that hard for me."

He clutched the necklace in his hand and stood. Something surged through him. Power of some kind, electrifying the atmosphere. He seemed to grow larger, more intimidating.

That wasn't quite how I'd hoped it would go. But it did explain why Tsenaha wanted the necklace.

I bent my legs and clutched my sword, waiting for him to attack.

He leapt, not at me, but over me. I whirled around just in time to see his claws extending toward me. I stepped back just enough so he only raked my arm.

It still burned like fire, making my hold on the sword waver. But I couldn't stop now. He was off balance from his attack, and I pressed forward, slashing with the sword.

I nicked his arm, but it didn't slow him. He barreled toward me again. I ducked down and rolled as he jumped, so I ended up behind him, and he had to turn to avoid the swipe of my sword.

This time I made solid contact with the back of his shoulder.

He snarled. The medallion surged, a glowing gold aura emanating from it, and the cut on his back sealed itself shut.

TWENTY-THREE

Well, shit. That could not be good. No wonder Tsenaha hadn't been able to get his hands on it. But it wasn't like I could quit now. I'd never make it out alive. It was him or me.

I backed away to get my bearings, but N'merygor didn't give me any room to recover. He leapt at me again, landing on top of me, pinning my sword between us, against my chest, where I couldn't use it.

What would happen if I let go? Would I automatically bounce back into my dimension? Would the sword come with me? Or would I just pass out here, like most people did?

I decided not to experiment in the middle of a fight. Releasing the sword with one hand, I swung at his face.

Hurt my hand way more than his face, but it startled him, which gave me just enough leverage to pull the sword up.

Despite his magic healing amulet thing, the sword did burn him. He hissed and drew away instinctively, giving me space to move the sword even more. I jabbed it at him.

I sliced a gash in his torso, which almost immediately closed up again.

I would have to make a killing blow—something he couldn't recover from. I stabbed again, causing him to release me. Then I warded him off with my swinging blade until I could pull myself to my feet. My eyes darted to the door. I couldn't be sure when or if reinforcements would come, but either way, I had to end this quickly.

I backed away slowly, angling toward the door.

"Okay," I said. "I can see we got off on the wrong foot. I'm just going to…" I feinted like I was going to make a break for the door.

He fell for it, diving toward where he thought I was going to be, while I ducked back the other direction and swung my sword around, slicing for his neck.

His head rolled away, thudding against the ground before disappearing, while the rest of his body crumbled to the ground. In its place stood his spiritual form—the part of him that was only present in this dimension, but was still every bit as dangerous. The necklace lay on the floor. I snatched it up and stuffed it in my pocket, then ran for the door.

"Stop!" he bellowed. Once in the hall, I slammed my sword into a yellow light on the wall. Elemental power surged out from the space where the light had been. I broke another yellow light.

Fire erupted behind me. I ran down hallways, breaking lights and releasing elemental power as I went. Sweat broke out on my back and soaked my hair from the heat.

The air power wouldn't slow them down much, but mixed with fire or water it would. I just had to make sure not to release water and fire at the same time and have them cancel each other out.

Occasionally, demons emerged from rooms or other hallways, but between my momentum and the element of surprise, I took them out as I raced along, trying to find my way back to the surface.

Bonus, since I'd already smashed lights in the hallways I'd been through, it helped narrow my options moving forward through the labyrinth.

I eventually came to a circular room, like a central hub from which several other hallways protruded, similar to the area before where N'merygor's throne room sat.

Damn. I had no idea which ones would take me up toward the surface and which would lead me deeper into the fortress.

Eight hallways. One I'd just come from. That left seven. Demon voices came from the hallway three to my left. That meant that probably wasn't the way to the surface, but that still left me with way too many options.

I dashed across the hall to the passage just beyond where the demons were coming and smashed two of the water lights in the entrance, then ran back across the room to the hallway directly opposite and ducked around the corner where I could peek out into the central room.

A few moments later, six demons emerged. "She went that way," one of the demons shouted, pointing toward the hallway where I'd smashed the lights.

Good. They fell for it.

"You two follow her," the first demon said, motioning toward the hallway. He pointed to two more. "You two, go that way and see if you can cut her off at the communications hub. We'll go secure the exit in case she finds her way there."

The demons split up, not noticing me hiding in the shadows across the room.

The first demon and his partner pushed through the water, while the second pair took a hallway two down from the one I'd exited, and the last pair angled toward me. I ducked deeper into the shadows in the hallway, sword ready in case they came this way.

They didn't. They disappeared into the hallway just to my right. Heading to secure the exit. That was the way out.

I waited a moment, then crept down the hall, staying far enough behind that I could duck out of sight if they turned around, but close enough that I wouldn't lose them as they marched forward.

A short trek later, and I saw the door I'd come in, slightly ajar, the red, otherworldly sunlight filtering in.

"Check outside," the lead demon said. His partner stepped through the door.

I ran down the hall, sword raised, reaching the demon just as he turned around to examine the hallway. My sword sliced cleanly through his neck and he disappeared in a cloud of smoke. I pushed through the door and slammed my sword into the back of the demon who stood out there examining the landscape.

And then I took off running. With any luck, I'd be back to Tsenaha's domain before they even realized I was gone.

The ground bent underneath my feet, and before long Tsenaha's fortress appeared in the distance.

Behind me, a shout rang out in the air.

I glanced back long enough to see a swarm of demons flying straight toward me.

"Tsenaha!" I yelled, forcing my feet to move faster, the alternate dimension to bow to my will. "Open up!"

The door to the fortress opened and the sentry on duty gaped.

"Let me in!" I yelled.

I barreled past him, thudding against the wall in the entry hallway as I jolted to a stop.

The sentry slammed the door closed behind me. "What have you done?"

"Get Tsenaha up here, now!"

The demons outside banged on the door. It quivered, like they would knock it down if they kept this up long enough.

The sentry darted away, and a moment later, the hallway swarmed with Tsenaha's demons. Some of them eyed me as if they'd love to slaughter me right there, but they apparently knew of the arrangement I had with Tsenaha.

They opened the door to the flood of demons on the other side and began battling them back, away from the entrance. I scooted around a corner, out of the way of the fighting, to catch my breath.

A few moments later, the hallway was clear, and the battle had moved outside. Tsenaha rounded the bend and walked toward me.

"I didn't say bring N'merygor's entire army to my door," he sneered.

I shrugged. "You didn't say not to. You only said to bring you the amulet." I fished it from my pocket and held it up.

He lunged for it, and I snatched it away. "We had an agreement. Information first."

He snarled. "Let's go into my office."

I raised an eyebrow. It sounded strange to hear a demon in a desert fortress casually mention his office.

Nodding toward the front door, I asked, "Do they need help?"

He shrugged. "Is N'merygor alive?"

"In a manner of speaking," I answered. "But only here. His physical body that would be present in my world is dead."

"If he doesn't give up by the time we're finished, then I will be able to defeat him once I have the amulet on. This way."

I followed him down the hallways, keeping careful track of the turns. This fortress wasn't set up to be quite as labyrinthine as N'merygor's, so I was pretty sure I could find my way back without too much trouble. If I needed to. As long as I had the amulet, I had leverage.

He led me into a room with a bank of monitors along one wall, a lab table opposite, and a throne of sorts.

He sat on the throne and did not offer me a seat. "So, you want to know about Inanna."

I leaned against the wall and rested my sword on the floor, though still with the hilt firmly in hand. "That's the idea, yes. But also the sword."

"I already told you everything I knew about the sword when I gave it to you."

"You didn't tell me anything about it."

"Exactly."

I narrowed my eyes.

He gave an exasperated sigh. "I don't know anything about it. I acquired it when I killed the being who wielded it in a battle long ago."

"What kind of battle?"

He waved his arm. "The battle for this land."

"How long ago?"

He shrugged. "Three or four thousand years."

I tried to keep my face neutral. "And so you just kept it hidden in your attic for a few millennia until I came along?"

"That's right."

The lights along the wall behind me dug into my back, and I shifted position while still trying to appear in control. "That's quite a relic to just give up as leverage in a battle you weren't even part of."

"As I'm sure you've figured out, it's not like I can use it myself. And better someone with whom I can establish an alliance than a being who would kill me with it as soon as he got it in his hands."

"Like the one you took it from?"

"Precisely."

"What was he? It?"

"What do you mean?" Tsenaha asked.

"You can't touch it, and neither can any of the other demons I've encountered. Who did you take it from? A god?"

He shook his head. "No. Something else entirely. The point is, by giving it to you, I have ensured some level of protection against its power—but I couldn't tell you where it comes from or what it's capable of."

So, it wasn't my imagination. The sword was inherently powerful, and getting stronger each time I used it. But there might be more he could tell me if I pressed. "It couldn't be that powerful if you killed the guy who had it before me."

A harsh, guttural laugh erupted from his throat. "I assure you, that endeavor was not without its casualties. And I had more than one artifact of my own to increase my strength against him."

Artifacts again. "If you had so much power, why were you afraid of Dionysius?"

His claws drummed against the throne that I now realized looked like it was made of bone—but not human. The pieces were too large for that. But demons disintegrated when they were killed, so what in hell—literally, maybe—were those from?

Tsenaha placed his hands on armrests that resembled skulls. "One thing I have learned in my years is not to be overly ambitious—to not start a fight I can't finish. The more you acquire, the harder it is to keep."

"But you wanted N'merygor's territory."

"I can hold on to that. His claim has been wavering for years, his followers ready to revolt at the slightest provocation. I just needed a little extra... leverage for negotiating."

"That's where I came in."

"Indeed. Dionysius was an indirect threat. Powerful, yes, but so were his enemies. By helping you, I eliminated a potential threat for myself without drawing attention to my own plans. But this conversation isn't about me. You want to know about Inanna."

"Yeah, okay. Let's talk about Inanna. What can you tell me about her?"

He took a deep breath, as though thinking. "Her history goes back several thousands of years. She was one of the more powerful goddesses of her time."

"Wait, what's the difference between a goddess like her and a demon like you?"

He shrugged. "There isn't much of one, really, at least practically speaking. Think of it like a military hierarchy. Certain beings were given more power and more authority. We're also different... I suppose species would be the closest word. The gods and goddesses had power and certain domains. They made names for themselves among you humans, many of which are still known today in the form of myths. Although, to be fair, much of the mythology that surrounds us is what you humans attributed to us, not necessarily what we earned or claimed for ourselves."

I nodded. Most of this was stuff I'd already learned. "But Dionysius was a demon, not a god."

Tsenaha shrugged. "In a manner of speaking. The walls between dimensions used to be more fluid. We could go in and out between dimensions with relative ease. About five thousand years ago, a change in the earth's atmosphere made the walls begin to close, making interdimensional travel difficult. A couple thousand years ago, someone made a sacrifice in an attempt to cast a spell that would reopen the walls, but it backfired. Beings that your legends call gods and goddesses were killed in the attempt. Almost none are left now."

"Except Inanna."

Tsenaha nodded. "She was already trapped in her tomb when this happened, so the spell didn't affect her the same way. With those beings gone, creatures like me—what you think of as demons—set themselves up as deities, taking over from the ancient ones, even adopting the legends as their own. Like I said, it's a hierarchy. And you can climb your way to the top, using any means deemed necessary—manipulation, murder, you name it."

"Or stealing their magical amulets," I said.

Tsenaha nodded. "Or that."

"Okay, so Inanna was a goddess, with inherent power and a region she controlled. You said she was trapped in her tomb so she didn't die off with the others. What happened to her?"

"Several thousand years ago, her domain was razed by invading forces. As has been happening since the beginning of time, gods and demons have been vying for territory, and finally one amassed an army large enough to destroy hers."

"Okay, but how did that trap her? Why did she disappear and lose her power?"

"You are familiar with the laws of physics—enough to know that every action causes an equal and opposite reaction?"

I nodded. That much, apparently, was universal.

"It's a similar concept. The ancient gods figured out how to control the human world. In addition to being in the world, being stronger and more powerful than the humans, they figured out how to manipulate weather, crops, even life and death, to an extent. But in order to control the physical world, they had to be tied to it. There was a cost to joining to the earth. In some ways it made them stronger, but in others, it made them weaker. Inanna's power was tied to her temple, where she was worshipped and received sacrifices. Specifically, her idol was the conduit between herself and the natural world. When her temple was destroyed, she was, in a way, cut in half."

That sounded both encouraging and terrifying. "What do you mean?"

Tsenaha paused as though trying to figure out how to explain it to me. "Sort of like when you kill a demon in your reality, but his spirit is still alive here. Her connection to the earth was severed, and she could no longer access it or control it. But since she had tied herself to the earth through her idol, she was trapped inside it, in a way."

"So, when her idol was unearthed, she was set free."

"Yes."

"Why couldn't she get free anyway, then? I mean, the idol was buried, but the landscape is different there, and you can make it do what you want. Even I can make the land move."

Tsenaha snapped to attention. "What do you mean you can make the land move?"

"I—reality is different here. I can make myself move faster, and I can make the ground move under me. You guys can do it, too."

184

Tsenaha shook his head. "No, we can't."

"Yeah you can. That's how I knew I could. I watched Chet—or whatever his demon name was—rip apart a rock wall with his claws, and fly through the air at, like, Mach speeds."

His fingers tightened around the skull-shaped throne arms. "We are strong and we are fast and we are used to this dimension. But we cannot control it, not like you're describing. Are you certain you're not just stronger and faster here?"

"No. It was a conscious thing. I am only so strong, so fast, but then I willed the earth to move, so I could cover more ground. How do you think I beat N'merygor's demons here?"

Tsenaha's eyes landed on my sword. "That may be more powerful than we realized before."

"No, I could do that before I had the sword."

His eyes widened, betraying just a hint of horror before he controlled his reaction. "I see. Well, it's not important now. Where were we? Oh, yes. Inanna. She couldn't break free from her idol and escape, because she was attached to it, so when it was buried, so was she."

"Then how did she escape when it was unearthed? Because she's not attached to it now—she's wandering through your dimension pretty freely."

"Someone must have performed a ritual or sacrifice that enabled her to walk free."

Someone.

The gears in my mind started turning. Like the someone who had killed a worker at the dig site. Which probably meant it was the same someone who uncovered her idol in the first place. They knew what it was, and they knew what it meant, and they'd set her free?

"Okay, so *someone* set her free, and now she's trying to regain her power. I know she's planning a huge ritual, and I'm pretty sure she needs all the icons and attachments to be in place for it to work."

Tsenaha tilted his head to one side. "Yes and no. She can do the ritual without them. But they each will have inherent powers that will make her stronger in some way."

"Like what?"

He gestured toward my pocket where the coyote amulet sat. "You saw what that can do?"

I nodded.

"There are many such objects. You'd call them magical, although human understanding of magic doesn't begin to encompass all its intricacies. At the height of her power, Inanna had created and

185

acquired many such items. That was why she was so hard to defeat for so long."

"How do they work? I mean…" I patted my pocket. "I saw *what* this does, but why?"

Tsenaha waved his arm around the room. You have seen our technology—at least some of it. You know that it is powered by the elements, and you know we've developed many things, including the ability to mingle our DNA with that of humans. Creating artifacts is the same. We make objects and infuse them with power, much of which is beyond anything you could compare it to on earth. And we can bind them to ourselves. The one in your pocket, for example, is still bound to N'merygor. It was something that only he could use, until you killed his physical body. Even still, it is infinitely more powerful for him than for me. But when I kill him, that bond will break, and I will be able to bind it to me."

"How do you bind it?"

"Various rituals. Blood is always the strongest and most powerful."

The ever-present nausea intensified, and a chill ran down my arms despite the unnatural heat. "Why is always blood with you people?"

"Because blood is life, my dear. And life is the most powerful magic there is."

"That brings me to what I think is probably my final question," I said. "Inanna is after my son. Something about him specifically. What is it she needs? What is so special about his blood?"

"I can't answer that directly," Tsenaha said, "but I can give you my best guess. There was a Babylonian king named Naboplassar who united several nations to march against Assyria—Nineveh. He was believed to have fulfilled various prophecies, and it is from his line that a race of people has been carefully cultivated. One of his descendants is prophesied to be the most powerful human on earth."

"The antichrist."

"That is one name for him," Tsenaha said.

I exhaled. "So, the descendant of the man who originally defeated her is the one who can give her back her power."

"In the most simplistic terms, yes."

"Okay." I exhaled again. Not exactly the best news, but at least now I knew what I was fighting and why.

"Is that it?" Tsenaha asked.

I wracked my brain, but my mind was already full with this new knowledge and I couldn't think of anything else.

Except one thing.

TWENTY-FOUR

"How do I stop her?"

"Last time it took three armies and countless demons." Tsenaha leaned back in his throne, the tips of his fangs showing through an almost bemused smile. "If you don't have that, then... best of luck."

"Seriously? That's all you've got?"

"There's nothing else I can tell you that you don't already know. Destroying her artifacts will prevent her from acquiring various powers—and no, I don't know what they do, but I suspect there is one that will help her heal, much like the coyote does, and probably one that will give her greater strength, one that will let her wield some other power, like the elements. But that's all just a guess."

One more thing popped into my mind.

"Last question. I've heard she wants to make the world hers. My world. Any idea what that's about?"

If a demon gargoyle face could be said to blanch, his did. Terror flashed clearly in his eyes before he controlled it, his mouth again forming into that fang-baring, amused smile.

He said, "That is not a thing you want to happen. If she succeeds, your world will essentially be absorbed into this one. Everything you know will be subject to her. She will be a goddess again, and the most powerful one your world has ever seen. The myths of Greek and Norse gods and all their powers that your culture has embraced and glorified will be nothing compared to what she will achieve. I suggest you stop her before she can get to that point."

He held out his hand. "May I have my amulet now?"

"Take me to the surface first," I said.

He nodded and led the way out through the halls and up to a door—but not the one I'd come in.

I raised an eyebrow.

He opened the door and pointed to the burning desert beyond. "This entrance faces northeast. You can circumvent the fighting out front if you go out this way."

The distant sounds of battle rose up from the other side of the compound. Tsenaha held out his hand again.

I pulled the amulet from my pocket and handed it to him, still keeping my grip on my sword, just in case he tried anything.

He didn't. He just bowed his head slightly. "Thank you. Now, if you'll excuse me, I'm going to go expand my domain."

The door slammed behind me. I jogged until I was far outside the compound, out of sight of the demons that still fought. I thought I caught a glimpse of N'merygor, but I wasn't going to stay around to watch. I suspected his time was limited. N'merygor wouldn't quit until he either retrieved the amulet or died, and I didn't think Tsenaha would let him go quietly.

I'd just given Tsenaha a whole lot of power he didn't have before, and our alliance was tentative at best. I'd have to watch my back with him. But that was a problem for another day. Right now, I had a goddess to stop.

It was late evening by the time I got back to Phoenix. I emerged into my world near my truck and inhaled the air that seemed so fresh and clean after being in the demon dimension for so long. I picked Beck up from Gen's and took him home.

I kept waiting for the crash after having been in the other dimension, but it never came. I felt energized. Was it the difference between being there under the control of a demon and being there with the sword?

It had something to do with the sword. There was no other explanation. Except that Tsenaha had seemed genuinely surprised when I said I could bend the reality without it.

Early the next morning, I called Chase. We met for coffee at our spot near his church, and I told him everything Tsenaha had said.

"You're saying preventing her from getting the artifacts won't actually stop her," he said.

"Apparently not. But I think that's still our best chance of weakening her."

"And Beck is the sacrifice that will complete the… spell or ritual or whatever it is."

"That seems to be the case. Or, Beck and the others, like soon-to-be Senator Harding."

"Many of whom she's already killed, if Floyd's information was correct."

"Not just Floyd's," I said. "Desiree's, too."

"Oh, right. And there are those we don't know anything about, I'm sure. Inanna probably has a complete set by now."

"Or close enough," I agreed. "Except Beck."

Beck paused in gnawing the pastry I'd given him to look up at me at the sound of his name. I kissed him and turned back to Chase. "I need something, but I don't know what. With Dionysius, I got the sword, and that's pretty damn powerful, but... just me against an army of demons plus a goddess? There's no way. I've lost my element of surprise. And I can't even pick them off one at a time—there's just too many. By the time I got through some of them, she'd just recruit more."

"And he couldn't tell you anything else about the sword?"

"Nothing useful."

Chase stirred copious amounts of cream into his already pale coffee. "Okay, so the ritual is supposed to give her access to this world again, right?"

I nodded.

"How is that going to remake the world in her image? She wants our reality to be absorbed into hers, right? Just because she has access to our world doesn't mean her reality can overtake ours."

"You know more about this stuff than I do," I said.

"Okay. I'll start researching that, I guess." A pained look crossed his face. "I wish Floyd were here."

I reached across the table and took his hand. "I know. Me too."

He exhaled.

"How is Desiree?" I asked, figuring we were both ready for a change in topic.

"Better. She was awake last time I went down there. They think she's going to be okay, but she still has a long way to go."

"I'm sorry, Chase. I... I never meant for her to get hurt."

"I know. It's not your fault."

"It is, though. I asked her to come. She had no idea what she was going up against or why."

"She swore to protect and serve, same as you. Even if she knew everything, she would've gone with you. And you were ambushed. It wouldn't have changed the outcome."

I appreciated his attempt to help, but it didn't change the facts, either.

A year ago, my indecision had cost the life of my best friend. Now, my hasty decision had almost cost the life of… if not a friend, at least an ally. No matter what I did, I screwed things up, and people got hurt and killed.

I had to do something… but how did one stop a goddess?

"I should go in to work," I said after a few more moments of awkward silence. "And I need to check in with Desiree, if she's up to it, or whoever she was reporting to."

Chase stood when I did and pulled me and Beck into a hug. "We'll figure it out," he said.

"I hope you're right," I said.

I dropped Beck at Gen's and headed out to Mesa.

Desiree was awake and allowed to have visitors when I arrived. She looked surprised to see me.

"You're okay," she said. "They didn't tell me anything. Last thing I remember, you were surrounded by giants and you were lashing out with your stupid sword. I don't even know who shot me."

I ran a hand through my hair. "We were ambushed. I don't know how, but they were expecting us. I think… I think it was my coworker Ken who hit you."

She winced and her hand pressed against her side. "You've got to be kidding me. I get taken down by friendly fire? I'm not admitting that, if anyone ever asks."

I gave her a slight smile, glad she was able to joke a little. Also, I wasn't sure the fire was in any way friendly, but I still hadn't seen Ken. I had no idea his role in what had happened.

"I'm sorry I left you there. I just… I had to get out so I could get help."

"I would've done the same," she said. "But… one thing… who are they? You said they were expecting us. I thought I was on the trail of a single thief who was killing his lackeys. I thought the goal was a collection of priceless artifacts. But that… that was an army."

I nodded. Again, I debated how much to actually tell her.

But she'd been shot. I needed to give her something to explain why it was worth it.

"They're Inanna's followers. Her cult."

"I haven't seen a cult this big or devoted since… well, ever. The ones I'm familiar with often rife with various abusive behaviors, they're not usually aggressive toward outsiders. And they're rarely situated in the middle of the city. They're usually in remote areas surrounded by razor wire and protected by vigilantes."

191

I sank into the uncomfortable chair on the other side of the small room. "Yeah. This is different. They're determined to revive her worship, and they'll kill anyone who tries to stop them."

"But the statue is in the museum. Are they planning to steal it?"

"I don't think they have to. I think they have access to the museum and are planning to perform their rituals there."

Desiree pressed the buttons to adjust her bed so she was sitting up a little straighter. "What did your friend say? The archaeologist? Is she okay?"

"She's fine. She was attacked from behind when she opened the door. She doesn't know anything about the cult accessing the museum. They... they must have an inside man or two. Who knows, some of the museum staff may even be her followers."

"They must have a powerful set of beliefs to have their army guarding her statue."

"Yep," I said.

"We've got to be able to get a warrant," she said.

"I'm pretty sure you're not going to be allowed to work for a little while," I said, offering a small smile to soften my words.

She *thunked* her head back against the back of her bed. "I hate that. I'm perfectly fine. Give or take."

I grinned. I actually did admire her some. That was exactly the kind of thing I would've said if it had been me. Wait... it was exactly the kind of thing I did say when it was me.

"As soon as they let me, I'm going to demand to be allowed to work from my bed," she grinned back.

"In the meantime, is there someone I should talk to about the case? Your superior or partner or someone?"

"I'm... between partners at the moment. You can talk to my boss, Peter Kingsley."

"Okay, thanks." I paused, wondering what exactly I could say to her that wouldn't sound trite or patronizing. "I'm glad you're going to be okay. And I'll keep you posted if I find anything out."

"Thanks."

I drove to Desiree's field office and found a spot in the covered parking garage. I left my sword in the truck—not because I thought I wouldn't need it, but because I thought I might forfeit my chance to get a meeting if I carried it inside a federal building—and marched up to the front desk. "I'm Detective Jack Davidson. I'm looking for Peter Kingsley."

"Just a moment," the receptionist said.

She typed something into her computer, waited, then stood and looked up at me. "He's free now. This way."

She led me down a hallway banked with offices to the corner office at the end and rapped on the door, opening it without waiting for an answer.

A man stood from behind a mahogany desk and extended his hand. "Detective, it's nice to meet you. I've heard interesting things about you."

Interesting things? Was that good or bad? And from whom— Desiree or someone else?

I didn't ask, instead grasping his hand in a firm shake. "Thank you for seeing me, sir. I was consulting with Agent Escobar on her murder case."

"Yes, she told me. How can I help you?"

"Is there anyone else who was on this case with her, someone I can talk to about what I'm working on?"

He shook his head. "Her last partner asked to be reassigned, citing irreconcilable differences."

"What does that mean?"

Kingsley chuckled. "It means that, while she is very good at what she does, she does not like to compromise and has a tendency to create a somewhat difficult working relationship."

"Don't I know it," I muttered. "Sorry."

Kingsley waved his hand dismissively. "No need to apologize for having an opinion. Agent Howell did have some of her notes. While she's on leave, I'll probably put him back on the case, I just haven't had time to make it official yet. I'll instruct him to utilize your help on this. Agent Escobar said you were competent, which, coming from her, is high praise."

I smiled. "Thank you."

Kingsley picked up his phone and dialed an extension. "Howell, I'm assigning you back to the Sezate case. Can you bring the file and any notes you have to my office?"

"Thanks," I said.

"My pleasure. I want to get to the bottom of this as much as you do."

I doubted that, but I just nodded.

"Escobar said something about a cult?" he prodded.

"Yeah. I can't prove it yet, but I believe it may be linked to another murder case I'm working on. A man was killed at the airport, a symbol carved in his chest. All the victims Agent Escobar has linked died right after they stole an artifact, and all the artifacts are linked to the idol of a goddess called Inanna. We believe her followers are trying to revive her cult. Bring her back to life, so to speak."

He rested his elbows on his desk and steepled his fingers. "And killing people will help?"

I shrugged. "They certainly think so."

He exhaled long and slow through his lips. "I hate zealots. They're the most dangerous kind of criminal. People who kill for money or power or revenge… they make sense. But the ones who really believe that what they're doing is right? They scare the hell out of me."

"I know what you mean," I said.

A moment later, the door opened, and I was almost overwhelmed by nausea. My stomach roiled, goosebumps popped up on my arms, and an oppressive smell of sulfur permeated the room.

Demons, and lots of them.

I didn't even have my sword and I knew they were there. I turned slowly, bracing myself for what I would see.

A man stood in the doorway holding a file. Perfectly ordinary, human man. Brown hair, trace of a five o'clock shadow, friendly smile. There was absolutely nothing suspicious or dangerous about him— except that he reeked of demonic activity.

What fresh hell was this?

"Oh, sorry," he said to Kingsley. "I didn't realize you were busy."

"Not at all," Kingsley said. "Come in. This is Detective Davidson. Detective, this is Agent Howell."

"Oh, you're Des's contact, right?" Howell smiled.

I forced a smile. "Right."

Des? Not even Chase called her Des. And especially coming from someone who couldn't even stand to work with her, this endearing nickname felt particularly odd.

"So sorry to hear about what happened to her." He came over and sat in the other chair in front of Kingsley's desk. "She's going to be okay, though, right?"

I nodded, still trying to swallow the bile that bubbled inside me. "Her prognosis is very good."

"Great. So, in the meantime, I guess I'm working with you now, yeah?" He glanced at Kingsley for confirmation.

"That's right," Kingsley said.

"Great!" How could he be so… jovial? What was even happening right now?

Howell opened up the file on Kingsley's desk. "Here's what we have so far."

There was nothing there I didn't already know, and plenty I did know that wasn't in the file. But how much could I trust a guy who smelled like demon?

On the other hand, I had to give them something or risk being kicked out of the investigation. Whatever Desiree knew was likely already in their files, or would be if they asked her about it. That was a safe place to stay.

"Inanna's idol is being housed at the Natural History Museum, under the care of Dr. Smith. The museum is restoring it. They have received several anonymous donations of artifacts related to it—but not specifically the ones related to the murders, so we can't directly tie the murders directly to the cult or the museum. Everything we know is speculation, not proof."

"That is going to make stopping them more difficult," Howell said.

"Exactly," I said. "But we did have a lead that Agent Escobar was looking into. One of the artifacts was delivered to the museum by messenger. The package had some sort of smear on it, that may have been human remains, specifically those of the last victim's body we found in the warehouse. Agent Escobar was getting it analyzed. Do you know what the status of that is? That would give us enough to get a warrant."

Howell thumbed through the file, a frown on his face. "I don't think she mentioned anything about that, and I don't see a report in here on any findings, or a copy of a request for the lab or anything."

Based on his tone of voice and mannerisms, I would swear he was genuinely concerned about what had happened to that piece of evidence and why it was missing. But somehow, I knew beyond a doubt he was lying.

He'd done something with it, and I would probably never find out what. I'd have to find another way to get into that building.

If I could. Even with a warrant, it might be a suicide mission. But I still had to find some sort of evidence that wasn't subject to Howell's mishandling.

And I had to think of something to say that would divert him away from realizing I was onto him.

"Agent Escobar was also looking into any connections between the victims other than the way they died. Anything new there?"

Howell rifled through the file. "Ah ha, here it is. Prison records—all three had them, but none of them were in the same places, let alone at the same time. Sezate was in prison with a fellow named Caggio, and Caggio was also did time at the same prison as Earl in New York. No evidence that they knew each other, but it's possible."

"Where's Caggio now?"

"Died from a drug overdose over a year ago."

"So even if that was a connection, there's no way to tell for sure. And that's pretty thin."

"Very," Howell said.

"I'll keep looking for a connection—anything actionable," I said.

"Great." Howell thumbed through the file one more time, paused, and looked up at me. "This is interesting. Do you know a guy named Brandon Harding?"

Alarm bells rang in my head. Again, his physical form seemed genuine, but something coming from the demons within him told me he his motives were somewhat less than pure.

"I met him last year. He'd been kidnapped and brought here, and I rescued him. Why?"

"Apparently he thought someone was following him and asked to be put into protective custody."

"In Illinois?"

Howell nodded. "He said he'd been contacted by a cult. And he mentioned your name."

My heart thudded against my chest. I fought to keep my face neutral. "When was this?"

He glanced back at the file. "Friday afternoon."

"Did they? Put him in protective custody, I mean?"

"I'm not sure. I'll look into it. You don't know anything about this?"

I shook my head. "I haven't heard from him, and nobody contacted me to tell me he asked for me. Let me know what you find out, would you?"

"Of course." Howell pulled a business card out of his pocket and handed it to me. "I know the museum isn't in your jurisdiction, so if you need anything, anything at all, give me a holler."

"Thanks," I said. "I will. And feel free to contact me if there's anything I can do to help with this investigation, even grunt work."

"Will do," Howell grinned.

I nodded to Kingsley. "Thanks for your help. I appreciate you taking the time."

"Hey, we're all on the same team here, right?" He stood and leaned over his desk, extending his hand.

"That's the theory." I shook his hand. "I'll be in touch."

I turned to go.

"I'll walk you out," Howell offered.

His voice was so charming, helpful. But cold dread clenched my stomach. Whatever he wanted with me was not going to be good.

I pulled out my keys when we left the building, mentally calculating how long it would take me to get to my truck and get my sword.

But he hadn't made a move yet, and it would be good to see if he revealed anything.

"Crazy that it's still so hot, am I right?" he asked in a tone that suggested he was legitimately interested in small talk. "I mean, not like the heat wave last year—that was a doozy—but I'm originally from the Midwest, so October hits and I wonder why the trees haven't started to change color yet, you know?"

We passed from the bright glare of the sun to the shadows of the parking garage. I forced a laugh. "I'm from here, so I just assume it's going to be like this until Thanksgiving."

A few more rows until my parking spot.

My gaze darted across the spaces as I planned my route. Passenger side was closest—which was good, because that would make grabbing my sword easier.

I walked a little quicker. "Well, thanks for sharing your notes with me. Anything you're at liberty to copy and send me for my own file would be great."

"Oh, yeah, sure. My pleasure," he said, still with that insufferable grin on his face.

I pressed the button to unlock my doors. "I'll be seeing you."

In an instant, his grin changed from a jolly, Midwestern dad-vibe to a dark, sinister leer. "Oh, I know you will. Sooner than you think."

TWENTY-FIVE

I bolted for my truck, yanked the passenger door open, and pulled out my sword. "I know what you are."

He just laughed, his human voice discordant against the screech of what had to be a dozen demons speaking with and through him. "That won't do anything. This body protects us here."

I knew that—the sword hadn't worked at the museum the other night. But the question was, how?

The sword throbbed, vibrating with the proximity of the demons. "You have no idea how much power I have," I said.

"We know. We have seen you. You are nothing to us, and if you come after us, you will be destroyed."

"Us. You mean Inanna's followers."

"We see all. We are many, we are hidden, and we are inevitable. The world will fall before us."

"Whatever." I thrust the sword at his chest.

It bent, the metal useless in this dimension. And yet... the demon voices screeched as one, and I felt the searing pain that pulsed out from their emotions. The sword worked.

But not entirely.

Howell seemed to change before my eyes. He was still human—not a Nephilim like Dionysius had been, but fully human—and yet his eyes took on a yellow hue, his face contorted, and his fingers looked like claws. He lunged at me, shoving me down with superhuman strength. My sword clattered to the side, and he leapt on me, hands around my throat.

I thrust my hands around inside his and pushed out, making his elbows collapse, and whipped my head forward at the same time, head butting him.

He grunted, but didn't lose his grip.

So strong. Stronger than any human. Demon-powered and angry as hell. And I was choking.

I pulled a foot up in between us and shoved it as hard as I could into his groin. Demon-infested or not, no human man could take a direct hit there and not feel it.

He groaned and loosened his grip enough for me to get some leverage and shove him to the side.

I rolled away from him and grabbed my sword. Then I pulled my gun. I stood and edged my way to my driver's side door.

"You come at me again and I'll kill you. All of you."

Howell snarled at me but didn't lunge again.

I jumped into my truck and peeled out of the parking lot, racing back to my side of town. Straight to Chase's church.

"I think I know where the leak came from," I told him when I was safely ensconced in his office. "Desiree's former partner is definitely possessed."

Chase stepped forward and reached toward me, grabbing my hand. "Are you okay?"

"Yeah, just rattled." I told him the whole interaction, both in Kingsley's office and in the parking garage afterward.

"You think he's the one who told Inanna you were coming?"

I nodded. "It's the only thing that makes sense."

"But you also thought your coworker Ken might be possessed," he said.

"True, but I'm not sure he was before we got there. I think something got into him at the scene."

"Have you seen him? Talked to him since then?"

"No. I haven't been in to work. I've checked in with my captain a couple times. Told him I was going to the FBI field office today to compare notes. But I haven't gone down to the precinct."

He released my hand and stepped back, but his posture still radiated concern. "That's something you should probably do. You need to know for sure."

I sighed. "I know. I guess... I'm just a little reluctant to discover the worst. And I definitely don't want to walk into another ambush. I just wish I had any idea what they're planning next. Every step I take, I feel like I'm ten steps back from where I was before. They're so far ahead, how can I possibly stop them?"

"I'm still working on that. I wish I had more to tell you."

"I know. It's not your fault," I said.

"Still, there's got to be *something.*"

"You'll find it," I said more confidently than I felt. What if he didn't find it? What if neither of us found anything, and Inanna took control of this entire dimension? How could we do anything, anyway? Two humans against an ancient and powerful goddess? Not to mention untold thousands of her demon minions and human agents.

"I guess I'll go into work and see what I can find out about Ken," I said.

"Call me and let me know how it goes," Chase said.

I stood, still reluctant to leave the sanctuary of his office.

My phone rang. I pulled it from my pocket and glanced at it. Isaac.

Guilt flooded through me. I hadn't even thought about him—or his declaration—since I'd last seen him.

"I'll talk to you later," I said to Chase. I stepped out from his office and answered the phone. "Hey Doc. What's up?"

"Can you get down to the hospital right away? You're going to want to see this."

"Yeah, I'm on my way. I'll be there soon."

I raced down to the hospital where Isaac worked and hurried inside.

A flood of memories hit me as I entered. A year ago, I'd spent a lot of time here, dealing with young women who had been impregnated with demon spawn. This was where I'd first figured out what Dionysius was doing. Where Isaac and I had first kissed. Amazing how such an ordinary building, with its regular flow of doctors and nurses and patients weaving through halls and rooms, could trigger such powerful emotions.

Isaac was waiting for me in the main lobby. "This way."

"What's going on?"

He glanced at me and kept walking. "It's better if you see it for yourself."

He took me down a hallway to a surgical wing and to the viewing area outside an operating room. Several surgeons stood around what I was pretty sure was a woman, but it was hard to tell between the doctors surrounding her and the blood and viscera everywhere.

I watched as one of the doctors carefully put an organ back into the woman's stomach cavity and eased it into place.

"What's going on?" I asked.

"This woman appeared, seemingly out of nowhere, at the park down the street. Several witnesses. She appeared out of thin air, and a second later, seemed to explode from the inside out. We got to her before she died. Right now, they're trying…" he gagged. "Trying to put her back together."

A person who had come through the dimensions and exploded but survived? This was new. What made this one different? Aloud, I asked, "What… what's the prognosis?"

He shook his head. "No idea. We've never seen anything like this. I mean, obviously I haven't, I'm a labor and delivery doctor. But even last year, with everything… this is the worst trauma to a human body I've ever seen. But her heart was still beating, and she was still breathing when they brought her in."

"Did someone call police? Is there someone interviewing witnesses?"

Isaac nodded. "I think so. But Jack… there's one more thing."

He beckoned me to the side where a bin sat on a table with some torn clothing in it. He put gloves on and pawed through the clothes until he found what he was looking for. He held up what appeared to be a silver bangle with some sort of symbols etched into it. "She had this. She wasn't wearing it—she was holding it in her hand. We had to pry it out of her fingers."

I gestured toward the gloves. "May I?"

"Of course."

I pulled on a pair of gloves and took the bangle from him. Dark, oily power surged through me. It felt like… like the opposite of the sword. Powerful, but dark and soul-sucking rather than life-giving. Even through the glove, I could feel the taint. I wondered how much stronger it would be if I touched it with my bare skin…

But I didn't want to do that. Not until I knew more.

"Don't let anyone touch this, not even another cop. I'm going to bag it into evidence but I need it to be official."

"Not another cop?"

I shook my head. "I'm not sure who I can trust right now."

He raised an eyebrow. "You're going to tell me about it later."

"Promise," I said.

He leaned down and gave me a quick kiss that was somewhere between friendly and romantic. "I'll call you when I'm off work. I'll take you and Beck out, and you can tell me everything."

"Okay," I said.

I left the operating room and called the precinct to try to figure out who had jurisdiction on this case.

"You're downtown now?" the captain asked.

"Yeah, what've you got?"

"Ken is down there taking statements. Can you go give him a hand?"

Ken. So, he'd survived and was back at work. And apparently he hadn't given much detail about what happened at the museum. Did he remember what he'd done? How was I supposed to work with him if he did? That would be interesting.

"Of course. And there may be evidence at the hospital—I'll get that, too," I said.

"Great," my captain said. "I'll let them know you're coming."

"No need. I've got a contact there."

"Sounds good. Be careful."

I hung up and called Desiree. She was awake.

"I went to your office today," I told her. "Talked to Kingsley and your former partner."

"You talked to Howell? How did it go?" Desiree sounded worried.

"Why do you ask?"

"I don't know. He just… there's something off about him. I don't trust him. And I think he could tell. That's why he asked if he could have a different partner. It's nothing I can put my finger on. He's just off."

"I felt the same way," I said, relieved that she wouldn't think I was completely insane if I said he couldn't be trusted. "He showed me his notes from the case, but I couldn't help but feel like he was keeping some stuff secret. Kingsley put him back on the case, and I'm going to be checking in with him."

She sighed. "I really wish they'd let me work."

"I'll keep you up to date with everything I find out. Speaking of, there's another person with the same injuries as our murder victims—but she's still alive." I told her what I'd seen in the operating room. "I'm on my way to the scene right now. And she had a bangle that she was carrying. It looked ancient—it's possible we can connect it to Inanna's cult. I'm going to take it into evidence and show it to Dr. Brantley. See if we can make a positive connection to the deaths and the statue."

I hung up and made my way to the park where the woman had appeared. As usual, I had my sword holstered to my back.

A crowd of bystanders stood around the area cleared by police. Blood spattered the trees and grass and that putrid smell of death and rot filled the air.

I flashed my badge and pushed my way forward.

Ken saw me and waved me over, his big, puppy grin on his face and his eyes alight at seeing me. "Detective, I'm glad you're here. Everyone says they saw something. Can you help take statements?"

Ken seemed normal. No hint of the demonic presence that I'd felt outside the museum. No indication that there was anything off between us. Did he remember what had happened? What he'd done?

I started taking statements, collecting contact information, and gathering as much data as I could, keeping a close eye on Ken the whole time.

Most of the statements were more or less the same. Woman appeared out of thin air and then exploded. Some of the so-called witnesses clearly hadn't seen anything at all and were just basing their statements on what they'd overheard, trying hard to sound important. Some were homeless people looking for a handout by telling me what they thought I wanted to hear.

A few, though, had genuine information. They described the way the air seemed to shimmer and a tear seemed to form. The woman was thrown out—she didn't step or climb through the hole, she was tossed. A smell like sulfur permeated the air when the hole opened. The woman landed and rolled to the ground. Her chest cavity ripped open, like that scene from *Alien*, except all that came out was her intestines.

The woman who had first called 911 sat by an ambulance, clearly in shock. I gathered she'd been closest when the victim appeared out of the sky. The witness was a twenty-something who had been walking her dog—the barking rat still yipped at her feet—when the victim had appeared almost in front of her. She still had traces of flesh stuck to her skin and clothes.

I wanted to talk to her. But Ken had already taken her initial statement, and there were still half a dozen people standing around, so I had to wait to follow up with her.

We finally collected all the statements, and Ken and I regrouped.

"What do you think?" I asked.

"I have no idea. It's bizarre. The statements—at least the real ones, not just the attention-seeking ones—seem pretty consistent."

"That was my assessment too."

"There has to be a rational explanation," Ken said. "I just can't figure what it is."

"Yeah," I said. I looked at him, trying to look through him, see inside. I couldn't feel any trace of demons. But Howell was the only person I'd felt demons in without the sword. It was still strapped to my back, and my hand itched to touch it. But if Ken were possessed or whatever, I didn't want the demon to know I knew.

There was no real element of surprise anymore, but I still didn't want to give anything away that I didn't have to.

I made my way to the witness who had not yet been released. "Good afternoon. I'm Detective Davidson."

She raised tired eyes at me. "Melanie Ward."

"It's nice to meet you, Melanie. I know you already gave your statement, and you're probably anxious to get home and clean up, so I won't keep you, but I may need to call you with some follow-up questions, will that be okay?"

She pulled the blanket around her shoulders a little tighter, even though the weather was perfectly warm, and nodded.

I handed her my card. "If you think of anything—any other details, anything you repressed or forgot, no matter how mundane or seemingly unrelated—please call me. Even the smallest thing can be enough to put the pieces together."

She nodded again.

"Thank you. You can go home as soon as the paramedics give you the okay. Do you need a ride?"

She shook her head. "I'm... I'm okay. We don't live far."

"Okay. You can call me if you need anything."

"Thanks," she said.

I walked back over to Ken. "Did the crime scene cops get all the evidence?"

"I think so," Ken said. "There wasn't much—the paramedics collected most of her when they took her to the hospital. And the other parts were... not really big enough to be collected."

The spatter. The blood and gore that was flung who knew how far and was likely already being devoured by insects and birds.

"Do you have an evidence bag or two on you?" I asked Ken.

"Sure, why?" He retrieved a couple bags and a pair of gloves and handed them to me.

"Just in case," I said. "I'm going to walk around and see if there's anything here. You can go home if you want."

He nodded. "I've been here all afternoon—I'm going to head back to the precinct and file the statements and then call it a day."

I waved him off and began walking a slow grid from the place where the victim's body had landed, scanning the ground for anything she might have dropped, anything that might have come with her from the other side. As soon as Ken was gone, I pulled out my sword and went back to the opening. The scar between dimensions was still there, and I could see through. Probably even get through, if I tried.

The demonic presences I sensed felt benign. As though they wandered the park like any of the pedestrians, uninterested in what was happening over here, not projecting any particular emotion or focus in this direction.

Glancing through the tear in realities revealed nothing of interest, so I finished my search of the area, then went back to the hospital.

Isaac was on duty somewhere, but he had left very specific instructions that only I was allowed to retrieve the woman's clothes and the bangle. I showed my badge and ID and put the things into evidence bags. At least this was one item Inanna wouldn't get.

I snapped several pictures and carefully documented what I had for my files, then took the items to evidence. After logging them in, I left instructions that if anyone, especially FBI, asked for access, to call me immediately. Though I didn't plan to tell Howell about the bangle, there was no guarantee that he wouldn't find out about it, especially since I'd officially logged it. If he did try to take it and give it to Inanna, I wanted to know.

Finally, I called my captain to update him on what I'd done today and went to pick up Beck. His general fussiness hadn't been too bad the last few days, the fever was mild, and his pediatrician hadn't been able to find anything on the tests she'd done, so I'd still been sending him to Gen's, but that vague sense of worry gnawed at me.

What was Inanna doing to him, and how?

TWENTY-SIX

I had just gotten home when Isaac called me.

"You still up for dinner?" he asked.

A sense of peace washed over me. Being with him felt safe, and I was looking forward to decompressing after the day I'd had. "Yeah, I just need to shower," I told him.

"Perfect. That will give me enough time to clean up and come pick you up."

Isaac took us to a small '50s-themed diner, and we sat in a corner. The smell of deep-fried everything filled the air, making my mouth water.

I scooted into the red vinyl booth with Beck, across the table from Isaac.

The waitress handed us water and took our drink orders.

I waited until she left to speak. "Do you know how the woman is? Did she make it through surgery?"

"She's still alive. The damage was extensive. Not sure whether she'll make it."

"Any ID on her?"

Isaac shook his head. "Not yet. She wasn't carrying any."

"I'll send someone by tomorrow, if it's okay, to check her fingerprints. Assuming she hasn't been able to identify herself."

"I'll let her doctors know."

We sat in awkward silence for a few moments. It was never hard to talk to Isaac. That was one of the things I liked about him. So, what was different tonight? Why were we staring at each other with nothing to say?

But I knew the answer. He wouldn't bring it up until I did—I knew him well enough to know that he wouldn't push—but the unspoken question hung in the air.

The waitress came back and took our orders. I ordered a burger and onion rings for me and fries for Beck, focusing my attention on him rather than the tension between me and Isaac.

"There's something about this case that I can't quite figure out," I said at last. "Inanna wants to open the door between dimensions and sort of… absorb this one into hers. But I don't know how she's going to do it. Beck is a key—specifically his blood—but I'm not sure what it will. As for why it has to be his, Tsenaha told me—"

"Who is Tsenaha?"

"The demon in Nevada. Where I was held captive last year. The one who gave me the sword."

He stared at me, the wheels in his head turning behind his eyes.

"Sorry. A lot has happened this week. I… didn't remember not telling you I went to see him."

"It's okay. Go on."

"Tsenaha told me that Trent's bloodline—and therefore Beck's—is descended from the king who banded together with a bunch of demons and gods to take over Inanna's territory thousands of years ago. So, because his ancestors trapped her, his blood is specific to the ritual. But she's already drained so much blood from other potentials. I don't know what's different about Beck's. On top of that, I know she's trying to take over this dimension, but I don't know what that means. Will humans be wiped out? Enslaved? And every lead I turn up is a dead end."

I looked at Isaac, the way his dark eyes studied me, but he didn't speak. He just let me rant, thinking out loud.

The waitress came back with our food. I gave Beck a fry to gnaw on.

"I have to stop her, but I can't get close to her statue to destroy it in either dimension. I can't get through her followers to even begin to get close enough to kill her."

"Why you?"

I looked up. "What?"

"Why does it have to be you? She wants Beck—but she's stuck here. What if you just left town? Hid for awhile?"

"I'm the only one who stands a chance. No one else even knows she exists. There's nothing the cops can do about demons. And the FBI—at least the agent in charge—is in on it. I can kill them with the sword. I can access the other dimension. Without me, she wins for sure."

"What about Chase? Isn't dealing with spiritual forces his job?"

"He can't use the sword, not in the same way I can. It's like... bonded to me or something."

Isaac raised an eyebrow but didn't comment on that. Instead, he asked, "Inanna can't do whatever she wants to do without Beck's blood, right? Well, make it impossible for her to get. My family has a cabin in Colorado. We could go and wait it out."

I stared at him, absorbing what he'd said. Considering it.

Would it work?

Inanna had the blood of the other potentials. Did she have enough without Beck? Tsenaha had told me she didn't need all the artifacts to make her ritual work, just some, but the more she had, the more powerful she would be. Was the same true of the blood? Was that the same as for the artifacts? Ellie Malone had called the statue haunted—was it doing something like the amulet I'd retrieved for Tsenaha had done?

And if I ran away, disappeared, taking Beck and the bangle I'd gotten from the woman in the park, would the world end?

"I... I don't know what to say."

"Say you'll think about it. The offer stands. I have plenty of time off saved up. I can take a leave of absence the minute you say the word."

"Okay. I'll think about it."

Isaac deftly steered the conversation to talk about a baby he'd delivered. The mom had preeclampsia and had to deliver early, and the baby, though small, was healthy. He took Beck from my lap and fed him bites of applesauce, talking about an article he'd read about the neural pathways in babies' brains and how something Beck did indicated high intelligence, but I was only half listening.

Could I really do it? Take Beck and hide until Inanna either failed or succeeded without me there to interfere one way or the other? Could I live with myself if I just abdicated my responsibility? Or was it even my responsibility to begin with? I wasn't a messiah, a chosen one. I wasn't a great warrior or demon hunter. I was a mom, and my first responsibility was to protect my son. After that, I was a cop—a local, insignificant detective, not someone with a destiny.

"I think he's got a tooth coming in," Isaac said, interrupting my thoughts.

"What?" I asked.

"He's chewing on my finger and it feels like there's a tooth coming in."

"He's teething."

"Yeah, seems like."

Beck was teething. I'd been so worried about demonic activity I hadn't even considered any normal explanation. Fever, fussiness, trouble sleeping. He was teething. Maybe Inanna hadn't even touched him. Maybe all my worry was unfounded.

And if that was the case, maybe it really would be okay for me to take him on vacation. Get out of town until whatever happened with Inanna blew over.

Isaac drove us home after dinner and carried a sleeping Beck inside for me. I carefully put him in his crib. Isaac was still in my living room when I came out, and he pulled me into his arms.

"I'm serious about leaving." He kissed me. Not the gentle pecks that he'd given me lately, but a full, deep, hungry kiss that hinted at both the deep affection and the powerful desire that he didn't usually let out.

I surrendered, opening my mouth to deepen the kiss, pulling him tighter against me, suddenly desperate for the connection, for the feeling of being completely wanted.

I don't know how long we stood there, mouths and arms entwined, before he finally pulled away.

"You know where to find me when you decide," he said.

And I knew that meant my decision about being in an exclusive relationship with him, too. Although I had no doubt he'd still take me to Colorado, even if I said no to a relationship.

He gave me a final embrace before leaving.

I sat on the couch for a long time, thinking it through. I needed a second opinion. Someone to bounce the idea off of, someone to talk through the implications. But who could I talk to? My first instinct was to call Bridget. She'd tease and probably insert some anecdote about someone she'd dated at some point who'd put her in a similar situation, but ultimately, her questions would dig deep and get me to focus on what it was I really wanted.

Thinking about her wove sharp pain wove through me. I missed her so much. Sometimes it was harder than others.

And now I didn't have anyone I could count on for this level of girl talk. Who else did I know? Dr. Brantley? Sure, she knew what was going on, but she didn't know the dynamics between me and Isaac, and besides, we weren't exactly the kind of friends who shared intimate details about our lives.

I could call Desiree—but she wasn't exactly unbiased. She'd be thrilled to get rid of me. And she also didn't understand the spiritual side of this or why I felt like I was the only one who could do anything about Inanna.

I finally called the only other person I could think of. The one person I trusted more than anyone else in the world. The one I knew I could count on to tell me the truth, no matter what.

I called Chase.

"I think you should go," he said after I told him about Isaac's offer and my thoughts about being out of Inanna's reach.

"What?"

Despite having wanted a completely unbiased opinion, I guess I wasn't really expecting him to be on board with that plan. A part of me was sort of hoping he'd talk me out of it.

"Don't get me wrong," he said, "I'm not thrilled with the idea of you holing up in a romantic cabin in the middle of nowhere with another guy."

A jolt of excitement rushed through me at that.

"But," he went on, "I want you to be safe. I want Beck to be safe. You can take the sword, just in case. I'll coordinate with Dr. Brantley and see what we can do here. But Dr. Reyes is right. The best-case scenario is that Inanna can't complete her ritual without Beck, and you being away from here will keep everyone safe."

"I guess you're right," I said. My mind rebelled at the idea of running away and hiding. Of not being part of what was going to happen. Of not doing something to stop it.

But all my attempts at being proactive had backfired. Trying to get ahead of the situation had turned out almost as bad as when I'd done nothing. I'd been ambushed. Desiree was injured. Pastor Floyd was dead. Inanna knew where I was and what I could do, and it was only a matter of time until she figured out a way to get to Beck. It didn't seem to matter what I did—either way, people ended up hurt or dead because I'd made the wrong choice. Was there even a right choice anymore?

"I'll think about it."

"Don't think too long," Chase said. "We know whatever she's planning is going to be soon. The quicker you get out of town, the safer you'll be."

"Yeah," I said. But it wasn't an agreement so much as an acknowledgement.

I hung up the phone and sat on the couch for several long hours before finally going to bed.

210

Beck woke up in the middle of the night and cried until I picked him up. He soothed instantly, his face lighting up with his big, beautiful, toothless smile.

Before anything and everyone else, I needed to protect him.

I called Isaac first thing in the morning.

"I'm in," I said. "I'll go with you to Colorado."

I could almost hear the smile in his voice. "I'll take the time off work. Let me take today to get things settled today. Can you be ready to leave first thing tomorrow morning?"

"I just need to wrap up things here, leave instructions for whoever takes the case, and get packed. I'll be ready."

The phone beeped. "Hold on, I'm getting another call." I glanced at the caller ID. It was the captain.

"I have to take this. I'll see you tomorrow."

"See you then," Isaac said.

I hung up on him and answered my captain's call.

"Good news," he said. "We've identified the woman who... the woman from yesterday. Her name is Naomi Crouch. She's part of what we believe is the cult you've been looking for. A search of her apartment found paraphernalia consistent with goddess worship, and we discovered her cell, for lack of a better term. They meet in a strip mall. I'll text you the address. Go down there and see what you can find out. Maybe we can finally get to the bottom of what they're trying to accomplish and why so many people are dead."

Finally, something to go on. "I'm on my way," I said.

I dressed quickly and dropped Beck off at Gen's, then headed to the strip mall where the cult was supposedly headquartered.

My sword safely strapped to my back, I walked toward the building. The sign on the door read *Fellowship of the Divine Protectress* and had Inanna's symbol—the ankh without the cross arms. Other than that, the building was unassuming and nondescript. Like any storefront church, it had neutral blinds on the windows and a little bell that jingled when I opened the door.

The front lobby was decorated with plush chairs covered in a soft floral pattern, a low coffee table strewn with magazines depicting nature and crystals and other things like that, and various prisms and crystals hanging from the walls and ceilings.

I looked around but didn't see or feel anything particularly noteworthy.

"Just a moment," a man's voice called from the back.

A few seconds later, he emerged. Tall, brown hair, and a thin beard, wearing a simple tunic-style shirt and jeans.

"Be blessed," he said with a slight bow of his head. "My name is Nathan. How can I help you?"

I flashed my badge. "My name is Detective Davidson. I'm looking for information on one of your members, Naomi Crouch."

He blinked, a flash of recognition crossing his face before he gave me a blank stare. "I'm sorry, but all our records are confidential."

"Are you aware that Ms. Crouch is in the hospital right now?"

He blinked again and swallowed.

"I got the information for this organization from her apartment. I'm just trying to figure out what happened to her."

"What… what did happen to her? Why is she in the hospital?"

"She exploded."

His face blanched. "She what?"

I shrugged. "Witnesses say she appeared out of nowhere in the middle of a park and then exploded from the inside out."

His fingers toyed with the edge of his tunic. "I see."

"I'm just trying to find out anything I can about her. Her habits, her friends—anything that might help me understand what happened to her. Do you know if she took drugs or had any chronic medical conditions?"

"I… no, I don't think so. Not that she mentioned. She definitely didn't do drugs. We are very focused on holistic healing here. We believe that drug abuse is a symptom of a much larger problem. We have successfully helped more than a dozen addicts to recover."

"Was Ms. Crouch one of them? Is there any chance she could have relapsed?"

"Oh, no. She was never a user. She's one of our founders."

"Okay," I said. "Can you tell me a little more about your organization? What do you do? What do you believe?"

His face lit up at that. "I would be delighted. Please, have a seat."

I sat in one of the plush chairs and he took the seat across from me, leaning forward just enough to look eager without being pushy. He folded his hands over his knees and made eye contact, his expression interested but not demanding.

"The Fellowship of the Divine Protectress was founded by a group of three women, who were searching for meaning in their lives. They tried various healing practices, such as yoga and meditation, and they incorporated crystals and herbs into their everyday lives, and they sought truth and fulfillment. And while they found some benefit from these other practices, they still felt as though something was missing."

The speech was rehearsed, yet conversational. Nathan had learned his lines, but he truly believed them—it wasn't a sales pitch, it was the most genuine proselytization I'd ever seen.

"Then, one day, they uncovered an old story that filled in the missing pieces. The story told of an ancient goddess whose power lay dormant, waiting to be unlocked by true believers. A patroness, if you will, who would grant them all their hearts' desires."

That sounded eerily familiar.

"The Fellowship of the Divine Protectress was born, and they've dedicated the last ten years to sharing knowledge of her to those who are open to the goddess' blessing."

"And you are one of those?" I asked.

He gave a slight nod, his smile radiant.

"What does the goddess give you?"

"Pardon?" Nathan asked.

"You said she granted their hearts' desires. What did she grant you?"

"My blessings are too numerous to count, but the most tangible, the things I share with those who are seeking, is freedom. I spent years in a cycle of debt and self-destruction. I lost my marriage, my kids wouldn't speak to me, and I found solace in drinking. When I met Leann Hart—she's one of the founders—I was at my worst, about to be evicted from my apartment, on the verge of suicide. To make a months-long story short, through the Fellowship, I was given a new job and the strength to put drinking behind me forever. I now have a high-paying job that enables me to contribute to my kids' college, and in my off time, I volunteer here."

Rainbows from the prisms hanging in the window danced on the walls, giving a vaguely aquatic feel to the room. "Why?"

"Why do I volunteer?"

"No, why does the goddess grant you these things?"

"I'm not sure I understand the question," Nathan said.

Pictures on the walls showed smiling people in flowing white gowns, embracing one another as if they didn't have a care in the world. "What do you have to do for the goddess in order to receive her blessings? What's in it for her? Is she just that benevolent, or does she require some sort of tribute, some sort of list of rules and things that you have to follow?"

Nathan chuckled lightly. "The age-old question. What do I have to do to get what I want. All of nature is a balance. Everything has a cost. The goddess provides material prosperity and emotional peace. The cost—though I hardly think it deserves such an unflattering term—is service to her. We worship her because of who she is, not because of what she can offer. Her worship includes giving to her that which she wants and needs."

"And what does she want and need?"

"Followers, for one. She desires devotion, and sharing knowledge of her to others is one of the ways we serve her."

"What else?"

The smile he gave me this time was indulgent and just a little patronizing. "Whatever she asks of us."

"And what is that?"

"It varies from person to person."

"What has she asked of you specifically?"

"That is between me and the goddess."

I paused. He clearly wasn't going to come out and admit that they sacrificed children or stole priceless artifacts or whatever. I had to try something new. "How do you communicate with her?"

"How does anyone communicate with a deity? Through prayer."

"Okay, how does she communicate with you?"

His eyes took on a distant, dreamy look. "It's hard to explain. When I am quiet and my mind is open, it's almost like I can hear her voice. Not audibly, but still distinct."

I knew that sensation all too well. I'd experienced demons talking to me in the other dimension. I could hear them clearly, yet my physical ears didn't seem to hear anything. And I'd seen them influence people. My old doctor, Dr. Campbell, had asked me a direct question that I heard a demon tell him to ask, so somehow, he'd heard, even though he didn't have any conscious knowledge of it.

It had to be something like that.

"How long have you been communicating with the goddess?"

"With the goddess herself? Only a few months. I had to work my way up to be worthy of her personal attention. I communicated with her acolytes, who relayed my messages."

"What about Naomi Crouch or Leann Hart or the other founder, what's her name?"

"Ellie. Ellie Malone."

TWENTY-SEVEN

My head snapped up. The lady with the haunted statue? "Ellie Malone is one of your founders?"

His welcoming expression disappeared as he closed off his emotions to me. "You know her?"

"We've met."

"I see." Nathan stood. "Well, if there's nothing else, I need to get back to work."

I rose and handed him my card. "Thanks for the talk. Call me if you think of anything else that might help me figure out what happened to Naomi."

"Certainly."

I walked slowly back to my truck. Ellie Malone worshipped Inanna?

Then why in the world had she given her statue to a pawn shop, of all places? She had to have known Inanna wanted it. If she actually worshipped Inanna, why wouldn't she have kept the statue safe? Given it to the museum? What was her game?

There was one way to find out.

I drove to Ellie Malone's house and stalked up to the front door.

The smell of cat piss struck me before I could even knock. This woman was disgusting. But I had to know.

I pounded on the door.

The shuffling of footsteps sounded, and the door opened a crack. "Can I help you?" Ellie asked.

"I'm Detective Davidson. I interviewed you about your statue that was stolen from the pawn shop, do you remember?"

She nodded slowly.

"May I come in?"

She paused for a long moment before finally opening the door. She led me to the living room and waved toward the stained couch. I sat, vowing to bathe in bleach later, and smiled at her.

"Can I get you some water or something?"

"No thanks," I said. "I just have a couple quick questions."

"Okay."

I decided to jump right in and hopefully catch her off-guard enough to get her to reveal something. "Did you know the statue belonged to Inanna when you sold it to the pawn shop?"

Her eyes widened and her breath hitched. "How… how do you know about her?"

"You'd be surprised what I know. For example, I know that you were one of the founders of a cult that worships her."

Ellie gaped.

"I know that she needs the statue to complete her collection, and the more pieces she has, the more powerful she'll be."

I waited a moment to see if she would respond. Her mouth moved, but she didn't speak.

"I know there's a ritual, and it's happening soon, and when it does, she'll be more powerful than we can imagine."

Finally, Ellie's expression changed, and her lip curled in a sneer. "If you know so much, why are you here?"

I shrugged. "There are a couple of things I'm still trying to piece together. Like why, if you worshipped her, you got rid of the statue."

"I told you. It was haunted."

"You didn't really inherit it from your uncle, did you? You've been worshipping Inanna for over ten years, and you just got the statue a few months ago."

Her head jerked up, and I could see the calculations happening behind her eyes, as though she was trying to weigh how much to tell me. "I did, actually. Sort of, anyway. He was where I first learned about Inanna. He had a lot of old things from his tour in Iraq. He told me the statue had brought him good luck. And he had it, too. Luck, I mean. A lot of men who came back from the war had PTSD and whatever, but he started a business and almost immediately made more money than he could count. It was because of him that I started worshipping her, and it was because of me that the others did."

"The others—you mean Naomi Crouch and Leann Hart?" One of her cats wound its way between my legs. It wouldn't have been so bad if it didn't look diseased.

Ellie reached out with her foot and nudged the cat away. "We were all searching, and Inanna was exactly what we were looking for. The very definition of woman power—a goddess of fertility and love and war. She took what she wanted, and everyone followed her. We strove to be like her, and through her, we were able to become that. Even before I got the statue, Inanna blessed us."

"Why did you need the statue, then?"

"Because it wasn't enough, at least for me. Naomi and Leann were always best friends. They accepted me because I was the one who had the knowledge of the goddess, the connection to her. But once they got that on their own, they didn't need me anymore. They started to push me out. The Fellowship was jointly owned, but they started finding loopholes in our articles of incorporation that gave them more power and pushed me aside. I thought if I had the statue, they would have to follow me instead of me always being the one clinging to hang on."

"So, you got it from your uncle."

Ellie nodded. "He had money, respect, women—everything he wanted. I thought… since he already had everything, then he didn't need it anymore. So last time I visited him, I took it."

"Did he notice?"

"He didn't say anything. But a week later, he died."

Shit. That was not something I expected.

"Was that when you got rid of it?"

Ellie shook her head. "At first I thought it was a coincidence. But then it started moving, and I started hearing voices. *Her* voice. She made demands. Things… things I couldn't do. Then my cats started dying, one by one. That's when I got rid of it."

"What did she ask you to do?"

"She needed things. She wanted me to submit to her control and to…" Ellie closed her eyes and swallowed. "There was a man. Tall, brown hair and eyes. He lived in Florida. She wanted me to kill him. Before, I always said I'd do anything for her. Even after I took the statue, I promised her I'd do whatever she asked if she'd make me the leader of the others, give me power over them. I even went to Florida and found the man. But… I couldn't do it. I chickened out at the last minute."

Tall, brown hair and eyes. One of the potentials? One of the men Pastor Floyd had said died?

"If it was just killing him, I think maybe I could've done it, but… she wanted his blood."

I sat up straighter, my attention again riveted to her. "His blood?"

She nodded. "She gave me a thing, like an old urn. I was supposed to carve her symbol in his chest and put his blood in there and bring it back to the Fellowship."

"Did she say what it was for?"

Ellie scoffed. "She never told me anything. Just demands and promises of rewards for obedience. I never knew any of her plans."

"But you were supposed to take the jar to the Fellowship?"

Ellie nodded.

The cat came back and rubbed against my leg again. I was definitely retiring these pants after today. "Tell me about the ritual."

"I just told you, I don't know anything. I wouldn't have even known there was a ritual if I hadn't happened to overhear Naomi and Leann talking. Something about Thes... Thesmophoria, that was it."

"What or who is Thesmophoria?"

"Hell if I know."

"What did Naomi and Leann say about it?"

"Just that they had to have everything in order before it began and they needed to get the sacrifice in order for the ascension to take place."

"Any idea what the sacrifice is or what the ascension means?"

"Not a clue. It was right after that when I stopped going to the Fellowship."

"Any idea where I can find Leann?"

Ellie shrugged. "Probably the Fellowship. She basically lives there."

I stood to leave. "Thanks for your help. Call me if you think of anything else."

"Like what?" Ellie asked. "I don't even know what you're looking for."

"Any information on Inanna or the ritual. Anything that would tie Leann or Naomi to the murder of the man you were supposed to kill or anyone else."

Ellie blinked and nodded. I had a feeling she still wasn't telling me everything, but I wasn't sure what to even ask. And I had enough information to request a search warrant for the Fellowship of the Divine Protector.

I called my captain and gave him a nutshell version of what Ellie had told me about the ritual requiring a sacrifice and the connection to the murder of the man in Florida.

"Great work, Jack," he said. "I'll see about getting the warrant."

"Thanks. There's one more thing I want to look into first, but I'll be in to the precinct in a little bit."

219

I drove back to the Fellowship and sat at the other end of the parking lot, just watching the building, and called Dr. Brantley.

"Hey Detective, I apologize for not being in better touch. After the incident at the museum last week, they've tightened security, and I haven't had access."

"That's not what I'm calling about, actually. What do you know about Thesmophoria?"

"Oh, um… not much. It's a ritual celebrating the goddesses Demeter and Persephone. Takes place in the fall, either having to do with fall planting or the harvest, it's not clear which, but it celebrates fertility and Demeter's ascension from the underworld, or something like that."

A ritual. In the fall. Celebrating a goddess' ascension.

"Who was Demeter?"

"A Greek goddess, why?"

"Any chance this ritual predates her? Could it have originated with Inanna?"

"Oh…" Realization dawned in Dr. Brantley's voice. "I don't know. I'll see what I can find out."

"Thanks."

I hung up and clutched my sword. Immediately, I felt the presence of hundreds of demons. I focused my attention. They were congregated in and around the Fellowship building.

More, there were dozens of tears in the fabric between realities where demons had come through. There was one such entrance not far from where I sat.

I got out of my truck and crept closer, listening. The demons milled around, but none appeared to have noticed me. The Fellowship building had some demonic barriers built up—not a full fortress like at the museum, but a few demon-brick walls provided some added protection to the building.

I stepped through the nearest portal and crept along the side of the building, which didn't exist in the demon dimension. Its shadowy reflection from the real world was enough to give me a little bit of cover. And there was what seemed to be a rock wall separating the lobby from the inner room. In the real world, it would be like an invisible forcefield, but here it made a perfect hiding place. I ducked into a corner behind the rock wall, next to what would be the wall between rooms in the real world. Out of sight, unless they were looking for me, but where I could see everything that went on in there.

A shrine sat in what would be the center of the building. It looked like an altar, upon which sat a giant bowl etched with swirls and designs that resembled some sort of ancient language. The top had some sort of grate over it. Crystals, gold jewelry, and an incense burner had been neatly placed there—I presumed they were offerings of some sort.

The shrine was present in both the real world and the demon dimension. The crystals and other things I'd seen in the Fellowship lobby were also present here, but they were different here. Like beacons of energy, they absorbed light and directed it to the shrine. The crystals hanging in the lobby seemed to draw energy from the surrounding landscape and power the crystals in the shrine, making them glow with an otherworldly luminescence.

A wave of energy pulsed out from the shrine, and a figure seemed to rise up from it. A portal within a portal?

What was that, and how did it work?

The figure coalesced, and I had to fight to keep from gasping. *Inanna.*

TWENTY-EIGHT

She was here. Her winged, six-armed body seemed to hover above the shrine.

A woman—human, with dark skin and hair—bowed before the shrine in the real world.

"You called me?" Inanna said.

"Yes, Great One," the woman said.

She didn't seem able to see Inanna through dimensions, but she could obviously hear her. I looked more closely at the shrine. Was it a conduit, somehow? An amplifier that allowed the woman to sense the other side?

"You told me to tell you of any new developments," the woman said. "A woman was here today, asking about our Fellowship and our worship. A detective."

Inanna hissed. "What detective?"

"Detective Davidson, Great One."

"She was *here*? You're certain it was her?"

"Yes, Great One. Nathan took her card."

"How did she—never mind. It doesn't matter. She knows where this place is now. How much did she see?"

"Nothing except the lobby," the woman said.

The tension visibly released from Inanna's form. "Good. We can't afford for her to come nosing around here. There's too much at stake."

"There's one more thing," the woman, still bowing, said. "Nathan mentioned Ellie's name. He said the detective seemed to think it was significant."

Inanna's wings twitched. "It is significant. Call Ellie. Find out what she told the detective."

222

"Yes, Great One," the woman said.

"And call the girl," Inanna said. "We can't delay any longer. We must have the sacrifice safely within our walls."

"It will be as you command, Great One," the woman said.

The girl? What girl? And what was the sacrifice?

Inanna disappeared back into the shrine. Or through the shrine? I really needed to figure out what that thing did. But I couldn't go in there while it was still surrounded by demons.

I stayed hidden, listening as the woman dialed a number.

"Ellie? It's Leann. Can you come down to the Fellowship for a bit?"

I couldn't hear Ellie's response.

"Oh, Ellie, you know better than that. It was your own actions that caused Her Greatness to be displeased with you. You were her chosen one. The one she counted on. You betrayed her. But she is willing to forgive you. To restore you to your rightful place."

Another pause as Ellie responded.

"Please, just come hear me out. Fifteen minutes, and if you still decide you don't want to be part of us, Inanna will release you from your vows."

Leann hung up on Ellie and dialed another number. "It's time," was all she said.

She paced around the office, checking her watch, sifting through paperwork on a desk in the corner, tidying up various surfaces.

A short while later, Ellie Malone pulled up in a car that looked as bad as her house. I almost panicked, then remembered she couldn't see me through the dimensional wall. She shuffled into the Fellowship building and made her way to the back room where the shrine sat.

"What do you want?"

Leann smiled, a look that seemed genuinely friendly and welcoming. "I'm so glad you're here. I spoke to Inanna. In person. It's almost time. Her servants are gathering, and we have an important part to play. She wants you to be among those favored when she returns to our world."

Ellie's face was a mix of skepticism and hope. "Why?"

"What do you mean, why? You were the one who discovered her. Without the knowledge passed to you from your uncle, we wouldn't have known she was real or where she was buried. Because of you, we could tell the archaeologist how to get her out."

The archaeologist? She couldn't mean Dr. Brantley, could she?

Pastor Floyd's words rang in my head. *Don't trust anyone.*

223

If the archaeologist was Dr. Brantley… but I didn't have time to think about that yet.

Leann was still smiling warmly at Ellie. "It's because of you that the goddess is freed from her prison, and she wants to honor you for your service. She is willing to forgive past mistakes. You will be her high priestess."

Excitement blossomed on Ellie's face. "High priestess?"

Leann nodded, beaming. "Above even me and Naomi."

At once, Ellie's look became guarded again. "What do I have to do?"

"Only return to us. Commit yourself to Inanna."

"Okay. I… consider me back, then, I guess."

Leann smiled. "Inanna hoped you would say that."

Ellie looked at the shrine. "Where is she now? Is she here?"

Leann shook her head. "I don't think so, no. She went to prepare for her ascension. By the way, she said something about a detective paying you a visit. What was that about?"

I leaned closer to the barrier that hid me.

"That same detective who interviewed me about the statue," Ellie said absently. Her fingers trailed the stone shrine. "She just wanted to know what I knew about Inanna. I didn't tell her anything useful," she said quickly. "She already knew basically everything. About the ritual. About what Inanna asked me to do to… to that man."

"And you filled in the blanks."

Ellie's eyes narrowed. "There were no blanks to fill in. She already knew what she wanted."

"I see. There is one more thing Inanna asked me to tell you," Leann said.

Ellie edged away, suspicion in her gaze, but Leann stood between her and the exit. She backed into the shrine, standing warily.

"This altar is a gateway," Leann said. "It wasn't when you were here last—we made it so after you left. It allows Inanna to travel between here and her fortress. The problem is, in order to keep it open, it requires fresh sacrifices."

"What do you mean?" Ellie's jaw tightened.

"You know what I mean," Leann said. She pulled a long knife from where it sat on her desk. "Rest assured, you will be honored."

She slowly advanced on Ellie.

Ellie's face paled, contrasting with the heavy layer of makeup she wore on top. She tried to scramble out of reach, but was too slow.

"Your blood will help set the goddess free, and you will be rewarded for your part."

I considered my options. I had to get in there, into the real world, and get Ellie out. But how? She'd pass out if I brought her in here and I'd have to carry her. Plus, that would reveal my position, and I couldn't fight off the demon sentries and carry Ellie out.

Or, I could go into the real world and arrest Leann. That was the best option. I started to open a portal into the real world.

In a last desperate attempt to escape, Ellie pushed Leann out of the way and made a run for the door, catching the knife on her arm and dripping blood across the floor.

She got about halfway when one of the demons standing sentry ripped open a tear between worlds, reached through, and yanked her back. He threw her across the top of the shrine, stunning her long enough for Leann to plunge the knife into her back.

I stifled the gag that threatened to rise up.

Ellie gasped. Blood bubbled up from the wound. Leann and the demon rolled her over so the blood seeped onto the bowl atop the shrine. Leann ripped open Ellie's shirt and carved Inanna's symbol into Ellie's chest, then rolled her back over so the blood dripped from the symbol into the bowl.

I was too late. My hesitation had cost another life. I squeezed my eyes against the sting of tears and peered out at Leann and Ellie.

Ellie's blood didn't spill onto the floor. It seemed to fizzle out of existence on the real world side of the dimensions. I could see it plainly on this side—running over the rocks, drenching them, absorbing into them, but on that side, even though Ellie's body was there, nothing.

Ellie's eyes grew vacant as she stared at the floor, gasping for every last breath. A moment later, the demon dimension seemed to open up and pull her in. She was here now, her body lying across the shrine, her blood still oozing into it.

In the real world, Leann jumped, clearly not expecting Ellie to just disappear. But instead of fear, I saw only amazement and awe in her expression.

The demons advanced on the shrine, closing in around Ellie's body. I had to get out of here before they saw me.

I crept away from the wall, out to the parking lot, and jumped through the portal back into the real world.

My phone buzzed in my pocket.

I pulled it out. Four missed calls from a number I didn't recognize.

It rang again and I answered.

"Detective, I've been trying to get a hold of you," a male voice gasped.

"Who is this?"

"It's Oscar—Gen's friend."

"Oscar, how did you—why are you—"

Nathan appeared from around the other end of the parking lot and burst through the door into the Fellowship building. Where had he been? Why hadn't I seen him?

"I got your number from Gen last week," Oscar said. "But that's not important. I overheard her, on the phone. I don't know what... but she's going to do something to your son."

My world crashed around me, and I completely forgot about Nathan and Inanna.

Gen—no, it wasn't possible.

I turned toward my truck. I had to get to my son.

Gen's car pulled into the parking lot—she was here? Why was she here?

I jogged toward her just as she pulled Beck from the backseat.

A cry split the air.

I screamed.

Gen sauntered from her car into the Fellowship building carrying Beck.

I didn't have time to think, just react. Drawing my sword, I charged toward Gen and my son, bursting through the door of the Fellowship building just behind them.

Gen jerked out of my path.

I whirled. "Give him to me."

Gen gave me a condescending smile. "I'm sorry, Jack. I have really loved working for you. Beck is a great baby. But this is more important." She held a hand to Beck's throat, ready to squeeze the life out of him. "I suggest you stand back."

I drew my gun, but there was no way I would risk firing and hitting Beck. She edged toward the back room and I followed, still with my gun out, but giving her enough space that she didn't strangle my son.

Leann straightened and wiped the knife on the shrine, though it, like the shrine in this dimension, was clean. The only sign of what had happened to Ellie was the few splatters of blood from where her arm had dripped on the floor.

"Bring him here," Leann said.

The door opened behind her and Oscar rushed in. He saw me. "I'm sorry, Detective. I tried to stop her, and then I followed her, and—"

My hand tightened on my sword. "You did the right thing. Thank you." I turned to Gen. "Gen, stop. You don't know what you're doing."

"Actually, I know exactly what I'm doing. I've been following the goddess for years. I will hold great power when she makes this world her own."

She stepped closer to Leann who still held the knife by the shrine. Oscar edged around Gen the other way.

"How… how could you?" I asked. "How can you fall for this kind of trick? You're an independent, educated woman. You're going to let some ancient goddess order you around?"

She eyed me. "You really think only uneducated, gullible fools would follow her? I follow her because I know what she can do. I know who she is and what she has to offer. This world is full of darkness and hate. When the goddess rules, there will be no more imbalance of power between men and women, rich and poor, white and minorities."

I recalled Gen's words when she was talking with her study group. "Someone strong enough to rule who will live forever."

"Exactly," Gen said. "Inanna will make everything right."

I took a step closer. "Please, Gen. That's my son. Is it really worth harming him?"

"Yes."

"No goddess who would demand this is worth following!"

Leann held her arms out, as if to take Beck from Gen.

Gen kept her eyes on me, though her gaze darted toward Oscar to make sure he wasn't getting too close. "I disagree," she said. "Think of all you've seen. All you've dealt with. The misery that infests the world. Inanna will fix that. She's the only one who can. And Beck is the key. It's necessary." Looking past me, she said, "I'm ready."

A horde of demons surged into the room, coalescing right where Gen stood, still holding Beck.

"Gen, what did you do?"

She laughed, but it wasn't her. The voices of dozens of demons echoed through her lips.

She took a step, through a portal in between worlds and into the demon dimension. Awake. I jumped through after her.

Beck slumped against her chest, his tiny mind unable to stay lucid in this dimension, though with the demons inhabiting her body, Gen remained awake.

Here, I could see them all—Gen and the demons that possessed her all lumped together in one disgusting blob of human and monster flesh.

She—they—carried Beck toward the shrine.

"No!" I yelled. "You're not taking him!"

Gen ignored me and kept walking. My attack was intercepted by the other demons in the building, all swarming around me at once.

I slashed my way through them, my rage fueling me, but there were so many.

Someone yelled, and some of the demons behind me howled in rage and pain.

I turned.

Oscar?

In this dimension. Awake. Slashing at demons with a weapon that looked like a scythe.

How?

But I didn't have time to ask. I was just grateful he was ripping into the demons and charging toward Beck.

I don't know how many I killed, my sword ripping through them like they were made of jelly, but at last I reached Gen, just before she got to the shrine.

I grabbed Beck from her arms with one hand and prepared to jump through dimensions back to my own side.

"Give him to me," Oscar shouted.

I looked at him—really looked at him.

Through his human shell, I could see the gargoyle bodies of multiple demons infesting him. His eyes glowed yellow with the reflected glow of demon eyes. He was possessed.

Of course he would be—how else would he have gotten here? And that meant he couldn't be trusted.

"Thanks for your help," I said, "but I've got this."

I turned the other way and was stopped by Gen, who cut off my escape. I backed toward the far wall.

"Jack, please!" Oscar shouted. "We can help. We will keep him safe."

"Who?" I demanded.

"My master. His name is Dumuzi."

Dumuzi. I knew that name. The demon at the daycare had told me he was Inanna's top lackey. "Dumuzi works for Inanna." I slashed with my sword to fend off the demons—at least a dozen still alive— that edged closer.

"No."

Oscar swiped with his scythe and killed a demon, getting a step closer to me.

Gen kicked my knee, sending me tumbling to the ground, clutching Beck to my chest.

228

Oscar fought closer to me. "Dumuzi infiltrated Inanna's cult, but he's been working against her. How do you think you've gotten this far? All the information passed to you through Dr. Brantley, the FBI, even your own human contacts? Dumuzi gave you that information. And what about Beck? All the times he came home sick—Gen had every opportunity to take him to Inanna. It was us who kept her from harming him, but that kind of battle took its toll on him."

I scrambled to my feet, now trapped between Gen and one of the walls. "Why?"

"I think you already know that. We want Beck to live."

"You're trying to finish what Dionysius started."

Oscar—and all his demons—smiled.

"We can protect you. Keep him safe. We're even willing to let you be with him. Not like it was with Trent."

"I just have to let you groom him to be the antichrist."

Oscar shrugged. "But he would live."

Before I had a chance to even be tempted, one of the demons lunged at Oscar and ripped his head from his neck with his bare hands. His body fell to the floor, and the demons inside him were extinguished from existence.

Gen reached me, slammed a fist into my face, and grabbed Beck.

"No!" I clutched for him, but she tore all but the edge of his shirt from my grasp and dashed toward the shrine.

Without another thought, I swiped at her. The sword met some resistance as it ripped through her human flesh—pliant and almost rubbery in this dimension—but the slash was clean, cleaving her through the stomach and the dozens of demons that resided inside her.

Her bottom half crumpled to the floor, and her top half, still clutching my son, toppled onto the shrine next to Ellie's body. Gen's gaze landed on me, almost uncomprehending, as though she hadn't yet processed that I'd killed her.

I reached for my son, my fingers just brushing against his skin, when Inanna appeared through the portal in the shrine.

She picked Beck up in her six arms and looked me over. "I'm impressed. You gave it a noble effort."

With that, she—and Beck—disappeared into the shrine.

TWENTY-NINE

"No!" I screamed. I lunged at the shrine but was pulled back by more demons. I cut them down, but their claws still sliced into me as they tried to rip me apart. More demons erupted from the portal in the shrine, driving me backward faster than I could cut through them.

I wasn't going to rescue Beck this way. I retreated out of the demons' reach and sliced a hole through the dimensions, leaping back to my own side. I was still in the Fellowship building, though. In an office.

Leann and Nathan sat there, eyes popping wide at my sudden appearance.

How much did they know about what went on in the other dimension?

I didn't know and I didn't care. The only thing that mattered was getting Beck back.

I thrust my sword back into its holster and pulled out my gun and badge. "You're under arrest. Both of you."

Leann stood and eyed me. "On what charges?"

"Kidnapping, for one. And murder."

"Those are some pretty serious charges. What evidence do you have?"

"I don't need to share my evidence with you. You're under arrest. Hands behind your back."

When they were both cuffed, I called for backup.

Then I called Chase. "I need you to come," was all I could manage after giving him the address.

I turned back to my two prisoners.

Nathan looked worried, but Leann just sneered at me. "You'll never be able to hold us. You have nothing."

"You are part of a cult that kidnapped my son," I growled.

"Prove it."

"And I watched you murder Ellie Malone."

"Did I? Where's her body?"

"Don't mess with me, bitch. I'll get her body. Your fingerprints are all over the knife."

Plus, with the symbol carved in Ellie's chest, I could now connect Leann to the murder of the guy at the airport, and the feds could connect her to the other murders.

"What knife?" Leann smirked.

Shit. Had she done something with the knife? Last time I saw it, she'd placed it on her desk in the other room. Where was it now? I couldn't leave them alone to go check. If I needed to, I would go into the other dimension to retrieve it. And Ellie's blood was on the floor. She definitely hadn't had time to clean that up yet.

I kept my face neutral, but my mind raced a million miles an hour as I waited for my backup. Inanna had a specific timeframe in which to do the ritual. Thesmophoria, whatever the hell that was. I couldn't get to Beck yet—we would both be killed if I tried. I needed a plan.

"You won't stop us," Leann taunted. "You cannot kill us. We see all. We are many, we are hidden, and we are inevitable. The world will fall before us."

"What is it with cults and their dumbass taglines?" And what the hell was taking backup so long to get here? I had to figure out how to get my son back.

Finally. Sirens.

"Move," I said, shoving both Leann and Nathan out to the parking lot.

Leann sneered at me again as I pushed her down into the backseat of a cruiser. "It doesn't matter where I am. Inanna will come for me. Prison walls are no deterrent to her."

"True," I said. "But you forgot a couple minor details. Inanna can't yet get into this dimension, so she couldn't rescue you even if she wanted to. And I'm betting she doesn't care. All your work, all your sacrifices to bring her forth—she has what she wants now. She doesn't love you any more than she loved Ellie. And now that she has Beck, she doesn't need you. Not to mention that breaking you out of jail would invite way more attention than she wants right now."

For the first time, Leann's smirk wavered.

I decided to push it a little further. "You're expendable. She won't risk Thesmophoria for you. You're nothing to her. And now you're mine."

I slammed the door of the cruiser closed.

I would have so much paperwork to deal with, justifying my arrests, but right now—right now I was just numb.

Inanna had my son. And I couldn't get to him.

I leaned back against my truck and sank to the ground, letting the sobs overtake me. I don't know how long I sat there before a hand rested on my shoulder, jerking me from my despair.

"Jack, I just heard."

I looked up into Chase's concerned green eyes.

"She took him," I said.

"I know."

"I killed Gen."

"Okay."

"I don't know what to do. I don't know how to get him back. I tried, and I…"

Chase sat on the ground beside me and folded me in his arms. "We're going to get him back. I promise."

"You can't promise that," I said.

"Have faith."

But I didn't have faith. My son was gone, about to be a sacrifice that would release an entity on the world that would enslave us all.

Chase nodded toward the Fellowship of the Divine Protectress building. "That's where she was?"

I nodded.

"Show me."

He helped me to my feet and led me toward the building. I pulled my sword, ready to defend against supernatural attack, but there was nothing. No demons in the area. Only a handful of police remained at the scene.

I had to get evidence, though. Enough to hold Leann and Nathan. If I was lucky, enough to convict, but at a minimum I had to prove my charges weren't trumped up.

Chase and I wandered through the empty building.

But all the evidence except a little blood splatter was in the other dimension.

"Keep watch for me," I said. "Let me know if anyone comes in here."

"What are you going to do?"

"What I have to." I pulled my sword and jumped through one of the many rips in reality into the demon dimension.

Ellie's body still lay on the shrine, and Gen's on the ground right next to it. I gazed down at them, wondering how I would manage to lift and transport them by myself.

But, if I could bend physics to my will when it came to running across the country, maybe…

I bent down and willed Ellie's body to conform to my grasp—or maybe I willed my own body to be strong enough to lift her. Either way, I picked her up and hoisted her over my shoulder, carrying her easily. I found a storage closet at the back of the building. Locked in the other dimension. Perfect.

I walked through the walls that were mere shadows in this dimension, tore a hole in reality with my sword, and dropped Ellie's body on the floor of the storage closet in the real world. I returned to the main room and lifted Gen's body. I turned toward the desk.

Leann's knife still sat there.

In both dimensions. She was bluffing.

But that was good. The knife sat on the desk in the real world, and seemed to hover in mid-air where the desk would be in this dimension. I stepped around the shrine and picked it up.

A wave of filth washed over me, much the same as the feeling of dark power that I'd felt when I'd picked up N'merygor's amulet. It was more than just a knife, it was an artifact, like the amulet. What did it do? And was it just another article of power, or was it specifically connected to Inanna?

I suddenly remembered that Oscar had a scythe—was it the same? Where was it now?

There was no sign of it in the building. The demons must've taken it with them.

At any rate, the knife was every bit as solid here as it was in the real world. I wondered briefly if that was what my sword looked like when I didn't bring it into this dimension with me.

But I didn't have time to speculate.

I took the knife and Gen's body and deposited both in the storage room where I'd left Ellie. Even if they couldn't find any blood on it, they'd assume it was just cleaned well, if there weren't any prints, either. And the stab wound would match.

Oscar's body still lay on the floor near the shrine, so I found his head and put his remains in the closet, as well.

This would be enough to hold Leann and Nathan indefinitely.

I went back to the main room and touched the shrine.

It was solid. I couldn't follow Inanna through.

I couldn't get to my son.

I stepped through the hole back into the real-world dimension and put my sword back in the holster on my back. "Come on," I said to Chase. "We have to get the crime scene guys to check the closet."

I hurried out to the main part of the building where they were still tagging everything in the lobby. "There's blood in here," I shouted.

I led one of the techs to the main room and pointed at the floor where Ellie's blood had spattered.

"Look, what's through there? It looks like the trail is leading that way."

It didn't and it wasn't, but that was the direction of the storage closet. The bodies needed to be discovered there, and not by me. Especially since my sword was the weapon that had killed Gen.

The tech followed my pointed finger and found the back hallway.

"There's a weird smell coming from down here," he said, taking the hallway past a couple of offices and meeting rooms, which he glanced into. He stopped in front of the storage room. "It's coming from in here—and it's locked."

In a few short minutes, they would have it open, and I needed to be elsewhere.

"I'm going to head back to the precinct and start my report," I said.

The tech nodded. "We've got this. We'll call you if we find anything."

"Thanks."

I walked with Chase out to the parking lot, still feeling numb. "They're going to find Gen's body. They're going to know that I'm connected to her, and they're going to find out Beck is missing. What do I tell them? How do I…"

I couldn't speak anymore, couldn't think. I had to get into the museum, but I had no idea how to go about that without getting myself and everyone I loved killed.

Chase wrapped me in his embrace. "I have an idea. Call your captain. Tell him you'll finish the paperwork in the morning. Then call Isaac and Dr. Brantley and tell them to get to your apartment. We need to figure out a plan to get Beck back."

"I don't know if I can trust Dr. Brantley. What if she's the one who told Inanna? I thought she was trustworthy, but I just don't know anymore."

"Do you have any other choice?"

I inhaled. I really didn't. Trust or not, I needed her.

"Call her," Chase insisted.

He made sense.

I followed his instructions, saying the words he supplied to me.

"Good," he said. "Now, drive to Gen's house."

I drove, and Chase came in my truck with me.

"Now, go knock on her door."

He walked up with me, hanging out all casual, like he was just along for the ride.

I rang the doorbell. No answer, of course. I rang it again, then knocked and called her name.

At least one neighbor glanced out at me. I knew what he was doing, helping me to create plausible deniability. It was the sort of thing I should've thought of myself, but I was too numb to process it.

After a few more knocks, Chase said, "Now call her."

"The police will have her phone by now."

"Exactly."

I took a deep breath and called Gen's phone.

"Hello?" a voice I didn't recognize answered.

"Hello? Who is this?" I asked, trying to keep my voice as calm as possible.

"Who are you trying to reach?" the voice on the other end asked.

"Gen Levitt. She's my son's nanny."

"I'm sorry to tell you this, ma'am, but something has happened to Ms. Levitt."

"What? What happened? Where is my son? Who is this?" All the panic and horror I'd been feeling for the last hour flooded out of me.

"My name is Officer Pallen. I—"

"Pallen?" I interrupted. Good, someone I knew, sort of, despite not recognizing his voice over the phone. "Pallen, this is Jack. Detective Davidson. What happened to Gen?"

"Oh… oh shit… Detective, Gen is dead. She's been murdered."

I didn't even have to fake the horrified gasp that erupted from my mouth. "What? Where? How? Where are you?"

He gave the address.

"Are you serious? I was just there! How… never mind, I'll be right there."

Chase and I raced back to the Fellowship building. I flashed my badge around. "Where's Pallen?"

Pallen came out from the back room. "This way, Detective." He led me through the room with the shrine, down the hallway, to the storage room where I'd dumped the bodies.

Gen stared up at me with empty eyes.

"That's her. That's my nanny. What… what happened here?"

"We're still gathering evidence," Pallen said.

"These are the only bodies?" I asked.

Pallen nodded. "Two women who look like they were stabbed and a guy with his head ripped off."

I peered around, as though looking for clues. "What about my son? He's not here?"

"We haven't seen anyone other than the two we arrested."

"I was here for that. Leann and Nathan. I arrested them on suspicion of murder, but it wasn't Gen. It was connected to another case. I don't understand why Gen is here. And where the hell is my son?"

"We've got some people going through the files now. There's a complete member roster."

"Where?" I asked.

"This way."

He led me to an office off the hallway were a couple officers were meticulously sorting through piles of paperwork, photographing everything.

"Pallen said there's a member roster?"

One of the others looked up and nodded. He sifted through a couple things and handed me a sheet of paper, a list of names and contact info, updated a few days previous.

I glanced through the names.

There was more than one I recognized.

Jefferson Sezate. My first exploded victim. Rusty Hodge—my victim from the airport. Joe Dunkle—wait. He worked at the airport. Had Hodge been murdered by someone he knew? Someone he thought was on his side?

This just got more twisted.

I finally found Gen's name. "She's here," I said. "Member since..." I looked up at Chase. "She's been a member for almost two years. Long before I knew her, long before Beck was even born. How... how did I not know this?"

"Secret cults aren't usually keen to advertise themselves until they're ready to suck you in," Chase said.

"Okay. I need to file a missing person report," I said. "Come with me to the precinct."

"Detective?" Pallen said from the doorway.

"Yeah?"

"They found her car in the parking lot. There's a car seat in the back."

I followed him out and peered through the vehicle's back window. "That's Beck's."

"We're going to have to keep it in evidence for now." Pallen's voice was apologetic.

"I understand," I said.

What seemed like an eternity later, I had filled out the report. Amber alerts had been issued, but I knew it wouldn't matter. Beck was where no human could reach him.

Not even me.

Especially not me.

Chase followed me in his car back to my apartment. Isaac and Dr. Brantley were already there, waiting outside.

"What's going on?" Isaac asked.

"They have Beck."

"Who?" Isaac demanded.

"The demons. Inanna."

Dr. Brantley slapped a hand over her mouth, her eyes wide with horror.

"Good God," Isaac breathed.

"Let's get inside where we can talk," Chase said.

I pulled my keys out and promptly dropped them. Chase picked them up and unlocked the door for me. He gently pushed me down to the couch. "I'll make coffee. It's going to be a long night."

I told Isaac and Dr. Brantley what had happened with Ellie and Leann and Nathan at the Fellowship building.

"Leann called Gen and said it's time, and then Gen brought Beck, and…"

Isaac leapt to his feet. "Where is she? I'll kill her."

"Too late," I said. "I already did."

He sat down, his face a mixture of shock and admiration.

"But it was too late," I said. "Inanna came out of the portal in the shrine and took him. And now the portal is closed and her fortress is guarded, and I can't get to him."

Chase came in and handed me a cup of coffee, then returned and served the others.

"Thanks," Dr. Brantley said. She looked at me. "I've been researching Thesmophoria. This time of year is, in a lot of cultures and belief systems, traditionally when the veil between dimensions is thinner. There are a lot of theories, from the alignment of the stars to the moon to the weather to the equinox, and everything in between. The tradition of Samhain suggests it's because the natural world is preparing to withdraw from the realm of life and growth, so it's a time of transition, like a doorway between the season of life and the season of death. Thesmophoria is based in the same thinking. The veil is thinner, the worlds closer to colliding. Therefore, timing her ascension with this event is vital to her success."

"When?" I asked. "When is Thesmophoria?"

"Two days. Midnight on the night of the full moon."

Two days. Inanna and her demon army were holding my infant son captive for two days in their impenetrable fortress, at which point they would sacrifice him in the most horrifying way possible.

THIRTY

Isaac grabbed my hand. "We're going to get him back."

"Yes, we are." I looked at Dr. Brantley. "Can you get inside the museum? I need to know the layout. Where the statue is, where the other end of the portal in the shrine comes out, how many people are in there. Everything you can tell me."

Dr. Brantley nodded. "I think so. I won't be able to go after-hours, but I should be able to get in first thing tomorrow morning. Dr. Smith still owes me at least a couple favors. It should be enough to be able to take a look around."

"Thank you." I turned to Isaac. "The woman who… exploded. Naomi. Do you have any updates on her? I want to talk to her. Unless she's in a coma, I need to have some time with her."

"I will check."

I nodded and turned to Chase. "I need artifacts."

He tilted his head slightly to the side. "What do you mean? What kind of artifacts?"

"Like the amulet I retrieved for Tsenaha and all the stuff Inanna has been collecting, but not demonic, evil ones. Good ones. Like my sword."

The stare he gave me was completely blank. "I wouldn't even know where to start looking for something like that.

"I need to try an experiment. I need to go somewhere with a portal to the other dimension."

"Like where?" Chase asked.

"Closest place I can think of is the Fellowship building. There are lots of tears there, and they're fresh."

"I'll come with you," Chase said.

"Me too," Isaac jumped in.

"I have to admit, I'm pretty curious, too," Dr. Brantley said.

I nodded. "Okay. Field trip."

Everyone piled into my truck, and I drove to the Fellowship building. It was deserted now, all the police and crime scene investigators having gone for the night.

"What do you need here?" Chase asked.

"I need to test a theory about my sword."

There was a portal in the parking lot, so I didn't need to go inside the building at all. I stepped through, but left my sword arm on the real-world side. It was a strange sensation—always before I'd led with the sword, but now, though the sword enabled me to pass into the other dimension, it felt sort of like an out-of-body experience to leave my arm outside. My arm tingled, like it was asleep, and my mind felt fuzzy—like I was on the verge of passing out.

But it worked. I looked back through the dimensional wall and saw the sword, just as real here as there, but looking sort of like it was floating next to my ethereal hand.

I stepped back into the real world. "Now I know how to look for artifacts. But I just need to figure out where."

"Inanna was looking for relics related to her worship, right?" Dr. Brantley said.

I nodded. "The amulet I retrieved for Tsenaha has healing powers, and the knife Leann used to sacrifice Ellie also has some sort of inherent power. I'm not sure exactly what it does, but I could feel it when I touched it."

"Okay, so we need to look for holy relics, then, yes?"

"I guess it makes sense," I said. I looked at Chase. "Does your church have anything that might qualify?"

Chase opened his mouth and closed it again. He ran a hand through his hair. "I have no idea. I don't know what makes something a relic. Inanna used blood to... like... consecrate things. I highly doubt my church has anything like that."

"That may not be the only way, though. Tsenaha suggested that they used blood to bond it to themselves, but that it took a lot of time and skill to craft one. And we're talking about the opposite of Inanna, so, maybe there are other ways."

"We can look," Chase said.

"I have to go through the other dimension," I said, handing him my keys. "I can't guarantee I'll find another portal close by. Meet me there."

Chase took my keys and drove with Isaac and Dr. Brantley to his church, while I followed along, jogging through the other dimension.

Even here, Chase's church was like a haven. An aura of peace rested on it. I inhaled, feeling refreshed despite the stale stench of sulfur that permeated the demon dimension.

In the real world, Chase unlocked the doors and turned off the alarms. In the other dimension, I wandered slowly through the buildings—the main building with the sanctuary and classrooms, and then the second, smaller building where the offices were—looking for something that existed on both sides like my sword or the knife.

I'd almost given up when I saw it.

In Pastor Floyd's old office. A cross, hanging on the wall, seeming almost to glow in the dim light, and fully present in both the real world and the spiritual.

I ripped open a hole between dimensions and stepped through. "Chase, in here!"

Chase came down the hall and unlocked the door to Pastor Floyd's office. Dr. Brantley and Isaac followed close behind.

Chase exhaled deeply when he walked in. "I haven't been in here since... since the day he died."

"I'm sorry," I said.

"It's okay. I needed to come in here eventually. If it helps get Beck back, it's worth it. Did you find something?"

I nodded and pointed to the cross.

Chase walked slowly across the room and removed it from the nail where it hung. "That makes as much sense as anything. He got it on a trip to the Vatican several years ago. It's supposed to be a relic from the Renaissance."

"Good. Now I just have to figure out what it does."

"How?"

"I have no idea," I said.

"Let's go in my office," Chase suggested.

Dr. Brantley and Isaac followed him down the hall while I traipsed through the walls and met them there.

Chase had a couple of chairs opposite his desk, which Dr. Brantley and Isaac took, while he wheeled his desk chair around to sit by them. I stood next to him and opened a portal, stepping back into the real world.

"Where do we start?" I asked.

"Tell me more about the sword," Dr. Brantley said. "Understanding that might help us."

"Um... okay, I can use it to get into the other dimension. The only time I could do it before was when I had part of my soul trapped there, attached to a demon. With the sword, I can enter without being

242

possessed or whatever. But it wasn't always like that—it's getting stronger the more I use it. Like my connection to it is growing, and it's giving me more power."

"What do you mean by more power?" Dr. Brantley asked.

"I'm stronger, faster. And I don't get worn out. When I was there before, the longer I stayed, the more of a toll it took on me. I was passed out for almost a week after the last time I was there with the demon."

"Okay, that's a good start. Try using the cross instead of the sword. Can you still access the other dimension?"

I put the sword down and held the cross with both hands, really focusing on it and trying to form a connection with it, then felt the air around me.

I couldn't sense the other dimension at all, couldn't see the tear I'd made in reality.

"Nothing."

"Good, that's something."

I raised an eyebrow at her.

"It's science. And also detective work. We've just narrowed the possibilities. Now, hold the sword."

I obeyed.

Dr. Brantley picked up the cross and held it out to me. "You mentioned that when you held the amulet that you retrieved for the demon and when you held the knife, you felt power surging through you. What do you feel when you hold the cross?"

I took it from her and felt a surge of something, like a shock of static electricity, jolt through me.

"What was that?" Chase asked.

"I'm not sure. I didn't feel it when I held the cross by itself, but with the sword, it feels… warm, I guess. Like it has its own energy source."

"Good," Dr. Brantley said. "Now, when you feel the other dimension, is there anything different?"

Despite my misgivings about her, she genuinely seemed like she was trying to help. I turned my attention on the other dimension. Everything came into focus. The red haze that typified the atmosphere seemed to dissipate, and the colors seemed more distinct, more varied. "Whoa."

"What?" Chase, Isaac, and Dr. Brantley asked all together.

"I can see. Like I just put on a pair of glasses, or… binoculars. Usually the other dimension is dim and hazy, like walking through a really smoggy city. But things are sharper. Clearer. And I can see further."

I stepped through the hole I'd made and fully entered the other dimension. Even though it was now evening, it was as though a light had been turned on. I turned in the general direction of Mesa. Far away on the horizon, I could see what I thought was Inanna's fortress. Like a medieval castle, it rose from the red earth, defying me to try to enter.

"This is amazing. I can get intel long before they know where I am."

"Focus," Dr. Brantley said. Her voice came through with perfect clarity, even through the dimensional wall. "What other senses are enhanced? Can you hear further? What happens when you touch something? What does it smell like?"

She stopped talking so I could hone my senses. "The smell of sulfur is both stronger and easier to bear. I don't know how to explain it—I can smell more of it, but it's not making me sick."

I closed my eyes and listened. I could hear voices far away. Demons. I couldn't tell exactly where they were coming from, but it wasn't close. And it didn't seem like they were talking about anything relevant—something about needing to feed, looking for a willing soul. Gross, but not something that mattered to me at the moment.

I bent down and touched the ground.

The dirt felt hot, burning like the sand in the desert on a hot day, but without harming me.

"It's like everything is enhanced, but at the same time, it's less dangerous to me."

"Try hurting yourself. Just something small, like a nick with a rock. To see if the cross helps you heal like the amulet did for the demon."

I picked up a rock and scraped it against my arm. I could feel the pain like a distant echo of what it should feel like. Drops bubbled up on my skin.

I didn't heal.

I stepped back through the hole into the real world and showed off the scrape. As soon as I set down the sword and the cross, the sting of the scrape registered.

"Ow."

"It hurts now?" Dr. Brantley asked.

I nodded.

"Good. I mean, not good that it hurts, but good that now we know. The cross enhances your senses, but doesn't heal. It mutes pain

and negative consequences, but only as long as you're holding them."
She looked at Chase. "Do you have a Band-Aid?"

He jumped up and went into the other room, returning with a first aid kit.

Isaac took it from him and cleaned and bandaged my scrape.

"Ideally, we need to find another artifact, one that will help you heal," Dr. Brantley said. "But, if we can't, just make sure you don't let go of the cross until you are somewhere safe and can handle whatever damage you took."

"How am I supposed to fight when I'm holding artifacts?"

"That's easy enough," Isaac said. "As long as you're touching it, it should work, right? You don't necessarily have to have it in your hand?"

"One way to find out," I said. I jumped through dimensions and stuck the cross in the back of my pants so it was touching me but I wasn't holding it.

The effects remained—all my senses were enhanced. I went back to my own dimension.

"It worked."

"Okay, so we'll just tape it to your body or something. Under your shirt or somewhere it won't be in your way."

"That's good. So now I have superpowered strength, and I can't feel when I get injured until after the fact. But it's not enough. I'm still just one human against legions of demons. And any wrong move could mean they'll kill my son. I wish somehow I could get some other people into the other dimension. Or that I had more weapons that could kill demons here to give you guys when I flush them out. Or... there's a thousand things I wish."

"One thing at a time," Dr. Brantley said. "We're making progress."

I knew she was right, but her methodical, scientific brain might actually make me crazy.

I stood up and paced my living room. "I can't afford for the progress to be this slow. In two days—if I'm lucky, it will be that long—a demon goddess is going to sacrifice my son to take over this dimension, and I have... nothing."

"We know she has legions at her disposal. We need a way to thin the herd, so to speak," Isaac said. "Last year, you were able to kill some of them by pushing them through portals. Could you do that again? Especially if your strength is increased?"

"Probably."

"Good," Dr. Brantley said. "That's a plan. If you can get close enough to the fortress without being seen, you could pre-open some portals to draw them through maybe. And we could be waiting on the other side."

Yes. This was good.

"That will take care of some. But there's only so many times the same trick is likely to work."

"So, that's Part A," Dr. Brantley said. "Thin the herd. Let's talk about Part B."

We stayed up well into the night discussing plans of attack and contingencies. By the time everyone went home to get some sleep, we had made some progress. And if everything went well, I might actually get close to the fortress.

But I knew too well not everything would go as planned. And my son was still in danger.

THIRTY-ONE

Early the next morning, Dr. Brantley texted me with pictures of the museum, the inner room, and Inanna's statue, which seemed to have all—or at least most—of the artifacts. The crown sat atop her head. The star was in one hand—wait, Dr. Smith knew what we were looking for and hadn't reported it? Had he forgotten? Was he being controlled by Inanna? But Dr. Brantley had sent me the picture, which meant she wasn't trying to hide information from me.

The small statue of the goddess herself, too, sat in an alcove on one of the larger statue's feet. The statue of the bull was in another hand, and a relic of her symbol, the armless ankh, was in another.

Dr. Brantley's part of the plan was to dismantle the statue. Not yet—we couldn't afford for Inanna to figure out what we were doing—but when I attacked in the demon dimension, she would separate the artifacts from the statue to hopefully weaken Inanna. She had what she called a catchpole—the museum used it to adjust objects on high shelves and for hanging and adjusting lighting or chandeliers or other things in hard-to-reach places—that she could use to grab the artifacts. I browsed through the pictures one at a time, studying the layout of the room.

I stopped and stared at one, and quickly texted Dr. Brantley back. *What is that in the corner by the desk? The thing that looks like a well?*

Her text came back a few moments later with close-ups. *It's an urn. It was found near the statue's burial site. There was another, similar urn that disappeared in transit.*

Symbols and crystals decorated this urn.

The shrine in the Fellowship building. That was the missing urn that went with this one. And unless I was terribly mistaken, this was the other side of the portal Inanna traveled through.

I filed that information away and continued to browse through the pictures.

Security guards were stationed at every doorway, and I was pretty sure, though I wouldn't be able to tell until I saw them in person, that some of them were demons.

There was no sign of Beck, but I didn't expect there to be. Inanna would be keeping him in the demon dimension and away from prying eyes. Plus, he'd be unconscious, so she wouldn't have to worry about feeding him.

My breasts hurt at the thought. I'd been pumping, but I ached to feed my son. Would he sustain long-term damage from lack of food or consciousness? Or would being in the other dimension keep him in some sort of stasis?

Either way, it did no good to worry. I would fight for him to the death. Just not mine, I hoped.

And for that to happen, I needed to focus on what I could control.

I still needed a way to kill hundreds, maybe thousands of demons. So, I went to the next place after Chase's church I could think of that might have random bi-dimensional artifacts.

The pawn shop where Ellie Malone had originally sold the statue.

The hole in the dimensional wall was almost sealed, but it was open enough for me to squeeze through. The red haze pressed in around me, but I was familiar enough with this place. I walked into the space where the pawn shop existed in the real world and scanned the room for anything that was present on both sides.

There were several items. Far more than I would've guessed. I walked around the room, touching small trinkets, crystals, and jewelry. Most of them had that oily, tainted residue. I wasn't sure whether or not I could use them, but I didn't like the way they made me feel. Even if I could channel the power, it felt wrong. Like the price would be too high.

Joy glanced up occasionally from where she sat behind the counter reading, as though she could sense me, or maybe she saw the objects moving from the corner of her eye, but she didn't investigate.

Finally, in the back corner of the room, I found a small necklace that felt right—not tainted like the other things. Gold, or at least gold-plated in the real world, I was pretty sure. It looked sort of like a cross with a snake draped over it. I didn't know what it meant, but the energy that pulsed through me when I picked it up felt clean.

A tingle ran through me, concentrating on the bandage on my arm where I'd scraped it the night before.

I pulled the bandage off. No sign of the scrape.

A healing amulet.

I set it down and went back outside to the original tear in realities. Using my sword to open it a little wider, I stepped through and went into the store.

Joy looked up this time, surprised. "Detective. Hi. Did you have more questions?"

"Nope." I walked straight back to the back corner of the store where the necklace sat in a glass case. "I want to buy this."

She brought her key and unlocked the case.

It was more than I'd anticipated, but no amount would have been too much.

My phone rang. It was Isaac.

"Naomi is awake," he said.

"I'll be right there," I said.

I drove down to Isaac's hospital. He was waiting for me, flashing his credentials to lead me through the hallways to where Naomi lay.

The hallways seemed unusually quiet. My footsteps echoed on the floor, sounding extra loud in my ears, the sensation feeling like the calm before a storm, that eerie expectation of impending catastrophe looming over me.

Naomi lay in her bed, bandages covering most of her body, her face purple and blue from bruising.

She blinked up at me. "Do I know you?" she asked.

"No," I said. "My name is Detective Jack Davidson."

Recognition flashed in her eyes.

"So, you've heard of me," I said.

She nodded.

"Good. Then we don't have to waste time pretending not to understand one another. Do you know what happened to you? How you ended up in the hospital?"

She shook her head. "Not exactly, no."

"You appeared out of nowhere in the park. I think you traveled between dimensions with the help of Inanna's demons."

Her eyes widened slightly as she comprehended how much I actually knew and that I was serious about not beating around the bush. "I don't know what you're talking about."

I clenched my fists. I *so* didn't have time for this.

Isaac stepped forward, his smile wide enough to reveal his perfect teeth. "Ms. Crouch, I'm Dr. Reyes. Your surgeons and nurses have told you what you've been through. But as I'm sure you're aware, they don't have any idea about the other dimension or what really happened to you. I am one of the few doctors in this hospital aware of the supernatural elements of your case. Please, we need to know everything in order to help you."

Naomi nodded and winced from whatever pain that motion sent through her. "I was sent on a mission to retrieve an important artifact for her."

"The bangle."

"Yes."

"Do you know what it is or what it does?"

She shook her head. "It was in a museum in Italy. All I had to do was get it out of the case."

"How did you get to Italy and back so fast?"

"I was... transported."

"Tell me about that."

"I don't know what happened exactly. I was told to meditate, to open my mind and allow Inanna's servants to transport me. I felt very sleepy, and it was like an out-of-body experience, where I could sort of feel my body moving, but I had no control. I think I was flying? Anyway, I watched the world pass under me in a blur, and then I woke up inside the museum. I broke the glass case and grabbed the bangle, then the same thing happened—I fell asleep and flew back here. I woke up in the park, and then... nothing until I woke up here."

"I need you to tell me everything you know about Inanna and the ritual she's planning—how it works, when it's happening, what she still needs—everything."

Naomi's face paled and she shook her head slowly. "I... I can't."

"Can't or won't?"

She looked up at me, pleading. "Can't."

I narrowed my eyes at her. "Did anyone tell you what happened to you?"

She looked a little green and nodded. "They said I was... turned inside out."

"Inanna did that to you. She used you, and when she was done, she left you to die. You're lucky to be alive. Others have died from this. I found one body that had completely exploded. Pieces of him were splattered all over a warehouse. Inanna got what she wanted, and he's in a thousand pieces in separate baggies in the morgue. That could've been you."

"You don't understand what she'll do to me if I betray her." Her voice cracked, and her body trembled.

"Is it really worse than exploding from the inside out? That's what she does to people who serve her. You really want to be part of that?"

She shook her head, but it wasn't the shake of not wanting to be part of Inanna's plan, it was a shake of refusal. She still had no intention of telling me what I needed to know.

I decided to try a different tack. "I raided your Fellowship building yesterday. Leann and Nathan have been arrested."

"On what charges?" Naomi asked. She sounded terrified. Seriously, how was getting arrested more frightening than being ripped inside out by demons?

"Murder. Ellie and Gen are dead. Killed with the ceremonial knife Leann had. And Gen gave Inanna *my* son."

Leann's eyes widened. "Oh, goddess. I—I didn't know that's what they were planning."

"Bullshit."

She stared at me.

"You worship an evil demon goddess. You know she's killed people. She almost killed you. Leann called Gen and told her it was time, which means Leann and Gen both knew Inanna wanted my son for something. You were Leann's partner, which means you knew too."

"I—"

She didn't say anything. Probably best for her that way. The less she incriminated herself, the better.

"The ritual Inanna is planning will kill a lot more people than just my son," I went on. "Inanna doesn't care about you. She's not going to keep whatever promises she made to you about power and glory. You think being turned inside out is bad? Just wait until she rules this dimension. She'll destroy everyone and everything. There is no torment you can imagine that will be as bad as what she has planned. I'm going to stop her, one way or another, and it's up to you whether you're on my side or hers when I take her down."

Naomi sat still for a long time before answering. "What do you need from me?"

Good. Covering her own ass. Cooperating.

"How does the ritual work? How is Inanna going to open the doors between dimensions?"

"Blood."

"Yeah, I got that part. *How?*"

"She's… I don't know how to explain it, exactly, but it's like she's still chained up. Whatever her enemy did to her to bind her, the effects are still lingering. She's bound to her statue, which is why she's here, not back where she came from."

"She can't be *that* bound. I've seen her travel. She killed Pastor Floyd, and she's been to the Fellowship building."

"Right, she's got, like, a diameter, sort of, I think? I don't know how far it goes, but the further she gets from her statue, the weaker she gets."

Good. That was good information. "And the blood will release those chains?"

Naomi nodded. "I don't know how. I just know that blood dissolves the barriers. And it's specifically the blood of her enemies, which is why she needed so much of it."

So much of it... Oh, right. She'd killed at least three, possibly more of the potentials.

"Where is she keeping the blood?"

"She has, like, urns or something. But she's had to use some of them up. They couldn't even transport her without loosening the bindings that held her. Airport maintenance logs said it was magnetic interference or routine maintenance on the planes, but she had to use some of her enemies just to get here. It weakened the chains, but didn't remove them. She couldn't even get all her artifacts without sacrificing some blood. She tried—Ellie had a statue that Inanna kept trying to get but couldn't. She had to send humans after them instead of retrieving them herself. She's been saving up, storing as much blood as she can to use all at once."

Gross.

But made sense in a weird, demonic way.

"But why Beck? He's tiny. He doesn't have that much blood in the first place. And why did she want him alive?"

"I have no idea." But her eyes and the set of her jaw told me she was lying.

"Take a guess, then."

She glared at me, but also seemed afraid enough that it was worth it to tell me what I wanted to know. "Hypothetically, based on something I read once, it may be partly because he's innocent. The more pure a sacrifice is, the more powerful it is. Also, since his is the most pure, she also needs it to be fresh. The ritual isn't just about the blood, it's about the action itself. She couldn't afford to keep a bunch of grown men trapped in her fortress indefinitely, but she needed the extra blood. Your son will be the catalyst that ties everything together."

She shifted slightly, her eyes darting away.

"What aren't you telling me?" I demanded.

THIRTY-TWO

Naomi's face paled beneath her bruises, and the fingertips that showed out of her bandages squeezed her sheets. "Part of what makes him so powerful is that he's not just descended from an ancient enemy. He's the child of her current enemy."

"What do you mean?"

"It's you. When you declared war on their kind a year ago, you made yourself a formidable enemy. She couldn't stay in her own land—it has been torn apart by war, between humans and gods, for centuries. She no longer has power there. But this place—it went unclaimed. As the conqueror, you were the first in line to claim this territory. But you didn't, so it's still sort of up for grabs, but it sort of belongs to you. So as long as she's in your city, she's at a disadvantage. Your son is tied to both you and her ancient enemy, so his blood…"

Well, shit.

But also, good. The fact that she feared me would give me an edge. *If* I could figure out how to use it.

"Anything else you can tell me? About the ritual, anything?"

She shook her head. "I know the timing needs to be precise, but I don't know exactly when that needs to be. The ritual itself is pretty straightforward. At the right moment, your son's blood will be poured over her statue, where she'll be present, and then she'll be able to cross over into this dimension."

"She's also planning to absorb this dimension into her own. How does that work?"

"I think that's a side-effect of her crossing over. When she opens the door between dimensions, the tear will just keep widening, until there is no veil anymore."

Great.

254

So, I had to kill her before she crossed over.

But I knew that already. Because if she crossed over, it meant she'd killed my son.

I stood. "You've been very helpful. Thank you."

I had a message from Cameron on my phone when I got back out to my truck, demanding that I call her.

I did.

"Jack, I saw the Amber Alert. I couldn't believe it at first. Why didn't you say something?"

A thousand emotions clashed inside me. The truth was, I was so focused on figuring out how to get him back, I didn't even consider any of the other people who cared about him. "I... I didn't know what to say."

"Are you home?"

"Not yet, but I'm on my way there now."

"I'm on my way over."

She arrived at my house a short time later. "Tell me everything. He disappeared when he was with Gen? And now Gen is dead?"

I told her everything. Actually everything, not just the everything that I would tell to the cops or anyone else who didn't know what was really going on, including everything about Inanna. She'd helped me last year take down a demon. She knew enough.

"What can I do?" she asked when I finally finished talking.

I inhaled deeply. "I don't want you to get hurt," I said.

"That may be the stupidest thing you've ever said," she told me. "This is my nephew. And from what you've said, you need all the help you can get."

I nodded slowly. "Okay. Here's the plan."

I told her where we'd go, what we'd do, how we'd do it.

"I'll be there," she said. She sat back on the couch. "I can't believe Gen would do something like that. I mean... there were odd things about her, for sure, but everyone has odd quirks, you know? She was very adamant about certain aspects of the things she believed, but I never would've imagined."

She looked up at me, tears in her eyes. "I'm so sorry, Jack. This is all my fault. I never should've recommended her. If I'd had any idea..."

I grabbed her hand. "Hey, no. Stop that. None of this is your fault. I knew something was off awhile ago, but I trusted her too. There's no way you could have known."

She nodded, but she didn't look convinced.

"We're going to get him back," I said.

"Damn straight." Cameron's jaw firmed.

"You should go home and get some rest," I said.

"What about you? Are you going to be able to sleep?"

I gave her a wry smile. "What do you think?"

"I think you need to be at the top of your game, and you can't afford any mistakes. Take a sleeping pill if you have to."

That was easier said than done. What if I overslept? What if…

I didn't have time for what-ifs. And I would be okay even if I didn't sleep.

Cameron went home and I lay in bed, unable to relax. The apartment felt empty without Beck in it. Too silent without his soft breathing or occasional cries. Oppressive without the assurance that everything would be okay.

I woke from a fitful sleep to the sound of my doorbell ringing.

I shuffled out of bed and opened it to Isaac.

"You look terrible." He kissed me on the cheek.

"Thanks."

"I brought coffee. What else do you need?"

"Nothing. Let me get dressed."

I dressed in the most comfortable pants that I could still attach a gun to, sturdy shoes, and a tank top. Last, I put the necklace I'd bought at the pawn shop around my neck.

I went back out to the living room, and Isaac taped the cross to my torso.

"How does that feel?" he asked.

I shrugged. "As good as it can, I think."

"Good. It's almost time."

A moment later, Chase knocked at the door.

"I brought coffee," he said.

A weird wave of emotion washed over me, stinging my eyes with tears. Such a little thing, but both of them knew that hot coffee would soothe my nerves and be a thing of comfort.

"I love you guys."

They both glanced from me to each other and back, shifting their gazes in discomfort.

"Shall we, then?" Chase asked.

I nodded.

Chase headed out the door, but Isaac put his hand on my shoulder to hold me back.

He waited until Chase was out of hearing, and turned me around to face him.

"Listen, what I said before… I meant every word."

256

"Isaac, I can't right now."

"I know. That's why I wanted to tell you. I know you don't feel the same way about me. And you maybe never will. But I want you to know it's okay. Even if you never feel for me the way I feel for you, even if we're only ever just friends, and even if you end up with him"—he nodded toward the door where Chase had gone out—"it doesn't change anything. I'm still here for you. I'll still be here for whatever you need. And I'll always love you."

Tears stung my eyes. As always, he seemed to read my mind. And I hated that he was inadvertently hurt, but part of me loved him even more because of it.

I wrapped my arms around him in a tight hug. "Thank you."

We headed out to the parking lot where Chase stood waiting. Isaac got in his car, but Chase grabbed my hand.

"I have something for you," he said. He reached into his pocket and pulled out a ring shaped into a dove intertwined with a snake. "This was my grandmother's. She never took it off, but she told me she wanted me to have it when she died. The dove symbolizes peace, but it also symbolizes hope. The serpent symbolizes cunning and wisdom. My grandmother told me she had great hopes for me, and that she believed I would be wise and do great things. I… I don't know what's going to happen today, but I know hope is what will keep you going, so this is just a small token for you to keep your hope alive."

He held out my hand and put the ring on my ring finger on my right hand.

The ring warmed, sending glowing strength through me. Was this… an artifact?

I didn't have time to test it, but even if it wasn't, it accomplished what he intended. I squeezed his hand. "Thank you."

He nodded. "You're welcome. Let's do this."

We each got into our own cars. Chase and Isaac headed toward Mesa, while I made my way toward the Fellowship building.

I pulled out my sword and stepped through one of the holes between dimensions, walking slowly toward the shrine in the center. The sword radiated strength through me, the cross at my back warmed, giving all my senses clarity.

The place was deserted. No humans, no demons—nothing. Not even a police presence. Just the waving strands of police tape marking it as a crime scene.

The interior was in disarray, numbers tagging everything as evidence, files left open on desks, fingerprint dust coating everything.

The shrine was just a big pot now, the grate that had held the offerings gone somewhere, probably into evidence or to the lab to check for traces of blood.

I wasn't entirely sure if my plan would work, but it was my best shot.

Someone approached from the direction of the parking lot, their shoes crunching on the asphalt outside, a sound I picked up with my artifact-enhanced hearing.

A moment later, I felt presences nearby, both human and demon. I turned.

Someone was in this dimension, coming closer, but I couldn't see them yet. I turned in a slow circle, scanning the landscape.

A shadowy figure came toward me from the other side of the building. Only one figure, accompanied by a host of demonic entities. A possessed human, fully in this dimension through their demon hosts.

I readied my sword, waiting for them to approach. Then almost dropped it as the person came into view.

"Ken?"

"Hello, Jack," Ken said. But not just Ken. It was as though he and the demons spoke together in unison. "We thought you might come back here."

Wait... I recognized one of those demons. I'd interacted with him before, but I couldn't place when or where.

"Yeah?" I asked, trying to sound casual. "Is there something here to find?"

Ken shrugged, a smile playing on his lips. "No. But you'll grasp at any straw you can."

He crossed his arms, and that's when I noticed it. His arms. Ken had them—one of the demons inside him didn't. He was working with the demon from the daycare.

"It's you," I said to the demon. He snarled, lust for revenge pulsing from him, overpowering whatever emotions the other demons might have radiated.

"I'm surprised it took you this long to figure it out," Ken said.

"You had me fooled," I said to Ken, though it sort of applied to the demon too. "I really thought you were, at best, a pawn. A willing victim. I had no idea you were in on all this. How long have you been spying on me?"

"A long time." Ken laughed, the demons' laughter echoing along with him.

"All those times you pretended to be interested in me, asking me out, asking about Beck, it was all just a ruse?"

"Oh, no, it was real. I genuinely liked you. But I chose my side."

"It was that easy? You're just an Inanna acolyte now? Sorry to break it to you, but you chose wrong. I'm gonna kill her, and then I'm gonna kill all of her minions."

"You are more foolish than I realized. I don't worship Inanna. And if you were half as smart as you think you are, you would realize we're your only chance."

Another presence materialized, flying toward us at an unearthly speed, and landed next to Ken.

"I know you," I said. "You were watching me outside the pawn shop."

"Indeed," the demon said.

I gasped as the realization hit me. "Dumuzi."

"Guilty as charged," the demon grinned. "I believe Oscar told you of my proposal before his untimely death. We will help you. Protect both you and Beck. Even allow you to raise him. But he must not know of his destiny until it's time. And he will fulfill the prophecies."

Something told me he was lying. Then again, demons weren't known for their honesty.

"That's not a choice," I said.

Ken bared his teeth in what was ostensibly a smile, but it looked feral with the demon fangs showing through. "That's why you'll lose. You have no identity, no structure, no one to count on. This is your last chance. Join us."

"No thanks. And honestly, I can't believe you'd fall for that shit after everything that went down last year. These things can't be trusted."

"I didn't fall for anything. But I know where true power lies and how to achieve it. I'd only served Dionysius a few months when you killed him. But Dumuzi has taken his place as the leader, and I am his most trusted servant. Together, we will rise."

I considered it for a long moment. I had a treaty with Tsenaha. Would a treaty with Dumuzi be so much worse? At least Beck would be alive. They wouldn't kill him, and that would buy me time to figure something else out.

"Let's say I agree. How will you help me take down Inanna?"

"We'll transport you to her fortress," Dumuzi said. "I can get you inside. I have followers, demons who are loyal to me within her ranks. At my word, they'll turn on her and her minions."

That was a lie.

I wasn't sure how I knew—but he was definitely lying.

About which part, though? About having followers? About letting me raise Beck? About transporting me? Was he even really against Inanna, or was this a ploy to deliver me to her?

"You're almost out of time," Dumuzi said. "You can join me now. Serve me and let me protect you and your son."

The ring—Chase's grandmother's ring—on my finger pulsed. That's where the sensation was coming from. The absolute certain knowledge that he had no intention of keeping his end of any bargain we made was amplified through the ring.

I edged toward the shrine and the agitation coming from Ken grew stronger.

Either way, it was a trap.

Ken wandered closer, angling so that he stood between me and the shrine. He stuck his thumbs in his back pockets, the very picture of casual, but the ring pulsed stronger.

I sidestepped toward the desk, or the ghostlike representation of it that I could see here. Nothing currently on it was present in this dimension, so I just scanned the paperwork that littered the surface.

"I still don't quite get what your endgame was," I said, trying to buy time. "Why keep me from knowing all this time, only to reveal yourself now?"

"The time for secrecy and hidden agendas is past. In a very short while, Inanna will complete her ritual, and everyone will know who she is. It's more important that I serve Dumuzi now rather than try to maintain a façade."

The ring throbbed more powerfully than it had yet.

He was here to distract me, but not from that.

He still stood between me and the shrine. Guarding it, while trying to seem like he wasn't. For whatever reason, he and Dumuzi didn't want me going through.

Dumuzi stepped closer to him, and he opened his arms, as though in a welcoming embrace.

A moment later, Dumuzi had entered him, joining with both him and the other demons that possessed him.

I lunged toward him, jabbing with the sword.

He dodged easily, knocking the sword to the side, jolting my whole body with the force of his blow.

He was strong. Too strong. The demons inside him laughed, their voices echoing around the atmosphere.

It wasn't just Ken I was fighting, and it wasn't just a demon. It was the strength and speed of a whole army of demons, including a demon who had the strength and power of a god.

I lunged again, slashing with my sword, which he batted away without even seeming to notice. I did get him—his human hand bled and some of the demon hands somewhere within him sizzled—but it didn't seem to matter. They were too strong.

I managed to land a blow to his stomach, slicing a gash in it, but the countless demons were almost like layers of armor. I'd gotten through the first one—maybe even a few—but there were dozens left that I would have to cut through in order to actually harm him.

He advanced toward me, demon claws extending from Ken's human hands, circling slowly, as if debating whether to attack or waiting for me to make the first move.

He decided on attacking, launching toward me with the strength and speed of all the demon power he possessed, his hand making contact with my stomach.

I barely had time to react, let alone defend.

I stumbled back, my side bleeding from where his demon claws had penetrated my skin, and though I felt where the injury was, the cross taped to my torso kept me from registering it as pain.

The necklace I wore warmed, sending a healing glow through my body, and in a moment I couldn't even feel the wound. I'd killed a demon wearing a similar artifact, though, so I couldn't get too cocky.

Ken's eyes widened, but it didn't stop him. He rushed me again, and I sidestepped, my sword still raised, slashing wildly. Again, I cut through a couple of layers, but not enough to even wound him significantly.

There had to be a way to level the playing field.

Shifting my body so my feet were solidly under me once again, I edged around in a circle, as though trying to make my way toward the shrine.

Ken snarled and rushed me again. Just as he got close, I used the sword to slash a hole between realities. Ken fell through the hole and rolled, stumbling to his feet as I jumped through after him and stabbed his body with my sword. The sword bent, his human body withstanding the now-rubbery texture of the sword. But the supernatural element still worked. The demons screeched, writhing in pain.

Ken's face registered shock for a fraction of a second before his body contorted, then seemed to peel open. The demons rushed out from him, like being snapped from a rubber band from this reality to

261

the demon dimension, causing his intestines to burst outward, being flung to the far reaches of the office, splattering on the walls, the floor, the ceiling, the shrine... me.

I gagged at the stench that the demons left behind in their effort to flee.

Somehow, the sulfur and evil residue mixed with the human gore made it a million times worse. Like it had in the warehouse.

But I didn't have time to deal with that at the moment. I still had to get to my son.

I jumped back through the hole I'd made into the demon dimension. The demons were still there, surrounding the shrine.

"I'm so done with you," I said.

I charged, swinging my sword.

They were much easier to take on one at a time. In moments I had cut my way through them, their clouds of dust billowing around me as they disintegrated. Some of them fled, including Dumuzi, but they were no longer my priority.

I jumped up on top of the bowl-shaped shrine. The top was covered by a bubble, of sorts, almost like a glass lid over the top, holding me up.

It needed fresh blood to keep the portal open.

I used my sword to slice open a gash on my arm.

The necklace I wore grew warm and my arm healed almost before I could get any drops out onto the shrine.

Damn it. I did *not* have time for this.

I removed the necklace and shoved it in my pocket, then tried again.

My blood dripped from my arm, sizzling as it hit the invisible lid over the shrine. Light shone from the crystals still hanging in the front lobby, the prisms dancing across the growing puddle that seemed suspended in midair above the urn.

It hung there for several long seconds, until I was certain that I'd been wrong and it wouldn't work. But then the barrier beneath my feet became squishy, like Jell-O, and a moment later I was plummeting through darkness.

THIRTY-THREE

My breath caught, and my stomach felt like it was going to come out my mouth, the way it does on that free-fall ride at Castles and Coasters.

And as quickly as I had time to register that thought, my body slowed, and I began to ascend through the other shrine, like swimming toward the surface of the water after jumping in.

My head broke through, and I was in the back room of the museum.

Inside Inanna's fortress.

Demons swarmed around, turning to gape as I materialized before them.

In the real world, at least a couple dozen humans, wearing white tunics, like the one Rusty Hodge had been wearing when I found his body outside the airport, circled the statue, holding hands and chanting. I recognized a couple of them—Joe Dunkle from the airport, Desiree's partner, Agent Howell, and… Dr. Smith? Jolly, white-bearded Dr. Smith, the museum's archaeologist?

I leapt from the shrine, swinging my sword at anything within my reach. Several demons fell to my slashing. At least a dozen more advanced.

I killed them all, the righteous fury inside me giving me strength and precision.

A slow clapping echoed throughout the fortress chamber. "Well done." Inanna's voice. "I genuinely didn't expect you to get this far."

I turned to face her. She stood by her idol, a metallic twin that matched her nearly ten-foot height, with its bat-like wings, arms snaking out, and evil, red eyes.

Beck lay in Inanna's arms. Naked except for his diaper. Unconscious.

I lunged toward her, but stopped as she raised a knife over his tiny chest.

I rushed forward, but a horde of demons grabbed me, holding me back.

"Sadly for you, you're too late. It's done now," Inanna taunted.

She placed Beck into a crook made by one of the statue's arms."

"I'm gonna kill you," I seethed.

Inanna ignored me and etched her symbol into Beck's chest. She smiled at me. "This way he'll bleed out slowly."

He remained blessedly unconscious. I strained against the demons who held me.

Blood bubbled out from him, dripping onto the statue.

Their claws dug into my flesh, and though the pain didn't register, I also realized with horror that I wasn't healing. The amulet was still in my pocket.

Inanna took the knife with Beck's blood staining it and used it to smash the urns that were held in three of the six hands, plus the ones nestled into nooks around the statue's body. Blood poured out of each of them, dripping down the arms onto the body, saturating it with the dark, viscous fluid. At the same moment, in the real world, the cult members broke their circle, and every one of them slit their own wrists, spilling blood all over the statue and the museum lab.

I lashed out with my sword, killing some of the demons holding me captive, but unable to make much headway against them.

Inanna chanted something in a language I didn't understand, then she stepped into her statue. Merged with it, much the way Dumuzi had merged with Ken. Became it.

I could see the change as it happened—the statue surged to life, and it glowed with an ethereal aura that transcended dimensions. The statue was alive in the real world.

"Midnight! It's supposed to be—midnight!" I screamed, slashing to try to get close to her.

Inanna just held Beck. "You humans and your insistence that things be exactly as you demand. Midnight is a construct of your limited understanding of time. The exact moment of midnight is hardly different than the minutes or even days leading up to it or away from it. There's nothing inherently powerful about that moment more than any other." She grinned, showing her fangs. "Besides, where I'm from, it is midnight."

She still held Beck with that one arm, but now she moved, statue and all, stepping slowly at first, then more fluidly, as if the blood she'd drenched herself in created the lubrication for her joints to be able to move.

She took a step toward me, then another.

The demons holding me parted enough for her to come through, while the humans in the other dimension collapsed from blood loss. She backhanded me with one of her arms, sending me stumbling into the army of demons.

"Kill her," she said.

She turned to walk away, still holding my bleeding son.

"No!" I screamed.

I lashed out with my sword, slashing at the demons that grabbed for me, hacking off arms and legs, slicing through torsos, lopping off heads.

And still they came. Still they swarmed around me, another one closing in as soon as I killed the demon in front of it.

I sliced through the air and opened a portal, then kicked a demon through it. He couldn't survive there, and he evaporated almost immediately.

I kept kicking, slashing, fighting my way toward Inanna, but even in her slow, statue-state, she made more progress than I did as she stomped through the museum—in both dimensions—knocking down doors as she made her way outside.

Someone screamed.

Someone human.

In this—the demon—dimension.

I pushed through the demons holding me far enough to see.

In Inanna's wake there was a strange shimmering in the air. Sort of the way it looked when I peered through a tear in the dimensional walls. Reality bent behind her, this reality bleeding into the other.

Visitors to the museum seemed stunned, staring at her as she tramped through the halls, seeming to wonder if she was an exhibit or a stunt of some kind.

Until Beck cried.

When she'd shifted to absorb the real dimension, she'd taken him with her, so this one was no longer keeping him unconscious.

His tiny, bleeding form shocked people into action—some of them running away, others grabbing their own children and huddling out of sight, while still others stood still, as though unsure whether this was a gimmick.

One man approached the statue. "Hey, stop! Give me the kid. He's hurt!"

Inanna turned slowly to look at him, then swiped at him, sending him flying across the room.

The others who'd been frozen until that point seemed to snap out of their indecision, running toward the exits.

I slashed a hole in the dimensional wall and shoved a demon through it. He was one of the solid ones, that turned into his human form on the other side.

Where were...

Dr. Brantley and Chase burst into the building through the door in the back. Dr. Brantley clutched my police-issued taser and zapped him. It barely slowed him, but it did startle him enough that when I jumped through the hole after him, he didn't have time to react before I pulled my gun and shot him.

His human body fell to the ground, and his spirit materialized in the demon dimension.

Dr. Brantley was already moving on to her part of the plan. She held the taser ready, but didn't use it. She wouldn't, as long as Inanna still had Beck.

Using the catchpole, she circled around to Inanna's other side, out of view when Inanna was glaring at me.

She knocked one of the urns from Inanna's hand.

It crashed to the floor, but it was now almost empty.

One of Inanna's cult followers rushed at Dr. Brantley, and she shoved her taser in his chest, sending him crashing, writhing to the ground.

Inanna ignored the distraction, moving toward the front of the building—the main exit.

Dr. Brantley reached with the pole again, this time grabbing the miniature statue that sat nestled in one of the statue's nooks. The one that Ellie had sold to the pawn shop. The statue came away, and almost immediately, the Inanna-idol seemed to lose some of its luster.

Inanna growled, but it didn't seem to faze her.

Dr. Brantley grabbed the statue from where it tumbled to the floor.

Inanna turned. I thought she might be moving more slowly than before.

From her other side, Chase attacked, running toward her and knocking the eight-pointed star to the ground. He dashed to pick it up, then darted out of reach.

Inanna turned that direction, as though unsure who to go for.

Her attention divided, I moved in, diving through the hole into the demon dimension. Using all my supernatural speed and strength, bending the reality to my will, I ran with my sword pointed ahead.

I slammed my sword into her stomach, expecting it to bounce off, metal on metal. Instead, it sank deep into her.

I looked up into a face that seemed just as surprised as mine was, and pulled back, taking the sword with me. Something seeped out, greenish and putrid, from the hole.

Ignoring that, I swung my sword again, this time aiming for the arm that held Beck.

The sword sliced straight through, not even seeming to slow. I let go with one hand and caught Beck—demon arm and all—and pulled him to my chest.

I slammed the sword into Inanna's torso again, this time pushing her back to give myself some leverage, and bounded away. Inanna had built up her fortress in this dimension, so it wasn't as simple as jumping through immaterial human-dimension walls. And demons surround the perimeter. I would have a hard time getting out this way.

"Jack!" Dr. Brantley's voice came through the din. "This way!"

I turned to see her running down a hallway and followed. The hallway in the demon fortress mirrored that in the real world. But there were demons at my end of it.

I sliced open a hole in reality and ran through, almost bumping into Dr. Brantley.

"Here," she said, using a key card to open the door at the end of the hallway, revealing an office.

There was a window on the opposite side of the room that looked out onto a greenspace that was, at the moment, unoccupied. I pulled my gun and used the butt to smash the window. Dr. Brantley jumped through and held out her arms. "Give me the baby."

A jolt of fear ran through me, along with Pastor Floyd's words. *Don't trust anyone.*

I'd already been betrayed by Gen. And I'd just gotten my son back. There was no way.

Dr. Brantley nodded, her eyes filling with compassion. "Okay. Here." She extended her hand to me. I shoved the sword into the holster on my back and I took her hand, clutching Beck to my chest with my other hand, and jumped out the window.

"I'll get Dr. Reyes," she said.

She darted around the building to where Isaac was supposed to be waiting.

I tossed Inanna's arm to the side and slumped against the wall. The stucco already felt mushy, like a sand castle.

I could deal with that later. Right now…

Beck was unconscious again, but he was breathing. I pulled him away from my chest to examine his wound. It wasn't as deep as I'd worried it would be. It would need stitches, but it didn't look like she'd punctured anything vital. I wadded up the bottom of my shirt to put pressure on it, then gently stroked his face.

"Beck, baby, Mama's here. Wake up, honey."

No response.

Tears streamed down my face. Where the hell was Isaac?

I continued to jiggle him, trying to entice him with milk, anything to get him to wake up.

I moved, and something jabbed me in the hip. Something in my pocket.

I shifted slightly and stuck my hand in. The healing amulet.

I pulled it out. Maybe…

Moving my shirt, I pressed the amulet against the gash.

Nothing happened. Maybe, like the sword, it only worked on me because I was connected to it.

Or maybe it only worked in the other dimension. I pulled myself to my feet and, holding the sword, searched for an open portal.

Nothing. The closest one was back through the window, the office, the hallway—the one I'd come through. There were more on the opposite side of the building, the back lot where the loading bay was—but that was too far, and it was guarded by demons.

"Come on," I screamed aloud. "Can't I get a break?"

THIRTY-FOUR

I slashed at the sky with the sword.

The sky glowed, bent... and opened.

What in the... that had never happened before. The doors only opened one direction. *That would be like... chopping down a tree while it's still an acorn.*

That's what the demon had told me when I'd first tried to open a portal from my side to the demon dimension. *You have to create the portal there for it to be open here.*

But I'd done it. I'd opened the portal from the wrong side.

Without stopping to wonder about it, I stepped through, clutching the amulet in my hand.

Golden warmth spread through me. Aches I hadn't even registered because of the cross and the adrenaline eased, and I felt whole again. I pressed the amulet against Beck's wound. The glowing warmth flowed through me. Before my eyes, the gash sealed, and the skin knitted back together, leaving a thin scar.

Beck's eyes opened, and he gasped for air, then let out a beautiful, angry wail.

I stepped back through into my own dimension, Beck's hollering echoing around me. I laughed and cried and gasped for breath. Beck screeched and rooted for food.

"Okay, baby, I'm working on it," I laughed through my tears.

Part of me worried that demons might come after me, but they all seemed to be on the other side of the building, following Inanna.

By the time Isaac and Dr. Brantley rounded the corner a few moments later, I was sitting in the grass, and he was happily eating, staring up at me with his big brown eyes that looked so much like Trent's.

"Thank God," Isaac said, screeching to a halt beside me.

I nodded.

"How is he? Let me look."

I moved my hand so he could see the scar.

"I don't understand," he said.

"Healing amulet," I said, holding it up. "I got it from the pawn shop."

His mouth dropped open, and for a few moments he examined Beck's tiny body, looking for any sign of anything wrong. He caressed my face with his hand. "I'm glad it worked."

"Me too," I said. "But it only works in the other dimension."

"Speaking of…" Dr. Brantley said. She paused, glancing from Beck to the museum and back. "I know you need to take care of your son. But you should know Inanna is about half a mile down the street now. Things are… weird."

"She's opening up the rift between dimensions," I said. "The destruction is following her. She's marking her territory, in a way. Everything she touches is falling into her domain."

"Is she just going to walk forever, until the whole world is under her control?" Isaac asked.

"Fly," Dr. Brantley said. "Once she got outside, she started using her wings."

"I don't know," I said. "This is her home base now, her point of origin. So, I suspect it will grow from here. Watch." I touched the wall behind me and my hand squished into it.

"What is that?" Isaac said.

"It's this world fading. The stronger she gets, the more will fall to her."

"I'm sorry, Jack, but you need to get out there. You're the only one who has the slightest chance of stopping her," Dr. Brantley said.

She was right.

I hated it. But if I didn't stop her, what I'd done to save Beck wouldn't matter anyway.

"Help me up," I said.

Isaac grabbed my outstretched hand and pulled me to my feet.

"I'm sorry, baby, but Mama has to go to work."

He wailed when I stopped feeding him, but his eyes drifted closed a moment later, into what seemed to be a normal, healthy sleep.

"Have you seen Cameron?" I asked Isaac.

He nodded. "Last time I saw her she was in the main parking lot."

"Perfect. Let's go."

I found Cameron in a crowd of people who all scurried around like a mob waiting for Black Friday sales, but with no real direction. Some of them had cell phones out, recording the devastation. Cameron was trying to shoo people away, telling them to get out of town as quickly as possible. A few listened, but most of them stared at the trail of destruction growing behind Inanna.

"Cam!" I yelled.

She turned, and her eyes landed on Beck in my arms. Relief flooded her face, and she pushed toward me.

I handed Beck to her. "Get him to your parents' house, and all of you stay there until you hear from me. If you don't hear from me by tonight, start driving and don't stop. Get as far away as you can."

"What are you going to do?" she asked.

"I'm going to stop this."

Cameron nodded, her jaw firming. "See you tonight."

She put Beck in the car seat in the back of her car and drove the opposite direction from where Inanna had gone.

When she was out of sight, I clasped the healing amulet around my neck again. "You ready?" I asked Dr. Brantley and Isaac.

They both nodded.

"Where's Chase?" I asked.

"He was in the front of the museum last time I saw him," Dr. Brantley said.

I made my way toward the front of the museum.

Chase lay on the lobby floor, blood pooling around his head. "No, no, no!" I murmured, rushing to him and sliding to my knees by his side. I felt for a pulse and found one, weak though it was. The two dimensions had melded here, enough so that I didn't even have to cut through the dimensional wall to feel the amulet working. It heated up against my skin as soon as I touched him, sending energy through me into him. The bleeding stopped, and his heartbeat grew stronger. A moment later he opened his eyes.

"Jack."

Relief flooded over me. "You're alive."

"Apparently. Inanna knocked me down and took back the star. Beck?"

"Safe. I'm going after Inanna."

"Let's go."

"You've been injured. You should stay."

Chase looked at me like I'd said the stupidest thing he'd ever heard. "Let's go."

I smiled despite myself and handed him my second gun. "Hopefully this will slow her down enough for me to get to her."

He took it and held it like he'd been practicing for this.

I stalked down the street in the real world toward Inanna, trailed by Chase, Dr. Brantley, and Isaac, taking in the full scope of what she had done, the damage she wreaked in both dimensions.

Bodies littered the sidewalk—humans—dead, with huge gaping holes in their chests, but apparently drained of blood, since nothing seeped out from the wounds.

How? What was she doing?

She was getting stronger—faster. The bodies along the street were more frequent, and the bubble where the dimensions bled together was getting wider. I was fully inside both now. The others, too, were absorbed into the demon dimension, awake, as the demon dimension absorbed the human.

And if I was inside the demon dimension, that meant I could exert some control over it.

I started running, bending the earth under me to catch up to Inanna.

But that meant leaving my team behind. I paused, closed my eyes, and willed the ground to fold under them, as well. Willed it to move as they ran, like a treadmill, so they covered more ground alongside me.

Seconds later, I drew close enough to the goddess to shout at her. "Hey, bitch, where do you think you're going?"

She turned, gazing down at me from where she hovered in the air. A smile that sent my stomach into a spin cycle spread across her face that was somehow both metallic and demonic. "Back so soon?"

"I had such fun last time we hung out."

She swept a few of her hands around in a circle. "What do you think of my kingdom?"

"At this rate you won't even have a kingdom," I said, nodding toward a heap of bodies.

"Oh, don't worry. This will level out. I just need a little more power to make the transition complete." She emphasized her words by aiming the star she held down at a man who stood crouched over a woman on the sidewalk. A beam like a laser bolt of lightning shot out from the star. I could almost see—more like seeing with the same sort of perception that allowed me to sense the demon dimension than seeing with my physical eyes—the soul of the man being sucked from him and powering Inanna. With every life she took, she grew stronger. Her wings beat more rapidly, and the statue seemed more a part of her. And where the man lay, crumpled on top of the woman who gasped for breath under his weight, the wall between dimensions crumbled.

The woman was fully absorbed into this dimension now. She finally got out from under the man's body, and her eyes landed on

Inanna, then darted around at the landscape that was somehow both hers and the barren desert landscape of the other dimension.

She turned to run, but Inanna aimed the star at her.

"No!" I shouted. I did the only thing I could think of. I dove between Inanna and the woman, my sword raised like a shield to stop her bolt.

The sword seemed to absorb whatever power she sent through it. It grew warm in my hands, but not too hot to hold, and seemed to quiver with energy.

Inanna screamed and the energy bolt cut off, her body wavering as she tried to keep aloft.

She snarled in rage. "Get her!"

A contingent of demons converged around me. My sword still throbbed with light, as though still radiating whatever energy Inanna had pulsed into it.

Behind her, Chase and Isaac and Dr. Brantley moved into position. Good. If I could distract the demons long enough…

I grinned at the demon closest to me. "Come on, then."

He charged and I swung. I barely touched him, but the gash I sliced in his torso widened and spread. Choking, he gazed down at the wound as it consumed him and he died.

Awesome.

I took the offensive now, lunging and slicing. If even a nick was enough with my super-powered sword, then I could dispatch these guys almost effortlessly.

Okay, that was an exaggeration.

Despite the energy pulsing through me from the sword, my body was beginning to tire from the constant movement, but I couldn't stop. I had to get closer to Inanna.

She trusted her minions to keep me away from her, but I was making progress. It was working.

But I had backup of my own.

My team was in place.

I nodded to Dr. Brantley.

Using the taser, she targeted the various artifacts attached to Inanna's statue, starting with the crown.

The electric charge sped through the metal.

Inanna was a physical and spiritual being, even inside the protective shell of the statue, so that much voltage had to do something… didn't it?

I sliced through another demon. The super-powered energy that I'd somehow stolen from Inanna into my sword was starting to dull, the wounds it inflicted no longer instantly fatal with a scratch.

I thrust my sword deep into a demon's chest and pushed past him.

Inanna had recovered from whatever the taser had done and swung at Dr. Brantley with one of her many arms. Dr. Brantley soared through the air, crashing into a wall—or the mushy substitute of a wall that it had become.

That was a small relief, at least—she was less likely to be injured that way.

A moment later, Chase came at Inanna from the other side. He fired my gun, striking her straight at her chest.

Nothing.

The bullet glanced off and fell to the ground a few feet away.

It did draw her attention, though. She turned toward him.

He fired again, this time aiming for the statue of the bull. The impact was enough to jar it loose from her grip and send it tumbling to the ground. That left the opening for Isaac—he now had the catchpole. He reached in and yanked the bull out of reach.

Inanna hissed and turned toward him, but he was already running. He turned down an alley that was still completely in the real world and threw the bull into a garbage dumpster. Then, he poured a can of gas over it, struck a match, and tossed it in.

Flames erupted, enveloping the refuse and the statue of the bull. Inanna shrieked, and her bronze-toned flesh darkened in the spot where the bull had been.

It was working!

Another demon rushed at me from the side. Too quickly. And I was too focused on Isaac. The demon crushed me to the ground and lifted a clawed hand, aiming for my neck.

I writhed, but couldn't move enough. His hand came down, slicing a deep gash from my chin to my chest. The cross on my torso warmed first, blocking the sensation, and the amulet around my neck heated as the skin knit itself back together.

I rolled against the arm that held him up, making him lose his balance, allowing me to slide out from under him and stab him with my sword.

In clear view, Chase fired again and again at Inanna, sometimes hitting artifacts, sometimes not. A couple of the urns were smashed, and Dr. Brantley had managed to tase her again, this time hitting one of her wings. Inanna slowed as her body absorbed the shock, sending her thudding to the ground. But she found her feet and stalked toward Isaac.

Isaac saw her coming and braced himself, the pole sticking out. She aimed the star toward him, and he dove behind the dumpster. The blast hit the brick wall behind him, causing it to melt.

I ran that direction, for the moment free of Inanna's minions. I got close enough to jab at her with my sword, slicing a gash in one of her arms—one that held the artifact shaped like an ankh without the arms.

That putrid goo seeped from the gash, and Inanna turned toward me.

Good. I hacked again, this time severing the arm. Reaching down, I snatched it from the ground and tossed it toward the dumpster.

I missed.

Inanna grabbed it and put it back in place.

Another artifact—one I hadn't seen yet, a small flower of lapis lazuli embedded in her thigh—glowed. The arm sealed itself back on.

So that was her equivalent of a healing amulet. I had to get that off of her. Easy. I just had to get past the five arms she still had and the soul-sucking star she was aiming at everyone who came in range.

Also, the next wave of demons that was about to tackle me.

I sliced with my sword, cutting them down as they came at me. Too slow. She was almost to the dumpster where Isaac cowered.

Chase shot at the healing amulet and almost hit it, but his bullet pinged off her outer thigh, leaving the amulet intact. He aimed again, but nothing happened.

"Jack, I'm out!" he hollered toward me.

I had a spare magazine but I couldn't get it to him.

Dr. Brantley sent another jolt through the taser, hitting Inanna in the leg, but this one barely fazed her.

I dove through the demons and charged toward Inanna. She reached back with one of her arms and shoved. My sword pierced her hand, but she pushed me with enough force to send me thudding to the ground.

She flung the dumpster to the side and aimed her star at Isaac.

I scrambled to my feet and stumbled toward her. The star glowed, and light pulsed from it. Isaac dodged, but there was no refuge, no sanctuary to shelter him.

THIRTY-FIVE

"No!" I screamed.

Isaac convulsed as the beam hit him.

"Stop!" I dove in between her and Isaac, raising my sword.

She screeched and the pulsing halted as my sword began to glow with stolen power. I glanced at Isaac. He wasn't moving. No!

His chest rose and fell—he was breathing. Maybe I could heal him…

I started toward him, and Inanna turned and aimed her star toward Chase.

"No! You're not killing anyone else." I ran toward her, slashing at her arms, letting that weird fluid escape. The cuts sealed over almost instantly, but I managed to remove one completely. Down to four attain. She didn't fire the star, though—she must know that I'd intercept it and steal her power.

She stepped around me.

That was the opening I needed.

I leapt, removing another arm and kicking it out of reach. That made three.

"I've had enough of your interference," she said. She reached behind her and pulled something from her back that seemed somewhat reminiscent of a throwing star, and she hurled it at me.

It nicked my arm. Because of my own artifacts, I hardly felt it, and the cut was gone in seconds, but the jolt was enough to send my sword flying away from me.

I winced, waiting to either be hurled back to my dimension or to feel the crush on my mind that would send me into unconsciousness. Nothing happened.

The dimensions were too entwined now, and the bubble continued to widen.

Inanna grabbed my sword from the ground.

She yelped, and her skin—if it could be called skin—smoked. She hurled my sword the other direction. Far, far out of my reach. And then she turned on Chase again.

I screamed, powerless to do anything without my sword.

"Jack!" Chase yelled.

I looked at him as the pulse struck him.

He writhed in agony, but kept eye contact. "You... don't... need... the sword," he gasped. "You can... control... this... reality."

He crumpled to his knees.

I didn't have time to think. Just act.

I jumped, willing this dimension to bow to my demands. The space between Inanna and me closed as I leapt toward her, curling my hand into a fist. I was strong. Stronger than this demon.

I slammed my fist into her face. Her head snapped back. Her eyes widened.

Mine narrowed. "You're done here." I gripped her throat, my fingers bending both metal and flesh.

She flailed with her remaining arms, pumping her wings and lifting us both into the air.

"How..." she gasped.

"Don't know, don't care."

She turned the star toward me. I knocked it away.

But as strong as I was, as much as I exerted my control here, I couldn't kill her. Couldn't strangle her or rip her head off.

She managed to get one of her hands around my throat as well. She had the advantage of size. And immortality. And so many damn arms.

She lifted me up higher into the sky, getting another hand around my throat, cutting off my air.

I kicked.

The first shot struck her in the knee. She winced but didn't let go.

Only a few more seconds before I passed out and would be at her mercy. I willed all my strength, all my control into one final thrust and aimed it at her healing amulet.

It shattered beneath the supernatural force of my kick, and she stumbled backward, loosening her grip on my neck. I sucked in air and launched my foot again, this time aiming for her other artifacts. She grew weaker with each one I destroyed. How many were left? Three or four?

The next strike dug a dent into her hip. She instinctively let go of my arm as her hand went to the place where I'd injured her, and we fell from the sky, crashing into the hard earth below. Inanna pulled me up with her to a stand.

"Jack!"

I turned my head just enough to see Chase holding my sword. He staggered toward me, his body looking like he'd been run over, but still he willed himself to carry on.

I reached and he tossed it. I commanded the world to bend, drawing the sword right to me.

As soon as it touched my skin, power surged through me. I sliced off one of Inanna's arms and she dropped me. Rolling, I hacked at her legs.

The sword lanced straight through. Though she still balanced atop the severed limbs, they didn't heal.

Inanna roared. She reached out with one of her two remaining hands and grabbed a bystander off the street.

His scream silenced as Inanna ripped his head from his body. She tossed the head to the side and used his body like a ketchup bottle, dousing herself in his blood. Even without the healing amulet, her flesh and metal started to fuse back together.

The blood from the man spattered her crown and the metal started to glow.

I shuffled backward, trying to get out of her range.

She closed her eyes, focusing on I didn't know what.

Energy coalesced in her crown and burst, like a bomb, sending me, Chase, Dr. Brantley, and everyone else nearby flying backward.

I skidded against the dumpster where Isaac still lay. I couldn't see what happened to Chase or Dr. Brantley. But the world... the world was almost gone. I couldn't see the edge where the demon dimension ended and the real world began.

Dark clouds amassed in the sky, and thunder rumbled, shaking the buildings that were already unstable due to the dimensional spread.

"You will all bow to me!" Inanna yelled, her voice echoing through both dimensions, over the sound of thunder.

People screamed. The whole city of Mesa seemed to be wailing in unison.

Lightning—searing and dry—lanced from the sky, striking people and buildings and the dry remnants of trees that had shriveled up when they were sucked into this dimension. And it was hot. So hot. Like hell itself was erupting from Inanna's crown. Inanna stalked—slowly on her legs that were healing themselves even without the amulet—away

280

from me, toward a cluster of people cowering by a restaurant. Sweat broke out on their foreheads, and their skin seemed to sag more the closer she got to them. She reached out and grabbed the woman nearest her, choking her as she'd done to me. The woman's skin blistered and bubbled, her eyes bulging. Her essence drained into Inanna, like when she used the star, and a moment later, the woman slumped over, her life gone.

Inanna dropped the body and reached for the next person. The man scrambled to the side, trying to get out of her way.

Too slow.

I heaved myself up. Despite my own healing amulet and the cross that kept me from feeling damage, I could only handle so much before I gave out. But I couldn't allow myself to collapse yet.

I willed my muscles to move, told the world to bend to me. Gripping my sword, I ran toward her. I yelled, a primal, guttural scream as I buried my sword into her back, right where her heart should be.

She turned to look at me, her eyes glaring hate.

I stood my ground, wrenching my sword through her body even as she turned to face me, creating a gash halfway through her chest. The metal exoskeleton looked aged, corrupted. Almost rusted. And that yellowish demon pus oozed out.

Inanna reached for me, snagging my shirt and ripping it. Her hand brushed against the cross taped to my back, and she drew away quickly, like she'd been burned.

With one hand, I grabbed the cross, ripping the tape from my skin as I did so. Then I leapt forward again, wielding both my sword and my cross, pursuing Inanna, driving her away from the people, trying to slow her down, injure her, anything I could do.

She backed away, but even as much injury as I inflicted upon her with my relentless attacks, she still had so much power.

Lightning arced down and struck my sword, sending me tumbling.

As soon as I was out of her way, she reached for another person and drained their life from them, then sent more lighting my way.

I rolled out of the strike's path, and struggled to my feet.

Tired. So tired. I couldn't keep up. No matter how much I damaged her, the people in her path were nearly unlimited. They couldn't move as freely through the dimension, couldn't run fast enough or far enough to save themselves, and with every life she took, she healed and strengthened. With every death, her reach extended farther.

A shot rang out, and Inanna's body jerked.

Who shot her? Chase was out of ammo.

I turned to see Chase, but he wasn't holding my gun. It was someone else's. Where had he… never mind, I didn't have time to worry about that. I nodded to him and he fired again.

While Inanna stumbled, I rushed forward.

From the other side of her, electricity pulsed. Inanna had stumbled into range of Dr. Brantley's taser.

Inanna jerked back and forth, reeling between the taser and the blasts from Chase's gun. Keeping her distracted enough for me to rush toward her.

Chase stepped closer as I lurched forward. "You can control this dimension. That means you can control her. End this."

THIRTY-SIX

I… I could control *her*.

I absorbed Chase's words. Was he right? Could I? She was part of this dimension, born of it and trapped inside it. I could control the dimension. Did that mean I could exert some control over Inanna?

It was worth a shot.

I ran toward her, picking up speed. This dimension—this city—was mine, and I willed it to propel me forward. Willed my own body to keep moving.

She turned to face me, bracing herself for impact, flexing a couple of fists, preparing to grab me again.

I focused all my willpower on one of her two remaining arms and pushed it away, bending it behind her back. Inanna's head jerked up, her glowing red eyes losing some of their luster, confusion pulsing from her.

She screamed something that sounded like, "*Ettiri*," her voice thundering over the dimensions. Demons swarmed in from wherever they'd been—fighting or hiding or whatever they were doing—converging in a circle around us. Humans in white tunics emerged from the museum, now several blocks away, shuffling like zombies, but still determined to help her.

"Not today, Inanna," I growled.

I inhaled and pulled power in through the sword, then channeled it back out through the cross, sending a pulse, like the one Inanna had used, out toward the demons.

A shriek rose in a wave that was instantly silenced as the pulse burned through them, leaving a mist of dust and ashes billowing in the air.

More demons filled the gap left behind by those I'd killed, apparently far enough outside of my blast's reach that they weren't hit. But that meant they were still far away. And they moved more slowly than the first wave.

I stalked toward Inanna. My surge of—whatever it was—hadn't seemed to affect her at all. But there was genuine fear pulsing out of her now.

Good.

She grasped toward me with one arm, and I shoved it back with a shove from the sword. Another step, another pulse with my will—powered by the sword and released through the cross—until her remaining arms were pinned behind her back, and I was within striking distance.

"Wait!" She relaxed her posture. "Join me! Together—"

I swung my sword, slicing through her neck. Her head tumbled to the ground, her red eyes fading to powerless rubies as it rolled away. The statue stiffened, becoming nothing but metal once again, though the putrid, sulfuric odor of dead demon still seeped from the pus that discharged from her neck.

One by one, I smashed the rest of the artifacts with my sword, just in case.

I turned. Chase slumped to the ground.

I ran toward him. The demon dimension was still merged with the human—killing Inanna hadn't sent things back to the way they were, at least not yet. So, he wasn't passing out just from being in the demon dimension. "Chase! Are you okay? What is it?"

"I'm fine, I'm just…" Blood stained his shirt, belying his words. I stuck the cross in my pocket and touched the healing amulet around my neck.

I pressed my hands against Chase's side and felt the power emanate from the amulet, through me, into him. He gasped for breath, but a moment later sat up, stretching.

"Where's Dr. Brantley?" I asked.

He nodded the other direction. Dr. Brantley leaned against a tree that bent under her.

I jogged to her side. "Are you injured?"

"I don't think so. Go see to Dr. Reyes."

Oh, shit. Isaac.

I ran back the few blocks back toward the dumpster and slid to my knees by Isaac's side. "I'm here," I said.

I pressed my hands against his skin, feeling for any sign of movement, any warmth.

Nothing happened.

"No... no, no, no. Isaac, come on!"

He wasn't breathing. I felt for a heartbeat. Nothing.

I pressed my hands against his chest, starting compressions. Still nothing.

I yanked the amulet from my neck and thrust it against him, starting chest compressions again, with the amulet digging into my palm and his chest.

Not the faintest tingle of warmth trickled from my skin into his.

No. Not Isaac. My best friend. The one who was always there, waiting for me. The one who let me dictate how much or how little our relationship progressed. The one who never judged, never thought I was crazy, no matter how many rants I subjected him to. The one who loved me completely and never let go, even after I hurt him more deeply than I had ever hurt anyone in my life.

I kept doing compressions long after I knew it was useless, clinging to the hope that there was still some spark of life that I could connect to. Unwilling to admit that I failed him. That he died for me.

At long last, I collapsed, my head against his chest, and let the tears flow.

I don't know how long I sat there before I could move. When I finally lifted my head, Chase pulled me into an embrace.

"I'm so sorry," he murmured.

We sat there for a few more minutes, but around us, people were starting to move. Demons and humans eyed one another as they crept closer to the stinking statue that had almost been a goddess.

At least no one was fighting at the moment. I didn't have the energy to deal with that.

But I had to pretend I did.

"Help me up," I said to Chase.

He stood and reached down to pull me to my feet. I put the amulet back around my neck, made sure the cross was safely tucked in my pants, and gripped my sword.

Inhaling deeply, I stood and walked toward the remnants of the statue. I picked Inanna's head up from the ground and held it up in the air. "In case anyone wasn't aware, this is my city. My territory. This is what will happen to anyone—human, demon, god, or goddess—who tries to hurt it. Any questions?"

The mass of demons slunk away into the shadows, while the humans stared at me, still looking dazed for the most part.

I threw Inanna's head into the still-flaming dumpster, then dismantled her body, slicing it into chunks until it was a heap on the ground.

"Help me," I said to Chase.

Dr. Brantley joined us, as did a few of the onlookers. One by one, we tossed the pieces of Inanna's statue into the flames.

The pieces melted and swirled together.

As they did so, the air started to change.

"What—what's happening?" Chase asked.

"I'm not sure." I paused to look around.

The demon dimension that had encroached upon the real world was beginning to heal itself. In the distance, I saw a body slump over as the demon dimension disentangled itself from the real one and the person's mind could no longer function here.

"We've got to get these people out of here," I said.

I found a spot where the two worlds were distinct and ripped a hole.

"This way!" I yelled. "Hurry!"

Chase and Dr. Brantley herded people through the opening and into the real world. They stopped, blinking at the sun which shone so brightly on what was a pretty ordinary October day in the real world.

"Keep moving," Chase shouted.

The extra dimension bubbled in almost as quickly as it had bubbled out. Humans limped toward me, some of leading or carrying their injured companions.

Still, dozens, maybe hundreds of bodies littered the ground in the alternate dimension. I had no idea how many of them were still alive and how many were just unconscious.

There was no way to tell, no way to get to them all before the dimensions separated completely.

And before long, I would need to get Chase and Dr. Brantley out too.

"Let's move!" I yelled.

People scurried toward the hole, helping those behind them through in a steady stream.

And still the dimensional bubble grew smaller.

I ran toward the outer edge of the bubble, looking for stragglers. I found a few and willed the ground to move under them as I pushed them toward the opening.

But there were too many, and I didn't have enough time.

I ran toward the museum, the epicenter of the chaos. In the room in the back, the lab where Inanna had most fortified her fortress, I found a cluster of demons.

Good. I focused my attention on one demon—one of the ones that was still alive, so it could move between dimensions.

"Hey!" I yelled. "You're going to help me get all the humans, alive or dead, out of this dimension."

His gargoyle lip curled in a sneer. "Is that what you think?"

"I *so* don't have time for this," I said.

I slashed through him with my sword, then when his physical body died, leaving only his demon body, I slashed through that, too.

There was one more dual-dimension demon in the group. "You. Want to try your luck?"

He dropped to his knees and bowed his head to the ground. "No, Mistress. I will obey you."

"Good. Humans. Dead or alive. Take them to the hole I made on the other side of the street. I want every human out of this dimension unharmed."

He bowed and made his way out of the fortress.

"You guys too," I said to the others. "You can carry them to the hole."

One of the four remaining demons eyed me with a glare, but they all obeyed. I searched the museum, looking under tables and desks, in exhibits, anywhere I thought people might hide.

"It's safe now," I hollered every few moments. "Come on, we're getting out of here."

I found Dr. Smith in what had once been a storage closet but was now a collapsed heap of walls and debris in both worlds. He was unconscious, so I lifted him up and carried him out. The dimensions had almost completely sealed themselves back up. Only a small area remained right around the museum.

"Chase, Dr. Brantley, you need to go through. I'm going to keep checking for people. Start getting things organized so we can get people to their families."

I said people, but the look Chase gave me said he understood I meant *bodies*.

This was going to be a long process. But I couldn't leave people here. They would die or decompose much too quickly.

I pointed to the physical demon. "You go through and take the people the others hand you."

The demon bowed. "Yes, Mistress."

He leapt through the hole. Those still in line inside the demon dimension started to collapse, unconscious as the area returned to its normal, separated state.

"You, keep handing people through the hole," I said to one of the other demons. I pointed to two more. "You to go together, go that way and bring back whoever you can find." I gestured the way opposite from where Inanna had gone.

Finally, I looked at the last one, the one who had glared at me. "You, with me. Come on."

We made our way slowly down the street, collecting the bodies Inanna had left in her wake, carrying them back to the hole for the others to pass through into the real world, then coming back again and again until the streets were clear.

One upside to the dimensions being separated again was that all the buildings and trees and other things from the real world became translucent, ghostly reflections here. Easier to see people inside buildings and things. My enhanced vision because of the cross helped too.

Night was falling outside in the real world by the time we finally made it to the dumpster near where Isaac's body lay.

I knelt beside him, tears rising to the surface again.

I looked at the demon who'd been working with me. "Check the perimeter one more time for anyone else. Then you can go."

He acknowledged me with a brief nod of his head and went toward the edge of where Inanna's bubble had extended. A slight scar marred the landscape, as though an echo of the real world lingered here. I watched him for a moment, to make sure he was doing as I'd instructed, then turned back to Isaac.

I brushed my hand against his face. "I'm so, so sorry," I whispered.

Standing, I used my sword to slice a huge hole in the dimensional wall, then shoved the dumpster through it. I didn't want to leave Inanna's remnants here within easy access to the demons. I didn't think she could be put together again, and even if her statue could, she herself was dead. But I didn't know how much inherent power might be left in her artifacts. There wasn't much I could do about that, but at least if it were in the real world, there was a tolerable chance that the demons couldn't get to it for awhile.

Some dumpster diver was about to have the best day of their life. With any luck, the pieces would get melted down and sent to different ends of the earth.

Once the dumpster was all the way through the hole, I picked up Isaac's body and carried him through.

I collapsed as soon as I was in the real world, forgetting for a moment that my super strength only worked in the other dimension.

I still held Isaac, now on top of me like I was cradling him, and looked at his beautiful face.

Chase found me a few moments later.

"I saw the smoke from the dumpster," he said. He knelt and lifted Isaac up.

I tried to stand, but fell immediately back down, all the injuries and wear on my muscles fully hitting me now that I was fully back in this dimension. The amulet had healed wounds, but apparently I still had to deal with regular wear and tear, and the battle had taken a huge toll on me.

Sights and sounds from all around me began to register.

Sirens—all of them, from police to ambulance to fire truck—rang out, lights flashed with a rave-like intensity on the buildings, and people shouted to one another.

"Did everyone get out of the other dimension?" I asked.

"I think so," Chase said.

I nodded and tried again to stand. I managed to get my feet under me this time, and pressed against the wall of the nearest building for support. It still felt a little mushy, like foam instead of Jell-O, but seemed to be hardening by the moment.

There was no telling what kind of long-term damage would be done here. But I couldn't do anything about it, at least not right now.

I trudged along beside Chase as he carried Isaac's body toward where the medical personnel congregated.

I paused before we got to them and put my hand on Chase's arm. "I... I can't do this right now. I need to get away from here."

He nodded. "My car is that way. I'll meet you there."

"Thanks."

I touched Isaac's face one last time. "Good-bye." Then I turned toward where Chase had indicated and left him to take Isaac to the front lines.

THIRTY-SEVEN

Chase got to the car almost as soon as I did, as slowly as I was walking. Opening the passenger door, he offered me his hand and helped me to sit, placing my sword carefully in my lap.

He got in on the driver's side. "Where do you want to go?"

"I need to see Beck." I gave him Deanna and Dave's address.

I dozed in the car until Chase nudged my shoulder.

"We're here."

I jolted awake and shook the exhaustion from me.

Chase came around and helped me out of the car and almost carried me up the walk. The front door burst open before we reached it, and Deanna rushed out to embrace me.

"We were watching the news. Jack, what happened down there?"

"We'll fill you in in the morning," Chase said, helping me inside.

"Beck," I said.

Cameron came out from the kitchen carrying him, Dave hovering just behind her. "He's here. He's fine."

Beck started wailing when he saw me, and I pulled him into my arms, collapsing onto the sofa at the same time.

"She needs food and sleep," Chase said.

Deanna nodded and bustled into the kitchen. Knowing her, I'd have an eleven-course meal in front of me in minutes.

Cameron sat down beside me. "I had everyone packed and ready to go, but by the time police and news were on the scene, it looked like everything was over."

Beck rooted until I fed him.

"He just ate," Cameron said almost apologetically.

I stroked the soft hair on his tiny head, gazing down at him. "It's okay. Right now, he needs comfort more than food."

292

"Anyway, the news is saying rioters and looters. They're linking it to the cult, saying the cultists were trying to loot the museum to gain access to what they considered sacred artifacts that belonged to them or something."

"That's… about as close to the truth as they're likely to get," I said.

Deanna came out with salad, bread, and hot tea. "I'll have something more for you in a minute, this is just to tide you over," she said. She looked at me, then. Really looked at me. "Oh, honey! What happened to your face?"

I lifted a hand and felt the scar that now ran from my chin to my chest. "Demon claw."

She looked concerned for my mental health. I knew that look way too well.

Oh, well. I could come up with a better story tomorrow.

I reached for the plate she still held. "Thank you."

I tore into the bread, not aware until that moment just how hungry I was. How much the day had depleted me of everything.

I leaned into the soft couch cushions and finished the bread, then started on the salad.

The tea was chamomile. Soothing. Chase sat across from me, just staring at me, as though worried I might disappear.

"Thank you," I said. "For everything that you did today."

He reached out and put his hand gently on my knee. "You too."

My head lolled back against the back of the couch. "I kind of did save the world, didn't I?"

He grinned. "Again."

I smiled back, enjoying that we could just pick up where we left off, even after months apart, and after an otherworldly battle that left a good portion of an entire city decimated.

I thought about Isaac and all the reasons I had chosen not to pursue a relationship. All the reasons why I wanted to be with Chase. Preferably before the next monster tried to destroy my city.

"Can I ask you something?"

"Sure," he said.

"Why aren't you dating Desiree?"

"I'm not dating anyone."

"Yeah, I know, but… why?"

"Because I don't want to date her."

I wasn't sure how much more I was going to get out of him, and I didn't have the energy to push, so I just sat and waited to see if he'd go on.

Deanna brought steaming plates of spaghetti to both of us. "I'm sorry, I didn't have time to make something. This is just left over from dinner."

"This is great. Thank you," I said.

"Thank you, ma'am," Chase said.

"Oh, you," Deanna grinned. "Ma'am. Just call me Deanna."

"Thank you, Deanna," Chase smiled.

Deanna stood there awkwardly for a moment before deciding it was better to let us be alone. "We'll be in here if you need anything," she said, disappearing back into the kitchen.

"She's nice."

"Yeah. Always treated me like a daughter, not a daughter-in-law."

"That's good. Nice to have a good relationship with the people you're going to be related to."

I nodded.

"Pastors have certain expectations set upon them," he said after a moment. "They're supposed to look a certain way, have certain things in order. Perfect middle class life, perfect wife, a couple of well-behaved kids who rebel in high school but end up going into the ministry when they're older. My dad fit that image pretty exactly."

I raised an eyebrow at him. "Your dad was a pastor?"

"Still is."

"And you rebelled in high school?"

He shrugged. "My brother was the black sheep of the family, but I had my moments. My rebellion came later."

Chase had never talked about his family. I sort of assumed, somewhere in the back of my mind, that he had one, but he'd never mentioned any of them.

Beck fell asleep, and I adjusted him so he was resting against my chest and straightened my clothes while Chase stuffed a few more bites of spaghetti into his mouth.

"I never wanted any of that. Never wanted to be a pastor at all. Never wanted to get married or have a bunch of kids."

He hadn't wanted to be a pastor? He always seemed to fit that role so naturally. I couldn't imagine him as anything else.

"Anyway, when I realized I was called to be a pastor, despite my preferences, I decided I was not going to be the kind of pastor everyone expected. I didn't want to fit into a specific mold. I wanted to be myself. And that kind of ended up meaning being single. There were girls in my undergrad classes, girls in my seminary classes, and women in church who all thought I'd be the right guy for them."

"Like Desiree."

"Among others. I can't go a week without some well-meaning old woman trying to fix me up with a niece or something. But I didn't want that. Thought I never would. And then you came along."

My head snapped up at that.

"You were... so different. Traumatized, and yet the strongest woman I'd ever met. Smart and capable and driven. And even though you made it clear you were interested, you didn't try to connive your way in. You weren't looking for a perfect little romance or life as a pastor's wife, and that was... nice. And I thought we might have a future, but then..."

"Then Beck."

He exhaled deeply. "Yeah."

"I understand." And I did. "So where does that leave us now?"

"I have no idea." He gave me a sheepish grin.

"Okay." I exhaled. No idea was not the same as no. I could live with that. "I'm going to go to bed, then."

He jumped to his feet to help me up.

"Deanna?" I called out. "I'm going to go to bed, okay?"

Deanna hurried out of the kitchen. "Sure, honey. Your room is always ready for you. Are you... do you..." Her eyes darted between me and Chase a couple times.

"I'd be very grateful if I could crash on your couch," he said.

"Oh. Yes, of course. I'll grab you some sheets and a pillow."

"Thanks."

Chase pulled me in for a hug then released me to go to my room.

I spent most of the next couple days in and out of sleep, my body catching up to the rigor I'd put it through. Beck stayed with me for the most part, except when he was too active for me to get any rest. He was recovering way faster than I was, so Cameron took him for frequent trips to the park and played with him so I could sleep.

I watched the news—Cameron's summary of the official story was the one that was sticking. Rebuilding was happening in Mesa from what they'd concluded was a concussion bomb of some sort.

Chase had gone home the next morning, but he returned a couple days later to bring me my truck. He dropped it off, and Cameron drove him back to his car.

There were a handful of people still on the missing list, so when I felt a little better, I made my way down to Mesa. I stopped first at the police department to give my official statement, then went on to the museum.

There were still several tears in reality, but the dimensions themselves seemed to be in their own places.

I went through one of the holes with my sword and spent the next few hours searching for bodies.

I found two. One, a young woman, was still alive but unconscious. The other, a middle-aged man, was dead and decayed enough that I just hoped he'd be easy to identify.

I took them both to the hospital, leaving them with the appropriate personnel.

Finally, I made my way up to Desiree's room. She was out of the ICU now, in her own room. Flowers and stuffed animals littered every surface. So, she did have people who loved her.

I chided myself for still being that petty. But I couldn't help wondering if any of the bouquets were from Chase.

"You made the news again," she said when she saw me.

"Yeah, once a year. I've got a quota to keep."

She laughed, then winced.

"How are you?"

"I'm okay. I've got a long recovery ahead of me."

"Yeah… about that… I think I can help."

She raised an eyebrow.

I used my sword to tear a hole in dimensions right by her bed. Because apparently I could do that now.

She jerked back, wincing again as she strained her wounds, backing away from me and my sword.

"Trust me for once, would you?" I said.

She nodded.

I stepped through dimensions.

"Jack? Where'd you go?"

I reached through and pulled her halfway into the demon dimension. I could see her vision clouding as she fought to maintain consciousness in the demon realm.

"This will just take a minute," I said. I gently pressed the healing amulet against her side, feeling the warmth flowing through it into her body.

She gasped like I'd thrown cold water on her, and her eyes widened.

I stepped back through the hole and set her back on her bed.

"What… what was that?" she asked.

I smiled. "The doctors will probably say it's a miracle."

With that, I turned and left her room.

"Jack?" Her voice echoed down the corridor, but I kept walking.

I went back to Deanna and Dave's to get Beck.

I held him close to me. My perfect, precious son. "Are you ready to go home?"

Other Books by Avily Jerome

Jack Davidson Case Files
The Breeding

Fairly Dark Tales
Swimmer

The Amulet Saga
The Heir
The Defector
The Silver Shores
The Prophecy
The Sorceress
The Beginning
The End

Acknowledgements

Special thanks to Catherine Jones Payne and SD Grimm, whose spectacular edits helped make this story what it is.

Thank you to my Wonder Women—Lindsay, Catherine, and Sarah, my dear and wonderful friends whose support is what keeps me going.

Thanks to my husband, for all he is and all he does.

Thanks to Kirk, my amazing cover designer, for making this cover even more spectacular than the last.

About the Author

Avily Jerome is a writer and freelance editor. She spent five years as the Editor of *Havok Magazine*, an imprint of Splickety Publishing Group. Her short stories have been published in multiple magazines, both print and digital. She has judged several writing contests, both for short stories and novels, and she is a book reviewer for Lorehaven Magazine.

She is also a writing conference teacher and presenter, and she enjoys speaking to local writers' groups and going to SFF cons.

She loves all things SpecFic, and writes across multiple genres. Her writing heroes include Joss Whedon, Robert Jordan, and J.K. Rowling, among others.

She is a wife and the mom of five kids. She loves living in the desert in Phoenix, AZ, and when she's not writing, she loves reading, spending time with friends, and experimenting with different art forms.

www.ingramcontent.com/pod-product-compliance
Lightning Source LLC
Chambersburg PA
CBHW020646030726
47498CB00002B/394